Riccardo Stephens

**Mr. Peters**

A novel

Riccardo Stephens

**Mr. Peters**
*A novel*

ISBN/EAN: 9783337000332

Printed in Europe, USA, Canada, Australia, Japan

Cover: Foto ©Andreas Hilbeck / pixelio.de

More available books at **www.hansebooks.com**

THE ARRIVAL OF MR. PETERS

BY

RICCARDO STEPHENS, M.B., C.M.

WITH ILLUSTRATIONS

BY E. M. ASHE

NEW YORK
HARPER & BROTHERS PUBLISHERS
1897

# CONTENTS

# CONTENTS

# ILLUSTRATIONS

# MR. PETERS

THE rapidly rising town of Bonville, U. S. A., was about
to prove its hatred of law-breakers by taking the law into its
own hands. It was also prepared to mark its recognition of
the sacred laws of hospitality by giving a stranger and a
foreigner a handsome swinging. In spite of the late hour
and the darkness, the citizens of Bonville had forsaken
whiskey-saloons and quiet card-parties, feeling that whiskey
and euchre were always with them, but a horse-thief, once
hanged, could not be relied upon for further entertainment.

He had been opportunely met by the Sheriff, caught red-
handed, so to speak, riding one of the two stolen horses and
leading the other. The Sheriff had tried to get his prisoner
quietly away to the nearest jail, Bonville having none. But
they were Bonville horses that had been stolen, and when
the citizens of Bonville heard of the Sheriff's intention, a
sufficient number of them crossed his path, some six miles
out, and, by unanswerable argument, persuaded that stout
and conscientious little man that Bonville could and would
attend to her own affairs. The Sheriff now watched the
progress of these affairs, rueful and carefully guarded, spit-
ting now and then in contemptuous disgust as he saw how
things went. They went badly for the prisoner. He had

been found in the hands of the Sheriff, who could not deny,
though he would not own, that he had acted because he
knew the stolen horses.

The judge, a lean, long man, sitting in a buggy, with a
rifle across his knees, pointed out to the jury, who clustered
in a wagon that had been unhorsed and deprived of its tilt,
that this was not contradicted, and, what was still more important, that the prisoner could give no satisfactory explanation in spite of the help given to him by their able and
eloquent fellow-townsman, Mr. Joshua Buncombe. True,
the prisoner, a tall, long-bearded Swiss from one of the
Italian Cantons, could speak only his own language and a
little French, but Mr. Buncombe translated for him and to
him with a rapidity, a feverish fluency, which testified both
to his powers and to his eager and anxious sympathy.

"Whar did he *git* them hosses?" asked the judge, and
the prisoner's answer, which was a long one, was evidently
unsatisfactory to his friendly interpreter and advocate.

"Speak up!" a juryman told him. "Say it as he says it,
and don't stop to patch up," and this being evidently the
popular feeling, Mr. Buncombe spoke.

"Gentlemen, he says that he found them. On my honor,
gentlemen, I believe him."

A roar of laughter greeted this profession of faith.

"Does anyone know the man?" asked the judge.

No one knew him. He was thirty miles away and heading for the next county when the Sheriff, coming home
from another errand, had met him. Not a bar loafer or
farmer recognized him. The man was clearly a marauder.

"Where does he come from?"

Again question, translation answer and translation, the
translation always, owing to Mr. Buncombe's linguistic
ability, much more concise than the prisoner's explanation.

"Sweet Springs."

Again a howl went up, for Bonville lay between Sweet

Springs and the spot where prisoner and booty had been found together.

" Did he come by here? "

The prisoner, frowning this way and that as the jeer rippled round him, waited, haggard, for the question, and his answer was long.

Again his protector hesitated and stammered, and again he was urged to speak out quickly, lest, it was even suggested, he should find a place beside his client.

With a shrug of his shoulders, and an action as if washing his hands of the whole thing, the answer came.

" He passed through last night, he says, and saw no one."

" Nor wanted to, I guess," remarked the judge, and from that moment he seemed to pay less attention to the proceedings, letting his eye rove among the branches of the tree under which the prisoner stood.

The case was clear to those who listened.

There were the two horses for all to see; a gray mare and a chestnut gelding, with a white star and a white stocking, going lame when met, recognized by the Sheriff, now claimed by the owner. There was the man who was found trotting them away, meaning to get rid of them as, no doubt, he had got rid of the other six which, always in couples, had gone during the last few months.

Mr. Hector Inch, a young Scotsman recently arrived from the mother country, stating the evidence for the prosecution, and anxious to show his neighborly sympathy for the horses' owner, pressed these points and more also.

" Let them look," he told them, with a long, accusing forefinger pointed at the prisoner, " and judge if that was the face of an innocent man ! "

The jury looked, the outside audience looked, and the prisoner, shifting his restless eyes from one face to another, moved uneasily in his place. While the citizens of Bonville had persuaded the Sheriff, they had also man-handled the prisoner, and he showed marks of it. His clothes, shabby before, were tattered now, his face was bruised, his mouth swollen and cut. He blinked in the flare of the pine-knots, looking very like a wild animal dragged from the darkness against its will, and a surly hum running through the crowd told the orator that his audience was with him. His blood stirred at the sound, as it had been used to stir when he gained the applause of the Philomathic Society in his gray native city.

When he lashed himself into further denunciation, it was applause he spoke for and thought of, not a man's life. He ended with trite words on tempering justice with mercy, but if there had been any hope for the wondering, uncomprehending prisoner, there was now no more.

The judge, recalled by the silence from his meditation, brought his eyes down from their speculative wanderings among the branches, and asked if the prisoner had anything to say. His interpreter replied hurriedly that the prisoner begged for mercy; whereat the stout little Sheriff spat once more and cursed under his breath.

The judge, grinning sourly, took a quid from a neighbor, told the jury to consider their verdict, and, beckoning to one of the crowd, whispered in his ear and sent him away into the shadows beyond the circle of light made by the pine-knots.

The young fellow who had prosecuted stood with a pleased smile, and listened to the rough compliments of those by him. The prisoner glanced about uneasily, and then, turning, asked a question of the interpreter. He, however, had moved off, and was now haunting the shadows, flitting from place to place as men noticed him, and wiping his pale, sweating face with his coat-sleeve. The jury did not retire, having no particular place to retire to, nor did they take long to consider.

" Guilty " was the verdict, given unanimously in less than

five minutes, and the interpreter mopped his face again in the shadows as he heard it, while the prisoner stood waiting and wondering what would come next. The man Inch who had spoken against him stepped a little forward, with a jaunty air of self-satisfaction.

" That being the case, sir, I propose that a little of your well-known local remedy of tar and feathers will be given to this gentleman, and that then he be handed over to the recognized law."

He pointed, laughing, to the Sheriff, but the judge, scarcely moving, caught his eye, and pointed to the branch directly over the prisoner's head. There crouched the man to whom the judge had spoken while the jury consulted, and presently a rope uncoiled from above and hung swaying and serpent-like from the bough.

" Not that! My God, not that! "

Inch's voice rang out, startled and entreating, and the prisoner, turning sharply to him, followed his glance and looked upward.

The next moment the prisoner had leapt silently at the nearest neighbor, bearing him down by the suddenness and fury of his attack, and was struggling to get the man's revolver between his roped hands. The attack was as useless as it was savage, and two minutes later he was hauled to his feet and stood breathless, but gasping broken words in his unknown tongue, while a revolver pressed hard against each ear.

They noosed his neck, and bringing up the gray mare which he had ridden, they made her stand, and hauled on the rope and set him upon her back.

" Now ye can pray, sonny, if you know how," said one. " She's onstiddy, and that's straight !" remarked the mare's owner, peering up at him. " A touch of the heel will start her, I reckon. So long ! " and he strolled slowly away.

The light now flickered around the tree some twenty

yards off. The moon was rising, and her rays fell pale on
the man's face. Sitting erect, he could just feel the pres-
sure of the rope tightening as the mare pricked up her ears
and stamped uneasily, whinnying to her stable companion.
Then the man, staring at the moon wide-eyed, began muttering to himself, and presently burst into a low vacant
laugh.

" Darn the skunk," muttered the judge, shifting his rifle;
" what's the fool laughing at now ?   If he don't shift that
mare for himself, I guess I will," but the man was singing,
in his own tongue, a song he had heard years ago among his
own people, and stared at the moon all the time :—

> Oh! cold and pale
> My mistress wanders
> O'er hill and dale,
> And nightly ponders
> On all things else in earth and sky
> But me, who love her till I die.
> Oh! pale and cold.

There was a flash from among the shadows, and the crack
of a revolver.   The gray mare, startled at the whistle of the
bullet as it flew by to bury itself in the tree, winced and
broke away at a gallop.   Her burden, jerked from the saddle, twisted convulsively to and fro, a mark for more bullets,
as the revolvers of the crowd were emptied.   Presently it
swung with pendulum-like regularity, and at last, slowing
down, hung motionless, the face, twisted into the semblance
of a mocking smile, still turned to the quiet moon.

There was a sigh, which might be of content at work well
done, and the crowd was scattering, when a fresh comer, a
small, wiry, gray-bearded man, cantered up.

" Well, sonnies, what's the fun now ? "

" Lynching," said the nearest man, briefly, and nodded
toward the tree and its dead fruit.

" I swar ! " ejaculated the little man, rising in his stirrups and peering across. " Who's the fool, and what's he done ? "

" Furriner ; sneaked Joe Brown's hosses last night."

The rider dropped back into his saddle and trotted gently through the moving crowd to satisfy his curiosity, but in a minute he was back again, calling to the man who had answered him:

" Miners ! where are ye ? "

Miners halted in his track with a grunt and waited.

" When did you say he stole 'em ? "

" Last night."

The little gray man sat and thought slowly, with his hand on the other's shoulder, so that he should not go. At last he spoke with great deliberation.

" I was with that chap last night from, lemme see, nine o'clock till sunrise ; yes, I was. If these hosses was stole last night, why—you've hung the wrong man ! "

" Shucks ! " retorted the other, loudly, so loudly that those who were still about drew near and listened.

" From nine till sunrise," the gray man repeated, after refreshing his memory, " me and him [and he jerked his thumb at the tree] was side by side."

One or two, cursing loudly, ran toward the tree, the rest crushed close round the gray man, who sat still.

" 'Taint no manner of use," he said, " you're sich durned fine shots, some o' you boys, that there's two bullets through his head, anyway. I've seen that," and he sat thinking, while a babel of tongues rose all about.

" I didn't know any of you gents could parley-vous," he said at last, raising his voice and speaking loudly. " I can a bit, and I had all the world's trouble to make him out. How did you work it ? "

" Buncombe spoke for him," chorused a dozen voices. " Did it fine, too," said one, and there was a loud " hear ! hear ! " to that.

" Who nabbed him ? "

" Tom Fraser; leading the horses he was, and heading straight away."

" What in thunder did Tom bring him *here* for ? " demanded the astonished catechiser.   There was a silence, and then——" He was fetched ! "

" Fetched, was he ? "   The man's temper was rising, and there was as much sarcasm as his voice could throw into the question.   " What made you fetch him ? "

" Buncombe happened to say in Sadler's bar that he'd seen Fraser heading across to Terenceville," said one man sulkily, after a pause; " and some of the boys allowed we could see to these things ourselves, and went out."

" Hope you're satisfied," snarled the gray man.  " Where's Buncombe ?   I want to see him—badly."   But Buncombe was not to be seen, though Bonville searched for him that night, and for many days and nights after.   He had drawn a freer breath as soon as he knew further interpreting was not necessary, and that his client was silent for ever.   He had been close by the newcomer when that inquisitive individual had started his questions, near him when he came back from his first look at the dead man, but what he heard then sent him into the shadows again, and he was riding for his miserable life five minutes later, thinking every moment that he heard the lynchers upon his heels, and seeing a dead man grin and swing from every bough.

The next day saw the little gray man, who had so disturbed the self-appointed law-givers, mount again and ride, grim and meditative, to Sweet Springs, the merest germ of another township, twelve miles away.   By his side, unwilling and remonstrant, rode one of the last night's crowd, who had, however, taken no active part—a lank, foolish youth who disliked his errand and said so.

" I dunno what to say," he repeated for the twentieth time, as they slackened pace within sight of a small newly built house. The little gray man gave him practically the answer he had given twenty times before.

" I don't keer," he said, staring towards the house, and shading his eyes with one hand. " That's the good of you, Jerry. I want someone by to see that I do the straight thing, an' to hear *me* talk. T'other chaps 'd chip in and tell their own story, an' mebbe their's an' mine'd get mixed. You stand by an' see me do the thing square; an' if you *must* speak, just foller my lead. I've had a deal to do with mares in my time."

They were now drawing up at the door.

The small man threw himself out of the saddle, lifting down a canvas bag that was balanced over the pommel, and rapped gently on the door with his whip-handle. Then he turned his head, clearing his throat in a dry nervous way, and found the younger man still mounted.

" What the hell are you doin'? " he blazed out; " climb down an' be ready."

" The hosses ! " explained the young man feebly, but his senior merely snarled, and was proceeding in highly colored language to condemn him and all his works when the door opened.

The woman who stood and looked at them from one to the other, was tall, handsome, and dark. A low, broad brow frowned a little anxiously over dark, melancholy eyes. Her aquiline nose and strong, rounded chin gave a masculine strength to the face, which full, red lips could not overcome. An olive-skinned youngster, a boy perhaps ten years old, peeped under her arm. After a moment she seemed to recognize the older man, and, drawing back, motioned him to come in, which he did when sure that the other was going to follow him. Seated on the edge of a chair in a clean room that showed nothing of the ornamental except a big bunch of grasses and wild flowers, the little man held tight to his canvas bag and cleared his throat again loudly, one

finger thrust between neck and shirt-collar as if he felt the
need of more room.

" You'll know our talk, I reckon," he said at last, politely,
" leastways so I've heard, which your good man didn't."

The woman, watching him from where she stood by the
little rough, unpolished table, nodded.

" My husband does not understand.   I do."

" 'Course he doesn't now," the little man agreed hurriedly.   " That is, p'r'aps he does.   I'm no hand at these
things.   'Twould have been more use to him yesterday may
be, I think anyway."

" What came yesterday ? " asked the woman.

" He took ill after I left him."

" And——? " said the woman, steadying herself against
the table.

" He died, ma'am, among strangers.   A hard thing for
you to hear—and for me to tell, I do assure you."

The suddenness of the stroke seemed to paralyze sensation.   The woman gasped and looked round her in a dazed
silence, while the man hurried on.

" He had a good deal of money about him, as no doubt
you'll know," he said, pleased at his own brilliant imagination, for the dead man had only four or five dollars.   " An'
when I turned up, as I did before he was buried, an' the
folk heard the lay of things, they sent the hat round, an' me
an' him (here he jerked his head back at his silent and staring junior) guv our word as how we'd bring the best respecs
of the rest, and ask you to 'low them to put their little pile,
as they did, to what your man had about him."

With that he stepped up to the table where the woman
was, and, untying the string and taking the bag by the
corners, he emptied its contents carefully out.   He had
spent the night in collecting this money from the penitent
men of Bonville, and in conducting a hurried but effective
funeral.   He now stepped back a pace, with a little sigh of

relief, feeling that, whatever might come of this matter when all was known, his share in it was creditably ended.

The woman's eyes rested dully upon the pile of coins, and gave little sign of feeling.

" My man ! " she said, " where is he ? "

" We gave him a big funeral this mornin'," said the man, " miles, miles from this, in the sweetest gully you ever sot eyes on, but it is a terrible place to get at, an' if I was you I'd let him be, and get away to my friends. If I can help you to that, Joe Flinders is my name, and Bonville City will find me any day next week that you send a message. I'll come over, with a boy or two, to get yer things together."

He looked round to see if a boy or two would be enough for the business, and came to the conclusion that they would not be overworked. After this he said good-day and went out, followed by the other, but came back directly alone, and spoke again.

" As I said, missus, he had a tremendous funeral, I give the boys credit for that, an' I'd made tracks, I tell you; but I promised Sheriff Thomas Fraser to say that, if you must see a man who was by him when he died, you must go to him. He ain't bent on seein' ye, but he holds himself in duty bound to be ready to answer questions. But you be a good soul, an' start for home."

The woman sat down with some word of thanks, staring quietly at the floor. The man turned, and, going out, swung himself into the saddle and broke at once into a gallop, watched by the child from the open door.

" Didn't seem much put about," said the younger man when they rode level again, but the other shook his head dubiously.

" She looks I-talian," he remarked, " which her man wasn't."

He pulled up at another door, and, hailing the woman of the house, told her to look up her neighbor.

"She's struck silly," he went on, as they broke away again, "but she'll come to. Then she'll feel, an' may be others will, if she can make 'em. She'll want to know more of this."

That proved true. A day or two later the woman interviewed the Sheriff, and heard what he could tell her. She was still quiet, but with a difference, the difference between a dead fire and a smouldering fuse.

" I can't git all Bonville City hanged, ma'am, for this business. If I could I believe I would at times. The worst of 'em's got clean away, an' that's Buncombe. I'd string him up if I cud ketch him, but I'll have no sich luck ! "

" Buncombe? " said the woman, carefully.

" Buncombe; that's the man. Seems he did the stealin' first, an' then got your man mixed up in it, though how he did that I dunno. Then, as he did the parleyvooin' at what the chaps called the trial, the Lord only knows what lies he told. An' though you may say in a way that your man was hanged, yet, in a way, he was shot, which we count more decent an' respectable. But two of the boys swear that it was Buncombe who fired the first shot, being anxious to git it done."

By his mother's side stood the boy, quietly munching an apple which the Sheriff had found for him. The woman turned and spoke earnestly in Italian, while the boy listened. She finished with the word " Buncombe," and he repeated it, at first incorrectly, then well, while the Sheriff wondered what was being said.

" Then, too," he went on, when the woman finished with the boy and turned to him again, " there's another bit o' comfort I can give ye, and I'll allow, missus, that you'll need it all. Your man was light-headed an' light-hearted in consequence, when he came to his end. He died singin', as you may say, bein' clean mad; though I've no head for music an' can't tell you the tune," he added regretfully.

But the boy, who had finished his apple and was listening

with his big black eyes fixed upon the Sheriff's weather-beaten face, began to hum quietly and the man whipped round upon him.

" That's the tune, sonny; you've hit it fair and square! Good Lord ! " he added, turning to the woman again, " I didn't calc'late on the kid's understanding all this ! "

" He must understand," the woman said in a dull way.

" He's a bright chappie," the Sheriff told her, admiringly; " he'll be a comfort and a help to you later on, missus."

" Yes," the woman answered, " I shall want help," and she rose to go as she spoke.

" The man who spoke against him was Inch," she said.

" That was the man," the Sheriff admitted. " But, mind you, that chap didn't know where he was landing. Tar an' feathers was in his mind, an' nothin' more. We can't touch him I reckon, missus ! "

But the woman was scarcely listening. She had turned to the boy again. " Inch," she said, " Inch," and the boy repeated the name after her. Then she went away, a strong, noticeable figure, with the silent, quick-eyed youngster at her side. The men of Bonville, guessing who she was as she left the Sheriff's house and moved down the street, mostly disappeared if they saw her soon enough. Where she came upon them unawares, they looked skyward or earthward, and remained contemplative until she had gone by. But she hardly noticed them. As she went she constantly repeated to the boy those two names, " Buncombe " and " Inch." He said these two after her, and a third that she had taught him to link with them, " stai," or " wait."

Folk wondered what would follow upon this visit, but a few days later the woman and her boy again disappeared, without any help from the well-intentioned Joe Flinders. Soon, as the population shifted and changed, these things were forgotten by Bonville City, or only vaguely remembered when a stranger made inquiries about what was known as the Gallows tree. So twenty-five years rolled by.

# CHAPTER I

Mrs. Jimps was expecting another Paying Guest, and therefore, as usual, she was nervous. Her House of Residence, as she chose to call her house in a familiar Edinburgh street, usually held four Paying Guests, and in the tourist season had been known to take eight, because Mrs. Jimps didn't like to refuse old friends, and knew very well that they wouldn't be comfortable anywhere else.

No *chef* in any Princes Street hotel could send in better omelettes and such like trifles than could fat Maggie, the cook. Her scones, porridge, haggis and cocky-leekie were also beyond reproach, and when Maggie raised up her shrill voice against " our Annie," the quick, pert table-maid, Mrs. Jimps, if possible, shut the double doors and gave them the kitchen to themselves until the thunder-clouds had melted into tears, valuing her domestics too highly for needless interference.

Mrs. Jimps, however, though prudent, was no coward, and when her tall, black-robed figure swept into the kitchen Maggie usually bestowed her wrath upon the kitchen fire, or maybe broke a plate, but abstained from words, while " our Annie " would suddenly recollect that a bedroom needed " sorting."

Nevertheless, to-night, Mrs. Jimps was nervous. Romance does not always lose its charm, as young people suppose, at forty, and she was barely that. Moreover, under a manner of great dignity and some reserve, Mrs. Jimps hid an impressionable heart, which always asserted itself on the advent of a male stranger. Her new Paying Guest was a

14

Mr. Peters, coming from the Continent, and recommended by a former lodger (I apologize, I mean Paying Guest).

Mr. Peters was already overdue. Mrs. Jimps, in a stiff, white widow's cap, had fluttered for a quarter of an hour between her own little sitting-room and the room set apart for Mr. Peters, and was about to flutter up the stair again, when the house-door bell sounded with a sudden jerk. Mr. Peters had arrived.

First there was the banging of a heavy trunk in the hall, followed by a second.

Mrs. Jimps, hesitating between dignity and curiosity, loitered behind her door.

Then came the clink of silver as the fare was paid, and then an astonished and contemptuous " Eh, what mon," from the cabby.

He said no more. Mr. Peters was, audibly, equal to the occasion. A deep strong voice repeated his number sonorously, the owner of the voice evidently making a note of it.

" Two shillings I have given you, my best fellow," the voice went on, " and one shilling and ninepence is your fare. Here is my card also. Shall we meet to-morrow at your procurator-fiscal's ? "

A word or two of choice blasphemy from the man, and the voice rose again.

" Will you swear before this young lady, my friend ? Outside is best," and with that there was a short scuffle, and the door banged upon the astonished Jehu.

" Bring me now to Mrs. Jimps," and " our Annie," her face still wreathed with the smiles called up by Mr. Peters' delicate respect for her gentility, ushered him into the room.

Mrs. Jimps saw bowing before her a man upon whom she would have looked twice anywhere.

He was tall and swarthy, dark-eyed and clean shaven. His age was really only thirty-five, but his large, well-shaped features were rather fat and had an air of immovable and

sphinx-like calm that seemed the mark of an older man.
As he bent over Mrs. Jimps' hand now, his face was unalter-
ably solemn.   Later, when Mrs. Jimps began to watch, she
found that Mr. Peters laughed often—the laugh of an easy-
going, big, strong man—but she never saw him smile.
When he spoke he watched her intently, and his big smooth
voice filled the room and was easily heard by the attentive
Annie outside.

" So this," he said, " is Mrs. Jimps ! "

Mrs. Jimps bowed, feeling, as she acknowledged to herself
afterwards, in a bit of a flutter under those unwinking black
eyes.

" Now I am aware," he said solemnly, " that friend Bergen is a man of taste."

" I beg your pardon," murmured Mrs. Jimps.   " I don't
follow you."

" Friend Bergen pictured to me my hostess, madam.   I
said, ' It is too much ! '   Now I say, ' It is not enough.' "

" Really these foreign gentlemen have a way with them !"
So Mrs. Jimps thought, and her manner softened to an extent that surprised herself.

" We are not accustomed to such compliments here, Mr.
Peters."

" Ah, excuse a foreigner, madam," and he turned.

In the hall there was much thumping and bumping.   As
Mr. Peters threw the door open, Annie was revealed outside,
red-cheeked and breathless, but tugging manfully at his box
which she had scarcely got half-way to his room.

" So, you cannot manage that !   See "—and he picked
up the box; then, seeing its fellow, picked that up too, and
marched contentedly up the stair, while Annie meekly followed, wondering whether her " young man," a corporal of
dragoons, could do the like so easily, and very much doubted
it.

Meanwhile Mrs. Jimps stood in her own little room, and

composed her face to the dignified expression it usually
wore. She looked at the mirror over the mantel-piece, and
wondered what Friend Bergen had said of her. Presently
she began to wonder, too, whether everything was comfortable upstairs, and whether she should go up and ask for herself. This was quite unprecedented. Mrs. Jimps had
great faith in the power of appearances, and studied them
carefully, not believing, as she put it, in making herself too
cheap. But here was a gentleman who knew how to behave,
and who must be shown that manners were not lacking in
Edinburgh, so she made a sudden and noiseless appearance
at the door of Mr. Peters' sitting-room, to the intense surprise of "our Annie."

When that young person was startled in the presence
of a male, or thought that she ought to be, she invariably
shrieked. It showed that her organization was just as sensitive as that of a real lady who never put her hand to anything heavier than a novel. So she shrieked now, and Mr.
Peters, who was bending over one of his trunks, turned,
though with deliberation, not being easily startled, and
faced Mrs. Jimps.

"I only came," said Mrs. Jimps, wondering at the sound
of her own voice, "to see if everything was comfortable."

Mr. Peters, bowing solemnly, waved his hand to compre-
hend all.

"Everything," he said briefly, and stood as if waiting for
her to speak further, or to go. Mrs. Jimps, anxious, as she
told herself, to understand her Paying Guest, tried to decide
which he wanted, and could not. The black eyes were
steady and unwinking and expressionless, the big figure
simply quiet.

"You will want some supper," she suggested, but Mr.
Peters shook his head energetically.

"Some coffee," he told her, "and a great smoke presently.
That is all."

2

" I will make the coffee at once myself," said Mrs. Jimps, at which Mr. Peters laughed loudly and without restraint, throwing back his head, with wide open mouth, showing a regular and strong set of teeth.

" There is no one in all Edinburgh shall make my coffee," he announced. " Would I poison myself? No! The fire here shall be lit, and the water, fresh and cold, look you, shall be brought, and I will make my own coffee now and always."

The idea of having his coffee made for him seemed hugely amusing. The man went off into laughter again, until, through sheer infection, Annie began to choke and to giggle; and Mrs. Jimps, her cheeks gradually flushing to flame, threw her such a look that she retreated hastily.

Mrs. Jimps stood biting her lip, obviously put out, and Mr. Peters must have noticed it, for he stopped laughing and spoke again.

" You shall make me your porridge and your haggis, and I will presently try your whiskey," he promised, " but your coffee, No ! "

With that Mrs. Jimps, not knowing what to say, had to be content. She went down, and, easing her mind considerably to Annie and Maggie in the kitchen, sent up water and ground coffee.

This provoked another explosion from above, and the coffee came back. Presently there stole through the house the aroma of roasting berries, then the distant sound of a coffee-mill. After that there was peace in Mr. Peters' part of the house until, just as Mrs. Jimps was making her nightly round, candle in hand, with Annie in attendance, there came a crash and the clatter of broken glass far down in the street below. To Mrs. Jimps' thumps at his door, and her agonized entreaties to be told what had happened, her Paying Guest made answer at last. He opened the door

wide and appeared in a dressing-gown, and apparently little
else, with a fresh-lit cigarette between his lips.

"How you did frighten us, Mr. Peters! What has happened?"

Annie gasped incoherently in the back-ground while Mrs.
Jimps put this reasonable question, and Mr. Peters surveyed them curiously.

"Your so damnable windows," he said, "will not open
above. I must have air, and I have therefore broken two.
That is all. Good sleep to you," and with that he bowed
and shut the door in their faces before Mrs. Jimps had recovered from the combined effect of his costume and his
comminatory adjective. Later, she found that, in what she
carefully explained to the two servants was his foreign way,
he used such words more often than her Paying Guests
usually did. It was with him no sign of anger or any other
feeling. He merely made his conversation picturesque
therewith, when he thought the words expressed his meaning best. In the future, one supposes, they may be left to
the time-honored imagination of our dear readers.

After this episode Mrs. Jimps' household was quiet, and,
let us hope, slept.

# CHAPTER II

If you were to do as Mr. Peters did on the morning after his arrival in Edinburgh, and take a car from the General Post Office down Leith Walk, you would find your surroundings very quickly, indeed immediately, changed. From Edinburgh, aristocratic, professional, and academic, you are moving towards her money-making mercantile sister, Leith. If Edinburgh is wedded to wisdom (as some of her inhabitants fondly suppose), and if Leith has married money (as she is popularly declared to have done), it is natural that you should see differences, and natural, perhaps, that their close relationship should emphasize the occasionally exchanged sneer. As you roll away down the hill, you see at once that Leith means business, and sticks to it, in business-like offices and in great warehouses, with whiffs of the salt sea to keep her wide awake, and weather-beaten sea-captains and strange, foreign, and seafaring men to keep her in touch with other lands. Perhaps these things, and the battered storm-wrecked ships that come panting into harbor, like spent swimmers, serve to keep some men soft-hearted in spite of bargaining, and with something of the child's wondering appreciation of the wonderful world that many of us rather yawn over at middle age. Let us leave Mr. Peters, impassive and imperturbable, but noticing most things from the top of his tram-car, and make our way before him to the Leith office of Mr. Moriarty, Swedish Consul, and a keen man of business, but with something of those less business-like qualities we have hinted at above.

Work just now is slack with Mr. Moriarty, and he is engaged in what, for him, combines business with pleasure. Watch him now, as with a pencil viciously nipped between his teeth, he rolls his eye ceiling-ward, following a fly as though it possessed the thing that he longed for. The fly, after some gyrations, pops out at the open window, and Mr. Moriarty says " Darnee ! " not unkindly, but with a pensive melancholy, having thereby lost the thread of his ideas.

He looks ruefully at the sheet of paper before him, and turns over some leaves of the dictionary at his elbow. The fringe of stiff, sturdy hair that stands on end, circling a bullet head and bald pate, bristles more than ever with the agonies of composition. What this elderly and highly respected merchant is at, we must find out some other time, for a stranger's voice is heard in the outer office, and Mr. Moriarty listens. " The young blagyard ! " he mutters, as the youngest clerk, announcing him as disengaged, can be heard bringing the stranger in, and dictionary and paper disappear in the nearest drawer as Mr. Peters is announced.

He came in with his usual air of polite solemnity, and, bowing in silence, presented his card and a letter together.

Mr. Moriarty, looking at him over the top of his glasses, waved his hand towards a chair, and opened the letter.

It was a formal note, introducing the bearer, Giuseppe Peters, " referred to in my former letter of the 16th August," and signed Olaf Bergen.

Mr. Moriarty, whose face was fast losing the fierce expression with which he had greeted his imprudent clerk, opened a letter-clip, and took a letter in the same writing from it.

" Hm-m," he read, " ' Consignment of pine '—No, no, that's not it," and then he found the passage he wanted.

" ' I also consign to your kindness, my good Moriarty, a what-you-call second-cousin of mine, Giuseppe Peters, of late visiting these parts from America, who tells me that he has family affairs to settle in your city. Do what you can for him on my part, my good Moriarty, and let him try that very particular whiskey. You will find that he has the head of a man.' Th' chap hasn't forgotten that whiskey yet," chuckled Mr. Moriarty, as delighted as if he had never read the passage before, and, rising from his chair, beamed upon the attentive Peters.

" You're welcome to Leith, and to all that I can do for you in it, Mr. Peters. What can I do for you now ? " He held out his hand and shook the other man's heartily enough, and the latter, rising from his chair with another grave bow, gave him such a grip in exchange that Mr. Moriarty surveyed his own fingers with some amazement, almost surprised to find them in their place. " Man ! ye've the divil's own fist," he remarked. " If your head's as strong as your hand, why ——," and he broke off as if words failed him, and sat down again. " I wonder how I can best serve ye," he went on meditatively, and looked at Mr. Peters, his head a little on one side, like a terrier, and waited for a reply.

" Bergen told me," returned Peters slowly, his voice booming through the office like strong wind down a big chimney, " that the name of Moriarty would bring me respect and attention at all times in this place."

" Did he now ? " asked the other, frankly delighted. " That's good of him, sir, though maybe saying a bit too much. Still, he knows me in office hours and out of 'em. If Bergen says that, why, maybe there's some truth in it among them that know me," and he nodded, while Peters went on.

" If you would do me the goodness to be my banker ? " he said.

" With all the world's pleasure, for as much as you like, and as long as you please, if so be as the Bank of Scotland isn't good enough for you," returned Moriarty, opening his honest eyes widely.

So the big man slowly and carefully unbuckled a belt from about his waist, and, taking packets of notes therefrom, he counted out five hundred pounds, and put back the rest. "There is something more," he said, as the other began to write a receipt, and, turning to the chair, lifted a black bag that lay beside it. He opened that, and took a canvas bag from it. This was old and dirty, with a letter or two and a number on it—J.F. 1000. "That is all," he said, and Mr. Moriarty added to his memorandum, "also a canvas bag, tied and sealed, marked J.F. 1000, contents unknown," and locked them up, then and there, in his safe.

"You'll dine with me on Saturday?" he asked, hunting for a card. "Pot-luck, at seven, mind—and no swallow-tails."

Mr. Peters, looking somewhat puzzled, had swallow-tails explained to him. "Never wore 'em in the States?" queried Moriarty to himself, and then, begging Peters to look in any time before Saturday when he happened to be passing or to be in want of any help in his family affairs, he showed him out, risking his fingers in another warm handshake. His conscience plagued him sorely as he turned back into the office. He was a temperate man in spite of any idea Bergen's letter may have given to the contrary, and the thought of spirits in the morning was abhorrent to him. But a foreigner, from the States, too! It was most inhospitable not to have offered it at anyrate, though he wanted badly to get back to his desk.

"Mackenzie," he said to the youngest clerk, who had been put by his seniors to sit opposite the door because there was a draught there when it opened. "Mackenzie! Run out, there's a good fellow, and, if you can see that gentleman, say that I'll be obliged if he'll step back for a minute."

Mackenzie tumbled off his stool, and rushed out hatless, to return in half a minute.

"He's not far," he explained. "I'll just take my hat——"

"Tut, tut," interrupted his master. "Let be! He'll be
calling again in a day or two. Remember, you, sir, that if
any gentleman calls to see me, you don't know whether I'm
engaged or not until you've asked."

He plunged back into the inner room, shut the door, and
pulled out writing pad and paper. His visitor had uncon-
sciously suggested the word that he wanted, and Mr. Moriarty longed to set it down.

Meanwhile Giuseppe Peters had made for the waterside,
and was strolling among the shipping. Cranes swung great
sacks of grain and flour and meal over his head, and puffing
locomotives threatened to run him down without his seeming to notice them. He strolled serenely on, and fell into a
brown study when he reached open water at a pier-head.
There he sat down, and looked across the Forth—which for
once happened to be sparkling in the sun—without seeing
very much. The steamers grunted and puffed past him, the
gulls, attracted by scraps tossed from some cook's galley,
fought in the water at his feet, and screamed harshly overhead. Morning became afternoon, and afternoon wore on
until the shadows lengthened, and still he sat idly. Sometimes he muttered a word or two between his teeth; once he
put up his hand to his throat, and, pulling out a gold coin
that hung about his neck, stared at it and laughed a little.
Perhaps he began to feel hungry, perhaps it was the clocks
of Leith striking five that roused him at last. He looked at
his watch and rose.

"Five," he said, "and I've had nothing to eat but my
breakfast! The dinner of Mrs. Jimps will be the worse for
my appetite." And that evening Mrs. Jimps watched him,
marvelling, and wondered whether he ate like that always,
and whether such a Paying Guest would pay after all.

# CHAPTER III

### MR. PETERS DECLARES HIS ERRAND

It was a quarter to seven on Saturday evening, and the household of Timothy Lucius Moriarty was as busy as he could make it. You would think, as the exasperated cook remarked, that he was giving a " bankit " to the Lord Provost of Edinburgh and all the Town Council instead of to one man from Amerikey, who likely didn't know grouse when he saw them, and couldn't tell hare-soup from ox-tail. " There's nothing comes frae thae pairts worth eatin' except Blue Points," she told the table-maid, turning her red face from the fire, " and ——, ther's his bell once more. Tell um, Jean, that if it's me he's wishing to see, I'll come, but the birds 'll be sinners," that at least was what it sounded like, but she meant cinders, and the message being duly delivered, her master left the cook in peace.

" If Miss Nelly'd make haste down an' pacify um," she confided to the hare-soup as she peered into it, " things'd gang a' richt," and Jean, the table-maid, inclined to agree with her.

Nelly Moriarty, the motherless child of the house, was in her room putting a finishing touch here and there, and trying, from various points of view and with hand-glass and mirror tilted at various angles, to decide whether her hair was as it should be at the back. This was not so easy as it might have been had she owned less, or had she been able to take it off for re-arrangement, but she was satisfied at last.

" Dad'll be in a fine fury by this time," she announced to the mirror. " Must be off, or he'll get as hot as the soup," and down she went.

Meanwhile, her father, his hair as much on end as when we saw him last, was pacing up and down the drawing-room, looking at his watch every two minutes. Twice he put his hand on the bell and twice he took it away, remembering cook's prophecy concerning the "birds." Over his own meals he was as meek as any lamb, but when a guest was concerned his hospitable soul knew no peace. As for Nelly, who ruled the house with smiles and a rod of iron, he alternated between forgetting that she was past the school-room and making her responsible for everything right or wrong. Whatever he might say or pretend, she was really like his heart's blood to him, though he often vowed her the plague of his life, and swore that she would bring his gray hairs in sorrow to the grave. From all which you will infer that Lucius Moriarty, owing to his Irish blood or some other cause of which I know nothing, was a somewhat unreasonable and unreasoning man, at anyrate where his daughter was concerned, but that he had his likable qualities.

And now let us follow Nelly as she goes into the drawing-room.

When she opened the door her father was standing in the middle of the room, watch in hand, and held it out for her to see the time.

" Five minutes to seven ! " he said solemnly. " It's dress —dress —— "

" Dressed ! "

Miss Ellen Moriarty finished the sentence for him, and rounded it with a smacking kiss.

" There, sir," she announced, " though you don't deserve it. How many times have you sent down for poor Carter? "

" Only twice," Lucius declared. ".At least, the next time I told her not to come."

" A queer thing to tell her ! " commented Nelly, gravely, " and one I didn't think she'd need to be told at her time of life. I think you mean three times, dad."

" What's a man to do," grumbled Lucius, " if the girl who should see to such things spends her time before her glass with her chignons and ——"

" Chignons ! " interrupted Nelly, remorselessly, " I may have heard of them in the nursery, dad, but never since. Why, you're *awfully* out of date, you old dear ! "

" If I hadn't given an eye to the table, what would one know about how things were ? " demanded Lucius, gruffly.

" Just as much as one does now, daddy, seeing that everything was done before I went up to dress."

" Then I had to see Carter and make sure that she put more pepper into the soup.    She always forgets."

" And I do hope and trust she has forgotten again, father dear, since I went down and seasoned it myself."    She was surveying her father critically all the time.    " I can't make out what's wrong with you," she said at last.    " Why, your hair's all on end !    Run away, there's a dear, and give it a good brush.    Off you go !    The bell hasn't rung yet," and she hustled him good-humoredly out of the room, and was sitting the very picture of a demure and somewhat reserved young lady when Mr. Peters was ushered in.

He was in swallow-tails, in spite of Lucius' injunction, and looked well in them, too, or so Nelly thought as she lifted her eyes and made a swift, but fairly thorough inspection, as was her habit with strangers.

" Big," she thought, " and strong, and what strong, white teeth he's got.    He's not shy before a woman, anyhow. He's very polite, too.    I'm not sure *yet* ——," and then dinner was announced, and Mr. Peters ceremoniously offered his arm, while Lucius followed on behind, thinking that, after all, there was no girl like his, and that in her way of walking and the turn of her head, she got more like her sainted mother every hour.

The dinner went on quietly and pleasantly in the comfortable dining-room.    If Nelly made a despairing little

mouth over her first spoonful of doubly seasoned soup, it
was only Jean who saw her, and the other two, as she re-
ported downstairs, " took them [soup being plural here-
abouts] as if they could ha' ta'en mair."

Nelly questioned Peters now and then about the States
and the places he had visited, while Lucius, satisfied by this
time that his guest was going to be well dined, beamed upon
both, and sent down a message of congratulation to the
kitchen.   Peters talked well, slowly, and with now and then
a quaint word or turn of sentence that showed he often
thought in a foreign tongue, but he seemed to know what
was likely to interest Nelly, and gave her picturesque little
sketches of life here and there.

" He's clever too," she thought, while she watched him,
" and he's attentive and entertaining, but ——"

She broke off, even in thinking, because she didn't know
exactly what her own " but " meant.   It really meant that
she was not quite sure of Mr. Peters—how to ticket him in
fact.   Women, especially young ones, like to classify us, the
simpler sex, and Mr. Peters did not lend himself to any such
arrangement.   He was absolutely polite, to her, but so he
was to her father, with precisely the same manner, and listened to the one as attentively as to the other.   She might
as well be a man, she told herself with mock indignation.
She tried such perfectly innocent feminine devices as she
knew to draw him out a little, but Mr. Peters could not or
would not be moved.   So Nelly pretended to think he must
be stupid, which she didn't believe for a moment, and was
again demure and retiring, and for her almost dull, until she
had had a glass of wine, and half an apple shared with her
father.   Then she rose from dessert, and, bringing cigars
and cigarettes, laid them at Lucius' side, and went to the
drawing-room—bowed out ceremoniously, but to all appearance without regret, by Mr. Peters.

Arrived at the drawing-room, she sat down at the piano

and practised one or two of the Irish songs that her father liked. She had a pretty voice, and sang with taste, but with not much more—as yet. Then she took up a novel and presently threw it down, and some fancy work, and threw that down, thinking that if Mr. Peters had not been so stupid and dull she could have wished the men would leave the dining-room. Later she decided that her dear dad at anyrate mustn't be neglected, and sent down to ask if they would have coffee there or upstairs. Meanwhile, the men had been chatting, while Lucius puffed a big cigar, and Peters slowly smoked one cigarette after another, listening to his host and watching the wreaths of smoke through lazy, half-closed eyes.

" You'll be staying here some time? " asked Lucius, pushing the decanters across, when Peters had closed the door behind Nelly and was back in his seat.

" Some time, probably," he answered, looking critically at the cigarette he had just lit. It was a fat one, with " Dream " stamped at one end.

" Does that suit you ? " asked Lucius, rising; " if not, I've another lot somewhere handy. I'm no judge of those paper things myself."

But Mr. Peters waved his hand in protestation. " The most excellent," he assured Lucius. " What did I do ? I thought, for the moment, of my business, which was most rude."

" Thought you didn't like it," explained Lucius, returning to his seat. " Here's to your business, Mr. Peters, whatever that may be," and they bowed to one another over their glasses.

" You'll find these parts lively enough for a winter. Dance, I s'pose ?—of course ! " as Peters nodded, " and no entanglements ? "

His guest's eyebrows went up a trifle as he looked for an explanation.

"No lassie weeping her eyes out for ye over beyond?" explained Lucius, and Peters laughed loudly.

"I have made no one weep—yet," he announced.

"D'ye know any Edinburgh folk?"

"By name, some. I shall know more of them later on."

"Of course, of course," assented Lucius. "If you've letters or anything of that kind for 'em, of course they'll make you welcome and you'll soon know more of 'em. Who did you say they were?"

Peters opened his mouth as if to answer, and then looked at Lucius' good-tempered face, and shut it again, trying apparently to think of something.

"I have forgotten the name," he said at last; "your Scots names are so strange. It was perhaps Mac Something?"

"Perhaps," said Lucius, chuckling at his own small joke. "There are one or two Mac Somethings hereabouts. But you'll find 'em later, no doubt."

"Oh! I shall find them," said Mr. Peters, with an air of quiet conviction that set Lucius off chuckling again.

"I'll show you the Macs presently in the directory," he promised him. "Are these the people you have business with?"

"Perhaps," said Mr. Peters.

"Good biz., I hope," said Lucius. "Money in it, I hope, Mr. Peters, since you've come so far." But Mr. Peters shook his head and said he thought not.

"A debt to pay; that is all," he told Lucius.

"Ey, ey! That's a different matter," Lucius sighed regretfully. "Still, it's a great pleasure, sir, to be able to pay one's debts!"

"It is indeed," Mr. Peters agreed solemnly, "and I have been compelled to leave this—(how do you business men say —standing?)—far too long."

"Old family business?" asked Lucius, interested, but not wishing to put unpleasant questions.

Mr. Peters nodded again. "My father died suddenly," he explained, "and in debt. I now wish to settle the account."

"Very right and proper spirit, sir," said Lucius, raising his glass and nodding his warm approval. "It 'd do honor to any merchant here, an' if it was my affair, Gad! I'd be glad to meet you half-way. When you've looked over your documents, you can tell me the name if you like, and I'll do anything to help you if they've business with me. They'd likely be ready to let you off something."

"Very true!" Mr. Peters considered gravely, and seemed to think that possible. "But I will pay them in full," he added.

Just then the maid came down with Nell's message and Lucius repeated it.

"What d'ye say? Shall we go up now and have our coffee with my Nell, as she's alone?"

Mr. Peters said he would be most happy, and rose, throwing away his half-finished cigarette.

"She'll give us a song if you're fond of music, and," said Lucius, chuckling, "Jeanie, get the directory from the library, there's a good lassie, and bring it to me in the drawing-room."

So they went upstairs and had their coffee with Nell.

Jean brought the directory, and Lucius, with great satisfaction, turned up the Mac's and the M's. They agreed that it was of no use bothering until Peters had looked over his papers. "Tho', anyway," said Lucius, dryly, "I'm thinking that if you were to put in to-morrow's papers that you'd come to pay a debt, and wanted your creditor's address, you'd not have to wait long!"

Then Nelly sang to them, while Mr. Peters sat very still, and he thanked her very politely at the end, but whether he listened to her, or thought about something else all the time, she couldn't tell. After that he said good-night, and went

away; while Lucius shouted after him from the door-step, to
be sure and speak any time that he, Lucius Moriarty, could
be of any use.

Lucius went back to a little snuggery of his own, where
he usually ended the evening with a book and a cigar, for he
was a careful and critical reader. There he found Nell
waiting, as was her habit, for five minutes' gossip, usually
conducted on his knee.

"Pleasant chap, Peters!" he suggested, as Nell settled
herself down.

"M'yes," said Nell, and Lucius, who always either hated
or loved a man, and cursed or blessed him with fervor accordingly, demanded what she found wrong with him.

"The rudiments o' hospitality aren't in you!" he insisted.
"Here's a poor fellow—a stranger an' a foreigner—comes
on an honest errand, with a letter from a man we both know,
and who thinks nothing too good for you when he comes
this way; an' yet, of this stranger—his relative—all the good
you can say is 'M'yes,'" which Lucius miaulled out as if he
were a tom-cat on the tiles.

"The man's good-looking, isn't he?" he went on.

"Oh, yes!" Nell allowed; "though I don't like a middle-
aged man to be so fat about the face," she added critically.
Peters was at most only thirty-five, but to Nell that seemed
quite middle-aged, if not past it.

"What's the objection?" demanded Lucius. "Would
you have us all like Irving in the Bells? He's a powerful
well-informed man, too."

This, we may say, was asserted on the strength of a monologue by Lucius, which it has not been necessary to repeat,
upon some hobbies of his, during which monologue Peters
had sat silent, but apparently appreciative.

"I daresay, dad, I don't understand him, that's all, and
so I don't know for certain if I like him or not."

"Conceit," says Lucius dogmatically. "How can a lassie

like you understand any man ? Be off to bed, my dear, and leave me to me book. The man's just a simple, honest chap, who pays his way, and owes no man anything but what he's ready to fork out. Be off wid ye."

3

# CHAPTER IV

## LUCIUS PROPOSES A QUIET EVENING

IT was early in September when Peters presented his letter of introduction to Lucius, and September drifted on without his showing any pressing concern about his business, so far at least as Lucius could see.

"An easy-going chap," he told Nell in the snuggery; "don't seem to know if he'll settle things next week or next month. Now, I guess my correspondents in the States aren't like that much. However, what d' you say to letting him meet some folks here? Quietly, y' know, and no fuss or bother for you?"

One of Lucius' theories was that, by guileful and steady practice, with gradual increasing of her responsibilities, he was training his girl to be fit to rule a house. A child like that, he thought (when do we cease to be children for our parents?), naturally timid of responsibility, must be led gently through the mysteries of housekeeping, and must not be frightened by having to give entertainments on anything but the most modest scale. Unfortunately for his theory, Lucius' hospitable wish to entertain everyone he knew, and a good many he didn't know, led him into practices which did not correspond; at which he would stare far more aghast than Nell.

"Everybody's away still," he said to comfort her further, "so you can do it quite quietly without offending 'em."

"Very well, dear," answered Nell serenely. "If they're all away I don't see how we can get them to come, but what do you want? Half a dozen or so in for a little music next week? People are beginning to come back, I can tell you."

34

" Ay, half a dozen or so in for a little music," agreed Lucius cautiously.   " And maybe one or two to come early for dinner.   Music's cold comfort to some folk.   At least (diplomatically) I know they enjoy your songs more as they ought to, if they've seen first what a grand housewife y'are."

Nelly gave his ear a pull for this attempt at diplomacy, and Lucius, thinking of another powerful reason, went on—

" The table looked lop-sided last time Peters was here," he remarked casually.   " I saw you noticed it, my dear, and one or two more would make it look more decent."

" One would, daddy.   Two would put it wrong again."

" Best make it three or five then.   Seven's a good number, for that would make ten," Lucius told her.   " But you mustn't think of more than that: of course, for afterwards ye'll make it as many as ye please.   It's as easy for you to please fifty with a song as fifteen, and sandwiches and a cup of coffee are no expense, thanks be."

" Aren't they ? " asked Nelly, innocently.   " I've got the bills for the last evening, and I'll fetch them, dad.   Somehow I thought ——"

" Tut, tut ! lassie, none of your havers.   With a housekeeper like you I can afford to see my friends now and then. It's time for you to be in your bed too, and I'll just finish this book."

" Dad !   It's my novel, and you told me only last week that I ought to be ashamed of reading it, when I couldn't give you a line of Goldsmith or Sheridan."

" Go off to your bed, ye besom ! " retorted her father. " How could I say that when I hadn't read it ?   I would be most unjust.   Here's a man writes a book about Constantinople who's never been in it, and it's most extraordinary life-like."

" I didn't know you'd been there either," retorted Nelly maliciously, but Lucius refused to notice this.

" The life and the learning a clever man will put into a

good novel—good, mind ye, none of your trash—is most surprisin'. None o' your slaughtering and cheap love-making, but a plain, honest story."

"There's a lot of killing and love-making further on," Nell warned him. "You'd better drop it. They called for the book to-day, and I hunted high and low for the thing."

"If you'd looked you'd have found it got mixed up with some papers in my bureau," Lucius told her, with one eye on the page.

"The bureau was locked."

"Ay, so it was. D'ye think I want all the maids routing round? Be off now, and let me get time to finish, or they'll call for nothing again to-morrow."

So Nelly planted a kiss on the back of her father's head, and went laughing to her room, and before Lucius went to bed he finished the book, with many ejaculations at the extraordinary knowledge of the novelist.

# CHAPTER V

MEANWHILE Mr. Peters, in spite of his obvious want of business-like push and despatch, was, like an intelligent foreigner, keeping his eyes open. Under the smiles of Mrs. Jimps he lost some of his elaborate gravity. The change did not show itself usually in any frivolous form of joke or laughter, but in the frank comments he made upon things in general. If these comments had been made with any appearance of spite or anger, they might sometimes have fairly been called brutal. When he did anything which might, by a stretch of imagination, be called a joke, it was certain to be practical, and such as was not likely to be forgotten. One night, for example, when he sat in the drawing-room, with the other partakers of Mrs. Jimps' hospitality, whom I need not describe, since they were birds of passage, there came sudden shrieks from the kitchen, with unmistakable oaths in a deeper tone, and then crept in a faint smell of burning, as Mrs. Jimps opened the door and indignantly swept out to investigate.

The others wondered to one another what could be the matter. If Mr. Peters wondered, he didn't say so.

When Mrs. Jimps came back, she had a strange and harrowing story to tell.

This, it seemed, was the night upon which Annie, by permission, was accustomed to receive her young man, who, I believe, has already been spoken of as a corporal of dragoons.

While that innocent couple sat before the kitchen fire

alone, it being cook's evening out, and talking, so she assured Mrs. Jimps, of the minister they had heard together only the week before, there came a live coal out of the fire and struck her beloved in the face, " and if you will believe me," Mrs. Jimps told her eagerly interested auditors in the drawing-room, " the poor young man's mustache is nearly all gone, and his face is quite scorched, while the smell of that burnt mustache, well—it might have been gunpowder, or sulphur, or anything."

" Really a cinder ? " asked Mr. Peters, much concerned.

" Yes, Mr. Peters, there it was on the hearthstone, as Annie showed me."

" Most miraculous," he told her, " and sulphuric smells, you have said ? While they talked of their minister ? It will be the Devil, do you not think ? "

" Well," said Mrs. Jimps cautiously, " in these parts, although one knows very well that there are Powers of Evil, still, one doesn't look for ——"

" I have known many such things," he said, gravely, " but the Devil has made one of his silly mistakes. This good fellow, being a brave dragoon, will have laughed."

" He didn't while I was there," Mrs. Jimps said. " His mustache, you know ! "

" These brave boys care nothing for their appearance," Mr. Peters assured her. " He will have been vexed that you were disturbed."

" Perhaps so," said Mrs. Jimps doubtfully, and the matter dropped for the time.

When Mr. Peters went to his room, he rang the bell. There was no answer at first, but he was always very patient, and he waited patiently now until cook answered.

" You ! " he said. " Where is my good friend Annie ? "

" She's a sair heid, sir," the cook explained, " and she's now away to her bed."

" Our poor Annie ! " Mr. Peters was most sympathetic.

"But I have excellent remedies for sore heads (it is that you said, is it not ?), and I will cure it."

So presently, Annie, seeing no help for it, made her appearance, with her head bundled up in a shawl, at which Mr. Peters laughed immoderately. "I have a message for your soldier," he informed her. "If you take any more of my best cigars for the pig, there will be gunpowder enough and plenty in the next to make him so that you shall see his face no more. Now, go !" and she went.

He came with a very good knowledge of English, though he used a foreign idiom now and then, with queer turns of sentences. Now he enlarged his vocabulary quickly, being ready to talk, at table or in the street, with anyone who was conversationally inclined, and he constantly asked questions where a meaning was not plain to him.

"My good Mrs. Jimps," he called up to her from the foot of the dinner-table one evening, "am I at liberty to put to you one little question ?"

"Why, certainly, Mr. Peters !" Mrs. Jimps said politely. There were ten at table that night, and Mr. Peters, being now the male resident of longest stay, sat facing Mrs. Jimps, and wrestled with a fowl as he spoke.

"This is an ancient fowl," he remarked casually, as he disarticulated a leg, and then, "What is a lodger, madam ?"

"A lodger, er—lodges in a lodging-house, and pays for board and lodging," Mrs. Jimps told him, after consideration.

"So ?" and Mr. Peters disposed of the other leg.

"What is a guest, my dear Mrs. Jimps ?"

"A guest is a friend who stays in your house."

"But a Paying Guest ?"

"A friend also, I hope, Mr. Peters," Mrs. Jimps said, drawing herself up and flushing a little. Poor woman, she did her best with her Paying Guests and her House of Residence. It was, after all, a harmless expression; and since it somehow made her feel superior to the ordinary landlady, her Paying Guests quite possibly profited in comfort, if not in coin. Mr. Peters asked no more, but openly lamented the difficulties of our tongue.

" Here," he said, " are two things which are the same thing. ' Lodger ' and ' Paying Guest,' also ' Lodging ' and ' House of Residence,' and the poor foreigner who wishes to learn is troubled over two, until he finds they are one. It is most devilish hard ! "

" Mr. Peters ! "

Mrs. Jimps had told him before, that certain words were not used in polite society—at anyrate before ladies; and this was one of them.

" Pardon ! " he entreated. " We may say ' deuced,' may we not? and that again is the same thing, and both refer to a thing in which I do not believe."

The conversation was then changed by some charitable tourist, but poor Mrs. Jimps noticed, after that, that when anything in the House of Residence happened to displease Mr. Peters, he took the next opportunity of alluding to his " lodgings " and to himself as her poor lodger. To do him justice, he was not readily displeased, and often seemed so preoccupied as to pass over, unnoticed, little discomforts that occurred with the coming and going of visitors, and which would have irritated most other men.

Every day he strolled, big, placid, and dignified, about the city, with apparently no other object in life than to quietly enjoy himself, and to listen in innocent silence to any lies which any guide chose to tell him. Sometimes he took a cab, and once imperturbably allowed a cabman to drive him from the Castle to Leith by way of the Queen's Drive, because the fellow began chatting about a celebrated trial, as they passed near the Parliament House, and went on to speak of the judges and advocates engaged. Peters rose from the seat of the open cab, and went up on to the box, where he questioned the man about the judges, some of whom, at anyrate, he knew by name already.

It was that evening on his return that he made the acquaintance of a lady whom I must introduce, namely. Miss Sophia Amélie Rivers, who asked her friends to call her Amélie, and was therefore known as Em'ly.

Mr. Peters had dined, and having gone out for an evening stroll, was roaming placidly along through the streets under a cloudy sky, when, having put a cigarette between his lips, he discovered that he had no matches. He grunted, and then, seeing that there was a tobacconist's shop opposite, he crossed the road and went in.

There was, there still is, nothing striking about the place to distinguish it from a dozen others. It stands in one of the lesser streets behind Princes Street, and is just a small, well-kept shop, with a wooden, genial-looking, kilted Highlander extending his mull to you at the door, and with a pigeon-hole of a room behind, in which a light must always be kept burning if one is to see anything there, since there is no window, and not much light comes through from the street. As for ventilation, except through the shop, there is none but the chimney. Of course Mr. Peters didn't know all this at once. He rapped on the counter, seeing no one, and presently the curtain which separated the shop from the pigeon-hole was lifted, and a frowsy-headed damsel appeared.

Her hair was the fashionable color, or as near as she could get it, namely, a sort of straw yellow. Her dress was brown velveteen, rubbed at the elbows, and very balloon-like at the shoulders. She had a wide, good-natured mouth, with good teeth, which she showed often by a broad smile. Her complexion was remarkable, considering the atmosphere in which most of her life was probably spent, and one felt that to match it, her hair, if she left it alone, must surely be red. She had a dirty novel in her hand, the back torn away, and she kept her place in it with her left forefinger while she gave Mr. Peters his matches.

" Anything else ? " she asked, and he said " No," and turned away, but stopped at the door. A few big drops of rain fell, splashing in great blotches on the pavement; people began to scatter and hurry for shelter, and Mr. Peters turned to the counter again. The girl was watching him from the back, with a woman's natural admiration for broad shoulders, and smiled again when he said he would smoke there until the rain stopped.

" W'y, cert'nly," she said, and, lighting a cigarette, he rested on the long, leather-covered seat that was placed against the wall opposite the counter.

" Reg'lar Scotch weather, ain't it ? " she said, genially. " 'Ow d'you like Edinburgh ? "

" I think your city most superb," Mr. Peters replied gravely.

" 'Taint mine," said the young person, with a somewhat disdainful projection of the chin. " I don't belong properly to these parts."

" Indeed ? "

Mr. Peters, having nothing else to occupy him, was much interested, or seemed so.

" What part of this country has the honor ? "

She looked at him suspiciously. " B'lieve he's fooling," was her first thought, but Mr. Peters was already lost in contemplation of his cigarette. " Just his forrin' way," she said to herself, for foreign he certainly seemed.

" London's my 'ome," she told him. " I'm a Cockney born and bred, I am."

" A great city ! " announced Mr. Peters politely, and lapsed into silence again.

The rain was now coming down like a water-spout, the empty streets were filled with the hissing of it on the flagstones and with the gradually growing gurgle of the gutters.

The girl looked out into the dusk and gave a little sigh, because she wanted to get back to her novel, where the heroine was wavering (though only through innocence and for a moment) between the villain with a coronet and the poor but extremely handsome and honest hero, who was to claim the coronet later.

" Can't expect the poor fellow to go out in it, I s'pose," she allowed, generously, to herself.  " Let's see who he is ! " and laying her book open, face down, on the shelf under the counter, she rested both elbows on some cigar-boxes, and resigned herself to social amenities.

" W'ere d'you come from ? " she asked.

Mr. Peters waved his cigarette widely and vaguely.  " A wanderer," he explained.

"A sailor, p'r'aps," she suggested.  "A sea-captain, say ? "

" I have sailed," he admitted, and let the question of capacity go by.

Miss Amélie Rivers grew interested, and thought over the matter a little, while Mr. Peters smoked on, and the rain rustled through the streets.   Now and then the faint sound of far-off thunder mixed with the rattle of passing cabs.

" Sailors go to all parts," Amélie sagely announced at last. " Now, I wonder if you've ever been to the States ? "

Yes, Mr. Peters had been to the States, and said so.

" I've had friends there," she went on, at which Mr. Peters laughed rather sarcastically.

" You all have friends there," he told her.   " Now you want very much to know if I have met your friends."

Amélie was nettled at his tone, being suspicious of sarcasm.

" I've only one of my people there now, anyway," she said, " and it doesn't matter what I want to know, and I think the rain's pretty well done."

The rain wasn't done, and anyone could tell that much, but she thought a broad hint to go was excusable.

Mr. Peters, however, was not the man to take a hint, unless it suited him, and he was only amused.

" Would you have me drowned ? " he asked pathetically. " Who is your friend, and where, in that so small place ? "

" My pa's there," said Amélie sulkily, " or was when I heard of him last. But I don't want to trouble you."

" How could I be so ungrateful ! " protested Mr. Peters gallantly. " Tell me your name. Certainly I may have met him."

He was so accustomed to such questions, and so prepared to say he had never met the man, that he struck a match noisily when he had spoken, and lit another cigarette.

" My name's Sophia Amélie Rivers," Amélie answered, waiting, however, until he was quiet again.

" That's not his name, though," she said presently. She had not realized that her question involved a small confession on her part.

" Your dear father is not called Sophia Amélie ? " suggested Peters.

" No, nor Rivers."

" How is that ? " Mr. Peters asked, scenting another mystery of the English language.

" Well, you see," Amélie admitted, " I don't like our name. It's a good enough name, but when I was in a London establishment, the young ladies made fun of it. Some girls are such fools, you know ! " and Mr. Peters nodding sympathetically, said " yes," and begged her to go on.

It was a stupid sort of thing to have to explain, though. Amélie was glad that she had forgotten to light the gas in the shop, for her cheeks were getting a little hot.

" It's something to be able to blush anyway, you silly ! " she told herself. " You know plenty who can't ! " and she went on defiantly. " So I just changed my name a bit when I came away. I says to myself, ' I shall have to change it some day, anyhow, I suppose ' ; " and here she

giggled a little, while Mr. Peters declared that she must
have had many chances already.

"While you're about it," she went on, "it's as well to
have a pretty one, and I found one in a lovely book. So I
just changed Buncombe into Rivers. What d'you think
of it?"

What Mr. Peters thought of it she couldn't hear at the
moment, for just then a flash of lightning that flickered into
the little shop, followed at once by a thundering peal, made
her shriek.

"Good Lord!" she ejaculated, directly the thunder had
rolled, muttering, away. "I'll light the gas at once, and
close that door. Why, it made you look awful! I wouldn't
have another flash like that in the dark for anything. I'd
be afraid to look at you." She bustled round and lit the gas,
but did not close the door. Mr. Peters stood in the doorway, looking out upon the street.

"I wonder, now, if I looked as queer as you did?" she
said, but got no answer.

"It is stopping," he told her presently, "and I will go."

"Wait till it's finished," suggested Amélie.

"It is late," returned Peters, and stepped into the street.

"P'r'aps you'll look in some time when you're passing,"
screamed Amélie after him.

"I will certainly come back," he shouted over his
shoulder, and Amélie picked up her novel again.

"Don't know that I want to see him either," she remarked, as she ran her finger down the page. "He doesn't
seem to have met pa, anyway," and presently she was lost in
the sorrows and joys of her heroine.

# CHAPTER VI

## A LITTLE DINNER

As Nell Moriarty had told her father, people were beginning to come back to town, and settle down for the winter. She had no difficulty in finding friends ready to come, and Lucius' limit of ten for dinner was quickly reached. Imagine them then in the cosey, old-fashioned dining-room, which we know already. Nell has been brought down by an elderly bachelor friend of the family, Donald Dee, a counsel at the Scottish Bar, who was at school with Lucius, and who, being of a sanguine temperament, is quite ready to flirt paternally with Lucius' daughter. His legal training gives him a ready tongue, and Nell rather enjoys the flutterings of this ancient butterfly. Also, maybe, although she would not acknowledge it to herself, she is interested to see how far some other people are affected by these philanderings.

On his right hand, Lucius has a widow of comfortable proportions and sufficient income, Mrs. MacQuestra, whose manœuvres are watched apprehensively by Nell. For it is Nell's secret belief that her father is the innocent quarry of all unattached females, and doomed to a melancholy slavery, unless she be for ever vigilant.

Lucius tortures her with his open admiration and enjoyment of the widow's lively badinage, while the widow herself, expanding figuratively in the warmth of his smile, looks to Nell horribly and deceitfully young and traitorous.

Mr. Peters is quietly studying his partner, a lady of whom we shall see more. She is a Miss Margaret Murray, a woman of perhaps twenty-seven or twenty-eight, who professes to have a great admiration for Nell, and has recently cultivated her acquaintance. Madge Murray states that she is fond of truth because anything else is so much trouble, and that no one believes anyone else in any case. I think we will let her speak for herself, and one never has to wait very long for that.

On the other side of Madge sits Tom Dunbar, student of medicine at the University of Edinburgh, now in his final year, and very well aware that he ought to be reading in his own rooms instead of dining sumptuously here. But what would you ? Tom doesn't care a ha'penny for the dinner, at least he thinks not, being just now " a bit off his feed," as he would put it ; he also certainly doesn't care a ha'penny for the lady whom he has brought down, and who privately fears that all students, and especially medical students, are in a bad way.

But Tom is honestly and head over ears in love with Nell Moriarty, and since, as he tells himself a dozen times a day, he's nothing to her and never will be, why what's the good of work or anything else ? Nell, of course, is quite unconscious of his feelings. Young ladies always are in such circumstances, I know. She treats him in a sisterly way which is horrible and delightful torture to him, and Tom listens far more, just now, to her chat with Mr. Donald Dee than to the question of the lady by his side as to how he spends Sundays. It's mean, he knows, to listen, but he does so, and is no happier : in fact, rather the reverse.

The other man of the party accepts, from conscientious motives, all invitations to dine out, thinking it his duty to be sociable, but being on principle a strict vegetarian, makes his hosts unhappy by refusing fish, flesh, and fowl, and inquiring shyly but persistently into the composition of all sauces and puddings. On this particular occasion he is confining himself to bread and asparagus, much to Lucius' dismay.

His partner is a not very brilliant, though tender-hearted

dame, who enjoys a good dinner, but feels abashed before such asceticism. She apologizes hurriedly at intervals, and cannot be made happy.

"A charming little gathering, Miss Nelly," says Dee, "and I am the most fortunate member of it."

Poor Tom Dunbar catches this, and mutters, "I should think so," when his neighbor asks if he ever works on Sundays.

"How well your daughter manages everything for you," says the widow to Lucius. "You cannot expect to keep such a good housekeeper always, Mr. Moriarty."

"She's young yet, ma'am," says Lucius, "an' has a lot to learn. Maybe, when she settles down, there'll be a corner for an old man."

"My dear Mr. Moriarty, you don't expect to keep her so long as all *that*, surely!" says the widow.

"Or I'll get me lady friends to advise me," adds Lucius, and the widow, with her eyes fixed upon her plate, after just the least little fluttering glance at him, says that she is sure he has plenty of lady friends who would do anything they could.

Madge Murray, who had noticed the plate of the vegetarian gentleman, turned presently to Peters.

"Don't you think vegetarianism a fraud?" she asked.

"I have heard," said Peters, gravely, "that your asparagus shouts (or shrieks, is it?) when he is cut."

"Doesn't that spoil your dinner?"

"Why should it?" asked Peters philosophically, helping himself to vegetables. "First, I don't believe it; second, if it is true, I do not hear it."

Madge surveyed him more carefully than before at this frank statement, and lost a trifle of the supercilious and *blasé* air with which she had greeted him on their introduction.

"I don't believe you'd care if you did hear it," she remarked, and Mr. Peters, not perhaps much interested in her beliefs, shrugged his shoulders a little, and turned to hear the explanations of the lady who was apologizing for her carnivorous habits and expressing her ardent desire for a strictly vegetarian diet.

" I assure you," she told her neighbor, contritely, " I should *love* it, if only I might be allowed. But my doctor, a most charming man, who understands my constitution thoroughly, won't hear of it. ' It's nourishment that you want, and nourishment you must have,' he told me only yesterday. He says my brain is so active, you know, that my nervous system needs more support than most people's."

" You cannot imagine the tranquillizing effect," the conscientious man told her.

" Oh, I sleep well enough," she insisted. " He told me I must, and I always nod a little after dinner—when I'm alone and at home, of course," she added hurriedly, and the conscientious man sighed.

So talk went on, growing more lively and general as the champagne went round, and even Tom Dunbar began to feel that stars could be looked at, aye, even climbed for, though one might not expect to reach them.

" P'r'aps if a fellow got the ' Ettles,' or even did a first-class pass," he thought, " she might listen to him," and at the second glass of champagne he began to make great plans for steady work. Time passes quickly when one is building castles in the air, and from this point he didn't pay much attention to the dinner's progress. He answered vaguely when spoken to, and smiled foolishly when his neighbor informed him that she didn't think it a good thing for young men to live alone in lodgings. Evidently she was not a bad sort after all.

" It's awfully dull at times," he told her. " A fellow can't help wanting to go out a bit. Of course," he added, bash-

4

fully, " a fellow can't even think about settling down until
he's capped and properly started."

" Of course not," the lady asserted, heartily. "I quite
agree with you, Mr. Dunbar, that such notions are criminal.
I'm glad you think so. So many people talk of 'settling
down,' by which they mean marriage, as if it were the great
object of life. What I say is, look at me ! "

Tom looked hastily, and muttered " Yes ? "

" Has marriage been my object in life ? " demanded his
neighbor, severely, and answered " No " for herself, since
Tom took so long to think it over.

" Now, especially for young men and women," she went
on, delighted to find so sympathetic a listener, "I would
suggest such surroundings as should protect them from
wrecking their lives at the outset."

Tom, watching Nelly, who at that moment laughed over
something extravagant in the way of a compliment laid at
her feet by the insinuating Dee, muttered incoherent words
that might mean anything.

" For you, for example, I would provide dwellings, somewhat on the collegiate system, with respectable, indeed re-
fined, matrons, who would supervise where necessary, and
make the place so attractive by their society that you would
no longer wish to go outside for less praiseworthy pursuits
and less improving companions."

" Really ! " Tom protested, startled at being taken in
charge so swiftly, " I ——"

" Of course, I don't mean you, Mr. Dunbar. You and I
are, I am glad to see, practically at one on these matters.
I mean your average fellow-student, whose moral back-bone
is, I have reason to fear, less—what do you call it ?—ossi-
fied. Thank you."

Tom was conscientiously trying to decide how far he was
obliged to give his views to this evangelist when Nelly began
to smile in his direction. Thinking that she was going to

say something to him, he forgot all else, and bent forward
only to find that she was trying to catch the widow's eye
and make the signal for moving. Dinner was actually over!
What had he been saying and doing, not to have known it?
Evidently he had eaten and drunk, for there was a half-
finished bunch of grapes before him and his glass was empty.
He got up quickly, and was in time to open the door, thereby earning a little smile and a nod from Nell as she passed
out. Then he made his way back to the table, thinking
what idiots men were not to go up with the ladies, and wondering how soon he might be allowed to join them, if he became his own medical adviser for the moment, and declared
himself warned not to smoke.

The other men came up towards their host's end of the
table and lit their cigarettes, all, that is, excepting the conscientious man. He applied himself energetically to a plate
of bananas.

"How are things getting on, Peters?"

The question was put by Lucius, from whom Mr. Peters
was farthest. It consequently drew everybody's attention to
him, and Lucius thought an explanation needed. He introduced him formally to the rest, and particularly to the Law,
as represented by Mr. Dee.

"Here, Donald, here's a wonder for you. A man from
the States looking for his father's creditors."

Mr. Dee bowed, and raised his glasses, astonished.

"Gad, sir!" he ejaculated, with a genial grimace, "if
your complaint spread, what would become of our profession? But it's not catching, I warrant. Our clients are
more likely to cross the water before than after their creditors."

"He may need help yet," suggested Lucius, but the legal
gentleman sighed doubtfully.

"Not from the Bar," he told them. "There is no plead-
ing needed by the man who wants to pay. Good Lord! and

what credit is to be gained by counsel in such a case ?" He sighed again, with a cheerful and whimsical expression, as though sure that he was surveying a " freak," and that his bread, with thick butter, was secured.

" Glad to take you over Parliament House any time after the Courts sit," he told Mr. Peters, and Peters replied that he would take advantage of the offer, and fell into a conversation that drifted on until Lucius suggested the drawing-room.

There Mr. Dee oscillated between Nelly and Miss Murray, while Tom Dunbar loitered around and tried not to look sulky. The widow openly beckoned Lucius to her side, and by so doing agitated Nell far too much for that anxious young hostess to bestow any attention upon poor Tom. The widow, in a review of recent Celtic literature, had just read a good deal about Celtic Gloom, and was anxious to hear from Lucius whether he was much troubled by it, and to let him understand that, if a woman's sympathy availed anything to a man with such a dismal inheritance, he might always count upon hers. The Designing Creature, as Nell always called her in soliloquy, succeeded in holding Lucius a pleased and willing captive until she made the mistake of insisting upon her passionate love for Irish music in a loud voice while Nell sang.

" Don't you love it ? " asked the widow.

" Ay, ma'am, when I can hear it." Lucius acknowledged, and was overcome by a gloom, possibly Celtic, which lasted until the end of the evening, though unnoticed except by the cause of it.

# CHAPTER VII

WHEN the swallows, following summer, cross the seas to escape the northern winds and frosts, the well-to-do residents of " Auld Reekie " turn homeward. They grumble maybe, but they come. Some of them because they must work, others because they must pretend to, if their fat bank balances are to remain such as will command respect. Others, again, come as they went, because they are accustomed to do as their neighbors do, without thinking for themselves, thereby, no doubt, wisely conserving such nervous energy as they may possess.

With the rest came Hector Inchiquin Inch, one of the Lords of Council and Session, that is, Judge in the Supreme Courts of Scotland. We met him five-and-twenty years ago in circumstances which he at anyrate has not forgotten, although for a time he flattered himself that he should do so. He came home to Edinburgh almost directly after that night of which we have told, and astonished his friends by the steadiness and sobriety with which he set to work to qualify for the Scottish Bar. Hard work he found to be the best remedy for unpleasant memories, and gradually he grew more lenient towards himself, especially as success came.

What had the doggedly persevering student, still less the keen advocate, to do with the shadow of a single night, always growing more shadowy ? His reputation increased, his appetite for work seemed insatiable, and now a year had passed since he had been raised to the Bench. Then, almost at once, the old trouble returned. Whether it was that with

more dignity came less strain of perpetual work and less to
try for, or whether physical trouble pricked conscience, one
cannot tell, but the Lord of Session was often occupied in
self-reproach when smart young advocates flattered themselves that their eloquence commanded, and received, his
entire attention.

Now he came back from Switzerland, where he had spent
the vacation, thin and sallow, looking more as if he came
from prison than from the playground of Europe. With
him came his son, Archibald, a young fellow of nineteen or
twenty—a youngster who in face took after his dead mother,
who had been a silly, pretty woman of fashion, with a full
purse when the young advocate married her. So the brown
paper came down from the windows of 45 Drumsheugh
Gardens, and Morris, Lord Inch's footman, standing on the
doorsteps after a holiday in the country, looked around him
to see if there were any changes, and noted with satisfaction,
being a man of taste, that No. 46 had engaged a pretty
housemaid. He also saw a foreign gentleman stroll quietly
past, with the air of a stranger who was admiring Drumsheugh Gardens as they deserved to be admired.

If he seemed to pay special attention to No. 45, that was
only natural. Morris stood there, and Morris was of opinion
that his figure and livery could not be matched, outside the
British Isles at anyrate.

" We must introduce ourselves to the young lady at No.
46," said Morris to himself, and thought no more of the
foreign gentleman, who strolled quietly on.

It was Mr. Peters, who had passed the house more than
once before, and knew perfectly well who lived there.

The quiet repose of Drumsheugh Gardens, or the sight of
these preparations for habitation, interested him so much
that the following morning, at about half-past ten, Mr.
Peters chose to smoke a cigar in that direction again. He
had scarcely turned in at the eastern end, when he saw a

boyish figure run down the steps of No. 45 and come towards him. There was a good distance between them; the young fellow turned to call back some order to a servant, and if after that he saw anything at all before him, it could only be Mr. Peter's back, that gentleman having suddenly decided that he wished to go the other way.

So Mr. Peters reached the end of the street first, and was surveying a passing *char-à-bancs*, as if in doubt about a ride to the Forth Bridge, when young Inch, for it was he, went by.

Mr. Peters, looking, saw a fair, lank young fellow, with close-cropped yellow hair, and a somewhat vacant expression, and receding chin.

He was in a light riding suit—breeches, gaiters, and spurs—the spurs longer and sharper than most horsemen care to have them. They jingled as he went, and he flicked his little cane against his gaiter, seeming in excellent spirits.

Evidently the boy, for he was very boyish, was going for a ride, and therefore one could not follow him far, even if anxious to do so. But Peters turned, wishing to see what he could of him, and was led into Princes Street.

The youngster was in no hurry. Twice he stopped to chat with people he met. Then he turned off Princes Street, and presently, to Mr. Peters' surprise, marched into the tobacconist's shop which was presided over by Miss Sophia Amélie Rivers.

Mr. Peters was surprised, and then spoke to himself in uncomplimentary terms for being so. No doubt the boy had gone in for cigarettes or matches, and would be out in a minute or two. So he lit another cigar and waited like the patient man that he always was. The cigar was finished, and still there was no sign of Master Archie Inch. So Peters, apparently quite contented, threw the cigar-stump to a waiting ragamuffin, with a few words, unfortunately in

a foreign tongue, on the value of patience. Then he went
back to his rooms.

Meanwhile there were tender passages in the little tobacconist's shop.

When young Inch tramped in past the silently grinning
Highlander, whose face, to an imaginative spectator, might
have suggested a sneer, his spurs were jingling as though
he represented a whole squadron of dismounted dragoons.
Miss Amélie rushed from her retreat like a plump and good-
natured spider, and said " Lor' ! " likewise " My ! "

" I thought you was a cavalry officer ! " she explained,
which was not displeasing to Archie, though he affected indifference, and a certain amount of suspicion.

" I s'pose you have that sort of fellow dangling round at
times ? " he suggested, but Amélie suddenly remembered
business.

" Wot can I give you, sir ? " she asked, and destroyed the
first faint sketch of a very flowery compliment that had just
occurred to Archie.

" Dreams ! " he said, a little suddenly, for fine compliments were difficult to him, and he disliked to feel one
spoilt in the making.

Miss Rivers seemed neither to notice his sulkiness nor to
think his request for " Dreams " peculiar. She turned to
the case behind her, and brought out a packet of cigarettes.
Archie threw down his cigarette-case on the counter, but
held out his hand for the packet.

" Let's see the wrapper ! " he demanded, and Miss Rivers
gave it to him.  " It's nothing new," she said.

" ' We are the stuff that dreams are made of.' "  Archie
read this out aloud, and then gave her the packet again.
with a sniff.

" The fellow's got no imagination ! " he told her.  " It's
always the same old thing."

" Thirteen Dreams for a shilling," Miss Rivers said, with

an absent-minded air, and then returning to business, " Good thick uns too, and just as good cigarettes as there are in the market. What more do you want, Mr. Inch ? You gentlemen expect so much."

She said this with a little flutter, and a sigh that made Archie inclined to suggest that a kiss into the bargain would make a packet of " Dreams " a satisfactory investment. He had, however, got a swinging box on the ear just before the summer vacation for trying to snatch a kiss over the counter, and the memory of it and of the accompanying threat to refuse to serve him, made the young man restrain himself.

" The cigarettes are good enough," he grumbled, " though I don't suppose anyone knows of 'em or buys 'em but me. What I say is, the fellow misses his chance. Say a chap comes in for a cigarette, just to smoke on the way down Princes Street, or something of that kind. ' Dreams ! ' he says, and picks up the packet and reads—

' We are the stuff that " dreams " are made of.'

' Same old motto,' he grumbles, and picks out his cigarette, and lays down his penny, and off he goes. But s'posin' now he comes in for one, and sees somethin' fresh an' fetchin' like—oh, well, somethin' like those scribblin' fellers can run off as easily as winkin', about, say, dream and gleam (of hope, don't you know), or cloud and shroud (of despair or death, or something of that kind), and smoke and, well, something cynical and bitter, ten to one he'll buy the whole packet for the sake of the wrapper, an' take it off to his girl."

" Well ! " said Miss Rivers, admiringly. " I didn't know you were so clever, Mr. Inch, an' that's a fact. My ! I believe you could make 'em up yourself as easily as anyone."

" I don't say I couldn't if I was to sit down and give myself up to it. Specially as I feel sometimes," and here he cast a woful glance at Amélie that made her look a little self-conscious in spite of attempts to keep business-like.

"There's more variety on the ounce packet of pipe mixture," she said, just to turn the conversation, and she took down half a dozen packets and laid them out on the counter for Archie to read—

> Smoke and forget, for day by day
> Trouble like smoke will pass away.
>
> When tired of fame, and wine, and kiss,
> Turn to your pipe, and dream with this.

"H'm, h'm," he went on over two or three more. "They're all very well, I daresay, Miss Rivers, for old chaps who've had their fling, you know, and think everything's a farce because they don't feel it like they did. I don't know that a man's sure to be right either because he don't think as he used to, you know. They're not the rhymes for young chaps anyway."

Archie shook his head wisely over this, and Miss Rivers secretly admired his wisdom more than she cared to own even to herself, so she talked on.

"That's a notion o' yours about the cigarettes, Mr. Inch, though whether the young men dropping in here for a box of matches or an ounce of Dream Mixture think so much about the ladies as you suppose, I can't say I'm sure. I can't believe all young gentlemen are so silly."

"Perhaps they aren't," Archie allowed, "perhaps they've no reason to be."

"Well," Miss Rivers promised, "I'll see what can be done about those Dreams anyway! My master's due round to-night, or some night soon, to look at the books and things, and I'll be sure to tell him of your idea."

"Who's your master?" asked Archie.

"That's private," Miss Rivers answered promptly. "He's

a gentleman, Mr. Inch, and that's all you or I need to know."

" A gentleman, is he, and keeps a tobacco shop ? Tell us another, Miss Rivers ! "

" Yes, a gentleman," persisted Miss Rivers angrily, leaning a little over the counter, her weight upon her tightly clenched fists. " P'r'aps you'll say next I'm no lady 'cause I see to the shop for him ? "

" Don't be angry, Miss Rivers; I was only chaffing. It's awfully hard to say what a gentleman is nowadays."

" Is it ? I'll tell you then—a gentleman's one who minds his own business, Mr. Inch. I don't care to know no other sort either."

She glanced over the counter at him, and he glared back, his temper and his color beginning to rise too.

" I wish your master, since he's such a fine gentleman, would teach you manners," he retorted, moving towards the door.

" You might go and get some lessons yourself since you've so much money to pay for 'em," Miss Rivers informed him, haughtily. " I needn't go to him for lessons either, Mr. Inch. There's other gentlemen come in sometimes who could teach you a lot. They don't go insulting a poor girl because she tries to earn an honest living either ! " And satisfied with that parting shot, she bounced behind the curtain, and plumping down upon the little settee, thrust fingers into both ears, lest he should retort in such fashion as to bring her out again. But Archie Inch did nothing of the kind. He stared blankly at the curtain for half a minute, and then, jingling his spurs more than ever, strode out of the shop with what little chin he had thrust well forward. He didn't dash on to the back of any fiery steed and gallop off his perturbation. In truth, I can't swear that he had planned a ride for that morning. But he went home, not so ready to greet friends as he had been earlier, and telling himself that, by Jove, though Emily was always A1, he didn't know how ripping she could look until that morning. Nevertheless, he wasn't altogether satisfied with the result, and spent a long time, and several " Dreams," in trying to remember exactly what all the fuss was about, and in wondering how he could put things right.

# CHAPTER VIII

At Mrs. Jimps' table that evening Mr. Peters was un-
usually silent; and Mrs. Jimps, who considered him in
many ways the pattern of a Paying Guest, noticed that silence, and was uneasy. Finding that partridges were plentiful and cheap that day, she had bought a brace, and had
carved them herself, marking them on the *menu* as a hors
d'œuvre.

"Our Annie"—perhaps through carelessness, perhaps
through malice, for she had never forgotten or forgiven the
cigar-trick—had bestowed upon Mr. Peters a drumstick,
instead of the wing with a slice of the breast which Mrs.
Jimps had intended for him.

That better portion had been practically wasted, thrown
away upon a mere wanderer who was to leave for the ends
of the earth to-morrow morning, while Mr. Peters, to all
appearance, might be considered in the light of a small
annuity.

Was he vexed?

"I hope," said Mrs. Jimps, hiding her anxiety with a
smile, "that the partridges were good? There was not
much of them, I know, but 'little and good,' I do hope.
Mr. Peters, was your partridge good?"

"He was an active bird," said Mr. Peters sententiously.
"I hope he was good, madam."

Mrs. Jimps gave a little sigh of relief under her breath,
for this, from him, was quite a joke.

"A most sarcastic gentleman," she said, playfully, to her
right-hand neighbor, who, being an American tourist, and
acquainted with "Brown of Calaveras," puzzled Mrs. Jimps

by surveying Mr. Peters with a well-affected air of terror,
and saying that he was sorry to hear it.

As dinner proceeded, she was quite sure there was nothing wrong—that, if anything, something had happened to
please Mr. Peters. Much to her delight, he joined in a little discussion on Providence, which began in an undertone
between two new-comers, who didn't know or didn't regard Mrs. Jimps' dislike for the introduction of such topics
at table. Someone was sure to be offended, she always
thought, but since it had begun she was glad that Mr.
Peters' voice boomed in from the other end of the table,
silencing the dilettanti by a pious declaration of belief. He
spoke of Fate, instead of using the word Providence, but his
tone left no doubt in Mrs. Jimps' mind that he meant the
same thing, and spoke from some striking personal experience. Mrs. Jimps loved a story, and as she rose from the
table she made up her mind that Mr. Peters should give her
the benefit of his experience, but she was not to have the
pleasure that night.

"Mr. Peters, if it isn't too much trouble for you to look
in at my sitting-room as you go upstairs, I would like to give
you a receipt and some change that I owe you. Or may I
come up with it? I never like putting temptation in the
way of servants," Mrs. Jimps explained, for the benefit of
the world at large, "however honest they may be."

"It is safe in your hands, my dear madam," said Peters,
waving the matter aside with an expressive movement of
a very muscular hand. "For me, I have promised myself
the pleasure of meeting a lady friend and cannot stay."

So frank! as Mrs. Jimps pointed out to the others who
were present, and with such a pleasant foreign way with
him. Suave? Yes! That expressed it exactly, and she
retired, smiling, to her little sitting-room, whence she presently heard Mr. Peters go out.

That same evening Lucius Moriarty grew restless after

dinner. He hummed and ha'd in the drawing-room, taking up and throwing down, one after another, the new books which Nell had put there for him to look over. The two had dined together at seven, and by half-past eight Lucius was fidgeting with the drawing-room blinds and commenting on the weather.

"It's a fine night for a stroll," he announced at last.

"I'll go for a walk with you, dear, if you like," Nell told him, dutifully, and Lucius was rather discomfited.

"H'm! I don't know," and he shook his head suspiciously. "It's the night for doing up your books, you'll remember. I can't have ye neglecting these things just to give me company."

"They're done!" said Nell proudly. "Balanced to a ha'penny, and I've not had to put in anything to make up."

"Well, well, you'll do in time as well as any of 'em, I daresay," Lucius allowed, with a gruffness that he thought made him a perfect imitation of the Roman Father. "I don't want any cheese-paring, you know, but I can't have waste. Those women downstairs 'd send us to the workhouse in twelve months if you and I didn't keep an eye on 'em, remember that!"

"Yes, dear. Cook wants two pounds rise next month."

"Two pounds rise! She wants the sack, that's what she wants," said Lucius defiantly, "and she'll get it too."

"All right, dad. I'll tell her to-morrow morning."

"Tell her what?"

"Tell her she'll get the sack. That's what you said, wasn't it?"

Lucius looked at her and gaped in amazement. "You've got a heart of stone!" he decided. "I never saw such a girl—though I know you're all the same nowadays. You've no compassion. Are ye your mother's daughter? Why when she was your age I was courtin' her, an' her heart was as soft ——"

" Dad, how young ! "

Nelly threw up her hands, and Lucius, perceiving when it was too late that he had been rash, fled speechless.

" Sha'n't I come ? " Nelly called down over the stair as well as she could for laughing, but all she got back was a broken murmur, " Telegram—news—club on way back—can't take you in," as the door banged. So she had her laugh out by herself, and then called up cook to settle the question of higher wages, and to mention one or two little things which she would expect to have more carefully seen to in consequence.

Meanwhile Lucius, whose gruffness seemed to have somehow got left behind as he banged the hall door, went chuckling upon his way.

" A woman could always do what she liked with you," he acknowledged to himself. " And she's 'cuter than most by a long way."

It was a fine night, as he had told Nell, and at first Lucius went along in the breezy, open way which was natural to him, he being always glad to meet a friend, and generally finding one before he had gone far. But to-night this could not last, such shameful changes are wrought by a wish for secrecy. It was not long before Lucius' coat-collar was turned up, and his face bent down. By the time he reached the narrower by-ways at the back of Princes Street, he was a figure at which any observant constable would look with suspicion. He slunk along on the more shadowy side of the street, and seemed to be passing Miss Rivers' premises as carelessly as any other place, when he suddenly made a dive at the door, as a rabbit dives for shelter in its burrow, but drew back hurriedly.

" A customer, begor ! " said Lucius, very much flurried, and slunk on to the next shadow, where he waited with an eye on the little path of light that led through the open door into the presence of Miss Rivers.

" By golly ! " he thought, as some such figure of speech occurred to him. " Something might be made o' that. Shrine, dine, no, that won't do; wine, no, divine's better, but what's an old chap like you got to do with such things ? The Dream-Mixture things ain't so bad, quite philosophic, some of 'em, but if ever this fad o' yours got known among the boys at the Exchange, an' any such like things could be fathered on you, begor ! you might as well get into one of your own flour sacks an' go off the far end o' Leith Pier at once. Long time that chap is buying a cigar or a box o' matches ! "

That was quite true. Mr. Peters, whose broad back Lucius had not given himself time to recognize, was taking what would have been an unnecessarily long time to buy a box of matches, but then he had more important business on hand.

When he first reached the shop, Miss Rivers was what she herself would have called " stand-offish."

Mr. Peters, in bowing over the hand not too readily extended to him across the counter, had playfully pretended to kiss it, and Miss Rivers was wroth.

" I 'ate those nasty foreign ways," she snapped out at the aggrieved Peters. " Give me the ways of an honest Englishman—or Scotchman, for the matter o' that."

Mr. Peters, who had called there more than once lately in passing, kept a philosophic silence, and, taking a match, sat down, while Amélie regarded him almost with hatred. Hadn't she, as she put it, cast him up against Mr. Inch only that morning, though not by name, and hadn't Mr. Inch said more than he meant because of it ? Wasn't Peters, therefore, justly to be blamed for tears that had fallen since ? So she jerked about a little, putting things straight behind the counter, while Mr. Peters smoked on in silence and humility.

" You might *speak*, Cap'n Peters," she said at last, rather

5

pleased at his complete submission, " I don't know as I told you not to."

" I do not know that I have anything to say, now," meditated " Cap'n " Peters deliberately. " It is so easy to be wrong and to offend."

This was obviously a thing he would do anything to avoid, and Amélie was gratified.

" If you don't know that you've anything to say, now, say what you had to say, then," she told him. " You know I don't always mean all I say. The shop gits on one's nerves sometimes. Sometimes it's lonely, too."

" It is exercise that you need." sagely suggested Mr. Peters, who had never felt the need of it in his life, though at times he had been forced to take a good deal.

" You are losing your so good color," he added, with a concerned air.

" Exercise ! me ! " ejaculated Amélie. " What'd you recommend ? A 'unter, an' will you mind the shop ? "

" A bicycle," he suggested, ignoring the sarcasm.

" 'Oo are you gittin' at ? " asked Amélie, her temper beginning to rise again. " 'Oo's goin' to let me have a bike ? D'you think I can pay for one, or lessons either ? "

" One may hire, and one may teach," returned Mr. Peters, dropping the short stump of his cigar into the spittoon at his feet. He then leant forward, and, taking a " Dream " from the open box upon the counter, laid down a penny and relapsed into silence.

" Who'd hire and who'd teach ? "

" I might," said Mr. Peters, calmly.

" You ! What's your little game, Cap'n Peters ? "

Amélie flushed slightly, and, drawing herself up from the counter on which she had been leaning, looked at him suspiciously, but Peters smoked on unmoved.

" My very little game is exercise," he confided to her. " I am a big man, and I grow fat. It is not good. I eat. I drink, I smoke, I sleep, all too much in this city. Soon Giuseppe Peters will have a fat heart and die."

" Lor' ! " said Miss Rivers, rather touched by this. " you mustn't say such things, it's wicked."

But Mr. Peters nodded his head with an air of mild desperation. " It will be so," he predicted, and relapsed into silence again.

" See me biking ! " ejaculated Amélie, and became lost in contemplation of such bliss.

This was a joy that Mr. Inch had never hinted at. Her color was going, too, she knew, and Amélie cared as much for her complexion, strangely enough, as any fine lady.

" I feel my heart after dinner," explained Mr. Peters, and thought of the partridge drumstick.

" Course I'd love it—awful ! " admitted Amélie. " If 'twould do you good, too, why so much gained ! But you men, who's to believe you ? What'd my young man say, too ? "

This last was an inspiration, and she watched Peters narrowly for the effect, but he was quite unmoved.

" Ah ! " he responded, " I did not know. My best congratulations. Why has he not seen to this ? Let him come too."

" I didn't say I had one," retorted Amélie, and then she considered the matter, while Peters smoked and watched. After all, she thought, Captain Peters had never been rude. Now she came to think of it, she was as mild as milk with Mr. Inch until he as good as said she couldn't be a lady because she kept a tobacconist's shop. Seemed to think, too, that he could have everything all his own way. Well, she'd show him.

" How could I get out ? " she asked a bit fretfully. " Eight-thirty to eleven. Them's the hours for this place. You wouldn't teach me down Princes Street after that, would you ? "

" We will not have all the world to see your first efforts,"
Mr. Peters told her, gravely. " They will be comic. But in
the Queensferry Road, for example ? We would meet at
half-past seven. That is quite possible. You after your
breakfast, for digestion, and I before mine, for appetite.
Think of your color ! " and he got up and passed out.

" Well, ta, ta," said Miss Rivers. " I'll think about it,"
and she was doing so, carefully, a couple of minutes later,
when Lucius walked in.

# CHAPTER IX

## LUCIUS LOOKS INTO THINGS

HE nodded to Amélie, and, giving a quick glance round to see how things looked, went, as usual, straight into the little room beyond. Here the gas was lit, as, indeed, it was almost always, unfortunately for poor Amélie's complexion. The books in which she kept her accounts were put out upon her little table.

Once settled down to them, with Amélie at his elbow to give any necessary explanations, Lucius adopted somewhat of that stern, inquisitorial air which he thought the correct thing at home, while Amélie, poor girl, not knowing him so well as Nell did, trembled a little. She wished she could have had a more profitable month than was shown by the books over which Lucius pursed his lips and shook his head.

" There's no profit here, Miss Rivers," he said at last, and poor Amélie had to admit it.

" I believe trade's bad everywhere just now, sir," she suggested, and Lucius nodded more gravely than ever. ·

" That's true," he said. " A man can't afford to chuck money away on fads nowadays," and Amélie's heart sank.

" I do my best," she told him. " I don't know as I can do more, or as anyone else could do better, but if you could tell me anything, sir, I'd try it."

" No doubt, no doubt," agreed Lucius gruffly; "wouldn't have you here else," and he bit the end of the pen, which was a habit of his, and glared at the figures as if they had personally insulted him.

" There was a young gentleman in this mornin'," Amélie went on, trying to be hopeful, " an' I thought he said something *very* clever."

" Hey ! What's that ? " asked Lucius, waking up from a brown study.

" If we could get different verses to put on the Dreams, he said, young chaps might buy 'em to take home, and so they'd sometimes take a packet. or a box even, instead of one or two. As it is," she added, " they'd rather, I mean a'most as soon, take Dimitrinos or Melacrinos."

" Would they ? " returned Lucius gruffly. " More fools they. Mine are just as good, and bigger. Special brand. Can't get 'em anywhere else ! "

" They're awful good they say," Amélie told him earnestly, " and this young gentleman was very friendly like, an' give me this idea."

" Very friendly like, was he ? " grumbled Lucius. " Hope you don't encourage young gentlemen to come round here, Miss Rivers. Bad for them and bad for you, ye know."

" I can't drive 'em away, sir, can I ? " objected Amélie, her voice quavering a little. " It would spoil the business, wouldn't it ? "

" Of course, of course," agreed Lucius hastily (" You darned old fool ? " he muttered to himself under his breath). " Only, of course, you've yourself to think of as well as the shop, don't you know. That's all, my dear. I'll think over what you say about the Dreams. Never touch 'em myself."

" They're *awful* good," repeated Amélie, with conviction, somewhat cheered.

" Don't smoke yourself, I hope ! " suggested Lucius sharply.

" I tried once, sir," Miss Rivers had to admit. " I thought I'd like to be able to say I *knew* they was good, but—but I wasn't well after, an' I haven't tried again. I put a penny in the till, sir."

" Tut, tut, I didn't mean that," said Lucius testily. "Let's think now. D'you miss anything by closing early ? Or, often a man wants baccy on the way to his office. D'you open in good time ? What are your hours ? "

" Eight-thirty to eleven, sir," Amélie told him. " I'll try eight to eleven-thirty, if you like. That would give us the chance of an extra half-hour each way after the rest have shut up."

" Eight-thirty to eleven, and a half-hour tacked on each way to that ! Good Lord ! Does the girl think I'm a slave-driver ? Nonsense, lassie, this must be seen to."

Lucius then got up and put on his overcoat, stamping as he did so, to ease his mind a little.

" The others do it, so we must," Amélie insisted. " And I hope you know I'm doing my best, sir. I've never thought to complain, for I gets time to myself here for readin' an' so on. I'm glad to have such a place. There's lots would jump out of their skins to-night to get it."

" Good Lord ! " was all Lucius felt inclined to say, and he was out looking round the shop before he spoke again.

" It's stuffy in there, my dear," he said at last. " Better read your book out here most times. You keep it clean and tidy out here, I can see. And, lemme see, I haven't paid you your month's wages, have I ? Here they are," and he stamped back behind the curtain, and counted them out.

" Five shillings a month more now," he explained hurriedly, " because you're doing so well. Good-night, good-night. Shut up at once an' go home, an' damn the other people—I mean good-night."

He hurried out, not waiting to hear her thanks, and went away muttering down the street.

" Good Lord ! Eight-thirty to eleven. Fancy my Nell doing that. Might have been Nell's luck, I s'pose. A stuffy

little hole like that. It's as dull as ditch water. Why I'd
get screwed every pay-day, and leave the shop with the first
chap that looked at me, if that was me ! And to think I
thought I was doin' the girl a charity. Plenty to jump out
of their skins for it ? Good Lord ! I must talk to Nell.
She's a woman, and she'll know more than I can about the
girl's chances."

He forgot all about the club, which he had intended to
call at for conscience' sake, and went straight home.

There, over a glass of toddy and a pipe, he pretended to
read, but puzzled Nell at intervals with such questions as,
how would she like to keep a tobacconist's shop, what hours
the servants kept, and what holidays they got, and so on,
until she said good-night and went wondering to her room.
He threw down his book and went off too, soon after, muttering " eight-thirty to eleven. Good Lord ! " as he went.

# CHAPTER X

## A PROFESSIONAL CONSULTATION

In a house not far from No. 45 Drumsheugh Gardens, that confirmed bachelor and well-known physician, Dr. Maitland, was sitting down to his dinner the same evening, when his man handed him a note from No. 45. It was very short. Its substance was that Lord Inch had come home from his holiday and wished to see him.

"Will you, my dear Maitland, make a special exception for an old friend and school-fellow, and allow me to come round after dinner to have a cigar and a chat with you?"

When Maitland, who was very short-sighted, had peered into the note and mastered it, he sat back in his chair and thought for awhile, regardless of the fact that the cover had been removed from the soup-tureen, and the soup was getting cold.

"What's wrong, I wonder?" he asked himself. "The fellow hasn't been in here for years. At one time I thought his wife came between us. But she's dead long ago, poor, silly soul. What's wrong, I wonder?" He sat pondering; and then, "What an ass I am to think about a diagnosis before seeing the case. Hey, what, Ross?"—this last was aloud, as the man rather ostentatiously put the cover back on the soup.

"Yes, yes; wait a minute. Bring a card from my writing-table."

He took the card, and scribbling, "Come by all means; coffee at 8.30," settled down to his dinner.

The dark, strongly marked, intellectual face was like a mask to cover his thoughts. They disturbed neither his face nor his appetite, but he ate in silence without any of the little remarks he was used to exchange with his old servant, and in spite of his sagacious scouting of premature diagnosis, Lord Inch continued to occupy his mind.

"Coffee in the consulting-room, Ross, when Lord Inch comes," he said, as he rose from the table. "I'm not at home to anyone else to-night."

"The carriage, sir?" Ross suggested.

"I sha'n't go out. Can't! Tell Sandy he's not to wait. After all, for old fogies like you and me, our own fireside's best. Her ladyship's 'At Home' won't miss me, Ross."

Ross, who considered his master would be a catch, as he put it, "for ony lassie," and who was in mortal dread of any change in the existing order of things, grunted and went off gladly to tell the coachman, while Maitland crossed the hall to his consulting-room.

Here he was sitting by a wood fire, with a book in his hand, when Lord Inch was shown in, half an hour later.

He rose and shook hands, peering at the Judge as he did so, and pointed to an easy-chair on the other side of the fire.

"Make yourself comfortable there," he said, "and try those cigars. I got 'em a bargain, I think. Ross will bring us our coffee, and then we can chat. Where have you been?"

"In Switzerland most of the time," his visitor told him, eying the cigar, "and a fortnight in Venice."

"Much overrated place," growled Maitland.

"Where were you?" asked the other man, twisting his cigar about between his fingers.

"Fishing in my own country. I don't half know it yet," said Maitland, dryly, and Inch gave a little laugh.

"You've the same sarcastic way I see, Alec," he told him. "You should marry."

It cost Maitland an effort to avoid a home thrust at that, but he choked it down as the coffee came in, and looked on in silence while Inch stirred his without touching it.

" How's the boy ? " he asked presently.

" In rude health, I believe," answered the other, staring at the fire. " He won't set the Thames ablaze, Alec."

" Which of us will, man ? " retorted the doctor. " But we're both useful members of society, I think. Many youngsters would wish nothing higher than to have my practice or your place at the Parliament House. I don't suppose our young days were all they might have been either," he added meditatively. " We gained experience though, and made the most of that, I believe."

The Judge frowned a little, and Maitland noticed it.

" You were a canny lad, Inch," he said. " You always knew the worth of a good reputation too well to go wrong, and I don't suppose you've any shortcomings of your own to mind, when you're wigging a poor devil in the dock. I wish I'd as clean a record ! What can I do for you to-night ? Nothing professional, I hope."

" I don't know," returned the other, getting up and leaning against the mantel-piece with his back to the fire. " Probably it's nothing at all. I expect I just want a tonic and a chat with an old friend to cheer me up. A touch of liver, I daresay, Maitland ? "

" Very likely," Maitland agreed, scanning him. " Those beastly foreign hotels, with their vile-made dishes of the Lord knows what, except that it isn't honest beef or mutton —they're quite enough to account for anything, Inch. Now, next year you should come North with me, and rough it a little."

He switched on another electric light in a movable lamp as he spoke, and put that on the mantel-piece.

" Tell me all about it," he said, and leant with one shoulder against the mantel-piece facing Lord Inch, while he listened in silence to a slightly disjointed story, told in a somewhat apologetic way.

" It will be liver, won't it ? " Lord Inch suggested. " I'm

not an active man, you know, Maitland. Sitting still most of the day, you know, during session, and perhaps dining out too often. I found myself not so young as I used to be when we tried a little bit of climbing, the boy and I. Not in training, you know, I got fagged pretty quickly, and, in fact, gave it up. Short of wind, and stitch in the side, and all that sort of thing."

He began stripping the outer leaf off the cigar which he had all the time in his hand, and Maitland watched him curiously. As the story went on, and as he watched the other, his face, which had shown every little change of feeling while they spoke as old school-fellows, became more and more expressionless. It was a professional mask again, showing little movement, except in the bright peering eyes.

"I thought," Lord Inch went on, "of a little horse exercise with the boy in the morning before the Courts sat, and if you'd give me a tonic, that would probably be all I need."

"Ah, yes," Maitland agreed. "Very likely. We'll see presently. What more?"

"Oh, nothing, I think. I get stupid and depressed about nothing nowadays. I don't get through my work so lightheartedly as I did. I'm getting elderly and rheumatic, I suppose."

"What makes you suspect rheumatism?" asked Maitland.

"Oh, aches and pains, you know—aches and pains. Old bones, as my nurse Macgregor told us bairns in the nursery days. You never knew nurse Macgregor? She was before your time, Alec. A wise woman was nurse Macgregor."

"She was before my time," agreed Maitland. "They're rare cattle, Inch, are wise women. Whiles I doubt if ever I met one, save my mother. Rheumatism, you say. Where does it catch you?"

" Between the shoulders, just now and then," said Inch shrugging his shoulders as he spoke.

" Ay, anywhere else ? "

" It runs down the left arm a bit at times," the other explained, " and it seems to me I'm going to have a touch of it now."

As he spoke the man drew himself together, staring at the doctor with a look of unreasoning dread. His face was contorted, his lips ashy pale. He seemed terrified to move, even to breathe.

The doctor watched for a second or two, and then, moving quietly but swiftly to a cabinet in a corner of the room, came back with his handkerchief held out before him.

" Smell this ! " he said peremptorily, and held it in position.

A faint smell, as of pine-apples, spread through the room, but for some moments yet there was no difference in the man's attitude. He still clung to the mantel-piece, shrinking into himself, as it were, before some vague horror. Then a little tinge of color came back, and grew upon his gradually parting lips. He took a deeper breath, and even shifted his position a little, as a man might who had felt the ground slipping away beneath him, but now hoped it might be stable once more. When Maitland saw this, he wheeled a sofa before the fire, and then slipped an arm around the other.

" You'll do now," he told him quietly. " Lie down here awhile," and helped him to the sofa.

" There," he said, " it's all over. Just lie quiet for a few minutes, and don't worry, man. Then we can go on with our chat quite well, and I'll have a look at your chest where you are, as a matter of form."

Lord Inch's forehead was damp with beads of sweat. He felt for his handkerchief and passed it across his face, but did nothing else, and Maitland did nothing to disturb him.

" Better now ? " he said at last, and when Inch nodded, he knelt by the sofa, and began deftly to loosen his clothing about the chest.

" I'll just run you over and have done with it," he explained, and examined in different ways with the quiet and certain touch of a man who knew exactly what he wanted.

After that he rose from his knees and sat down again, a trifle behind Lord Inch's head, looking at him meditatively from under shaggy eyebrows, and rubbing the side of his nose with the right forefinger, which was a trick of his when perplexed.

" All right now ! " he suggested.

" Yes," Lord Inch answered, and moved as if to get up, but a hand on his shoulder kept him back. " I am all right, am I not ? " he asked, with a little laugh, turning his head to see Maitland's face. He might just as well have looked at the fire, burning quietly in the grate, or at the opposite wall. The face was wooden, impenetrable, stolid.

" I wouldn't say that quite," Maitland told him. " You might go off and do something fair daft on the strength of it. Laddies of our age, Inch, mustn't take up football, or mountaineering, at a moment's notice. Not many fellows are as right as they once were, at your age and mine."

" I'm only fifty," said Lord Inch pettishly. " I don't want to play the fool at football or anything else, as you know perfectly well, Maitland. As for that, I met Erlestoun last night at the club, and he told me he was tramping his moors after grouse for a month beyond the Twelfth : played a salmon for two hours and a-half, too, and landed him. Why, the man's seventy if he's a day ! "

" Yes, yes," Maitland agreed. " That's true enough. But, mind you, he's done that, or more, since he was seventeen. You and I couldn't afford that, Inch, then, so we pay extra for it if we try now. Man, all I want is for you to take it a bit easy for awhile."

"Is it anything more than rheumatism and liver?" demanded Lord Inch, sitting up and facing round.

"I won't say but what they might have a great deal to do with your bothers," said Maitland cautiously, "but you must treat them with respect for awhile. Take life easy, man, and take notice you're under doctor's orders for the time. Does your work press upon you? Could you put it aside this winter?"

"I should yawn myself to death," Lord Inch said fretfully. "I shouldn't know what to do. Besides, between you and me, who'd do my work in the Division? There's Doune and Sauchie, the Lord knows they aren't overworked, but you know them—and the President looks to me to read up most of the heavy cases. Between ourselves, as men of the world, do you suppose they could do more, or at least do it as the public expects and demands it should be done? There will be some stiff Jury Trials before the Christmas Recess. I can't think of putting work aside, Maitland."

"Ay, there's no one like our bonnie selves," muttered Maitland, but Lord Inch never heard him, and went on.

"Privately, too, and of course one can talk frankly to one's medical adviser, there's some talk of a Royal Commission coming my way. That's our only chance of promotion, Maitland, and I mustn't miss it. It isn't as if I were really ill, you know."

"Well, well," Maitland agreed. "You do as I tell you for the time, and we'll see how you get on. I shall give you a call in a day or two. You've things pretty much your own way up at the Parliament House, I expect," he suggested, smiling grimly. "The other fellows do the fighting."

"Yes, just so," and Lord Inch laughed dryly. "We give away the prizes, you know." He paused, and then spoke more gravely. "My heart's in it, Maitland. I'll go higher yet if I get the chance, I tell you. Just you help me to get

rid of the rheumatism and all the other 'isms, and you shall
see. I believe it would kill me if ever I had to resign. But,
of course, you haven't even suggested that."

" No, no," Maitland replied hastily. " I never thought of
it. But just care, you know, and keeping clear of worry and
excitement for the present. No personal affairs to trouble
you ? Of course not."

" No, no. Everything cut and dried, my dear Maitland.
I hear my cases, and draw my salary, and leave everything
else to my clerk."

" That's right ! " Maitland nodded approvingly. " Nothing like business habits, so I'm told, to keep a man clear of
bothers. Never had business habits myself, but no doubt
they're excellent things. I'll just make a note of a few suggestions, so that you may bear them in mind, and I'll see
you again in four days or so, after you've been taking something I'm going to prescribe."

He scribbled at his desk for a few minutes, while Lord
Inch sat and stared at the fire. The Judge, to give him his
due, was not a timid man or a hypochondriac. He had firm
faith, too, in his old friend Maitland, and was ready to place
himself unreservedly in Maitland's hands.

Something else was occupying his thoughts now. Maitland's remark on a clean record brought to his mind what
had seldom been out of it lately—the lynching of five-and-
twenty years ago. It was significant of the man's estimate
of himself that he never doubted but what he had been the
chief agent in bringing that trial to its unhappy end. This
feeling was now exaggerated by ill-health, and the Judge
felt very like a criminal.

Maitland finished his writing, and, slipping the paper into
an envelope, rose.

" Now that's done with for the time," he announced;
" let me tell Ross to bring you in something else instead of
cold coffee. I'd drop coffee and cigars, if I were you, for a

few days until you see how things go on. I've not told you about my fishing. No fights with salmon like Erlestoun's, but just daundering along after the trout, in the sweetest country I know, man! Quite good enough for me!"

"Yes, I'd like a chat well enough," Lord Inch told him, "but I've some papers to go over before bedtime."

"Off you go, then!" said Maitland. "You must keep good hours while you're under my thumb. Will you drop in again on Friday, or shall I come round and have a yarn with you?"

"Come round, if you will," said Inch. "Come to dinner. No one but ourselves, for the boy will be out. I want to show you some things I picked up in Venice."

This was agreed, and they moved through the hall. Maitland let his friend out himself, and stood at the open door watching him go down the street.

"Threatened men live long," he muttered. "The fellow lives a regular, quiet life now. It's not the strain of his young days, and I'll keep a quiet eye on him. I'm not going to frighten the man into his grave. I can say a little more when I know a little more. Lord, the mistakes I've seen made—by better men than myself, too."

So he went back to his consulting-room, and sat for another hour with a review, which, however, he often laid aside to stare at the fire, and rub the side of a hawk nose with a long forefinger.

6

# CHAPTER XI

## INTRODUCING AN OLD ACQUAINTANCE

IT was just about this time that Alfred Buncombe, *alias* Augustus B. Bunner, and as many other false names as he had sins on his conscience—almost, began to sigh for his daughter, and for the domestic delights of a home.

Most of us have a virtue of some sort, we are told, and Alfred Buncombe had such faith in his own virtue that he always believed, and particularly insisted when maudlin-drunk, which was often, that, with better luck and a mother alive to look after him, he would have been a good man. Since vice, one knows, is strictly confined to the poorer classes, and folly is the portion of orphans, he may have been right in saying this, but I never heard that he could get anyone to believe him. From the time when he had fled from Bonville, twenty-five years ago, he had been an Ishmael of the lowest type, a sort of human jackal, whining and snapping alternately, and living upon whatever he could pick up. Not that his degradation began anywhere near that date. He called himself an Oxford man, on the strength of having, at a very early stage of University life, been ignominiously hunted therefrom for swindling a fellow-undergraduate.

An uncle who had tried to help him before, then promptly closed his doors, sending Buncombe a check for a hundred guineas, with a note to the effect that there would be no more.

The last of the guineas, changed into dollars, went before he was stranded in Bonville, and soon after that Buncombe took to stealing horses, because he had special facilities, and saw nothing else to steal more easily. It had been a chance, which he really thought providential, that had put the Swiss into his saddle where the little Sheriff found him. For Buncombe had turned aside to rest for a quarter of an hour, and was hidden, gnashing his teeth at his luck, when the honest Swiss, after looking in vain for the owner, mounted and met the Sheriff.

After that escape, Buncombe came across the Atlantic again. Here he married a woman very much better than himself, a barmaid, who loved him, only herself could say why, and who supported him while she could. Then two years after Amélie's birth, finding the home not so comfortable, and his wife's allegiance divided, he got what money he could from her and went off again. He had wandered everywhere, and tried all dishonesty. Port Said knew him, and so did Galle. He had been in Cuba, and once, vain hope, had expected to outdo the innocent and unsophisticated Maltee in ship-chandlering on his own island.

Twice in fourteen years he came home, each time, as was quite natural for him, under a false name. His first visit was made because he found himself in Constantinople with no cash and less credit. So he shipped to London as a fireman, and went to see if his wife was any better off than he was. She hadn't tried to marry again, though ten years had passed. Perhaps her first experience was enough. Buncombe found her manageress at the public-house where she had been barmaid, and, sponging on her, lived in clover for three months. He stole the week's receipts from her one Saturday night, and went off, leaving her to replace them from a little store of her own.

Four years later he came again, believing himself to be reformed. He had managed a successful swindle, and would see what could be done, and how things would be for him. If his wife had saved as she ought, they might even

think of a business in a small way for themselves. But his
wife was dead, after a long and painful illness that had
finished her savings, and Buncombe cursed his luck again.
'Melia he found in a tobacconist's out Tottenham way, her
mother having made her promise never to enter a public-
house or bar. So he spent a pound or two upon her ; very
little, but quite enough to make her look back upon her
father's appearance as if he had come in a shower of gold.
Then he disappeared mysteriously and suddenly.

This time the cause had been more urgent. In a drunken
row in an east-end of London bar, where half a dozen were
at rough and tumble, he had whipped out a knife and killed
a man who was struggling and swearing on the top of him.
The man suddenly, with a jerk, became quiet, and Buncombe disappeared from a locality where he had never been
before, and never meant to go again.

The papers said that the murderer was unknown to the
police, but that they had a clue—which they hadn't—and
Buncombe, after waiting a twelvemonth or so, being sure
that his name was not known anywhere except where his
daughter was, wrote to her. If he had any virtue at all, it
was a sort of fondness for and pride in the girl. So he wrote
saying that she must address to him, post restante, New
York, and let him know of any change of situation, as he
had been called away to take part in a splendid speculation,
and would come home to make a lady of her soon.

So poor 'Melia had written persistently, though she got
no more letters in reply, and read such novels as she could
get hold of, to keep her posted in the ways and doings of
that brilliant society which she was some day to surprise.

Buncombe got her letters, however, and the occasional
*Scotsman* which came with them after 'Melia migrated from
London to Edinburgh. He had access to and taste for little
literature beside, but letters and newspapers were carefully
read. In one of the latter he had seen that Hector Inch,

Esquire, advocate, had been raised to the bench, with the title of Lord Inch. He remembered Inch perfectly well, having attempted to prey upon him in the Bonville days on the score of their both being university men, and he wondered if this Hector Inch could be the same.

If so, he foresaw possibilities, but a sharp attack of delirium tremens cut short his speculations, and when he came out of hospital, the task of merely keeping body and soul together from day to day used up all his energy for some time.

We meet him now, however, in New York in flourishing circumstances. By a stroke of fortune, and the confiding nature of a youngster from the old country, Mr. Buncombe, posing as a land agent fond of a quiet game of cards, has become possessed of about four hundred dollars. This happened last night, and therefore, naturally, this morning finds him in a drinking saloon. He drank steadily last night ; he is drinking now, chatting with the bar-keeper, who is not pressed for time, and making maudlin references to his dear daughter in Edinburgh whom he so longs to see.

" Edinburgh ! " says the barman, " it's ma ain toon ! " and, producing a *Weekly Scotsman*, with the suggestion that he may like to look at it, turns to serve another customer.

The first thing that Buncombe sees is that the Courts, having re-opened after the vacation, Lord Inch is trying such and such a case, and then and there, braced to the effort by the four hundred dollars and a series of stimulating drinks, he makes up his mind to see 'Melia again, and at the same time to find out what he can about the past history of Lord Inch.

# CHAPTER XII

MR. PETERS had not thought it necessary to tell 'Melia that, before teaching her to cycle, he had to learn. That did not trouble him. He had every confidence in himself as perfectly able to do what other people did, and he was not mistaken.

The morning after his chat with 'Melia he made his way, soon after breakfast, to the Waverley Market, and, going to the gallery there, looked down upon the picture of struggling humanity that presented itself. Here were learners in all stages of desperation and despair, and Mr. Peters watched them with grave interest.

A stout lady, perspiring and breathless, with a fixed stare, and hair that was gradually coming down and separating the false from the true, struggled between two struggling supporters, and occasionally overwhelmed them, while sarcastic and audible comments came down from the onlookers above. One or two men in knickerbockers wavered rather uncertainly around. Two girls in irreproachable costume, who had evidently come to practise together, were doing loops and curves in one corner with astounding earnestness and solemnity, and a child of thirteen or fourteen, fair-haired, and enjoying herself tremendously, was whirring about, frightening everybody but herself.

"Yon wumman 'll dee afore she rides," one interested errand-boy told a friend, as he leant over to watch beside Peters. "Ten days she's come, regular, an' yon lassie here's been five."

" She's no fear'd," said the other, craning over and chuckling with intense delight as the fat woman made wildly for a pillar, and collapsed under the gallery.

" Come on ! " returned the first. " Wait a meenit. Let's see the fat wumman again," pleaded the other, and they did so.

Mr. Peters listened, and laughed when they went away. Then he went down into the market, and the man in charge, after a critical survey of his proportions, picked out a bicycle to correspond.

" I'll tak' ye in hand masel'," he explained, but Peters would have none of that. He moved the bicycle backward and forward to test the steering, and then bestrode it with one foot on the ground.

" A fall will not hurt me, my friend," he told the fellow calmly.

" It's the bicycle I'm mindin'," the man explained ruefully, but gave way at last, and Mr. Peters began his attempt.

When he finished half an hour later, it was as if he had stepped from the hot-room of a Turkish bath, while every prominent point in body and limbs was sore and every muscle cramped, but he had gone, somehow, in the end at least half a dozen yards before falling, and he was content.

He did nothing else that morning, but after lunch went down to Leith, and called upon Lucius at his office. The junior clerk, who was beginning to take a gloomy view of trade generally, as autumn drifted to winter and he felt the draught more keenly, thought that his master was engaged, but Lucius, having recognized Peters' voice, opened the door and greeted him heartily.

" Come away in, man, come away in," and Peters, entering, found the room littered with invoices, bills of lading, charter parties, letters, and telegrams.

" Business is brisk ? " he inquired cheerfully, and Lucius
shook his head with a mournful air.

" Man, it's fair awful. Prices rising, an' business pressing on me till I scarce see me daughter or me home from
one Sabbath to the next."

" That is good," suggested Peters, but Lucius was not so
sure.

" After all," he told him, " I don't know. God never
meant a man to live in an office or a warehouse either. And
it's always no trade and no money to spend, or you're half
killed with your business and you've no time to spend your
money. Begor, it's insufferable. I'd retire an' live a decent,
quiet life if 'twasn't for the girl. A little farm in the country. Peters, an' a cow or two. That's my dream. But what
can I do for you ? Money ? "

Mr. Peters acknowledged that he wanted to draw some,
and Lucius sent the junior clerk out to cash a check for
a hundred pounds, which the junior clerk, naturally, being
cold, set forth to do in the most roundabout way, that he
might have the benefit of exercise.

" Anything else ? " asked Lucius, while they waited his
return, as if the only delight of a busy day was to turn aside
from business and serve a friend.

" Your courts of law are again open, I think ? " asked
Peters, and Lucius said they were.

" Your friend Mr. Dee kindly offered to show me all those
things," observed Peters.

" He did," said Lucius, " an' he's a man o' his word or no
friend o' mine."

" Where would I find him ? "

" Wearin' out the floor of the hall up there," said Lucius,
" unless he's helping an unfortunate man to play pitch-an'-
toss in the courts."

" Pitch-and-toss ? "

" Ay, pitch-and-toss ! " growled Lucius, who had lately

carried an insurance case to the Parliament House, and was still wondering whether to gain a case might not prove more expensive than to let it alone.

" You aren't going to take your business there ? " he asked, as a sudden fear for his friend's sanity struck him. Peters assured him that he would not.

" I wish to pay," he repeated, and Lucius once more expressed admiration for such a desire.

" If all me creditors did as much," he said, " begor, I'd look for a farm to-day. I'd breed honest beef an' mutton, an' see to me education. Man, ye'd be shocked to know me ignorance, an' the books I haven't read. As it is ——" He stared disconsolately at the litter of business papers, and shrugged his shoulders apologetically.

" I'll take you up to see Dee to-morrow myself, if you like," he suggested. " I've got some fat in the fire there, an' I could see me agent then."

Peters expressed himself as grateful, but was unwilling to trouble Lucius.

" No trouble at all," he was told. " I'll wait for the midday post, an' go home. Lunch with me there at one, an' we'll go up an' see fools fight about nothing, an' part with good money after that."

Too much business was evidently affecting Lucius' digestion, and he smiled bitterly as he proposed this cynical form of amusement. He was equally cynical when the junior clerk came rushing in with every appearance of having run all the way to the bank and back.

" A livin' lie," he told Peters confidentially, " that I keep on for the sake of that decent widow, his mother," and Peters left him shaking his head bitterly over hypocrisy, as he settled down once more at his desk.

As for Peters, he turned away towards the harbor. It was a bleak autumn day, after a night with a keen touch of frost that had silently loosened the leaves on the trees, ready to fall with the next wind, and the wind had come—a keen, blustering nor'-easter, that was bringing down the leaves, shivering and whispering inland, and heaping up the waters of the Firth of Forth against the quays and piers of Leith.

Peters sniffed at the salt air, and made as straight against the wind as the turns and windings of the place would let him. The smell of the brine stirred him, and some sea-gulls, beaten inward, and screaming as they went, seemed to call upon him for action. The keenness of the air did no more than make him move a little more briskly against it, while he hummed under his breath some quaint tune, of a melancholy sound that was out of keeping with both place and weather. Down at the pier-head the sea was coming in in great green rollers, that broke against the stones and burst into spray, which the wind carried far inward. A steamer, a mile away towards the open sea, was plunging out through the waves in a way that washed her from stem to stern every few minutes, and Peters watched her for some time before he looked closer to hand. When he did so, he found that he had not the place to himself.

A woman, in a small, gray Tam o' Shanter cap and a waterproof cloak, was crouching at a place where the small lighthouse broke the force of the wind, and where she could lean over and see the water close beneath. She had neither seen Peters nor heard him, and she bent over, apparently watching the dizzy race of the twisted eddies and whirling bubbles, until his voice startled her. Then she turned so quickly that she lost her balance, and was rocking on the edge when his hand steadied her again.

It was Madge Murray.

" How you frightened me, Mr. Peters ! " she gasped, half-laughing ; " I thought I was over ! "

" A little more," said Peters, " and ——" He did not finish the sentence, but looked down at the water beneath, and laughed as if amused.

"It's all very well for you to laugh," Madge told him.
"What if I had gone ? Would you have fetched me —— ? "
She spoke lightly enough, but watched as if she meant her
question to be treated seriously. Peters, however, preferred
to think it a joke.

"At Mr. Moriarty's, where I had the honor of meeting
you," he told her, "you told me that you loved new—what
was it, sensations ? This would have been one."

"Yes, but my last," Madge retorted pettishly, "if you
were so cowardly as to let me drown. A big man like you
can't be a coward, surely ? "

They were walking down the pier now, and she turned to
look up at him coquettishly as she spoke, but Mr. Peters
shrugged his shoulders.

"What is a coward ? " he asked, and Madge stared at him.

"You would have been one if you hadn't jumped after
me at once, without hesitation," she said sharply. "But
you would have got me out, surely ? "

"Oh, I would have tried," Peters allowed, but didn't
seem at all anxious to pose as a life-preserver, or to say how
far he would have gone in trying.

"You can't swim, then," she said at last, as if that could
be the only explanation possible, but Peters did not seem
to think it worth while to deceive her.

"I swim well," he told her ; "I once swam and floated
for six hours."

"Then, of course, you would have picked me out like
nothing. How exciting it would have been ! I almost wish
I had fallen in, if it wasn't so cold. One looks so bad in
wet clothes too."

"It is well that you did not," Peters assured her, pulling
calmly at his cigar. "When I swam as I tell you, it was
because I must swim or drown. Also, the water was not
cold. There is always a danger in taking out anyone who is
drowning."

" Which means that you would have stopped where you were," she asked indignantly. " Well, I give you credit for frankness and courage of a kind, Mr. Peters. A Scotsman would have been afraid to say that. I think I'm going the other way. Good-afternoon ! " and with that she picked her way across the docks in another direction, while Peters, after bowing politely, went on undisturbed. Once he stopped and spoke, though there was no one near him.

" As if a life mattered ! " he said, and then laughed and passed on.

# CHAPTER XIII

## A MEETING OF MINOR POETS

LUCIUS was discontented after dinner that night, and failed to find consolation even in a pipe of Dream Mixture, taken with his favorite authors. Nelly also was somewhat depressed, and even irritable. She sat with Lucius in his little smoking-room, and darned socks in melancholy silence.

" The business," said Lucius, with a disconsolate air, " is makin' me mind a blank ! If the trade don't get depressed soon, why—I shall be just a rich uneducated ass ! Why don't we ask some one in to brighten us up, Nell, my dear ? "

" I don't feel that I want brightening, dad, thank you ! " Nell answered, with some warmth, and Lucius, surprised at her tone, took his pipe out of his mouth that he might look at her the better.

" You do, though ! " he insisted. " There you sit with your needlework and not an idea in your head, to all appearance."

" I've an idea that your socks have got to be mended," Nell retorted, and held one up to prove it.

" Nonsense ! " said Lucius. " It'll be a darn—not a sock, if you mend that ! Put it in the fire, an' get me fresh ones to-morrow. What's the good of your father slaving his brains into a batter, if it only ends in you spending your nights mendin' his old socks ? Where's Tom ? "

The change of topic was so sudden that Nell may be excused for needing a few seconds before she could switch her thoughts into this fresh groove.

" Reading in his own rooms, I hope; " she said presently,
" but I don't know. How should I ? "

" I don't know how you should," Lucius agreed. " He
never comes here now to tell us what he is doing. Why
doesn't he ? "

The darn, which she persisted in, needed all Nell's attention, and she was looking at it critically when she answered—

" Perhaps he doesn't come because I told him he came too
often," she said at last.

Lucius gasped in his chair.

" *You* told him ! " was all he could shout at first, and he
snorted and choked for some time before he could go farther. " Why ? "

" I told him," said Nell, speaking with great distinctness,
bending towards the light, and examining the darn more
critically than ever, " that any young man who was worth
anything would spend his evenings working for his examinations, instead of wasting his time in drawing-rooms."

" Quite right, I daresay," allowed Lucius. " Quite right.
But you're a caution, Nell, you are ! You're as hard as
nails, you know. Begor ! it's unnatural in a woman ! " and
poor Nell had to be content with this verdict as a reward
for doing what had been disagreeable enough.

" When did you tell him that ? " asked Lucius presently,
after a few pulls at his pipe.

" About a fortnight ago."

" He'll need a night off. Send a note round, saying that
I want to see him, Nell."

" When is he to do his reading, dad ? "

" Double tides to-morrow," suggested Lucius. " What's
the boy done to you that you should grudge him a pipe with
me ? "

" Nothing." Nell answered him, and Lucius was more
disgusted than ever.

"I think I'll go round and call on Mrs. MacQuestra," he said, after some cogitation. "She brightens a man up most amazingly."

Now, Mrs. MacQuestra was the widow whom Nell abhorred, and the effect, to Lucius' secret delight, was immediate.

Nell went to his desk and seated herself there, with the appearance of one who acted against her better judgment.

"What shall I say?" she asked meekly.

"Say? Oh, you needn't say anything. I don't want her round here disturbing you. D'ye think I'd expect a lady to leave her home this time o' night for me? I'll just put on a decent coat an' go round. She'll make me as welcome as sunshine." All this was said with the air of a man who was driven out to search for what his own home denied him.

"I'm writing to Tom," explained Nelly, her pen racing on the paper as she spoke, and Lucius, sitting with his back to her, winked at the fire.

"Oh, just tell him to come. 'Twont be hanging about a drawing-room to smoke a pipe in here with me. Tell Jean to bring in the whiskey and the biscuits about ten. Bring 'em in yourself if you like, an' if you can behave decently to the poor fellow."

So Nell, who saw herself dismissed, wrote a dignified little note, saying that her father told her to say that he would be very glad to see Mr. Dunbar for a chat, if he was not too busy to come round, and Tom, deciding that he was by no means too busy, though he was working hard enough when the note came, was shaking hands with Lucius, and looking in vain for Nell, a few minutes later.

"Sit down there," Lucius told him, pointing with his pipe to an easy-chair on the opposite side of the fire, "an' tell me what you've been doing that you never came round."

"Cramming, sir," said Tom, taking the chair and Lucius' tobacco-pouch.

" Ay, ay, of course !   You're a lucky young fellow, Tom."

" How so, sir ? "

" Look at me ! " said Lucius pathetically, pointing to a comfortable waistcoat.   " I'm a business man, an' me life is one long anxiety.   May be ruined to-morrow through no fault of mine.   A bankrupt, sir.   A dishonored man, with Nell left penniless in a cold world.   But you ! sir, you carry your fortune in your head where no man can touch it ! Your profession'll keep you comfortably wherever you go ! "

" Glad to hear it ! " muttered Tom, whose spirits didn't rise easily as work went on.   All he said audibly was, " I'm not a professional man yet."

" No, but Nell tells me you're hard at it, and you're bound to do well.   Don't tell me but what it's a sure thing for any young fellow with any brains at all—if he works.   Work, Tom, regular work.   There's nothing like it."   Lucius suddenly recollected that he had called Tom from work that night, so he added, " But you can't do without a night off now and then.   So don't you try it, my boy, or you'll break down," and after that they puffed in silence.

" How's Miss Nell, sir ? " Tom asked presently.

" She's all right.   She owned that she gave you a wigging about your work, Tom.   The impudence of these women ! But she means well, I tell you.   Just don't take any notice. It's a way she's got into because I let the hussy think she can do what she likes with me."

" Awfully good of her, I thought, sir," stammered Tom. " I believe it did me good.   I've been swatting pretty stiffly since."

" No doubt you'll be all right," said Lucius, with an air of certainty assumed most readily by friends who know least of the work.   " Don't overdo it though.   What do you do to amuse yourself now ? "

" Football once a week, and a good walk on Sundays, if it's decent weather."

"Right, quite right," agreed Lucius. "Don't miss church I hope," he added hastily as an afterthought, but didn't wait for a reply.

"You can't do much reading outside your work, of course?" he allowed. "Some of you scientific fellows don't care for it either. Now that's what I enjoy."

"I do what I can, sir."

"H'm! Never wrote, I suppose?" which hit Tom on a weak point.

"I never did what you'd call writing," he admitted, with something very like a blush, "but I scribble a bit now and then. Just for a change and amusement when I can't get out."

"No! you don't say so!"

Lucius took his pipe out of his mouth, and putting a hand on each knee, bent forward a little in his chair to have a good look at Tom.

"Who'd ha' thought it!" he said, with a frank emphasis that plainly showed it would never have occurred to him.

"You're a bit of a critic, then?" he suggested, half turning his chair towards the desk, with, at the same time, a keen eye upon Tom.

"Well, I know what I like, sir," and, satisfied with that, Lucius went to his desk, and, rummaging therein, brought out rolls of paper, which he carried back to the fire and arranged on the mantel-piece, clearing his throat as he did so.

"There's a man I know," he told Tom, choosing his words with great deliberation, "who amuses himself that way too, at times. Nothing big, you know. 'Trifles light as air,' as Shakespeare says. At least, mostly. I've got 'em to read over and criticise."

"I'd like to hear them," Tom assured him, and Lucius said that he should.

"I'd like your candid opinion," Lucius asserted. "I

7

think some of 'em are pretty good. But then I'm preju-
diced, the writer being a man I know."

"Let's have a specimen, sir," suggested Tom. "One of
those you think best," and he leaned back in his easy-chair
with a fine air of impartial and critical attention.

Lucius put on his glasses and searched among the papers,
clearing his throat again.

"I'm no reader, you know," he said.

"Shall I read them myself?" asked Tom, but Lucius
declined.

"The writing's a bit difficult," he explained, "and I've
got used to it. Here's one that's better than some of the
others, but I won't say it's the best—

> "When Chloris set my heart ablaze
>     With saucy looks and winning ways,
>     I lost my sleep, went off my feed,
>     And clean forsook the soothing weed.
>     But when the minx, with fleer and flout,
>     First quenched the fire, then put me out,
>     I filled my pipe. 'Go to!' said I,
>     'I'll smoke Dream Mixture till I die!'"

When Lucius had finished this production, he looked
anxiously at Tom, who maintained a disheartening silence.

"I don't know that it's so good as some of them," Lucius
said. "Let's find another!"

"Wait a bit, sir," Tom insisted. "Let's finish them off
as we go, if you want my opinion on them. Do you mind
reading that over again?"

So Lucius, standing with his back to the fire, read it
again, with more emphasis and a louder voice.

"Who's Chloris?" Tom asked at the end.

"It's a way a lot of them had of calling their girls Chloris
and Phyllis, a couple of centuries ago," Lucius explained,
but Tom shook his head cynically.

"Won't do, sir, tell your friend. It's nineteenth-century

stuff people want now—if they can't get twentieth; and I wouldn't call that ' went off my feed ' seventeenth-century, or poetry either, would you ? "

" Perhaps not, perhaps not," said Lucius, glaring over his spectacles at the unconscious Tom. " The rest is better, isn't it ? "

" ' I'll smoke Dream Mixture till I die ! ' " quoted Tom remorselessly. " Sounds awfully like an advertisement, doesn't it ? "

" Perhaps my man meant it for one," suggested Lucius. " Let's try another ! Here's a short one !

" Smoke! since a finger, stretched to touch the wheel,
    May crush a moth, or make an empire reel,
    Or count as nothing. Let the world go by,
    And leave the playing cards to those who deal."

" A weak copy of Omar Khayyam," Tom said coolly. " It's better than the last, though. Let's have another, sir."

" Like cures like, I hear them say,
    Smoke drives other clouds away."

" Short, and to the point, eh ? " said Lucius anxiously, after reading this, but Tom laughed.

" If you love me as I love you,
    No knife can cut our love in two,"

he quoted. " Sounds awfully like a motto out of a Christmas cracker, doesn't it ? " and Lucius waxed honestly angry.

" I've seen worse things in print," he said, bringing his hand down with a thump on the mantel-piece.

" Have you ? Where, sir ? " asked the incorrigible, while Lucius, not able to trust himself to speak, tugged at the old-fashioned bell-rope, meaning to order up the whiskey, and brought the rope down upon his head.

" Ah, you should have electric bells," suggested Tom.

" Damned tinkling alarums ! " Lucius declared angrily, glad to have a topic started upon which he might speak

freely to relieve his mind.  " I don't want to be reminded of
the telephone and the office while I'm at home for a little
quiet," and he wasted several matches over his pipe, to cover
his perturbation.

" So you don't think much of those things ? " he asked
presently, when he felt cooler, and Tom said " No: the
man's a penny-a-liner, I should think.   Someone you're
wanting to do a kindness to, I suppose, sir.   I know you're
always trying to give some fellow a lift.   But I don't believe
that's his line.   Perhaps they're not fair specimens.   Evidently he writes them to order, for some tobacconist ——"

" You're wrong there ! " interrupted Lucius rashly, but
triumphantly.  " He's got a tobacco business of his own.
A sort of fad, and a damned expensive one, too.   He thinks
trade advertising, as it is, a disgrace to a civilized people.
He's doing his humble best to give the thing a touch of the
artistic; that's what he's doing, and he's dropping a lot of
money over it, too."

" Then it's a failure all round, sir," Tom said, with blind
obstinacy, for he was beginning to think that Nell was still
vexed, and didn't mean to see him.  " You'd better advise your friend to get someone else to do his rhymes anyway."

" Perhaps you'd do them ? " Lucius suggested, sarcastically.

" It's not in my line, but I could do as good," Tom asserted, and, having smoked his pipe empty, asked if he
might fill it from Lucius' pouch.   The pouch was almost
empty, too, and Lucius, going to a cabinet, took a fresh
packet of Dream Mixture, and tossed it over to him.

" Oh, that's what we've been smoking ? " Tom asked,
looking at the wrapper.  " Well, I will say I wouldn't wish
for better 'baccy, anyhow, whatever the rhymes may be.

" In blackest, starless night, and darkest day,
    Smoke! and in smoke your care shall drift away."

"Cynical beggar!" he commented, after reading this aloud. "Extravagant, too! Seems to recommend smoking at all hours. I wouldn't give a rap for a pipe on a dark night."

"He's had his good times an' bad times," Lucius said. "There are times when he's cynical, maybe, an' times when he isn't. Now you've had your turn at cutting him to little pieces, I suppose you've nothing of your own about you for me to hear? There's the whiskey coming, an' if it's Nell who's bringing it, she shall be a judge between you and me."

It was Nell, who, being able to choose her own moment for an appearance, was far cooler than either of the two poets. Still, when Lucius, flourishing a bundle of papers at her as she came in, told her that "she must choose between himself and that fellow there," pointing angrily at Tom, she was considerably flustered, and so, for the matter of that, was Tom.

"We've been reading rhymes," he hastily explained, as they shook hands. "We don't quite agree about them, because your father sticks up for his friend who wrote them; that's all!"

"Oh!" said Nell, much relieved, "father was shouting so, that I thought I must come in myself to see what was the matter."

"Have ye got anything, Tom?" Moriarty repeated. "Of course ye have, if ye scribble at all! It'll be in your pocket there," and he pointed to a bulge shown in the breast-pocket of Tom's coat.

It was quite true that there were verses in that pocket, but since there were along with them some little notes from Nell, thanking him for books lent and so forth, it took Tom a little while to get the verses out separate from everything else. He being now, as it were, the prisoner at the bar, Lucius the judge, with a theory to uphold, and Nell the

audience, Tom hesitated, and hemmed, and explained, much
as Moriarty had done before.

" This is a little thing I just did quickly as it occurred to
me," he told them. " I haven't had time to polish, so you
mustn't be hard on it."

" Oh, polish it while we wait ! " Nell suggested, as if it
were a case of boot-mending.

" Go on, go on, man, and don't mind her ! " Lucius told
him. " She doesn't understand the art o' the thing at all.
There's a power of interest in sketches which you won't get
in oil portraits," he added solemnly, and, nodding his head
as a sign for Tom to read, he leant back in his chair and
closed his eyes.

But Tom had already discovered a difficulty. The
rhymes were upon Nelly. Upon what other topic could
they be ? Her name, he now recollected, came in in the very
first line, and, for the life of him, with Lucius impatient and
Nell curious, he couldn't decide on another. He wanted
two syllables to replace Nelly. Moriarty seemed to like
Chloris. Chloris it should be; and he started off in desperation—

> " When Chloris goes down Princes Street,
> 　　I walk behind and watch her sadly,
> For Chloris looks so dear, so sweet,
> 　　That all men needs must love her madly.
>
> Oh, sure, some day, a prince will come,
> 　　With castles, lands, and heaps of money,
> To bear her off and leave me dumb,
> 　　With Princes Street no longer sunny.
>
> Oh, Chloris, when you venture out,
> 　　For go you will, though I would hide you,
> Go veiled, and then, to banish doubt,
> 　　Oh, let me always go beside you."

" Chloris ! what a pretty name," Nelly said, politely. " I
don't know her."

"Ay! Who's Chloris? who's Chloris?" Lucius quoted, with tremendous sarcasm. "It's out of date, me dear boy. Two centuries ago, at least! It's nineteenth-century stuff we want, Tom, if we can't get twentieth."

"Father! what a rude thing to say! I'm sure they're very pretty verses. Miss Chloris ought to feel flattered. You asked him to read them, too."

"Why, the fellow laughed at the name when I, that is me friend, used it!" objected Lucius. "Then he goes an' uses it himself. That's what he calls criticism."

"I've changed my mind after hearing it a second time," Tom explained. "I think it's an awfully good name!"

"You'd heard it a second time a long while before you said that," Lucius grumbled. "Of course it's a good name. You can't use everyday commonplace modern names in good poetry. Not, mind you," he added, in haste, "that I say yours is good. 'Heaps o' money,' indeed! D'ye call that poetry? It ought to be 'ruddy gold,' only you'd miss the rhyme. Whoever heard of a prince carryin' about his land an' castles with him? I've heard that, even if they want to buy an evening paper, they borrow the ha'penny from an aide-de-camp! Poor divil! I hopes he gets it back, that's all. What was I talking about? Oh, Chloris, yes! An' everyday names. Now, try Nelly's name instead, an' see how foolish it'll be."

"I don't know," Nell said, with some hauteur, "that I care to have my name put into poetry that's meant for a lady called Chloris!"

"Tut, tut!" Lucius told her. "Hold your tongue, lassie! The name's not copyright. It was Mrs. MacQuestra's name before it was yours."

"A long time before, I should think," Nelly interpolated; but Lucius went on.

"She's the Widdy, you know, Tom, that you met here at dinner t'other night. A decent body she is, too. Faith, 'twould be a fine notion to send her a copy with my compliments, and what did she think of them! Not that I believe I will," he added hurriedly, thinking from the way Nell's foot began to tap upon the floor that he was going too far. "She's not the ear for music a woman should have, so it's likely 'twould be wasted on her—all except the compliment. Come on, Tom, put in ' Nelly' and if my Nell doesn't like it, and Mrs. MacQuestra can't have it, why, we'll call it Poetical License, and no more said."

So Tom read the thing, amended according to suggestion, with great warmth, and a stolen glance or two at Nelly, who, being naturally not interested, except in a friendly way, about verses written to a lady called Chloris, whom she didn't know, kept her eyes upon the floor and studied the carpet pattern, and was only politely complimentary at the end.

Lucius, however, was more enthusiastic, having in his mind the question of rhymes for the Dream Cigarettes.

" I'd like some more, some time," he told Tom, " light love-making sort of rhymes, as short as you please, to show to the man I told you of. Nelly and I'll hear 'em together now and then when you've time. We'll educate her to understand poetry and enjoy a good verse yet, Tom. The lassie's ignorance is shameful."

" One can't get time for everything." Tom suggested, with a look of apology at Nell for even listening to such blasphemous accusations against her perfection.

" I've heard you say that Miss Nelly spends all her time about the housekeeping, sir. I expect she enjoys real poetry as well as you or I do."

With that he said " good-night " and came away, after, at Lucius' request, leaving his rhymes for further criticism. One result of the evening was that, when Tom came across the Dream Mixture elsewhere, as you will find that he did, he recognized it and profited thereby.

Another most useful outcome was that Nell straightway began to develop a strong interest in Poetry, so called.

To such an extent was this the case, that she quietly lifted Tom's verses to Chloris, the young lady whom she didn't know, from Moriarty's desk when she said " good-night " to him, and studied them with great care and high appreciation before she slept. The scrawl bore no signs of " Nelly " having been substituted for " Chloris," but " Chloris " was not there, and " Nelly " was, which, on the whole, made them perhaps more interesting.

# CHAPTER XIV

### LUCIUS IS DIPLOMATIC

NELLY read the verses again before she came down to breakfast the next morning, and either because, for once in a way, it promised to be bright weather, or else because she was amused at Tom's marked admiration for Miss Chloris, her face was full of dimples, her gray eyes full of laughter, when she seated herself to pour out her father's coffee.

Lucius, with the contrariness of man, was not responsive. 'Melia was weighing upon his conscience, with the little shop and the kilted Highlander, the Dream Mixture, rhymes and all. He had said nothing yet to Nelly about any of them. He was stubbornly determined that he would, because he wanted her to help him with 'Melia, but he didn't at all like the job, though he couldn't exactly say why. It was so difficult, he felt, to explain matters. He scarcely understood them himself, and affairs were as they were, through a chain of circumstances, the result of reasoning on his part more ingenious than sound. This little speculation in tobacco arose from a dread he had of being too much wrapped up in his very prosperous and well-managed merchant business.

If Lucius found that after a busy day he was not always able to enjoy and to decide such questions as, for example, the full and exact meaning of "Sordello," or to whom Shakespeare's sonnets were addressed, he imagined that all finer qualities of mind must be blighted by office work. So he sternly set himself to a carefully considered course of the poets, with a strict avoidance of the ballad-makers, whom he liked best, and a special attention to Browning and Shelley as a refining influence. He read the others, but not as part of these intellectual gymnastics.

Next came the jotting down of lines for himself. Just for exercise, you see. Then, alas! the, at first, scarcely owned wish to see his own rhymes in print. A typewriter satisfied him for the time, but not for long. Then he got verses set up by a printer, but the business-half of him protested. Here was sheer extravagance and folly, since no one but himself and the aforesaid printer saw the verses when printed, which they were on single sheets of hand-made paper, with rough edges, broad margins, &c. Then the sophist deceived himself, as most sophists ingeniously do. He would employ his fancy to some profit; harness his Pegasus and make it PAY!

The idea suddenly came to him in a London tobacconist's. He was in London on business, and dropping in for a cigar at this shop, saw Amélie for the first time. She served him and he chatted with her, as he chatted with everyone, gentle and simple.

As he talked, he looked at the colored advertisements, some funny, some commonplace, some vulgar.

"A good rhyme, now, round a cigar might please a man," he said, tentatively, to 'Melia; and 'Melia, thinking of a music-hall refrain that had taken the town by storm, and was remarkable for its want of everything but jingle, said, "Yes, sir! Oh, cert'nly; I should think so indeed!"

"Much experience at this sort of thing?" asked Lucius, looking round him; and 'Melia told him that she had.

"Wages?" asked Lucius, confidentially; and she told him her wages too, as most people told Lucius anything he chose to ask, because of the pleasant, insinuating Irish way he had with him.

"Nice place?" he asked next; and 'Melia, having found out three days before that her fellow shop-girl was, as she

put it, "a nasty, low, treacherous, backbiting person," said
with emphasis that it was *not* a nice place, not by no means,
and that she thought of making a change.

" Wait a month, me dear," Lucius had said, in a fatherly
way, with a half-sovereign as retainer, and, taking her address, marched off.

Within a month he engaged her to come North, and
within two months she was installed with the Dream Mixture and cigarettes (which really, the rhymes apart, were excellent) most prominently in the front, with various better
known (though of course less deserving) tobaccos in the
background.

Here she had now been six months, and Lucius, sitting
with his coffee and fish growing cold before him, wondered
how to explain the situation. It wasn't business, for it
wasn't paying, and it wasn't being pushed. It wasn't charity to 'Melia, for, though he couldn't entertain the idea of
dismissing her after getting her North from a situation
where she would very likely have otherwise stayed, he had
really sent for her because of her honest ways, and presumed
business knowledge. It wasn't a fad of his own, a mere
extravagant toy; he vowed it wasn't that, since the tobacco
was good, and sold, when anyone would buy it, at a fair
profit.

Nell, watching him from behind the coffee-machine, wondered what was wrong, but, being experienced, kept her
wonder to herself, and did not let it affect her appetite.

" What with business extendin' this way and spreadin'
that, a man can't eat or sleep in peace." Lucius blurted
out, and Nell knew that she was to hear of his troubles at
last.

" Pass your cup for some more coffee, dear," she told
him. " That's all cold, and so's your fish. Help yourself.
and give me a little bit more, and tell me all about it."

" I've got a young woman working for me now," grumbled Lucius, doing as he was told; " she's more bother to me than all the men. It's always so with you girls ! "

Nell was quite unmoved by this denunciation of her sex.

" What is she ? " she asked. " A typist ? "

" D'ye think I'd have a girl making a mess of my correspondence ? No; she's in a retail trade."

" I didn't know you had any retail trade," said Nell, calmly. She was quite unaware of the great gulf between wholesale and retail.

" What's the business ? " she asked.

" A little speculation in tobacco," Lucius told her.

" Well, is it a failure ? "

" Can't tell yet," was all he would admit. " I can afford it if it is, I suppose. The girl will be a failure though, if she isn't seen to."

He waited to be helped by further questions, but Nell said nothing, so presently he repeated it.

" An utter failure she'll be," he said.

" What's the matter ? " asked Nell. " Is she dishonest ?"

" D'ye think I'm such a fool in business as I am outside it ? " demanded Lucius angrily. " D'ye think I'd choose dishonest folk to work for me ? "

" What is it then, dear ? "

" The place is goin' to be the ruin o' the girl's health if I don't see to it." Lucius blustered. " Here, when I put her in there, I told her to keep the same hours as the trade, an' because a darned little tuppeny-ha'penny place near opens at half-past eight and closes at eleven, the silly fool does the same, and takes a Saturday half-holiday by keepin' the place open till midnight ! The sitting-room, if you can call it one, gets like an oven too, with the gas and the fire. The place isn't fit for a girl to be in all those hours."

" Why don't you close it ? " asked Nell, as a practical question, but that only made Moriarty worse.

" And turn the girl adrift, I suppose," he asked indignantly, "after taking her away from another berth and bringing her from London ? Is that all you can suggest ?"

" May I go in and see her ? " Nell asked quietly; and that being what Lucius wanted, he gave his consent with a fair amount of grace.

" If there's anything she ought to have," he said, " you know where to come for a shilling or two. And if you can make any suggestion, after looking round, that would be likely to make another better place pay, why, I'll consider it. I'm not going to drop the thing, mind you, once for all! I can make it pay if I give me mind to it, and so I will. It's a fancy of mine, and I'm not going to throw that girl over either. She's an honest lassie, and means well. Just you dress yourself nice an' quiet, so as not to seem too much the patronizin' fine lady, an' look her up this morning. She won't be busy, and if anyone is there you can buy me a packet of Dream Mixture Cigarettes. I want Tom to try them when he comes in again."

So Nelly got the address, and her father gave her a smacking kiss and went off to his work in high glee.

" It's the easiest thing to me to manage a woman ! " he told himself as he went beaming along. " It's me Irish blood, I s'pose. Though there's nothing else I can put a successful hand to outside of the office, when a woman is to be wheedled into thinking she wants to do, ay, and *will* do, what all the while *you're* for her to do, faith ! Lucius Moriarty, you're hard to beat." And, certainly, Moriarty had, and has, bless him ! a most persuasive and insinuating way with the ladies, even when he seems to bluster most fiercely. Whether the dear creatures are always so blind to the way in which they are led as he believes them to be, is another question, and one which the ordinary unpersuasive and obtuse male won't pretend to decide. Nelly smiled at the recollection of his methods, as she put on her hat, but you will recollect that she began the day smiling, and, having

"'I SHA'N'T SHAKE HANDS'"

started, was likely to keep it up on small provocation until bedtime.

She then sallied forth, most provokingly and enticingly charming, and if she wore her plainest dress that morning, all I can say is that one wouldn't have thought it.

As she went along Princes Street the sight of a long row of sandwich men made her positively bubble over with mirth. They carried boards announcing the theatrical performance for that night, of which all that I can tell you is that its name was " Chloris ! " The coincidence seemed to strike Nell as most amusing, and the way she smiled over it must surely show that she had no jealousy.

Presently she dived into the back lane, which I absolutely refuse to give a name to, and soon came in sight of the guardian Hielander, whom 'Melia had wheeled out upon his stand, to get the benefit of fresh air and attract the admiration of passers-by.

Nell was past that admirable work of art and in the little shop before she discovered that her entry was *mal à propos*. Miss Sophia Amélie Rivers was standing well back from the counter, with her hands resolutely clasped behind her, and a most scornful countenance, while a fair-haired, rather nice-looking, but melancholy youth vainly stretched a hand and an arm and a good deal of his body across.

" No, Mr. Inch," Amélie was saying, " I sha'n't shake hands, not if you stay there for ever. You've got to apologize first! What do you take me for ? Oh ! ——," which last was caused by the sudden appearance of Nelly, at the sight of whom 'Melia moved forward, and Inch drew himself up, with an injured expression.

" I—I beg your pardon ! " Nelly said, quite as much disturbed as they were. " I mean, I want a packet of Dream Cigarettes."

" Yes, miss," said 'Melia, who had recovered herself, and now was strictly business-like. " They're very mild. As good as anything in the market, and very much liked. But you'd save upon the box of a hundred. Two-and-six you'd save. Mayn't I send a box for you?"

"No, thank you," Nell told her, with rather a dignified air, because she suddenly felt shy. "I was only asked to get a packet. They're for my father, Mr. Moriarty."

To young Inch, of course, this name meant nothing; indeed, he hardly heard it, but it meant everything to 'Melia.

To be caught "fooling," as she put it, by Miss Moriarty! She'd think that was the way poor 'Melia spent her time, but Nell spoke on before 'Melia could imagine what to say or to do.

"I'm going farther, and, if I may, I'll leave them until I come back, can I? I told father I would come in and see whether you were busy or not."

"It's the slackest time of the day," explained 'Melia, with absolute ignoring of Inch. "I've nothing to do if you'd like to step in now, miss, and she moved to lift the curtain of her private retreat, letting her eyes pass over the embarrassed youth as if he were another wooden Highlander. But Nell was already stepping to the door.

"I'll come in again in about half an hour," she said, nodding. "I can finish my shopping by that time," and out she went.

"Now you've done it, Mr. Inch." 'Melia told that reckless young man, as he stared after Nell's fluttering skirts.

"Pretty tale my employer'll have now of the way I mind this show!"

"If you'd only shaken hands straight away it wouldn't have happened," he retorted. "I don't know what I've done to be treated as if I wasn't fit to shake hands with! I've tried to make out what you got so angry about last time I was in, and, for the life of me, I don't know."

"Very rude you were," retorted 'Melia, "very rude in-

deed.   And now you've made things worse.   I'm a woman,
Mr. Inch, if I'm not a lady, and if you can't remember
what's due from a gentleman to any woman, w'y, you
mustn't come here."

" I swear ——," the boy began, but 'Melia held up her
hands in wild horror.

" How dare you ? " she told him.   " You sha'n't swear
here anyway.   Go away at once, and if you *do* come back, let
me see that you've learnt how to be'ave.   I've something
more to do than listen to your swears ! "

With that she dived behind the curtain, and there stayed
until the disconsolate fellow had left, after which she
popped out again, and began looking around to see if anything could be made to look better before Nell came back.

8

# CHAPTER XV

As Nell went about her shopping she tried to think what she was to do and say when she got back to 'Melia, and for the life of her she couldn't tell.

She had imagined that 'Melia would be a timid, worn, humble sort of creature, who would need protection and encouragement, and a great deal of cheering up. The dubiously tinted hair jarred upon her, and so did the shabby brown velveteen. It was hard for her to associate these things and the presence of the melancholy Archie with anything approachable. If she had found 'Melia sitting alone, in a rusty black dress, and shaken by a hollow cough, her task would have seemed much easier. However, Nell was a healthy, practical young person who didn't, as a rule, worry much over stiles before she came to them. All the preparation that she finally made for her return call was to invest in half a dozen big feathery yellow chrysanthemum blooms, and, armed with these, she went back.

Now, when 'Melia, ten minutes before, had been smoothing her hair and surveying as much of herself as she could see piecemeal in some four inches of mirror, she had longed for a flower wherewith to adorn herself further, or, as she put it, "to gild the gingerbread." The sudden longing in her eyes, therefore, when Nell marched in with the chrysanthemums was unmistakable, and Nell, like an able general, saw the weak point and assaulted.

"I brought these for the shop," she said, holding them out, and I think it was rather a tactful thing for her to say "shop," and not "you."

'Melia gave a big sigh of satisfaction, and pushed them against her own delighted face.

" They've no scent worth mentioning, you know," Nell explained.

" I know. It's the soft, feathery feel of 'em I like," 'Melia told her, rubbing them gently against her cheek. " Where shall they go ? "

" I think I'd try one in my dress if I were you," Nell suggested, " that is, if you don't think the small yellow one is too big. It will show well against the brown velveteen, won't it ? Here, I've got a pin, let me put it in for you ! " and she pinned the smallest flower carefully in the breast of the brown velveteen, while 'Melia, to whom a cabbage would not have seemed too big, was loud in her delight.

" It brightens up the place, doesn't it ? " Nell asked when she had finished, and 'Melia, trying to get a glimpse of the general effect from the shadowy reflection in a glass case on the counter, said that it made all the difference.

" I'll put the rest in water at once," she decided, and fetched a tumbler of water from behind the curtain.

That, however, was not big enough to hold them properly, and at last she poured out a tumbler of water for herself and put them in the jug.

" I sha'n't want more than that for dinner," she explained, "and I've got some in the kettle for my tea, so *that's* all right. I'll take 'em home at night for a change of air."

She said " hair," through an over-conscientious effort to omit no aspirate.

" Where is your home ? " asked Nell, who had seated herself on the little red settee opposite the counter.

" Out Comely Bank way," 'Melia told her. " It's just a room," she explained, " and I'm not much in it, of course. But it's respectable, and I always call it 'ome, because that makes it seem more 'ome-like.

" Won't you come inside, miss, if you're going to stay ? "

she asked hospitably, pulling aside the curtain. "It's a bit
stuffy in here, but it's quite private if anyone should come,
though this is the slackest time."

Nell thanked her, and went in, and 'Melia, in whisking
round, managed to get a satisfactory glimpse, in the four-
inch mirror, of the brilliant effect produced by the yellow
chrysanthemum upon the brown velveteen. Then she sat
down, necessarily near Nelly, and, folding her hands in her
lap, waited for further developments.

" Mr. Moriarty," Nell said presently, "asked me to look
in and consult with you about the business. It isn't paying, is it ? "

'Melia shook her head dolorously, and acknowledged the
fault. " That's a fact, miss, though I do my very best, I do
assure you."

" My father told me so," said Nell, " but he thought if
we two talked it over together, we might hit upon something
that a man wouldn't think of. Why doesn't it pay ? "

'Melia frowned anxiously over this, and shook her head.
" Them that comes, comes again," she said; and perhaps it
was the thought of the frequency with which one in particular came that made her blush a little. " But there's so
few comes ! " she added regretfully.

" Can we bring them, then ? " was Nell's pertinent question. " Or must we go somewhere else to get them ? "

" Well, this place hasn't had a chance yet," 'Melia decided. " It's only six months open, you know, miss. Now,
if we only had a lot of sandwich-men, down Princes Street
every day for a week, dressed up, you know, and all smoking
hard—big pipes as long as your arm, and Dream Mixture
printed back and front, large on 'em, why that might make
a difference. But your pa won't advertise ! "

" Not that way, at anyrate," Nell decided. " But can't
we make the place look brighter ? "

" A coat of paint ! " suggested 'Melia, getting quite excited over these plottings. "If 'twas a pea-green outside, with a little yellow about the window, 'twould be marked off, as you may say."

"Perhaps dark green might look prettier," Nell thought. "You're quite right, and we'll have it painted. Then, inside?"

'Melia pushed aside the curtain and looked out and round her critically, trying to see how it would strike an outsider.

"Those chrysanthemums do light the place up wonderful," she admitted. "Give a sort of tone to the place, don't they? I've never seen flowers in any tobacconist's I've served in before," she added dubiously. "I don't know as it's professional, and would be a great expense."

"If we're going to do better than other people, we must do differently," Nell announced, with a dogmatic air. "You've not got much room, though, and one can't always get flowers. What do you say to a tobacco plant there in the corner?"

'Melia looked at a sort of ornament of dried tobacco leaves that hung over the counter, and was doubtful.

"They're much the same color as everything else in the place, aren't they?"

"No, no!" Nell insisted, taking out a note-book. "Those things are dried—not a bit the same. They're a splendid green, with pretty flowers, only, I don't know if they'd live here. I'll find out for you," and she made a note of it.

"There's another thing," she said, "that my father told me to see about—only it's not so easy. He thought the hours were longer than they need be."

"It's that mean ijiot 'igher up, miss, that makes me do it," 'Melia explained, warming at the memory of her grievance, and letting her h's go to ruin in consequence. "Mister Moriarty brings me 'ere, and this is wot 'ee says, says 'ee, 'I'm not up in this trade, an' I don't know the ways an' customs of it yet, but you're a honest lassie, or I'm a fool!'

'Ee said that miss, standin' there by the counter, with 'is
'and in 'is trowsies pockets, jinglin' 'is money free 'an easy
like, and I says, ' Thank you, sir,' an' feels pleased, 'cause
where I'd been they 'sposed one was natchally not to be
trusted."

" My father's honest, of course," Nell said with pride,
" and so, of course, likes to be trusted and to trust other
people."

" 'Taint always safe," 'Melia told her, shaking her head
decidedly, " but I told myself 'ee 'adn't made no mistake in
me.  So I said, as for hours, I'd just find out an' do like my
neighbors, an' my neighbor is that ijiot 'igher up."

She paused, not for want of breath, but because, suddenly,
she became aware that she was excited, and had dropped
into a rapid h'less monologue.

" Well ? " asked Nelly, who didn't understand.  " What
happened ? "

" So the night before we opened the shop," said 'Melia,
speaking slowly, and trying to be correct, " I came round,
and I watched.  At nine, up went the shutters, and I went
home.  ' Nine,' I said, ' it shall be,' and nine it was, for a
week."

'Melia sighed, and being roused, muttered something
about a darned little fool, which Nelly paid no attention to.

" Why didn't you keep it at nine ? " she asked.  " That
seems long hours to me," and 'Melia launched out again.

" The little man that keeps the place," she said, " was
curious, an' I daresay 'ee was riled.  But there was nothing
to see from his place, being the same side, so in slack
times, of which there's plenty, he'd go in his slippers an'
a dirty old smoking cap, an' take a look at our place
from over across.  I seen him from behind the 'Ighlander
often."

'Melia was now completely carried away by the recital of
what, to her, was a thrilling tale.  Her aspirates had gone

hopelessly, one word gliding into another in a swiftly moving stream, accompanied by appropriate action.

She bent forward toward Nell, and raised a dramatic hand.

" One day," she said, " 'ee came in ! "

" What *did* you do ? " asked Nell, and 'Melia, seeing that she held her audience, told her.

" I never let on, not I ! ' Wot can I show you ? ' I ses to 'im—an' 'ee larfed ! ! "

" What a rude fellow !  Yes ? "

" It's easy to see," he told me, " from your tongue an' your cheek, where *you* come from."

" ' Well,' I says, " ' I ain't got no nasty Scot——,' I mean, that is, miss, I told 'im that was quite right, for I came from the south.  Then I asked 'im again wot I could serve 'im with.  ' I'd like to know how you're getting on, my dear,' he told me (one doesn't need to notice these men, miss, they knows no better), and I told 'im ' very well, indeed.'  ' I'm the proprietor of the Divan 'igher up,' 'ee says, ' an' I'm afraid there ain't no room for two.' ' Oh ! ' I says, quite innercent like, ' when are you goin' ? ' and the little ijiot was that savage that 'ee turned an' went."

Nelly burst out laughing.  She couldn't help it, as she seemed to see the owner of the dirty smoking cap depart; and 'Melia, pleased at the success of her dramatic recital, smiled, and then became gloomy.

" That night," she said, " that shop was open till midnight, tho' 'twas Monday.  So was this."

She sat, an unconquered Napoleon brooding over past victories and future fights, while Nelly watched her curiously.  The girl had more determination than Nelly had thought.

" It was twelve all that week," she went on, " an' my landlady started askin' me where I spent my evenin's.  ' I spend 'em alone,' I told 'er, ' and if you'll be so good as to bring your work and spend 'em with me, you'll be doin' a favor that I won't forgit.' So she came, once, and no more. But she was satisfied, an' never asked no more questions, not even when the worst came."

" It was bad enough already," said Nell. " What was the worst ? "

" One day the Smoking Cap came bobbin' in again, quite polite, an' asked 'ow I was. ' Bloomin' !' ses I, that is, very well. ' 'Ow's yourself ?' ' Oh,' he said, grinnin', wicked, ' I've the awfullest toothache, I 'ave. I can't sleep a wink. So I shall just keep my shop open for company.' ' Funny !' I told 'im, quite cool. ' You an' me can sympathize. I'm sufferin' from insomny, awful, and I'm going to do the very same thing this very night. There's the pleeseman, an' a lot of night watchmen, the people goin' to work early in the ware'ouses, not to mention the milkman, which is a girl in this street, I b'lieve. We'll make our fortunes !' That was the end, miss !"

" Quite time, I'm sure," Nell agreed. " How did it end ? "

" That night I called to a baker boy an' got 'im to bring me rolls and butter, and to tell the milk girl to bring me a penn'orth. He got two cigarettes for doin' it, and I thought I was right. I made myself tea that kept me so on the jump, I couldn't wink an eye for fear of bein' murdered in my sleep, an' I kept all the gas turned up, and a good fire, and the door wide open. I had the awfullest book that night, with five murders an' two suicides, and at two o'clock in the morning, when the pleeseman came in to see what was wrong, I screamed an' thought I should ha' died ! "

" You silly thing," said Nelly, not unkindly though, " what on earth was the use of it all ? "

" I don't like to be bested," explained 'Melia. " Anyway that ended it as I told you. ' Wot's wrong here ?' says the pleeseman, an' when I said I had insomny because my neighbor had toothache, I thought he'd 'ave died, an' serve 'im right for terrifyin' poor me.

"'You'd better go in with my compliments an' ask for 'is toothache,' I told that pleeseman, which he did, an' presently he come back. 'You kin go 'ome,' 'ee ses. 'The toothache's better, an' your friend had a warnin' from me for leavin' the shop open to thieves while he was snorin' on his bed. He's puttin' up his shutters, and I'll help you to do the same, 'cause you're a plucky one.'

"That's what he said, but I'd made up my mind to a night of it. The tea made me that jumpy I couldn't sleep if I'd wanted to, ever so. So I told 'im, with a cheap cigar for his trouble, and he told the other pleesemen he met on his beat, an' they told more. I got eight of 'em in for a laugh one time and another, and the inspector. They all bought an ounce or two ounces of Dream Mixture, which one told me I ought to be taking myself, and I got one or two early folk too. But my! I was bad the next day."

"You silly girl," said Nelly again, but she said it so that 'Melia didn't mind.

"As the Smoking Cap didn't come bobbin' round next day," she went on, "an' as my landlady did, I just got her to mind the shop two minutes, while I called. ''Ow's the toothache?' I asked, slipping my head in, an' he told me to go to —— blazes, but I took no manner o' notice. 'You're quite right,' I told him. 'I got a dozen people in, 'ow many did you get?'. Then I was 'bliged to leave because 'is language wasn't fit for a lady to 'ear. But we don't keep open after eleven now, that being his bedtime, I s'pose."

"You aren't going to keep those hours either," Nelly said as she got up to go, "but we can't decide and change everything at once. I may come in for another chat soon, mayn't I?"

"And welcome," 'Melia told her with emphasis, and watched her out.

As Nelly went up the street the man in the smoking cap—
a miserable, weakly specimen, was standing at his shop door.
Nelly laughed to herself as she thought of his discomfiture,
and then felt cruel because he was so utterly overcome.  She
became lost for the time in vague speculation, which
touched, without her being aware of the fact, on Free Trade,
Protection, Competition, Monopoly, Co-operation, and a
great many other debatable subjects.  But her thoughts
ended as she reached home in a resolution to see 'Melia again
very soon, and find out how matters could be improved.

# CHAPTER XVI

WHEN Nell had gone, 'Melia's first movement was to the little mirror. She could now get a fair idea of the chrysanthemums' effect, and she studied it critically. The result was a smile upon 'Melia's face, already bright after her account of the Smoking Cap episode, and an unexpressed wish that Archie would find his way back. Then she moved round, dusting a box here and a tin there, critical to discover dirt, though she had swept the whole place as usual on her arrival.

Then she went back to the chrysanthemums in the jug, and after pulling them about, and arranging them in different ways and places, at last took the comparatively small one from her dress, and replaced it by the biggest. Then she settled down to a book, careful at the same time that the flower shouldn't be crushed.

She was thus occupied when Mr. Peters dropped in, on his way, or, strictly speaking, a trifle out of his way, to lunch with Lucius according to appointment.

He complimented her elaborately upon her decoration. " Happy chrysanthemum," he told her. " It will no doubt live forever, at least, until you change it for another," at which florid compliment 'Melia beamed, and said, " Go along, Cap'n Peters ! "

She had persisted in giving him this title from the beginning, and occasionally asked him when he was going another voyage.

Peters looked at his watch, and then sat down.

" One little cigarette," he told her, " before I take myself from this pleasant place," and he took one accordingly.

" What about my bike ? " 'Melia asked presently, after the exchange of one or two more pleasantries.

So far, her experience in life had been that if you want a thing you must ask for it, and usually ask often. So she was quite prepared to remind Peters of the promised lessons as much as was necessary. In this case, however, she did not need to be anxious.

" It is of that," Peters told her, " that I come to speak."

He had spent another hour at the Waverley Market, and he was satisfied that four or five hours more would make him able to ride and to teach.

" Let us arrange ! " he told 'Melia, and she was overcome with gratitude.

" Why you trouble 'bout teachin' me I can't think," she remarked. " 'Tisn't as if I hadn't a young man."

" No," said Peters, who apparently didn't care whether she had a " young man " or no, which rather disappointed 'Melia.

" Is he coming ? " he asked, but 'Melia said " No," telling herself that it was no lie, and that whether there was one to come was quite another matter.

" When I can bike," she told herself, " I'll hire one to come to business one mornin', if I've to go without dinner for a week to do it. We'll see what the dirty Smoking Cap thinks o' *that*. He'll think trade's looking up ! "

" Let us say Wednesday morning," suggested Peters, " and where shall it be ? "

" Lemme think ! " said 'Melia, reflecting. " I'd like something soft to fall on ! " but Peters assured her it was not necessary.

" My arm is strong," he pointed out ; and 'Melia said, after a casual look at that muscular limb, that there wasn't a doubt of it.

" Say in front of Fettes then," she decided. " There's room to flop there, isn't there ? "

Peters, on having Fettes geographically placed for him, decided that there was room to flop.

" At half-past seven," he suggested.

" Say quarter ! " 'Melia begged. " I'd like a good go while I'm at it. Maybe you won't take me a second time. I can't make out why you're doin' it."

" It is for my health," Peters assured her, " because of my fat."

" Well, it don't matter anyway, Cap'n Peters. I may bring my young man when I like, mayn't I ? " and Peters saying " Yes, by all means," went on his way.

All he wished was to keep on chatty, intimate terms with 'Melia, for more than one reason. He did not yet know what might be the advantage, but Peters was quite ready, in a slow deliberate way, to take a great deal of trouble, in certain directions, with a small possibility of return. So he went to lunch with a good appetite and a consciousness of time well spent.

That morning was fated to be full of surprises for 'Melia, and the kilted gentleman at the door would have winked if he had been able to do so, as one person after another turned up to assist in 'Melia's astonishment. She had scarcely settled to her book again, after clearing out the corner of the shop and trying to imagine Nell's tobacco-plant there, when the postman came, a very infrequent visitor.

" Name of Buncombe ? " he asked, and, on 'Melia's nodding, threw down a letter upon the counter, and went off to distribute other sensations of various kinds along the street. If it were permitted to moralize while 'Melia gasped, one would like to consider the postman for awhile, second as he is only to the angel of death, in the fatefulness of his mission. But since 'Melia wasted very little time in gasping, perhaps one had better follow her example, and leave

the postman to be considered from various points of view,
without our valuable aid, by those who care to do so.

'Melia gasped, first because letters for her were very rare,
and if the postman had asked her name she would almost
certainly have said Rivers. Next, on looking at the letter,
she knew the writing to be her father's. It was a very long
time since she had heard anything of that estimable person,
though, as we know, she had tried to keep him informed of
her own movements. She opened the letter at once.

It ran as follows :—

" MY DEAR DAUGHTER,—

" Fortune, which, as you are aware, has been against your
poor father all his life, has ceased for the moment to frown,
and my first thought is of my child. I hope to reach you
soon, after a few days which I must spend in London on
business [the business was a little enjoyment, while his
hands should have time to recover from ten days' work in
the engine room]. It may soon prove necessary for you to
arrange to give up your menial occupation and take the
position suitable for your father's daughter. But that must
be left until I see you. I will write again.—Your loving
father,                              JOSHUA BUNCOMBE."

'Melia read this once, standing there behind the counter
where she had opened it, and a second time sitting on the
sofa behind the curtain. Then she jumped up, and, with a
shout, executed a series of jigs, that only ended when she
had knocked down a jar and smashed it upon the floor.

" Now you've done it ! " she told herself. " That don't
come under the head of necessary wear an' tear ! " and she
sat down a little subdued, and read the letter again. It was
vague enough, as you see, but a great deal more sanguine
than was justified by the possession of a diminishing four
hundred dollars. The fact is that Buncombe was building

upon what he thought to be a surer foundation. Immediately on reaching London, which he did with a clear head owing to ten days' enforced sobriety and physical exercise, he set to work and obtained the necessary information about Lord Inch. Old files of papers, and a pound or two spent in private inquiry, satisfied him that there was an interval of twelve to eighteen months, in the judge's early life, which had been spent in the States.

It remained to be seen how far the judge cared for this to be remembered, and what he would pay to have it forgotten. Here was a widower with one child and a large income. Buncombe knew his professional salary to a shilling, as anyone could who wished, and guessed also that there must be a fair amount put by from the advocate's fees. A part, and a large part, of all this should be his and 'Melia's, he promised himself, though how to manage this he could not decide. Yet what did he risk by meeting Lord Inch ? What did Lord Inch know of his share in the business he wished to recall ? In what capacity should he appear ? All these were important questions over which Buncombe thought carefully and often, with cigars and curiously compounded drinks to help him. The drinks, however, were taken in comparative moderation. Buncombe had been at some trouble to make himself realize that he really must be careful. This was less difficult than it would have been across the water, because of the expected meeting with 'Melia.

He was an unmitigated cur, and utterly selfish ; but, like a great many such people, he liked to create a good impression, when that did not involve too much self-sacrifice, and where it might, in the end, work for his comfort. Besides, he was very anxious to stand well with 'Melia.

After all, the girl was his child. He had cared for her mother so far as he could care for any one besides himself, and 'Melia had given him no trouble. When he saw her last, he had posed as an unfortunate man, worthy of a much

more exalted position in society, who, at the worst, was nobody's enemy but his own. That character he was very
anxious to hold, and since 'Melia, with increasing experience, would be less easily convinced, Buncombe felt that he
must be more careful.

So in London he lived a not outrageous life, and to prepare the way, not seeing how it could harm his prospects in
any case, he one day dropped in at a type-writing office, and,
hiring a machine, typed for himself the following letter
upon the unstamped paper which he had been careful to
bring with him.

" One who believes that he had the privilege of meeting
Lord Inch at Bonville twenty-five years ago, promises himself the pleasure of calling when in Edinburgh."

" It will pave the way," he said to himself, and decided
that in about a week's time he would probably go north.
After that, with great expectation of a profitable visit, he
wrote to 'Melia as we have seen.

Having read the letter three times, and broken the tobacco jar, 'Melia didn't know what to do next. She tried to
read, but her own prospects were so much more uncertain
and interesting than those of the heroine (called a Blood-
stained Bride) that she put the book down again, and set to
thinking of them. What did her father really mean?
What, to use her own expression as she thought of him, was
he " good for "? Had he come to stay? She, of course,
could not help thinking of his last sudden disappearance,
which had never been explained. To say the least of it, he
might have written all these years. She went to the door at
last, and hailing a child that played with a rag doll upon the
opposite pavement, sent her for a sheet of paper and an envelope. Then she sat down and wrote a letter which, if not
brilliant for spelling or composition, was at least sincere.
It did not please her, however, when finished, and she wondered why. She thought it seemed stiff and cold, and then,

wondering whether it would please her father or make her seem silly, she stuck in a row of crosses for kisses at the end.

What she said to the Highlander, as she stood at the door waiting for some one to pass who would post her letter, really showed her state of mind. " Our Menial Hoccupation," she confided to him, with considerable emphasis, " will suit us very well for the time. I'm not such a Juggins as to quarrel with my bread and butter till I sees cake," which tends to show that 'Melia, in spite of her foolish liking for highly imaginative literature, had a practical side to her character, and knew the value of a bird in the hand.

9

# CHAPTER XVII

WHEN Peters, leisurely strolling along in his customary way, at last reached Moriarty's hospitable door, he found another guest, who greeted him as he went up the steps. It was Madge Murray, in a costume which, from an ignorance of the lady-tailor's phraseology, I can only describe as striking. If the word "hitting" be permitted, I will use it instead, since a singular thing needs a singular word to define it. The colors were dark blue and a very deep, rich red, which showed itself in what I suppose would be called a waistcoat, in the facings of her jacket, in the underskirt, in the hat, and even in the stockings, where the short skirt let her ankles be seen. Red showed against her black hair : the whole costume emphasized a dark, haughty, self-conscious face, that itself seemed to challenge inspection.

Peters inspected, therefore, as he came, but showed no sign of conclusion upon what he saw, and bowed when Miss Murray condescended to notice him.

"I have forgiven you !" she announced, holding out a hand, and Peters thanked her, after a moment's pause, with just the least appearance of having been on the point of asking what for.

"I'm sure you would have done it if necessary," she told him, and Peters said "Yes ?" and asked if she had come to lunch.

"To meet you," she told him, as the door opened, "so you must be more polite," and they went in without any promise or protestation from him upon that point.

Lucius, who had come home in time to hear of Nell's interview with 'Melia, was in great form. Madge was by no means a favorite of his, but he never denied her good looks, and to-day tried to atone for occasional inward doubts of her, by open admiration and complimentary adjectives. She was a butterfly, a poppy, a volcano, and a comet by turns, according to him, and Nell at the foot of the table, and Peters at the side, had little to do but listen. Peters, as usual, took all this with immovable gravity, but Nell laughed heartily, partly at her father's extravagance, partly perhaps because Madge seemed almost inclined to take him seriously.

"Miss Murray wants to see the Parliament House too, father," she told him. "Are comets admitted?"

"Faith then they are," declared Lucius, "an' tails are provided free of charge. You'll have all the idle boys at your heels, Miss Madge, an' that's no small number!"

"But a volcano, dad!"

"Ay, I'd see a volcano, or an earthquake there, with all the pleasure in life," Lucius asserted, "specially if 'twould undertake to swallow up the lot. Keep clear of the Parliament House, Peters, as you'd keep clear of h——," he paused, stammered, and gasped for a word to fill the suggestive gap, until his eye fell on his plate, "hot potatoes—which are very good, too."

"It is hell to get into, I have heard," suggested Peters, and Lucius told him heartily that those were his sentiments.

"An' hell to get out of, too," he said, "an' all the divils up there with their own fish to fry, an' nothing else expresses it, savin' your presence, girls!"

"Father, father," said Nell, reproachfully, "what about friends like Mr. Dee?"

"Oh, here a one an' there a one is saved, may be, in spite of himself," Moriarty allowed grudgingly, leaning over to fill Peters' wine-glass, "an' the judges are most wonderful, I will admit. How such good things come out of Nazareth is a most miraculous providence."

" Your judges, then, are all just men ? " asked Peters, curiously.

" Ay, all just men according to their lights," Lucius admitted, " tho' what they may think when they remember the scoundrels they've tried to keep unhung, an' the innocent folk they've made to suffer one way and another, what they may think when they remember these, beats me. But maybe they don't remember."

" Unless they are reminded," suggested Peters, and sat eying his wine as if it showed him something.

" We may come then ? " Nell asked, rising from the table as she spoke.

" Ay, you may come," Lucius told her. " Though," he confided to Peters as they went, " what a couple of bonny lassies, like those, want up there is a conundrum. Woman's curiosity, I suppose. It's strong in Madge Murray or I'm mistaken, and she'll go her own way. Let's get along up there at once, for I've to be at the office again," and, sending for a cab, he packed them into it.

Mr. Dee was standing with his back to the fire that afternoon in the Parliament Hall, exchanging anecdotes of various descriptions, legal and otherwise, with his fellows among the unemployed. To hear, with an immovable face, a narrative that would move others to tears or laughter, is most excellent exercise. So, also, is the telling of a pointless story, with the air of one who knows that he can rely upon your common sense to see the point that is not there.

In these and similar intellectual gymnastics, Mr. Dee was engaged, and was in fact at the critical point of one of his very best ——, " and she," he told them, " came a little closer, so close that I could see an inverted image of Donald Dee, advocate, looking sentimentally out of her splendid eyes. ' And they told me, Mr. Dee,' she murmured, ' that you legal gentleman had no hearts.' "

" ' My dear madam,' I answered her ——"

"By Gad! there's a stunner!" muttered one of the younger men, whose attention had wandered, and Donald Dee's audience, to his disgust, turned and looked across, as one man, at one of the doorways, where dark blue and rich red stood out boldly against the wall.

Dee himself, to avenge his shattered romance, with lifted eye-glass and a fixed stare, was making comments more caustic than polite upon the apparition, when a familiar form darted forward and seized his hand.

"Here y'are then, Dee," said Lucius, "an' here we are. Peters, that ye've promised to show round, an' the girls who'll show themselves round if ye don't. As for me, I'd already like to be sure I knew the way out of this rat-trap!"

"Your father's always ready with his little joke, Miss Nell," said Dee, fluttering forward, and wondering, as he went, whether his wig was straight. "Mr. Peters, my dear sir, I am at your service, yours and the ladies', but I can show nothing so well worth your attention as what you have brought with you!" Bowing, while his hands gently rubbed one upon the other, Mr. Dee pointed the compliment by smiling glances, divided between Nell and Madge.

Behind him, at the fireplace, all this was watched with envy and disgust.

"Who are the girls?" asked one young advocate of a fat friend whose eyes were immovably fixed upon Madge, not at all disconcerting that self-possessed damsel.

"Don't know," returned the other. "Wish I did! Can't that dark one dress, and doesn't she fancy herself, hey?"

"More than I do," said the younger and quieter man. "See how she poses! The woman could draw every eye in the place without blushing. Give me the one in gray that's keeping back a little. I wonder if Dee wants any help? See, he's going to take 'em round."

This was true. Mr. Dee, paying special court to the red and blue that swayed so graciously towards him, was expati-

ating upon the beauties, architectural and otherwise, of the
hall. He even had the impertinence to wave his hand in a
general way towards the little group he had left, *à propos* of
some remark, all that reached their eager ears being something about *pas perdus.*

" Nous ne sommes pas encore perdus," muttered the
younger man who had spoken previously. Then louder,
" Come away, Maclean, I'm going to do some reading."

" My dear fellow," said the fat man, " your young energy
is worthy of a Sabbath school. What, in the name of the
Faculty, are you going to read ? "

" Something, anything ! " returned the other. " Even
Dee's stories, and yours, pall upon one after a time. I'm
going to find something dry."

" That won't be hard to find ! " said the fat man imperturbably, and turned to watch the red and blue on a sort of
slow triumphal progress down the hall, with a simple gray
figure almost unnoticed by its side.

With Dee as elderly, black-robed, bewigged guardian
angel, they wandered here and there unquestioned. They
lingered on the threshold of that sanctuary sacred to wigs
and gowns, and gazed through the glass half-door at these
sacred paraphernalia and their wearers, while Dee pointed
out the peculiarities which enabled law agents to decide at a
glance, and from side, back, half or quarter view, whether
any great man whom they wanted was to be found there.
They looked respectfully on the tons of books collected for
the information, solace, and delectation of the Faculty in
its library, or at anyrate all seemed to do so except Madge,
who devoted herself to the task of extracting from Dee an
offer to get out novels for her. This accomplished, she
yawned, and suggested that probably some of the Courts
would be more exciting.

Dee smiled politely, and said they must certainly take a
look in somewhere.

"But whether we stay or not, my dear Moriarty," he declared in an aside, "must depend entirely upon what is doing," to which Lucius agreed with a grunt, and something muttered about a pot and a kettle.

Nell and Peters went side by side, neither inclined to be very talkative. She looked more at those who were likely to be clients than at the legal part of the crowd, trying, as she went, to read their stories in their faces, and, needless to say, failing utterly. For the idea of self-preservation has taught hypocrisy to the more sensitive, while a good many show little because it is little that they feel. She gave up the attempt presently and looked at Peters, curious to see whether he was interested. It was difficult to tell. His face was as expressionless as ever—a mere placid mask, showing, if anything, a sleepy sort of indifferent, easy good temper.

Dee led them here and there through the narrow twisting passages, "as crooked as the law," according to Lucius, and, opening a swing door now and then, gave them glimpses of the Courts. Here three placid elderly gentlemen dozed side by side, nodding to the monotonous voice of a droning and dreary gentleman in wig and gown.

In another court four other judges appeared to be engaged in a trial of wit, while the counsel, on his legs before them, tried, vainly, to edge in some citations of legal authorities. They were very fierce or very funny, turn by turn, and caused vast amusement to all except the anxious and unhappy clients.

"It's Truthful James and the Innocent Abroad at it again," said Dee. "They've a pretty wit. You should hear the Innocent presiding in breach of promise cases!" This was to Peters, who, when they began visiting the Court rooms, had left Nell, and seemed to take more interest in Dee's explanations.

"Who are the judges?" he asked, but on being told,

turned away again, while the whole party was hurried out by the ever vigilant Dee, who had scented unsavory disclosures from the witness then under examination.

He led them farther, and then, suddenly, a bright idea seemed to strike him, for, with a finger on his lips to suggest silence, he turned aside, and, pushing another door open, went tiptoe up a few steps. Here he stopped before another door of green baize, with small glass panes, like bull's-eyes, let into it. At this door he turned, and, after an extravagant pantomime, meant to insure quiet, but rather provocative of laughter, he beckoned the nearest of the party to look. The nearest was Peters, who stepped forward noiselessly, and peered through one of the bull's-eyes.

He was looking into another Court from behind the Judges' dais, the spectators facing him. Row after row of faces, showing various degrees of interest and intelligence, were before him, gradually, in the nearest rows, becoming lost in the well of the Court. To his right was the jury box, in which were fifteen men whose faces just now showed various degrees of amusement or satisfaction, because a voice inaudible to him, whose owner was not visible, assured them, while Peters looked, that never before had the speaker addressed a jury so obviously intelligent.

Nearest to Mr. Peters upon the bench, and with its back to the door, sat a solitary figure, immovable and shadowy. No light fell upon it from behind, and from above the light was excluded by a heavy oaken canopy.

" A criminal trial," whispered Dee in Peters' ear. " Just drawing to a close. If you have finished looking, Mr. Peters, you might make way for the ladies."

But Peters had not finished. He was watching the heavy-robed figure near him that just now had turned a little side-ways, showing a glimpse of a long, clean-shaven, melancholy face. The figure leant a little forward and, it was evident, addressed the fifteen men slowly and carefully, though all this was dumb show to Mr. Peters at the bull's-eye.

He caught Dee by the arm and drew him closer, without turning his head.

" Who is this man ? " he asked softly.

" The Judge ?  That is Lord Inch.  As keen a man as we have on the bench, Mr. Peters.  We call him the Just Judge.  As keen as an east wind, and as impartial.  No bamboozling him, my dear sir, as we all know.  I can tell you some good things I've heard him say !  But the ladies are waiting, Mr. Peters.  Miss Murray is impatient.  Come away ! "

Still Mr. Peters did not hurry.  Lord Inch, emphasizing some point he thought important, had turned still farther in his seat, and, leaning a little more towards the jury, was obviously laying down the law with great care and delibera-tion.  With the movement the keen, sallow face leapt from the shadow, and stood out the very embodiment of clear-sighted justice, and Peters, through the bull's-eye, watched it as though fascinated, while Dee plucked uselessly and fretfully at his sleeve.  The point fully emphasized, Lord Inch sank back again into the shadow, and resumed a more conversational manner.  Then, and not till then, Peters obeyed the tuggings of the peevish Dee, and, stepping back in silence, allowed the others to take their turn.

That was the last of the sights.  Lucius was impatient to reach his office, and seemed to breathe more freely when once quit of the buildings, and outside the atmosphere of the Law.  Madge was longing for a cup of tea, and in her customary way, said so, openly, with special directness to Mr. Peters.  He, however, had suddenly become dull, and suggested that she would, in that case, be glad to get home.  It was the valiant and happy Dee who sprang, charmed, to the rescue, and begged that he might be allowed, as a reward altogether out of proportion to his services, to conduct them

to Princes Street, which he presently did, to the plainly expressed disgust of the fat advocate by the fire, who watched
the party leave, and cursed Dee for a dog in the manger and
an elderly reprobate.

As for Peters, gradually dropping behind, and getting
mixed in the crowd as he stared here and there, he presently
was separated from his party altogether, and made no great
effort to find them again. On the contrary, he wandered
back to the criminal trial at which they had last spied, entering this time by a door at the far end from the bench.
Here he stayed through the summing up, the verdict, and
the sentence, which separated a man from the outer world
for seven years. Apparently the prisoner fully deserved
what he got, and the Judge was impressive upon the patient
relentlessness with which justice had tracked him down and
secured punishment at last. " Let it be a warning to all ! "
he said, and then rising, while all others rose too, he went
away with a tired face to his robing-room, and thence to his
carriage which waited outside. Among the many loungers
whom he passed, as he stepped into the carriage, was Mr.
Peters, who, anxious apparently to see so great a man un-
robed and moving as an ordinary citizen, stood near and
watched until the Judge drove away. If Mr. Peters had
feared that, with the robe, the man's dignity would be laid
aside, he could now see that his fears were groundless. The
man, off the bench, was still unmistakably a noticeable and
memorable figure, and made a vivid impression upon Mr.
Peters' memory.

# CHAPTER XVIII

## A BICYCLE LESSON

A GREAT deal of 'Melia's spare time during the next few days was taken up in the preparation of a bicycle skirt. While the shape and cutting were under consideration, of course the skirt took up all her thoughts, but when the mere stitching began, she thought a great deal about her father.

Nelly found her at work the next time she came in. To speak accurately, she found her brooding over it, for 'Melia, as she humbly acknowledged to herself, was "fair bested" by the shaping.

" But 'taint business," she remembered, and laid the thing aside to consult further with Nell upon the means of increasing trade.

Nell came in to let her know, firstly that she might expect painters the next morning, and secondly that a plant or two were on their way to the shop.

The plants came whilst Nell was there, and some time was spent by the two girls in shifting them round from place to place, in order to judge where they would look best.

After these things were satisfactorily arranged, 'Melia invited Nell to take a seat behind the curtain, and allowed herself to think of the skirt once more.

" D'you bike, miss ? " she asked anxiously, and was discomfited when Nell said that Lucius didn't encourage it.

" P'raps Mr. Moriarty 'll object to me doin' it ? " she suggested.

" He won't dream of doing any such thing," Nell told her decidedly. " He told me already that you didn't get exercise enough. I've got a pony instead."

" If you don't bike, you won't know anything about cutting the skirt ? "

" Why ? " asked Nell. " Was that one for cycling that you were working at when I came in ? "

" Well, in a way, yes ! " 'Melia admitted, " not that I was fairly at it. I'm stuck, and that's the truth," and with that she leant over, and, dragging the embryo skirt from where she had thrown it, explained her difficulty.

The touch of nature which makes the whole woman-world kin, is the love of dress-criticism. It is the great common interest, and Eve's chief misery after the fall was probably based upon the fact that her fig-leaves went uncriticized. Nell and 'Melia grew still more friendly over a puzzling front-breadth, and Nell, once involved, felt the responsibility, and took it up in her own practical and masterful fashion.

" Leave that for the time," she told 'Melia, " and I'll try to let you know all about it to-morrow. If we're going to do it, it must be done properly, Miss Rivers. I think there are directions in a ladies' journal I've got at home, and, besides, I believe I can borrow a friend's skirt for a day."

With that she went off, but she came in again the next morning, carrying a ladies' journal and a pattern skirt, borrowed from Madge Murray for the day, and with these two aids they carried out the operation successfully.

The results were many. One of them—very important in 'Melia's eyes—was that she made her appearance near Fettes College on the next Wednesday morning at seven fifteen (she was there really at seven), knowingly attired. Another result was that Nelly's liking for the girl increased with further acquaintance, partly, no doubt, because one of the surest ways to create a liking for anyone, is to put that person under a small obligation. A third effect was that 'Melia, finding Nelly deft with her fingers and quick-brained, and " quite the lady." began to imitate her ways in

dress and behavior—always with modifications to suit herself—and she was a quick learner. After all, a girl who had
lived alone, first in London and then in Edinburgh, and still
kept, and deservedly kept, her self-respect, had already shown
a restraint and modesty that in better circumstances would
have stamped her at once as a lady. There are very few
of us who prove ourselves superior to our surroundings, but
'Melia, quick to recognize a better standard than her own,
if only in dress and manner, promised to be one of these ex-
ceptions. None of these little changes, barely begun, prevented her, of course, from devoting herself to the " bike "
light-heartedly. 'Melia turned up at Fettes that gray
Wednesday morning early, as I have said, and openly and
excitedly rejoicing.

" Thought you'd chucked me ! " she shouted, as soon as
Peters hove in sight on a lady's machine. " I'd have given
it to you proper, Cap'n Peters, if you'd brought me out 'ere
for nothing. I missed my second cup o' tea this mornin' for
fear of bein' late. Let's git on at once. I b'lieve *you're* late."

But Peters, dismounting, looked at his watch and declared he was punctual.

" Let's git on then. Ow ! ! "

'Melia had thrown herself recklessly into the saddle, and
was in the dust, mixed up with the machine, before Peters
knew what she was doing.

" You are a silly little fool ! " he remarked, in a casual
way, raising the bicycle and looking it over carefully, while
'Melia struggled unhelped to her feet. " What if you had
broken this thing ? "

" Silly fool yourself," said 'Melia, defiantly. " What if I
had broken my leg ? I thought you could hold me up, of
course ! "

Her leg was smarting pretty badly, and the tears stood in
her eyes, which rather amused Mr. Peters and put him in a
better temper.

"You have your reward!" he remarked, politely. "Now, try again."

'Melia felt for a moment inclined to give up cycling altogether, and stood frowning indignantly and alternately at him and the innocent machine. But the one was as indifferent as the other to her frowns, and presently she became amused and began to laugh.

"Thought 'twas my park 'ack!" she explained. "Let's go slow this time," and she mounted gingerly under Peters' direction.

That gentleman's heart, about which he had expressed himself so much concerned, was fairly well tested before the lesson was over. 'Melia was no feather-weight, and after her first tumble was forgotten, which happened quickly as she grew yet more excited, she flung herself about desperately, and with an *abandon* which showed a most complete and complimentary belief in Mr. Peters' strength and endurance. She rode at impossible angles, screaming, but going ahead nevertheless, until Peters insisted upon a rest, and, mopping his forehead, propped the machine against the railing and sat down.

"My!" said 'Melia, surveying him with interest, "you're fair done up! 'Ow's your 'art? Don't let me kill you!"

"Exercise is its best medicine," Peters assured her, polite once more, and panting.

"Glad to hear it," said 'Melia, "for that's wot you're getting. Say when you're ready for more of the same sort!"

"Five minutes!" entreated Peters, and 'Melia waited, though grudgingly, remarking that her time was short.

"Now, then, just a little turn!" she told him, not three minutes later, and Peters resisted no more.

"P'r'aps I'll be able to get help for you in a few days," she told him as they started.

"Ah! Who?" asked Peters, thinking that the fair-

haired boy from Drumsheugh Gardens, whose acquaintance
he intended to make, might have volunteered.

"Oh, there's someone besides you who'll be here in a day
or two, ready to give me a hand," said 'Melia, pedalling
away vigorously. "I'm expectin' my pa every day."

There was a moment's silence, and then 'Melia shrieked
with pain.

"Ow!" she yelled. "What are you *doin'*, Cap'n Peters?
Oh, stop, do! My fingers!" for Peters' hand, lying over
hers upon the left handle, had suddenly closed like a vice,
and the pain to 'Melia was unendurable.

When he understood what was the matter, Peters helped
her off, and apologized most humbly.

"It's fair crushed!" 'Melia told him, pitifully. "There's
no feelin' in it. Were you taken bad?"

"My heart," he told her. "A sudden pain, and besides I
thought you were falling off."

"Never was nowhere near falling off," 'Melia declared.
"And another time I'd *rather* fall off, if it's all the same to
you."

At this Peters expressed his penitence once more, and
'Melia forgave him.

"It's time to stop anyway," she said, "and now I come
to look at you, you are a bit white. Are you fit to ride?"

Oh, yes, Mr. Peters felt all right again, and thought he
would ride in to his breakfast. So he bowed ceremoniously
and went away down the hill. As he went, Mr. Peters, although no authority on Holy Writ, was recalling a sentence
heard somewhere long ago, about casting bread upon the
waters, and was more than satisfied with his morning's exercise, while his appetite struck terror to the heart of Mrs.
Jimps, who presided at the breakfast-table, and watched
his forays upon the dishes anxiously, from behind the coffee-
machine.

But 'Melia had to make straight for the shop, though, by

reason of a small and hurried breakfast and the unusual
exercise, she felt already hungry again. She hurried away,
stretching her legs, and stepping out as well as her high-
heeled, pointed-toed shoes would let her, with a hand now
and then placed delicately upon her right hip, which began
to feel stiff.

" I shall be one mask of brooses to-morrow ! " she told
herself, but hurried on cheerfully and in high spirits nevertheless.

She fancied herself very much, too, in the short blue serge
skirt, and began to wonder, as she walked, whether Fortune
had smiled sufficiently upon her father to guarantee, at anyrate, a pair of cycling shoes for her. This seemed a modest
and not unattainable piece of happiness, and she wondered
whether white shoes could be worn, or whether she ought to
content herself with brown. This she would consult Nell
upon, when a time came for her to choose; meanwhile
things seemed so promising, and the morning, for early
November, so fine, that she went smiling along the little
back street, and nodded in such a friendly way to her rival
in the dirty smoking cap, that the tobacco-dried little man,
watching her as she hurried by, had vague feelings of loneliness, and went back into his hole to day-dreams of partner-
ship and mutual profit, with enlarged premises, extended
business, and some one to pour out his tea for him. Meanwhile 'Melia, pressing on, had reached her place and gone in.
She laid and lit the fire, and put on the kettle, declaring to
the Highlander standing in the middle of the shop-floor
(whom she was accustomed to address disrespectfully as
Sandy, or Old Man), that she really must have some more
breakfast. Then it was time to sweep the shop out, take
down the shutters, and dust the jars and boxes, after which
she wheeled " Sandy " out to his post, giving him a good
dusting that he might look, as she told him, like a " shentle-
man." Then from the tiny press she hauled part of a loaf,

some so-called butter, and a tea-caddy. In a few minutes she began feeding ravenously, while her foot kept up a constant tattoo upon the floor, because she was still in such high spirits. Now and then she stretched out a foot and surveyed an ankle, more easily seen on account of the short skirt. She wished Miss Moriarty would come in and tell her how the skirt looked, and all the time she was drinking and munching away vigorously, wondering, too, when Cap'n Peters would give her another turn, and how long it would take before she could ride alone.

Hunger being at last satisfied, she put away what was left, which, she noticed with some self-reproach, was not much, and then, everything being ready for customers, she sat down again.

Her excitement was dying away, and she began to feel tired. The bruised hip made itself felt a little, and sitting in the tiny room behind the curtain she leant back in as comfortable a position as the old settee would allow, and began to half-think, half-dream, with closed eyes.

What was her father going to be like? What would he do for her? Not much, she expected, for 'Melia only let her fancy run riot when she chose, principally while reading, or when purposely making up stories for herself, as she sometimes did. Then fancy was legitimate, and she met with the best of fortunes, and moved in the highest circles, principally, of late, on a cream-colored bicycle with all the newest improvements. But when it came to the probable and the practicable in her everyday life, and for her everyday self, 'Melia dismounted from her two-wheeled Pegasus, and walked undismayed in the dust of a workaday world, and it was to that world that she believed her father to belong. A little wild she thought he had probably been, and possibly weak and selfish. Her mother had not encouraged questions about him, and had upon her death-bed given poor 'Melia most distinctly to understand that, if she wished

10

a firm footing in the world, she must make it apart from her
father, and keep it by her own efforts, and 'Melia had never
forgotten that. He was most likely coming by chance, and
would go as he had gone once before. A stray present or
two, gloves, even a dress maybe, or a hat, not forgetting
cycling shoes, and perhaps a night or two at the theatre;
these were the things she might, not unreasonably, hope for.
But, having more or less rigidly marked out the boundaries
of common-sense, surely one might go beyond them, openly
masquerading.

" Now, fancy, if ——" was the way in which 'Melia began
these wanderings, and off she went. The handle-bars of her
bicycle became solid silver, with a diamond set at each end.
The pedals were of pure gold, regardless of wear and tear,
for was she not rich enough to get fresh ones whenever she
wanted them ? The saddle was a happy and peculiar com-
bination of air and eider-down. There was a watch set in
brilliants at the back of the handle-bars, while in front
blazed a great diamond, like fifty crown jewels, instead of a
lamp. She wore the blue skirt, beautified with long rows of
great pearls, and there was a diamond buckle on each of her
white-kid red-heeled shoes, and another blazing in the front
of her hat, as the electric lights blazed on the heads of fairies
she had seen in last year's pantomime, while at the back of
the hat, she knew, though she couldn't see it, was the rarest
and reddest of rubies, to act as a red lamp.

And who was this by her side ? Who but Mr. Archie
Inch, booted and spurred, gallantly riding a bicycle that
pranced and reared, while Miss Moriarty and her pa looked
on, clapping their hands, and Cap'n Peters peered over their
shoulders from behind, looking white and ill as he did for
a moment in the morning. Where were they going ? Surely
that was a church, all lit up, in front of them ! As she dismounted at the door Miss Moriarty and her pa were clapping louder than ever. But why did Cap'n Peters,

stretching a long arm from behind them, squeeze her hand so hard ?

'Melia started up with the pain, and found that, in a doze, she had turned on the settee, and was crushing her bruised hand against the wall. But the clapping still went on, and presently realizing that there was someone in the shop, she screamed, " Coming ! " and with a hurried glimpse in the four-inch mirror, to see if her hair was straight, she lifted the curtain and went into the front shop.

# CHAPTER XIX

## A FOND PARENT

IT was a rather peculiar figure that faced 'Melia as she stood behind the counter. A flaming red tie formed as it were the key-note. Above the tie shone the glossiest and curliest-brimmed of " toppers," and between the hat and the tie curled a ferocious, blue-black mustache. Other items were a frock-coat faced with silk, a corded velveteen waist-coat, and a very yellow chain hanging across it. Also a pair of yellow kid gloves, the left one on, the right one held in a dirty hand. These things, mostly of tailordom, do not make a portrait, but they were the details first noticed, and led 'Melia to a hasty conclusion.

" A theatrical gent ! " she decided, and was not perhaps so far wrong as she imagined herself to be one minute later. The owner of the glossy hat raised it, showing an equally glossy head.

" Can you," he began, politely, " tell me whether a Miss Buncombe resides here ? " and then, before 'Melia could answer him——

" My daughter ! " he announced with fervor, and 'Melia found herself embraced across the counter, her nose, which was naturally a trifle tip-tilted, being made aquiline against the corded velveteen waistcoat.

" At last," said Buncombe, with a well-marked tremor in his voice, " I have got what I have so long worked for ! " and 'Melia, who, after all, had never been accustomed to over-much affection, or to the thought of anyone working for her, was moved to such an extent that she couldn't help snifling quietly—a very little—and letting a tear fall upon the red tie, which tear, however, she wiped away hastily, for fear it should take the color out.

Buncombe then held her off at arm's length over the counter, which was still between them.

" My little Em'ly ! " he protested, " I should have known you anywhere ! " which may or may not have been true, but Buncombe had spent almost every evening at the theatre lately, and had seen several stage-fathers greet their daughters.

" I'm glad to see you," 'Melia told him, wiping her eyes and blowing her nose without any attempt either to hide or to exaggerate her feelings. " I'm gladder than I thought I'd be. You didn't seem real somehow till you came in. Come into my room and sit down, Pa, so as no one will see me like this if they drop in," and, clutching Buncombe's hand, she led him behind the curtain. Then, carefully taking the glossy hat and a cane from him, and putting them respectfully in a place of safety, she sat down beside him on the old settee, half laughing, half crying.

Now that his lower half was no longer hidden from 'Melia by the counter, fresh beauties showed themselves to her in the shape of a bluish pair of trousers, white spats, and patent leather boots.

" You *are* a swell ! " she said, admiringly, and ventured, after consideration, to give him a little hug, which Buncombe took undemonstratively, being occupied in looking about him.

" Rather a hole for my daughter ! " he announced presently, and poked his head through the curtain, to have another look at the shop.

" I don't mind," said 'Melia, valiantly. " Beggars mustn't be choosers," and then she stopped with a jerk and a blush, because she had a dim idea that she seemed to be saying something that reflected upon her newly found parent. He, however, perhaps not being so sensitive, took no notice, but, stepping out into the shop, chose a cigar.

" No one to object to my smoking here, I suppose," he said, coming back.

" No," said 'Melia, and added promptly, after looking at the cigar from which Buncombe was biting the end, " that's fourpence ! "

" I'll put the money in the till, myself, in a minute," she went on, hurriedly, seeing that he stared at her. " I'm so afraid of forgetting a thing like that. Let me give it to you, Pa."

" You don't mean to say you'd pay Rivers for a thing like that ? " asked Buncombe, staring at her.

" Rivers ! " 'Melia repeated the name, puzzled, until the joke slowly dawned upon her, and she burst out laughing, while Buncombe stood, with the unlit cigar in his hand, waiting for an explanation.

" You spotted it over the door ? " she asked, presently. " That's my name, that is. It's only been up a week ! "

" Your name ! " asked Buncombe, as astonished as if he had not changed his own periodically. " Are you married then ? "

This tickled 'Melia's fancy immensely, and she laughed louder than ever, so loudly that neither of them heard a step on the other side of the curtain.

" Me married, Pa ! " she gasped, when she could speak. " Not much ! It was just a joke of mine. Miss Rivers, I'm known as hereabouts. But," she went on after a moment's hesitation, " I've thought lately I was a silly fool for my pains, and of course, now you're back, it's a different thing. I'll stop it, though," she added, regretfully ; " it's just new painted up. However, we'll see about that, and anyway I'll tell those as care to know."

She then proceeded to explain her responsible position, but Buncombe, as the state of affairs dawned upon him, looked at the question of the name from a different point of view, and seemed quite to enjoy the joke.

" Ah, Youth, Youth ! " he said, shaking his head smilingly over his cigar, " you've your poor father's love of the romantic, my dear. After all, where's the harm ? As you say, it would be a pity to have the painting done over again. Let the thing be, and say nothing for the time. I daresay it won't be for long, Emily ! "

" Yes," said 'Melia, who in the last week or two had really begun to feel rather ashamed of this fancy, together with one or two other things about herself which were not quite as they seemed. " Yes, but 'ow can we ? I'm your daughter, and if you're goin' to be about, as of course you are, why, 'ow can I be Rivers any more ? Unless you'd be Rivers too ! "

This struck her as more than ridiculous and impossible, and she went off into peals of laughter again, under cover of which the patient customer, outside, moved closer yet, until he was only separated from them by the curtain.

Inside, Buncombe joined in 'Melia's enjoyment of the joke.

" Good, very good ! " he told her. " I'd do more than that to see my little girl laugh as she laughs now. Rivers let it be, by all means."

" Oh, it isn't worth the trouble for you," said 'Melia, stopping her laughter, and beginning to consider. " If I've been a silly, why, I deserve to have people laugh at me, as they will."

But Buncombe's paternal feeling would not allow this.

" No one shall laugh at my girl while her poor old dad is near," he assured her. " Rivers it shall be, I insist upon it. Think how very foolish you would seem. Your employer might even think it dishonesty, when it is only a romantic girl's fancy. Emily, my child, I insist upon it—Rivers."

" Well, Pa, you know best," 'Melia agreed, enjoying the

change of having someone to give her peremptory orders, and decide for her. " But your clothes and things! It's always found out that way in novels. Not that it matters so much here. We've nothing to hide, 'cept the name."

" Everything fresh on me, my dear, from top to toe," said Buncombe, reassuringly. " I had a new outfit in London, and left it all for you to mark. I knew you'd wish to. My trunk is at the station still. I'll fetch it, tear off the label, put on Rivers, and there you are! *Eureka!* as we used to say at Oxford, and who is the worse or the wiser? "

The patient customer was the wiser, by a glimpse of Buncombe's black-mustached face, through a split seam in the curtain, and *Eureka* might have come more appropriately from him. It was as well also that he should know of this changed name before being introduced to Miss Rivers' Pa, since she herself had said, at their first meeting, that he called himself Buncombe.

Apparently the customer was now struck by the impropriety of listening, unseen, to conversation between father and daughter, for, the next time that 'Melia began to laugh, he moved away, and went out into the street while they chattered, as quietly as his own black shadow.

Mr. Peters, for Mr. Peters it was, went slowly some distance down the street. His eyes, as he went, were wide open, and quite as bright as usual, but he cannot have been using them very effectively, since he was only prevented from being run over at the first turning by a cab, through the yells of the cabman. The man's forcible statement, as to his opinion of Peters generally, and Peters' eyes in particular, roused him, but didn't ruffle him in the least. On the contrary, he politely waved his thanks, standing there on the curb, and, presently turning, went back to the shop, having remembered that his errand was unfulfilled.

" A pair of cycling shoes? " he heard a voice from the back room saying, as he passed in. " Of course, Emily,

The best that money can buy, in a few days, as soon as my business is set agoing."

But Mr. Peters, influenced no doubt by the delicacy which made him leave the place before, did not wait to hear further. He rapped loudly upon the floor with his umbrella, and 'Melia at once made an appearance.

" I came, Miss Rivers," he said, " to ask for you. Your fall has troubled me. Tell me, you are well ? "

" W'y, here's Cap'n Peters ! My Pa's come, Cap'n Peters ! "

" What a pleasure ! " said Peters, enthusiastically. " Tell me that you are well, Miss Rivers, and I leave you to him."

" Not a bit ! " 'Melia declared. " Pa, come out and be introduced to Cap'n Peters that I told you about."

So Rivers, as we must call him now, came out, and was formally introduced.

" My Pa, Cap'n Peters ! "

" Delighted ! " said her father, shaking hands affably. " Of what regiment, sir ? "

'Melia began to laugh, but Peters was untroubled.

" I am enlisted among your daughter's admirers, Mr. Rivers," he told him, with a profound bow. " It is the only regiment I have joined."

" Cap'n Peters belongs to the sea," 'Melia explained.

" Ah ! Royal Navy ? " suggested Rivers.

" No, a wanderer," Peters explained, " in the ships of many nations."

" Cap'n Peters has been in the States," suggested 'Melia.

" Ah ! Where, for example ? " asked Rivers, suddenly watchful.

" I have discharged cargo at Boston," said Peters, thinking carefully, " and have loaded at Florida twice, Mr. Rivers."

" A most honorable occupation," Rivers asserted, with a somewhat condescending air, having suddenly remembered Oxford. "The mercantile marine of the world, sir, includes many of its finest men. 'Those that go down to the sea in ships.' And when is your next voyage?"

Peters couldn't tell him.

"I have worked," he admitted, "too hard to have time to spend. But we sailors are a lot of silly, extravagant dogs. When we have a few hundreds we are foolish children. I shall wait a little, and enjoy myself a little, before I go far again. We are a careless lot."

Rivers inwardly quite agreed to this, but outwardly protested.

"A simple, straightforward body of men, taken altogether, sir," he insisted. "I have met with men of your profession in business, and have found them most satisfactory to deal with"—which was absolutely true.

While this was going on, 'Melia, who stood by, had been following her own train of thought. As soon as she told her father that Peters had been in the States, she recollected their first meeting, and their chat about her name. "A silly Juggins" was the mildest that she could call herself, and it puzzled her to know what she ought to do. But Peters showed no sign of remembering about it. Her father was at once "Mr. Rivers," and 'Melia, listening, gave a little sigh of relief. "I'm sick of these muddles," she thought, "I've told 'em both what a fool I was, and if Cap'n Peters chooses to forget, why it's not my business, and makes no difference anyway. We're Riverses now, once for all, me an' him, an' there's an end of it."

She was disturbed in her meditations by Mr. Peters offering to say good-by, and Rivers begging him not to hurry.

"Em'ly and I have had our little chat," Rivers told him, "and I must go off presently to hunt for lodgings. Before you go, Captain Peters, perhaps you could suggest rooms for me. Emily cannot help me in that, I fancy."

Peters thought carefully. "For you and Miss Rivers?"

he suggested, but Rivers put him right upon that point at once.

"Not yet!" he said, hastily. "I may tell you as a friend, if you will allow me to call you one, Captain Peters, that I hope to manage that soon. This—er—occupation is not suitable for any daughter of mine, but for a few days it will be best for her to make no change of any kind."

'Melia's face had lighted up at Peters' suggestion, and now clouded proportionately, but she had no thought of argument.

"Yes, Pa, you know best," she agreed, and Peters considered again.

"There is a most respectable lady, a Mrs. Jimps," he admitted, "who is excellent for a poor man like me, and I am content there. But for a rich man ——!" and he put aside the idea of the House of Residence, for such as Mr. Rivers, with a single shrug.

"Not so rich," Rivers insisted, modestly. "One may have prospects, and a little cash in hand to come and go upon, like yourself, Captain Peters, but one must economize in the meantime. Now, I think Mrs. Jinks might suit me admirably."

"There are no luxuries," protested the ungrateful Peters, who must have forgotten the partridge leg, but Mr. Rivers was persistent.

"I have roughed it in my time," he allowed. "I can do so again if necessary. Is it near by? I must not be far from my daughter's place of business, while she remains in it."

From the tone, and from the glance which he cast upon these modest premises, it was quite obvious that the aristocratic name of Rivers would soon be painted out.

It was near, Peters admitted, almost grudgingly, but it was dull to desperation. He had to come out of it to get amusement.

" Even then," he suggested, " these good Scotch people
are dull. Their Sabbath, observe, leaves a man only eating,
drinking, and sleeping. Whist is the only game I have ever
seen in the house of my good Mrs. Jimps—for counters."

" Ah, you sailors ! You must have excitement," Rivers
said, shaking his head over the sinfulness of the class, with
a fatherly smile. " A quiet place will suit me very well,
Captain Peters. A quiet, respectable place where I can rest
my old bones, and be near my daughter. You and I might
sometimes be company for one another, Captain Peters,"
and Peters had to allow that, as a pleasant possibility.

He made no more demur, but gave Rivers the address,
and indeed offered to go with him to fetch his luggage.
But Rivers, recollecting the label thereon, declined, and
Peters did not press the point. He bowed his adieu to
'Melia, after assuring himself that she was none the worse
for her tumble, and, leaving her father at the first street
corner, went away to prepare Mrs. Jimps for the advent of
another Paying Guest.

He had gone some yards when a loud " Hi ! " made him
turn, to find himself pursued by the breathless Rivers, who
laid a yellow-gloved hand upon his arm, and apologized for
troubling him.

" It has just occurred to me, Captain Peters," said
'Melia's Pa, " that to mention, at your House of Residence,
my daughter's present false and temporary position, is quite
unnecessary. In fact, shall we let her be unmentioned, except between ourselves ? " and this was agreed.

# CHAPTER XX

### TOM DUNBAR: POET AND STRATEGIST

To accuse a hitherto ingenuous youth of unblushing hypocrisy is no small matter, and yet it now seems necessary to do so, lest others should be deceived. Let it therefore be plainly stated that, at about this time, Tom began to play a double game. It would be almost equally true if one put the case another way, and said that, at about this time, he began to do double work. He "swatted," as he put it, most manfully, at his legitimate labors, but toiled in other fields as well, and under false pretences. Having found Moriarty's weak point, he set himself to attack it. He bombarded the unsuspecting man with Couplets, Triolets, Rondels, Rondeaus, Sonnets, and the Lord knows what besides. He began by dropping in on a Friday, which everyone, at least in Edinburgh, knows is supposed to be an off-night for all students. Whether it is or no, depends upon the particular student. The second Friday that he came, quite impromptu as it were, and with not the least intention of staying, unless asked to do so, a dispute arose between Lucius and himself about a certain quotation, which made it absolutely necessary for Tom to return with that quotation the next evening, which, of course, being Saturday, gave Nelly no excuse for scolding him.

As she said, when he offered a sort of apology, it was, after all, no affair of hers. He knew best what time he could spare, she told him, and then she sat dumb, working at a shaving tidy for Lucius, and took no part in the heated literary discussion that followed, though several efforts were made to get her entangled. The result was that her father, much puzzled and troubled by her neglect of their visitor, "a powerful well-read fellow too," as he told her afterwards, tried to atone and cover it by extra courtesy, and finished the dispute by asking him to dine with them next day, which, of course, would be Sunday.

When Tom refused, hastily, with a mutter of something about a little quiet reading, Lucius grew indignant, and called upon Nell, stitching in silence, to help him.

" Begor ! " he demanded, " is this a Christian city, and will you and I encourage a chap to work seven days a week? "

" We're out of date, dear," Nell told him, her eyes still fixed upon her work. " I don't suppose our opinion can make any difference."

" I'm so afraid of boring you," protested Tom.

" Any of our friends are welcome on Sunday," Nell said, still stitching, " if they don't find us too quiet."

Too quiet ! when to sit in the same room with her sent Tom's pulse up some ten beats a minute, while to suddenly meet her in the street seemed to make his heart leap to his mouth. Too quiet ! He tried to make his eyes express all this, while, in ordinary language, he said how pleased he would be to dine with them. The result was that Sunday found him there, at early dinner, according to the custom of the house, and Sunday afternoon, between dinner and tea, proved, for Nell at anyrate, anything but a quiet time. For after dinner she had to entertain their guest alone.

" It's me habit," Lucius admitted, after dessert. " to lie quiet, an' think of the sermon for awhile. I find that fixes it in me memory, an' I get good out of it that otherwise possibly I wouldn't. Maybe, after I've thought it over, an' the bearings of it, I go to sleep. But you'll not mind that, Tom ? We'll go up to the drawing-room, and Nell will amuse ye there, while I think on the sofa." So up they went.

So rapidly was Lucius, through long practice, able to review a sermon, and get the bearings of it, that five minutes after he had begun his meditation he melodiously proclaimed the fact by a hearty snore, which, coming suddenly upon the stillness of the room, made Tom start, and set Nell laughing heartily, though quietly enough.

"I didn't know you were so easily frightened," she told him softly.

"I don't think my nerves are as good as they were," Tom admitted, with somewhat the air of one who expected sympathy.

"Rubbish!" retorted Nell icily. "What's wrong with them?" but suddenly dreading that the imminent explanation would make matters worse, she explained for herself. "I'm afraid you smoke too much," she told him.

"Perhaps I do," agreed Tom meekly. "I generally smoke some of the Dream tobacco while I'm trying to make rhymes for Mr. Moriarty—to get the right spirit, you know."

"A lot that will help you for the Final!" Nell told him disdainfully. "Why do you do it? Then at the last you'll either break down or be spun (i.e. fail), and you'll blame us, and we shall blame ourselves, and neither will be any use."

"You might guess why I do it," Tom told her, thinking he saw his chance at last, and raising his voice as his hopes rose. "You know very well that I'd do anything ——"

"Sh-sh-sh." Nell interrupted hurriedly. "For goodness sake, don't talk so loudly. I know you'd do anything for him, but if you say it so loudly you'll wake him up, and it does make him so cross if he's wakened before the tea comes up. Would you mind putting some coal on, softly, because I don't want him to find the fire out, and if I ring up Jean, she's sure to rush in and make a noise before I can stop her? Oh, thank you so much."

Tom rose, I will not say willingly, to do as she wished, while Nell sat racking her brains for topics of conversation that would be safe. They seemed few, and not easily introduced. When Tom came back, after having nearly awakened Lucius by letting a large lump of coal smash on the fender, she was still groping for a really safe theme, and had to take what she could find, anxious above all things, suddenly and for feminine reasons not to be easily explained, that he should have no chance of steering the conversation.

"Have you any more of those verses with you?"

Yes, curiously enough, Tom had, and was decoyed into producing them, while Nell, settling herself into an attitude of calm attention, gazed fixedly at the fire.

"You're sure you want to hear them?" asked Tom doubtfully. "They're awful rubbish, you know. I'm afraid they'll bore you."

"Oh, not at all," Nell told him hastily, "I'd much rather hear them than anything else," and then, reflecting that her speech might be misunderstood, she fell into a rosy confusion, masked to some extent by the blaze from the fire, and hastily bade him be quick and read them before her father woke, "since he has heard them all before," she added.

We must bear with Tom while he reads one or two, because they are so symptomatic of his condition. At least we are better off than poor Nell, who had to face a big fire if she wished to avoid being noticed, as she alternately smiled and frowned, but persistently blushed through it all.

> Say, gentles, say, what good thing lack ye,
> Since having me, ye have good 'baccy?
> I feed the hungry, and with hope
> I cheer fond lovers when they mope.

"Dear me!" Nell chimed in, directly he finished. "That's very nice, but is it true? As a doctor, now, would you recommend tobacco for food?"

" It's better than nothing," Tom told her, a trifle gloomily, not being sure whether or no she was laughing at him.

" Then, cheering fond lovers with hope !" Nell went on remorselessly, because she couldn't stop to think. " Of course, if that's enough for them it's all right. But I shouldn't think it very satisfying in the end !  Now——"

" He's a lucky fellow who gets so much," interrupted Tom, leaning forward and trying to get a glimpse of the face turned towards the fire. " Oh, Miss Moriarty; Nell, if only——"

" Oh ! sh-sh-sh !" Nell told him ; " you *mustn't* speak so loudly. If you wake father before tea comes up, he finds it quite hard to be polite. Now he's stirring, and, if we suddenly stop talking, the stillness will wake him just as badly as a noise would, and he'll want to know what's the matter. *Do* go on, please !  The next piece, right straight on; they're so pretty !"

Tom choked down some words expressive of his state of mind, and, glaring furiously at the innocent scape-goat lying on the sofa, who turned uneasily in his dreams, read on in an aggressive way not at all suited to the sentiment of the piece—

> If you would see your fairest fair,
> Her dainty form and feature,
> Smoke ! and upon the clouded air
> Will float the mocking creature.
>
> But if you'd put a bruisèd heart
> Upon the torturing rack-oh
> Touch not the pipe ! but, sighing, part
> With all your sweet tobacco.

" What's a racko ?" asked Nell, swift upon the closing line. " Oh, I see what you mean !  I beg your pardon. How stupid of me !  What a comfort it must be to have a pipe. Why aren't women allowed to smoke, I wonder ?"

11

"They don't need comforting, I expect," Tom growled, feeling rather surly, and very much of a fool. "I think they'd have more pity on a fellow if they had any feelings."

"Dear me!" said Nell innocently, "I didn't know you had such a poor opinion of women! Has Chloris been unkind? There's father stirring again! The least little thing would wake him, and he is so cross when he doesn't wake up naturally, unless his tea is ready. But it will be up in a minute. Perhaps I'd better wake him unless you've anything more to read to me!"

"Mayn't we talk instead?" asked Tom dolefully.

"Not for worlds!" Nell told him hurriedly. "If he wakes he must have his tea at once, and he'll wake in a minute unless one goes on in a sort of reading sing-song voice, don't you know? Do read me just one more at anyrate! Have you any more like that pretty one to Chloris that you read us the other night? Perhaps you've got the same one there. I'd like to hear it again."

"Mr. Moriarty has it still," said Tom disconsolately, at which Nell smiled to the fire, knowing otherwise, "and I haven't another copy with me, I'm sorry to say. If you'd like one I'll bring it another time, but he's got that one in his desk; I saw him put it there."

"That's a pity," said Nell, philosophically enough, "and his desk is locked. But you might read me just one more before the tea comes up. If you've got another for Chloris?"

"Yes," said Tom desperately, "I've got another for Chloris, but whether she'll like it or not is another question—

> Chloris plagued me day by day,
>   Smiled, beguiled, and frowned, and flouted.
> At her little feet I lay,
>   Looked and worshipped, never doubted,
> Only raised my eyes to see
>   Chloris, my divinity.

Till at last, one careless day,
   'Neath those feet, she thought she crushed me,
Laughing.  When, to her dismay,
   Rising, straight, I shook and brushed me,
Knelt no more, no more did pray,
   Gave a yawn and came away."

"Bravo!" cried Lucius, huskily, from where he lay stretched, only half-awake.  "That's right, Tom, my boy! Don't stand any nonsense from 'em.  Nell, my dear, ring up the tea at once, will you?  I've thought it all out, and I guess I can tackle the minister next time he comes, an' make him feel he's got listening, thinking, practical men sitting under him, though they may not be so wise as some. Tom, that last was a fine piece, me boy, and ye read it most feelingly.  She's a sly minx, your Chloris, I reckon!"

# CHAPTER XXI

## PATIENCE!

THAT same Sunday, the second which he spent in Edinburgh, Rivers began to feel dull. The previous Sunday, he had managed to keep himself awake, by spending the greater part of his time with 'Melia. They went to early service at St. Giles', and took a long walk afterwards, and another in the afternoon, when Peters went with them.

But this time it was different. The latter part of that November was marked by thick fogs, one of which fell upon this particular Sunday, blurring all things to a colorless gloom, and rousing in Rivers an almost uncontrollable desire for strong drink. This, the man very well knew, was what he must above all things fight against, until he had settled, one way or the other, whether there were any prospects of making his visit a financial success. After that point was decided he promised himself a royal spree, whichever way things might turn out. Meanwhile he was sober and snappish, but in no great danger for that day, since he had carefully avoided bringing drink into his room, and it was not easy, on a Sunday, to get any outside it.

He met 'Melia in the morning, and lectured the poor girl peevishly upon her pronunciation and other little failings, until she was covered with shamed silence. Others might say what they would, and 'Melia light-heartedly held her own against them, but, to this *père prodigue*, she was all dutiful submission.

"I'll try, Pa," she said, humbly, in answer to his instruction as to the value of aspirates, but Rivers was not satisfied.

" That's another silly thing you say," he pointed out. " Why ' Pa ' ? It's American, not British. You never hear a well-bred British subject say ' Pa ' ! "

" I haven't met many real ladies," 'Melia suggested in self-defense, which only made matters worse.

" Are you going to complain of that, too ? " Rivers demanded, melodramatically, " and at a time when I risk everything for you ? This is a daughter's gratitude ! "

" I'm sure I never meant anything," 'Melia pleaded, scarcely able to pick her way through the mud because of the blinding tears, which she would not lift a handkerchief to wipe away. " I didn't think——"

" You should think ! " interrupted Rivers, sharply. " Thoughtlessness like that is what I cannot, and will not, stand. I shall go back to my rooms now. No, you needn't come with me. I need to consider my plans for your benefit. You might use a day like this as an opportunity for thinking over some of the faults I have spoken of ! "

With that, and a nod, he turned towards the House of Residence, which he had not yet allowed her to come near, and poor 'Melia, plodding her way alone to her little room, rejoiced in the fog, since it let her cry, unchecked through any fear of being observed by passers-by, who came towards her looming like shadows for one instant, and were utterly lost the next.

Rivers, letting himself in with the latch-key provided by Mrs. Jimps, paused at his own door, and then turning the handle, looked in. It was as he had expected. The room was still untidy, the fire unlit, and his limp mustache, damped and dulled by the foggy atmosphere outside, hung more limp than ever as he looked. He stood and considered, listening to the cheerful sound that came from the opposite room belonging to Peters. For Peters was evidently unaffected by the fog, and was singing in a cheery way that gave splendid evidence of an easy conscience, or a good digestion, or of both.

Rivers looked around his own room again, and noted how the fog had penetrated even there. He looked across the passage at the opposite door, behind which the cheerful voice boomed more loudly than ever, and at last stepped into the corridor and rapped.

He had to knock twice before he got any answer, so occupied was Peters in his own pursuits, but finally he was heard.

" Enter ! " Peters answered, and Rivers, pushing the door open, found himself at once in what, to him, seemed an earthly paradise. A roaring fire flickered up the chimney, a large oil-lamp was lit upon the table. The blinds were down, the curtains were drawn. Upon the hob steamed a kettle, and at Mr. Peters' elbow stood a full cup of his own particular coffee, while a spirit decanter was close handy. Peters himself lounged in an easy-chair at the fireside, with a low table before him, upon which he had put his coffee and spread a pack of cards. He was in a loose bright dressing-gown, out of which rose his big black head. He smoked a fat cigar, and was the very picture of one content with himself and his surroundings, and at peace with all mankind.

" Aha ! " he remarked, looking up with one hand upon the cards, " the good Rivers ! How is it with the good Rivers ? " He had adopted a free-and-easy style of addressing that gentleman immediately after their first meeting, and not altogether with Rivers' approval. The difference between a sea-captain and an Oxford man did not seem quite plain to Captain Peters, and the other at first tried to make it clear to him by a frosty politeness. But, in the first place, Peters took no notice, and secondly the manner was very difficult to keep up, and might, Rivers thought, interfere with certain little plans, with regard to this simple mariner, which suggested themselves to him. So he now merely smiled apologetically as he stood in the doorway, before explaining his errand.

"I pictured you at church!" Peters told him. "La, la, la, la-a, La, la, la, la," and he rolled out a scrap of a Gregorian chant with fervor and great enjoyment to himself. His big, plump, clean-shaven face, and close-cut black hair might have belonged to a jolly monk. The music seemed to catch his fancy, and the sonorous Latin of a full verse echoed through the room, before he stopped.

"Bravo! bravo!" cried Rivers, applauding in the doorway. "Quite operatic, sir! Latin, is it not? Your foreign accent puzzles an Oxford man."

"From one of the Psalms," explained Peters, lifting his coffee to his lips as he spoke, and looking at Rivers over the edge of the cup. "Enter, my good Rivers, and tell me what I may do for you. Let not the fog come also."

So Rivers entered, closing the door carefully behind him, and, crossing the room, took up a position on the hearth-rug, with his back to the delightful fire. What had he come for? The odor of coffee, with something in it, rising under the man's nose, suggested to him what he might get, even if he had not come for it.

"The fact is," he told Peters, sniffing gently, "the fog outside is simply vile. It has got down my throat, always a weak point with me."

"A weak point, is it?" demanded Peters, with an upward glance at what was to be seen of the part in question. "Ah, you should take great care of that, my good Rivers, and of your neck. Do not forget your neck, that is most important!"

"Yes," Rivers agreed, "I daresay that is important. One ought to wrap up more perhaps."

"You should certainly have something about your neck,"

Peters declared, rising and looking more closely. "See, it is all bare, exposed all about here!"

He passed both hands about the neck in question as he spoke, and closed them on it lingeringly, but took them away directly Rivers put up a hand in protest.

"I was thinking," said the latter, shifting his head from side to side, and clearing his throat experimentally, "that if I took a little something hot before a cold got hold of me, that might help to throw it off. But then you see it's Sunday, and I've nothing in my room. I don't keep anything there. Foolish, perhaps, but a matter of principle."

"Ah," Peters told him, "you should never go against your principles. But look you, I have no principles, and so I can keep brandy for such weather. Drink, my Rivers, and forget this so damnable climate."

"Now, this is really kind," Rivers declared; "you must let me replace it to-morrow, you really must, under the circumstances."

Peters bestirred himself hospitably. He got out a glass, and, suggesting that Rivers might think whiskey better for his weak point, produced some, together with sugar and a lemon. Then Rivers mixed himself a glass—a stiff one—and sat down in the opposite easy-chair to drink it, and to watch, with some curiosity, Captain Peters' little game at cards, which began again directly that hospitable mariner had supplied his wants.

The cards were, many of them. spread across the table, face up. Some he held, and dealt slowly, sometimes putting them among the exposed ones, sometimes adding them to a little pile at his side. As he played he talked, inquiring politely after 'Melia's health and other interesting matters. But Rivers' attention always wandered to the cards, and at last he expressed his curiosity.

"I've played a game or two in my time, when I was young and foolish," he explained, "and among friends.

But I'll be hanged, Captain Peters, if I know what that
is!"

This open expression of ignorance, for some reason or another, tickled Peters' imagination, not to all appearance
easily stirred, and shook him to fits of laughter. He first
showed his entertainment by deep chuckles, his black eyes
fixed intently upon his interested visitor. Gradually his
amusement grew until it was beyond his control, and he
rolled to and fro in the big easy-chair, as a storm-stricken
ship might roll in the trough of the sea, helpless under a
hurricane of laughter.

"Glad to amuse you!" Rivers told him, glaring with his
haughtiest manner, "but I'm d——d if I see what's the
joke!"

"That is better!" gasped Peters, with his hand against
his side as though fearful of internal damage. "It is your
so strange language. What do you say? You will be
hanged if you understand? What a strange thing! Would
one not rather say you might be hanged if you did *not* understand? Pardon! but your so rich and humorous language, though at times I have talked it much, is always full
of surprises."

"Oh, that's all right," Rivers allowed; "if that's all,
don't let me spoil your joke."

"You shall not!" Peters promised him gravely. "But
this game, that you say you will be hanged if you know, I
must teach it to you. It is Patience."

"I've heard of it," Rivers allowed, "but it's a stupid sort
of game, I suppose. You don't mean to tell me you spend
your time playing it all by yourself?"

"All by myself," echoed Captain Peters, dealing a card
as he spoke.

"Most confounded slow!" Rivers suggested. "Don't
you find it so?"

"Most confounded!" echoed Peters, and dealt another
card.

"What's the good of it all?" asked Rivers, bending over to see how the cards went.

"Ah! what's the good?" repeated Peters, as if these questions had set him questioning himself.

"You can't put money on it?" suggested the other.

"Not to win," allowed Captain Peters.

"Long to learn?" queried the other, satisfied with his inspection and turning back to the fire again.

"Years," Captain Peters told him, and dealt out his last card.

"Good heavens! Well, have you won?"

"No," said Captain Peters gravely, "I have lost."

"Then what the devil do you do?"

"Shuffle the cards and play again," said the Captain, imperturbably. "But not now, my good Rivers. There is the gong, and in five minutes it will be dinner. I will teach you this game some other day."

"I don't remember much of these things," Rivers told him, picking up the pack and shuffling awkwardly, "but I daresay I could remember a trick or two to show you some time!"

"I shall be most happy," said Captain Peters, who—perhaps at the thought of a Sunday dinner—had suddenly grown much graver. "I am always pleased to learn," and Rivers emptied his glass, and they went to the dining-room together.

# CHAPTER XXII

## MR. RIVERS ATTEMPTS SOME TRICKS

THE pleasing presence of Mrs. Jimps, black-silk-gowned and sedately smiling at the head of the table, seemed to have a cheering effect upon the company generally, on that fog-wrapped Sunday. She, too, like Mr. Peters, fought the weather with drawn curtains and a blazing fire, and Rivers felt his spirits rise still further as he looked.

Rivers, being one of the latest arrivals among the Paying Guests, and giving promise of being more permanent than many, was taken under Mrs. Jimps' wing, and sat at her right hand. Mr. Peters, in his recognized position as senior resident, faced her, thus getting the full benefit of the smiles which she frequently cast that way, for Mr. Peters, in spite of, perhaps even partly because of, a quietly masterful manner, still claimed Mrs. Jimps' earnest consideration. He seldom troubled about trifles. When disturbed, he proclaimed the fact at once, openly and loudly, and having carried his point, which, as a rule, he did quickly, the cause of complaint seemed to vanish from his mind altogether, and was heard of no more. Then, too, he was a tower of strength in the house. If an uncongenial male strayed temporarily into the place, as must sometimes happen in the best-regulated Houses of Residence, Mr. Peters could be reckoned upon to keep that male within bounds, or to make him feel the necessity for a move. True, Mr. Peters himself occasionally made use of a word or two of which Mrs. Jimps could not approve. But, as she acknowledged to herself when meditating over his virtues in her own little sanctum, he used them in such a gentlemanly foreign way that they really wouldn't frighten a child. In her softer moments, when the House of Residence was quiet for the night, when all necessary notes had been made of things to be done on the following day, when the boots of the Paying Guests, reposing outside the bedroom doors, mutely told her that their owners were safely settled until the morning, when in fact the worker could give place to the woman, and Head could yield to Heart, Mrs. Jimps had found herself acknowledging coyly that Mr. Peters as a permanent resident, paying or no, would not be unwelcome. His very boots, well-made, strong, and not over small, were masterful, every nail of them, and Mrs. Jimps, remembering " our Annie's " last vagary, or some would-be too free-and-easy Paying Guest, or the necessarily weak points of even the bravest of women, would own, with shyness and a sigh as she made her way to her own bed, that the House of Residence needed a master.

All this, however, was locked beneath the ample black silk, safe even from the gimlet eyes of " our Annie," and Mr. Peters knew nought of it, but Rivers, with a veteran's keen appreciation of a good base for operations, felt that his lines lay in pleasant places, and endeavored to show his feelings by what he thought his most winning and high-toned manner. It even occurred to him, sitting there at that Sunday dinner-table, that a man of his domestic tastes might, if greater schemes failed, do wisely to fall a little (it certainly, he believed, would be a fall), and drop softly into the lap of Mrs. Jimps. A quiet corner for himself in the House of Residence, where those whom he so far honored could share his quiet game at whist—or something more exciting—with modest refreshers, was not to be disdained. So Rivers was complimentary, impressively complimentary to Mrs. Jimps. What place 'Melia took in this vision, if she entered it at all, is not known.

" One would be glad," he said, under cover of a general conversation, " to relieve one's hostess of this trouble," and he nodded at the sirloin upon which Mrs. Jimps was then operating.

To be addressed as one's hostess was certainly pleasant. It showed that some people, at least, recognized a difference in such matters. It also showed manners, which maketh man, and Mrs. Jimps, who had not yet classified Rivers, marked him one up, and smiled appreciatively.

"So good of you!" she told him. "Many people don't seem to notice, Mr. Rivers. Would you mind tilting the dish a little? then I can give you some gravy. It's always best from the dish, don't you think?"

"Little home comforts and female society are so pleasant to a rough wanderer," said Rivers, sorry nevertheless that Mrs. Jimps had asked him to tilt the dish, since it exposed to view his hand still ingrained with oil and coal-dust.

"Dear me, I'm always so glad if we can make our visitors comfortable," said Mrs. Jimps, beckoning Annie to bring the vegetables that way. "Didn't I hear you say the other night that you were a widower, Mr. Rivers?"

"A lonely man, ma'am," Rivers told her; "widowed and homeless. What is the use of a home with no one to share it?"

"Very true," said Mrs. Jimps sympathetically, and the sentiment chimed in so far with occasional thoughts of her own, that she couldn't help casting a little glance down the table at Peters, who was making an excellent meal, as was his habit.

"And no family, I think, Mr. Rivers?" she asked, withdrawing her eyes quickly, and somewhat disconcerting that gentleman by her question. If he had been quite sure that there would be no danger in repudiating 'Melia, I fear that he would have added a childless condition to his other sorrows, but although it was agreed between Peters and himself that 'Melia's existence was not to be mentioned, yet some day she might turn up.

"One daughter," he acknowledged, "of whom, however, I do not see very much. The young birds quit the parental nest, Mrs. Jimps, when they think their wings strong enough to let them see the world, and make nests of their own"—which little admission, accompanied by a sorrowful smile and a shrug, somehow gave Mrs. Jimps the impression of a fond father heartlessly deserted by his only child, and bearing his loss in sorrowful but dignified silence.

"Young people go their own way nowadays," she admitted. "The world is not what it was when I was young, Mr. Rivers," to which Rivers, after a respectful glance, insisted that it could scarcely have had time to change since that date.

Mrs. Jimps colored just the least little bit, protesting, but wondering at the same time whether Mr. Peters had the same impression, and, feeling grateful to Rivers for suggesting it, helped him liberally to more gravy from the dish, when his plate came to her again. Her thoughts turned more or less to these matters all through the meal, though she superintended as keenly as ever, and let Annie see by a glance that she had found a plate not so bright as it should be, and did not fail to notice how the last new-comer allowed something to drop on the clean, glossy, white tablecloth. Before dinner was over she decided that she really must know how Mr. Peters' business was progressing, and she made up her mind to ask him to-morrow, while consulting him about something else. The politeness with which she listened to Rivers' tales of his old college days, after making up her mind upon this point, gave that sanguine gentleman an utterly false idea of the interest she took in him, and when he entered Peters' comfortable quarters again, which he did directly after dinner, he even decided that Peters' room would suit him best when the time should come for him to make a choice.

Peters this time had invited a visit. Not pressingly, but

suggesting that, if the other fire had not got up properly, his room might be the more comfortable. Rivers, whose mustache drooped less limply, and whose whole appearance was considerably brighter than when he had left 'Melia, went into his own room as a matter of form for a few minutes, and found a very cheerful blaze there. But there was no whiskey, and there were no cards, so, banking the fire up carefully with cinders, he knocked at Peters' door, and announced his own room as unendurable.

" Then," said Peters hospitably, " come, and I will teach you Patience ! " and they set to work, with a little more spirits for his visitor, about whose sensitive throat the fog was still hanging.

Rivers watched politely through a game, bracing himself to the task with frequent sips, but was not enthusiastic.

" You see," he explained, " I like a social game—or did when I played cards. Now, a game like Patience doesn't interest me—at least, not much. There's nothing in it."

" That is because you do not understand," Peters told him, chuckling softly and good-naturedly. " But teach me something, my good Rivers," and so Rivers tried to teach him something.

He attempted one or two card tricks, but, as he sorrowfully admitted, if he ever had known the way to manage the cards, he seemed to have forgotten. Peters could always tell, laughing hugely, and apparently much interested, what had become of the knave of spades or whatever card Rivers tried to hide. When, too, there was a dispute as to what card would turn up first in the pack, things never came as Rivers said they would, which was most annoying, and amused his host tremendously.

At last Peters suggested poker for a change, but his visitor needed a good deal of persuasion.

" I have played," he admitted, " but long ago. Really,

now, I don't know if I could tell poker from euchre—or are they the same?"

"We will attempt!" said Peters, shuffling the pack; "it shall not be expensive."

"Make it counters!" suggested his visitor, at which Peters roared again, and wouldn't hear of such a thing.

So Rivers, protesting that he didn't want another man's money, especially a friend's, if Peters would allow him to say so, was beguiled into a game for a small stake. At first Rivers won, and then he played a little longer to let his host win his money back, and Rivers won more, which made Peters insist upon continuing the game. So they played on until the tea-bell rang, and Rivers got up some few shillings to the good.

"Really," he protested most politely, "to come to a friend's room, and drink his whiskey, and take his money, really it's——"

"A what-you-call swindle, is it not?" asked Peters, unmoved by his losses and slapping his guest upon the shoulder as he spoke. "Tea! my good Rivers, and revenge another time."

"Oh, after tea if you really wish it," Rivers told him, "though the cards seem against you to-night, don't they?"

"Yes," Peters agreed that the cards seemed against him that night. "Another time," he decided, "I will have my revenge."

"You play a very good game," Rivers allowed, "though I didn't always understand your reasons for playing the card you did."

"I am a devil at cards," Peters asserted, with the air of a man who has unlimited confidence in himself, "but one cannot always explain what makes one play this card or that one," and they went off for their tea, dispensed on Sunday evenings by Mrs. Jimps in the drawing-room, where one is not so likely to make a hearty meal as if one sat down

at the dining-room table.   Much food being quite unnecessary at five on a Sunday afternoon, when dinner was at one,
it was on the whole very thoughtful of Mrs. Jimps to keep
temptation from those who, having nothing else to do,
might otherwise have possibly eaten more than was good for
them.

After tea it seemed unlikely that the two friends would
meet again that evening, but they were fated to do so.
Rivers grew restless in his own room, having been perhaps
a little excited by play.   After walking up and down from
one end of the room to the other, he at last made up his
mind to go out, and his feet wandered to Drumsheugh Gardens.   He was looking at the windows of No. 45, when a
hand, softly laid upon his shoulder, startled him.   Twisting round with an oath on his lips, he found himself faced
by Mr. Peters, who loomed huge in the fog.

"Ah ! my good Rivers," said that benevolent gentleman,
"this will not do.   What of your throat in this night-air ?
Is your neck well protected, my good Rivers ?   You are
rash, are you not ?" and he was so politely concerned about
his friend's health, that he insisted upon escorting him
home, and talked to an unusual extent, and most entertain-
ingly, all the way.

12

# CHAPTER XXIII

## HALF-CONFIDENCES

WHILE Rivers peered through the fog at the outside of No. 45, its owner, inside, sat restless and melancholy. New books lay at his elbow, but he could not fix his mind on any one of them. A large fire blazed before him in a big tiled grate, but the man was chilled and cheerless, and thought, perforce, of things which he would rather have forgotten.

Strange, foolish, absurd, it was for him to let his memory dwell upon the horror of a single night, blotted out, as it might have been, by the days, the darkness, and the dreams of twenty-five years ; but he was powerless to prevent it. The man was physically weak, with a weakness that, when he had nothing of powerful and gripping interest immediately before him, set his mind veering like a weather-cock before the contrary winds of fancy and suggestion. At the Parliament House he was still the Just Judge, dry, melancholy, unmoved, save against any attempt on the part of counsel to make words fill the place of arguments. At home he was a silent, melancholy figure : silent because he found himself curiously apt to speak harshly and irritably on small provocation ; melancholy because of that, and because of the hidden thoughts made more bitter than ever by the letter which, at this moment, he held smoothed out before him.

Who, that had met him twenty-five years ago, could remember and wish to meet him again ? Whom could he wish to see ?

The unsigned, typewritten sheet was threatening in every line, and yet what could he do but wait until the writer followed the letter ?

" Let him follow it to hell ! " Lord Inch thought, in a sudden gust of passion, crumpling the thing to a ball, and throwing it on the fire. Then he snatched it away again, and crushed out the flame that had begun to lick over the edges, and he had it again smoothed out before him when the door opened and Maitland was shown in.

The latter saw this scorched single sheet of paper directly he set foot in the room, and saw, too, the hurried way in which it was folded and put back into a pocket, but he said nothing of it. He spent the first few minutes in saying what he thought of the weather, and, from that, naturally turned to ask how it suited his patient.

" I don't notice it," Lord Inch told him listlessly ; " there's a fog, isn't there ? "

" Ay, there is," Maitland answered, drawing his chair nearer to the blaze, and bending over it with outstretched hands.

" The Cockneys may say what they will of their fogs," he added, " and I've heard them boast as though a fog was an Englishman's glory, but, man, I'd like to set them in the Meadows to-night, and bid them find a way here. But it's not worrying you ? "

" No," Lord Inch told him, " I saw it was bad this morning about church time, and thought I wouldn't go. I've not looked out since."

" Had dinner all right, I suppose ? "

" Eh, what ? No—that is, yes, I believe. Yes, of course."

Maitland saw, and indeed could not help seeing, the uncertainty with which the man answered, but he went on without seeming to pay any attention.

" I came in to tell you what Mackenzie said to me, after he saw you with me the other night," he told his patient, shifting about a little from the fire, and facing Lord Inch.

" Yes ; what does he think ? " asked the other, still to all appearance concerned chiefly about something else.

"What he thinks and what he says happen to be the same, with Mackenzie," Maitland replied, with a grim little smile, as if it might not be always so with all. But the smile died away as he watched the bent figure in the opposite chair, staring into the fire, and he laid a finger on the judge's arm.

"You've got to take a little holiday," he said, "just to put things right again, and get out of our hands quickly."

"Nonsense, man!" returned the other, frowning peevishly at him; "you can patch me up between you surely. I'll take anything you like to order."

"Ay, I know that well enough," retorted Maitland, not unkindly. "It surprises me, even yet, to see what some of you will take. But it's rest you want above all. Rest for body and mind, and you must have it." He may have laid stress on the word "mind," or the judge himself may have supplied it.

"How do you know that I should have rest by stopping work? How do you know but what I get most rest when I'm working my hardest?"

Lord Inch looked from the fire at last, and stared at Maitland as he said this, and Maitland stared back at him before answering.

"I don't know, Inch," he said at last. "How should I? I'm too old to make believe that I can read men like books, and God forbid that I should be able. 'Twould be no pleasure. Most men have their troubles that drugs can't touch, and the knife can't relieve. Then the medical man goes, and the old friend may take his place."

"You were always a good fellow," the judge told him, staring at the fire again, but the doctor shrugged his shoulders, and, getting up from his chair, strolled across to the bookcase.

"You've a book here that I'm going to borrow," he said. "See, I'm putting my card in its place. What was I saying? I remember. Well, you know, folk come to me with

all sorts of tales. Usually what they have to tell isn't half
so bad as they think. But it eases their minds tremendously, whether the story is worth telling or no. So, if there's
anything unsettling you, that you won't talk of to your
clerk and care to chat about with me, let me hear it some
day. It might help to pull you round quicker, though,
mind you, I don't know that, of course. I wonder if it's as
bad as ever outside."

He went across to one of the two windows as he spoke,
and lifted a lathe of the venetian blind. Looking down into
the night, for they were on the first floor, he became quiet,
and stayed with his eyes fixed upon the space he had made,
while his friend answered from behind him.

" You're a good fellow, Maitland. Yes, I've got my wor-
ries that medicine can't touch—like most other men, as you
say. I'll have a chat with you some time perhaps."

Maitland's attention seemed divided for the moment between Lord Inch and the window. He didn't answer at
once. Then he held the blind apart, while he turned and
spoke.

" I will admit," he allowed, with the air of one who was
making generous admissions, " that a wife may be useful
that way. They do say that all women are chatterboxes by
instinct, but that's unfair. They can keep their own secrets,
or their husbands', which is the same thing. It's only other
people's business that they must blab to all the world. A
wife is useful, maybe, at times." Having made this statement, he returned to his loop-hole of observation.

The man was not so garrulous as he seemed. He had seen
the judge four or five times since that first interview in his
consulting-room, and the impression had grown upon him
that, at the back of the very serious and probably incura-
ble disease, which was evident, his patient had some other
trouble, possibly curable, that made matters very much
worse.

Now that Lord Inch seemed a little more inclined to talk, Maitland's one object was to keep the conversation going, until the man had gained confidence and made up his mind to say more. For a certain amount of indecision was, in his opinion, due to the ill-health. Now, too, he began to get interested in what was going on outside, just below the window.

At his speech on the possible use of a wife, the judge laughed a little and dryly—and then made a rush at the subject.

"The fact is," he said, "I believe I'm being threatened, but I don't know."

"Ah! A disappointed litigant?" asked Maitland, still looking out upon the night.

"No, no, I pay no attention to that sort of thing," said Lord Inch impatiently. "I never did."

"Ah!" returned Maitland, and said no more for the moment, having all his attention directed to something else.

For, as he came along the street, on his way to this house, he had pushed against someone in the thickest fog, midway between two lamps, and both he and the other figure had apologized. Then, for some reason or another, perhaps connected with the damsel at No. 46, Morris, the footman, had not hurried to answer Maitland's pull at the bell, and, while Maitland waited, a figure strolled slowly past, following in his footsteps, and looked up at the door in going by. Maitland had his glasses on, and, standing with his back to the door, had looked down upon a man's face, on which a big black mustache hung limp. Then the door had been opened by the apologetic Morris, and Maitland thought no more of it until he went to the window. There he saw that a figure stood, beneath the nearest light, looking at the house, and, while Lord Inch talked, Maitland watched that figure and wondered what it did there.

It was a man, but he stood too much under the lamp for Maitland to see the face.

" Threatened ? " he repeated, and lost the vague reply that Lord Inch made, for at that moment another figure came within the hazy blur of light.

It was a bigger form than the first, and loomed huge through the fog. It stood behind the other, and, to Maitland's mind, had a watchful, threatening aspect.

If it had sprung upon the first he would not have been surprised. He saw it draw quickly closer, and he saw a hand raised. Then, before he could make up his mind to run the risk of startling Lord Inch by a shout, the hand came down—but only upon the other's shoulder.

Maitland quietly drew a long breath of relief, and, watching, seemed to see that the first man was as much startled as he himself had been. The fellow jumped and turned quickly. In doing so he came directly into the light, which fell upon his upturned face, and Maitland recognized the man whom he had seen from the doorstep.

The two figures stood together a moment, then turned away together, the bigger man, whose face had not been seen, affectionately clutching the other's arm.

Then Maitland, half-conscious that the judge was still talking, forced his attention back from those two shadowy forms, already swallowed up and buried in the thick mist.

Lord Inch was just finishing a sentence.

" —— and I may say, Maitland, that I have this evening had a stronger feeling than ever that there is mischief afoot."

Maitland hummed, and, coming back to the fire, took up his favorite attitude with an elbow on the mantel-piece. Standing there and looking down upon the judge, who still sat peering at the fire, he thought again of those two figures disappearing together. Yes, there might conceivably be mischief afoot.

But what had Inch said while he was watching them ?

" I want to be quite certain that I heard you correctly," he explained. " You think you're being threatened, but you are not sure, and you know it has nothing to do with any Parliament House business ? "

" Quite so ! " Lord Inch allowed that. " As I said, if I'm not mistaken, and indeed if it is anything at all, the thing must have its origin in my transatlantic days. Look at that ! "

He thrust a hand into the breast pocket of his coat, and drew out the paper, which Maitland recognized at once and read carefully, while Lord Inch sat and watched him.

" Well," he said, composedly, folding the thing and handing it back. " Some old friend."

" Man, man ! " said Inch almost fiercely. " Is that the way a friend writes ? No name ! No address ! "

The question was only fair, and Maitland felt embarrassed.

" Who else could it be ? " he asked. " You were there, I've heard you say, not much more than a twelvemonth, and twenty-five years ago. You had no time to make enemies."

" Are friends made quicker ? " almost snarled the other, and Maitland felt himself worsted again.

" How long does it take to make an enemy ? " Inch muttered, and then fell into a gloomy fit of silence, that Maitland found he must break if anything more was to come of their conversation.

" You've told me too much or too little," he decided at last. " This has not been enough to help you, Inch, but it suffices to trouble me. Can you say nothing more ? "

But the other, looking up gloomily, shook his head.

" Remember," Maitland urged, " I have not pressed this upon you. But now I may do you a serious wrong, if you leave me to imagine what I will, as the cause of this trouble."

"It's of the young fellow of twenty-five that you must imagine what you will, then," returned the other harshly, "not of me."

"Ay, Hector, but he was my friend too!" pleaded Maitland. "A good fellow he was, too, though a bit hard on those who didn't live as he did. Come, man! Me or another, it's little I care. But you must let another share your secret and the weight of it!"

Lord Inch, however, would not be persuaded that night, and Maitland could see it in his face.

"Another time, Maitland, another time," he said rising. "Think what you must, meanwhile. Maybe this fellow is, as you say, some old friend that I've forgotten."

"If it isn't, will you tell me?" asked Maitland. "Me or another?"

"You and none other," said Inch. "There's my hand on it." And with that Maitland had to be content.

"If your correspondent means mischief," he said, as he shook hands, "it's a promise that I'm to know as soon as you do."

"It's a promise," Inch repeated. "Twenty-five years ago, Maitland, and I was only twenty-five!"

Then Maitland went away down the street, growling and muttering to himself as he went, and peering right and left in the hope of again coming upon either of those two uncanny figures.

"I sometimes believe I'm a havering old idiot," he told himself as he searched for his latch-key, "but there! If I was one of those sharp chaps, maybe folk wouldn't tell me as much as they do. We're getting to the bottom of it all now, I think. He'll send for me if he's threatened. Ay, ay! it's thirty years ago that he and I got capped together in Arts," and Maitland, too restless to think of bed, smoked, solitary, until far on into the night.

# CHAPTER XXIV

## A SUPERIOR PERSON

On this highway of life, while some hurry along, eager for they scarcely know what, and busy, they hardly know why, others listen, and, looking cynically at their fellows and feeling vastly superior, don't do very much themselves.

By being fully convinced of one's own superiority, one can force some others to believe it. Not many maybe, but still some. Also, the Superior Person cannot be understood by the Inferior. Hence a splendid isolation, and the feeling that one is misunderstood, which is a great comfort.

Notwithstanding this comfort, one seeks the sympathy of other superior minds, and recognizes them by the fact that they at once see one's own superiority. They had better also proclaim it, and the louder the better.

The bother is that some of the less perfectly balanced among us, possibly the less pig-headedly self-satisfied, develop a craving for this recognition, turn aside into by-paths where they think to get it, and go far. Also, where it is not granted in large doses, they are hurt immeasurably, and curious as to the cause of this blindness. This was the case with Madge Murray. She had been spoilt as a child, with the result that now, as a woman, she had a slightly disguised contempt for the people who had spoiled her. With those people we have nothing to do. Madge had her own friends, or, more accurately, her acquaintances, her own pursuits, and went her own ways. After all, there is not much that can be done to thwart a woman of twenty-eight or so, especially if she has a small independent income. So Madge had found out, long ago, that so long as she made a regular appearance at meals, or foretold her non-appearance and came home at reasonable hours of night, there was nothing much said. Her father, above all things, hated " a row," especially as experience told him that victory therein always went the one way. She had taken up Nell Moriarty through the merest whim, and now, finding Nell unprepared to recognize her perfection, was ready soon to let the acquaintanceship die out. Interesting people were uncommon, she decided, at the Moriartys' house. Tom was only a student, and not at all bright, so she told herself after finding that he was openly devoted to Nell. Donald Dee, the advocate, was amusing because he paid such broad compliments, and Madge was getting to like them broad. But then he was far beyond middle age, a confirmed bachelor, and very selfish— this last being a vice which Madge abominated—in others. Then Peters came on the scene, and Madge's interest in the Moriartys grew a little warmer.

The first night that they met, she had thought him rather a dull fool. He said nothing witty; in fact, he did not seem anxious to talk at all. If this had been shyness it might have shown discrimination—for Madge considered she was brilliant that night. But it wasn't shyness, and Madge had no reason, on considering the matter afterwards, for believing that Peters was at all overpowered by her charms.

Then came the meeting at Leith Harbor, whence she went in a rage that served to keep the imperturbable Peters in her mind. His indifference was a silent challenge which should certainly be accepted. Hence her flaming appearance on the Moriartys' doorstep, and her interest in the Parliament House, which she had often visited before. Here again Peters had baffled her, by simple indifference, and she thought with naïve astonishment of the way in which he had let pass, quite unnoticed, her suggestion concerning tea afterwards.

It was on the morning after the Sunday's fog, which had

ended at night with a sharp touch of frost, that Madge
turned these matters over again in her mind as she went
from one shop to another in Princes Street, and she was
thinking of the almost expressionless profile that had irritated her while waiting for a turn at the little bull's-eye of
glass behind the Court that afternoon, when the man himself suddenly passed her, moving more quickly than she, in
the same direction.  He bowed, and was passing on, when
Madge held out a hand.

"We lost you in the Parliament House the other day,"
she told him.  "How was that ?" and Peters shrugged his
shoulders apologetically.

"A stupid foreigner," he said, "in a strange place."

"I think you were tired of us," Madge insisted.  "Very
natural, perhaps—but very rude to show it.  Come now, be
polite for a few minutes to make up for it, as we are going
the same way," and Peters silently marched at her side.

He was an aggravating man, Madge felt.  An un-get-at-
able man.  What was he thinking about ?  Did he think at
all, or was the enormous solemnity of this handsome face
merely the result of unmitigated boorishness and stupidity ?
She chattered on at a pace most unusual to her, for, as a
rule, she liked the part of supercilious critic : but she got
merely the replies that ordinary courtesy demanded, and at
last stopped talking, to see whether silence would have a
better effect.

It had the effect of making Peters halt, and raise his hat.

"I go to a shop this way," he explained, but Madge was
not so easily daunted.

"So do I," she told him, "so we may as well walk together a little farther," and they went together up Fred-
erick Street, and presently turned down the way that we
have so often been before.

Madge, talking a little for the sake of appearances, had
just noticed that, on the opposite side of the street, beside a

bland wooden Highlander, a red-haired girl stood looking this way and that, when the girl suddenly began to nod and smile across in their direction. While Madge stared Peters turned and bowed. "I go this way," he told her, and, straightway crossing the street, was hailed by the red-haired girl as "Cap'n Peters." Madge moving slowly on, with a side glance at the two, saw them go into the shop, a tobacconist's, together, and, if her astonished ears did not play her false, the girl asked Peters who his swell friend was, as they went in.

"A vulgar fellow!" was Madge's verdict, and she passed on, greatly annoyed, but, if anything, more curious about Peters than ever.

Peters, following 'Melia into the shop, chose a cigar and lighted it, payment, as usual, having been scrupulously exacted by 'Melia.

"Your father is not here?" he asked, looking round.

"No," said 'Melia, and did not offer any further information about that gentleman.

"You have not seen him since yesterday morning?"

"No," said 'Melia again, shortly, and, turning, began to rearrange the boxes which stood in the glass case behind her. She stood like this long enough for Peters, who was watching her curiously, to notice that there was a great change in 'Melia's hair. It was certainly redder, and a very pretty red, too. He said as much, solemnly, and 'Melia's cheeks, as she turned to him, matched it.

"I'm gittin' over my last attack of influenzy," she told him, and Peters congratulated her on a recovery from this illness, of which he had not heard before.

Suddenly 'Melia was frightened.

"You're not come to tell me Pa's ill?" she demanded, and was relieved at Peters' unsympathetic laughter.

"The good Rivers!" he ejaculated; "I have not seen him to-day, but he will be well."

"I was lookin' for him when you came." 'Melia explained. "I've got used to his turning in to see me of a morning. Pa's—father, I mean, is very good that way. It struck me, sudden, that you'd come to tell me something."

But Peters declared he had no bad news, and moved to the door that he might see if her father was near.

"I came because of that woman who was with me," he told 'Melia, tapping her friend "Sandy" on the head, as he spoke, to test his solidity.

"For shame, Cap'n Peters," said 'Melia; "she's a perfect picture."

"I do not care for pictures, when they must always talk," Peters told her. "See, here comes the good Rivers."

It was certainly Rivers coming down the street, with a small parcel in one hand, and in the other a cane, which he twirled with a jaunty air. On waking that morning, he had been so pleased to think of the friendly and familiar relations which he was establishing with Peters, that he thought kindly of 'Melia, and resolved to bring a peace-offering— paid for, so it happened, out of his last night's winnings.

He came in now, with a friendly nod to Peters, and giving a kiss to 'Melia, who greeted him carefully as "Father," he put down the parcel, and, with an air of gay mystery, told her to guess what was in it.

"Me!" said 'Melia. "What for, pa?—I mean, father;" but Rivers continuing to nod and smile graciously, she picked it up, and first felt it all over, then smelt it.

"Who's it for?" she asked, suspiciously, at last, looking up at the benignant Rivers.

"A young lady I know," he told her. "Open it."

So 'Melia opened it, and a pair of cycling shoes dropped out, much to her delight.

"For me?" she screamed, clutching at them. "Oh, pa! —father I mean, you're *too* good."

This was said with a fervor which was perfectly sincere.

and which pleased Rivers uncommonly. After all, perhaps, kindness and gratitude are relative terms. A wife who is kicked six nights a week by her lord and master may think him kind, and will almost certainly be grateful, if he leave her unkicked on the seventh. 'Melia, who had been left to her own devices for so long, and who owed nothing to her father's care, was quite unbalanced by this unprecedented behavior, and her extravagant gratitude caused such a glowing sense of self-denial and generosity in her father's breast, that he promised himself to renew it, if Peters continued to be as much of a fool at cards as he had been hitherto.

It was enough to make one wonder whether, after all, consistent kindness gains more gratitude in the end than a tolerable amount of neglect, varied by an occasional surprise. Speculation might go farther, and ask whether the first gives more happiness than the second. But Rivers did not carry his considerations so far, and what Peters thought about, as he puffed his cigar on the red settee where he was resting, no one knew.

" Now, I wonder," said 'Melia, looking out at the frosty street, " when I shall use 'em ! "

She dived behind the curtain, and reappeared with the shoes on. A cheap pair, white, high-heeled, and a trifle tight across the toes. But they were lovely, so 'Melia declared, with a private resolve to get them stretched, and she ached to use them, almost as much as she would certainly ache after she had done so.

Neither of the two men answered her immediately. Her father had no intention to make her any more presents just now, and Peters made no move until 'Melia looked at him appealingly.

" If you like," he told her at last, " you can have the same again, and—my want of exercise is great."

" There ! d'you hear that, pa ?—father, I mean. Cap'n Peters 'll take me out again. Ain't he kind ? "

"H'm ! ha ! yes," Rivers began, ready for 'Melia to have a pleasure that didn't cost him anything, and ready also to keep her on the friendliest terms with Peters, but trying, in a vague, groping way, to decide whether this would seem to be the correct thing.

"You'll come down and see me, pa—father ? " said 'Melia, and, feeling that that was enough, Rivers graciously gave his permission, which, strictly speaking, hadn't been asked.    He said that he must superintend his little girl's progress, but, of course, he never went.  'Melia did, however, regularly through the next week, always turning up at an hour which was too dark to do anything, and always pegging away until she had to scurry for the shop.  After eight days of it, in short snatches, she went alone, gasping and with great joy.  Then the mornings were too dark to do anything before shoptime, but 'Melia could ride, and managed on one or two fine Sundays to secretly get away alone, and to plod on in a way that proved her independence.

THROUGH all these exciting times 'Melia had often thought of Archie Inch, and wondered why he never came near the little tobacconist's shop. She took an interest in him which, at that time, was almost motherly, for she was only a year younger than he, and that meant that in experience she was a great deal older. Archie, who used to chatter freely as he leant over the counter, had told her long ago that his mother was dead, and 'Melia, who knew very well that in losing hers she had lost her best friend, pitied Master Archie far more than he pitied himself.

He, on his side, was thinking a great deal about 'Melia. At first he stayed away because he was vexed with her, and meant, as he said to himself, to bring her down a peg. But reflection told him that he was far more likely to come down than she was, and he respected her the more for the very independent manner which she showed—even to the rousing of his temper—whenever he was inclined to patronize.

So he very soon made up his mind to look in, and to make friends, which he knew would be an easy matter. For 'Melia bore no malice, and was as free and frank in her forgiveness as she was in her wrath. But still he did not go. For one thing he was working for his Arts degree, and even the Arts students of Edinburgh have to work sometimes.

For another thing, the young fellow had been very much sobered by a chat with Maitland, who, meeting him in Drumsheugh Gardens one day, had invited him in, and talked gravely of Lord Inch's condition.

Maitland had no particular liking for Archie. He had

13

some prejudice against him, in fact, because of Archie's resemblance to his dead mother, who, so Maitland believed, had kept two old friends apart.

But Maitland had to acknowledge to himself that Archie took the news like a man.

" You understand, my boy," he told him, " all I say is that your father is not so strong as he was, or as he should be, and I think you've a right to know it. He may do very well for a time, and after the New Year he promises us he'll take a rest. But meanwhile you've got to be very careful of him."

" What can I do ? " Archie asked, naturally enough, and Maitland wished he could tell him of the letter. This, however, could not be, and Maitland knitted his brows, rubbing the side of his nose reflectively, and wondering how far he could go.

" Well," he said at last, " I mind, when I was a youngster, I always wanted to have a hand in all that was going, and I daresay folk thought me a wild loon at times. Keep yourself well in hand, Archie, and avoid the appearance of evil just now, of all times, for your father's sake. If someone came along and told him you were in bad company—and there's plenty will say a thing like that for little enough—or if you chanced, by ill-luck, to be heard of at the Police Court for any bit row (I was there myself once, for there are times when a fellow's hand must guard his head), why, anything like that, coming upon him unawares, might just fell him as a bullock is felled in the slaughter-house yonder. More than that," he went on, with a hand on Archie's shoulder, " a man in your father's position has enemies always. Let him see, Archie, my man, that if he's got trouble abroad, there's peace at home."

" Who are they ? " Archie had asked, curiously.

" I don't know, but it's always so. A man's never up, but you may be sure some one wants him down. It's the

way of the world, man, and the penalty of getting up in it.
Say nothing to him of all this, for you'll do no good, and
maybe vex him, but just see that nothing troubles him that
you can prevent, till the New Year comes, and a holiday
with it. For a holiday he shall have then, or I'll eat my
diploma," with which blood-curdling threat Maitland shook
Archie's hand more cordially than he had done at meeting,
and sent him away.

This, then, was another reason why 'Melia had not seen
him. For Archie, glancing covertly at his father during
dinner that same evening, saw changes that he had not
noticed before, and that he by no means liked. It seemed
to him that, ever since their holiday (which, by the by, he
had voted uncommonly slow), his father had aged. His
hair was decidedly grayer, his face more yellow, and there
was less color than ever in the thin, tight lips. A cover
fell during dinner that night, and Archie, looking at his
father that very moment, saw how he started almost before
it touched the ground, and, half turning in his chair with an
angry frown, opened his mouth to scold the unlucky servant, and then closed it again, and kept it closed without
having said a word, as if he felt the need of saying nothing,
lest he should say too much.

After that Archie gave his father more consideration than
he had ever done before. He even went so far as to start
conversations at dinner, trying to be regardless of the somewhat contemptuous replies which he often received, and he
gradually found that his father's sarcasms were not so terrible as he used to think them. Then he went farther, one
night when Lord Inch was particularly friendly, and asked
whether he might bring his books to the study and read
there. Leave was given, though with raised eyebrows,
which expressed a kind of polite surprise quite as well as
words could. He flushed a little, but sat there for the evening, and the next night Lord Inch asked if he were coming

again, which Archie thought was intended for an invitation,
and worked at the table in the study that night, and for
several nights after. While he read, Lord Inch frowned
over processes sent down in his bag from the Parliament
House, or sat staring into the fire. A night came, however,
when Archie's self-imposed duties pressed hard upon him,
and, after he had been working for perhaps half an hour, he
rose to go out.

His father looked up, and asked where he was going.

" I want a walk," Archie told him, " and I'm going to get
some tobacco."

" There are cigars there," Lord Inch told him, nodding
towards a little cabinet near the mantel-piece, but Archie
said he wanted a pipe, and went out, while his father turned
to his papers again without any further comment.

In a quarter of an hour Archie passed the door which was
guarded by his old acquaintance Sandy, feeling so cheered,
by this little excursion, that he winked amicably at that
silent individual, as he went in. 'Melia, alone and a trifle
dull, was so much taken by surprise, that she had greeted
him cordially, and with a beaming smile, before she remembered the distant terms upon which they had parted. Then
she drew herself up a little stiffly.

" D'you want the same as you used to have, Mr. Inch ? "
she asked politely, with an air that suggested a lapse of
centuries since his last visit.

" The 'baccy, not the cigarettes, please," Archie told her,
and put down his pouch upon the counter.

'Melia gave a little sniff at it, before she put the tobacco
in.

" We sell *that* mixture too," she informed him with emphasis. " Would you prefer it ? "

" No, thanks," Archie told her, staring a little, " I'd
rather have Dream Mixture, please."

" Very well," said 'Melia. " It's a pity it isn't sold in

more places than one. It's such a long way for you to come
for it."

" It only takes me about ten minutes," Archie answered,
filling his pipe as he spoke.

" Oh ! " said 'Melia, with an air of polite surprise, " why,
I thought it took near a fortnight," at which Archie
burst out laughing, and 'Melia, pleased to see that the
point was appreciated, smiled somewhat more cordially
upon him.

" I'm an ass," Archie confided to her ; " I should have
been in before to tell you I knew it, but my governor's
seedy ; I've scarcely been out any evening after dinner.
Busy too, working for an exam."

" That'll be no trouble to *you*, Mr. Inch, I'm sure," said
'Melia. " I mean the examinations, of course. But I'm
sorry to hear about your pa—father I mean."

" Oh, he'll get a holiday soon, and the doctors 'll put
him all right again then," said Archie, puffing away philosophically.

" I can feel what it must be like to be anxious about him,"
'Melia said sympathetically, " since I got mine back."

" Your what ? "

" My father," said 'Melia, with some dignity. " A University gentleman like yourself, Mr. Inch, only Oxford."

" The deuce ! " said that astonished youth, staring more
than ever. " I mean, I thought you were an orphan, Miss
Rivers."

" So I might have been," returned 'Melia rather vaguely,
" and I didn't know but what I was. I didn't care to boast
much of my people till I could point to 'em if needs be. But
you do stare ! It's not so wonderful as all that, is it ? "

" It's not *that* I was looking at," Archie said admiringly. " By Jove, what splendid hair you've got, Miss
Rivers. Is it the light, or what ? Why it looks just like
what I saw in pictures abroad last summer. Or is it your

dress ? If your father has come back, what are you in black
for ? "

" Well, it's quieter," 'Melia told him, rather pleased that
he noticed the difference, " and the old velveteen was
rubbed to bits at the elbows through leaning on the counter,
talking to you, *I* believe."

" I wish you'd let me give you a new one then," said
Archie, " though I must say I like the black best—it looks
so ——" he was going to say " lady-like," but stopped in
time lest that too might cause trouble, and said " pretty " instead, and 'Melia was pleased because, after a little consulta-
tion with Nell, she had set off a black dress with big white
cuffs and wide collars, the ironing of which had given her
considerable trouble.

" But your hair ? " Archie insisted, looking admiringly
at that abundant ornament, which was now entirely free
from artificial color. The young man is either very bold—
or else very innocent—who ventures to ask questions upon
such a subject, but Archie's admiration was so open that
'Melia didn't mind very much.

" Well," she said, recollecting the answer she had given to
Peters, " I've got over the influenzy. They say that makes
a world of difference to the hair. I'm glad mine didn't fall
out. Then, too," she added, with some little effort, for
'Melia's ideas were changing in other matters than those of
dress, " I'm usin' a different lotion. Maybe the last was
colorin' it a bit."

" And are you going to drop the shop ? " asked Archie,
looking round discontentedly. But 'Melia shook her head.

" There's no hurry," she told him. " Father's come over
on business, which may be good, and then which may not.
I'm well treated here, and here I stay, till I know what
comes next."

" It's cosier than it was," Archie allowed, admiring the
tobacco plant and some cut flowers, while a dark, warm-

looking, new curtain hid 'Melia's little sanctuary from him.

"But what will your dad say?" he went on. "Oxford men don't care to have —— I mean, he'll be wanting you to keep house for him!"

"There's no house to keep yet," 'Melia explained, "and p'r'aps there won't be, you know. A gentleman may be a gentleman all round, and yet stay poor, you know, Mr. Inch."

"That's true," Archie said, quite cordially, "and I hope you won't think of running away, Miss Rivers."

"Well," 'Melia allowed, "I'm not going to-morrow. As for when I *may* go, here's father, and he knows more about it than I do," and Archie, turning from where he lounged over the counter, still lost in admiration of the red hair, found the benevolent Rivers looking at him curiously from the doorway, while on Rivers' heels, following him like an amiable shadow, came a big, dark, foreign-looking man, with a sleepy, placid, clean-shaven face—no other, in fact, than Mr. Peters.

# CHAPTER XXVI

'MELIA looked from one to the other of this strange trio, and seemed a little puzzled.

" Fact is," she announced presently, " I s'pose I should introduce you, gentlemen. Father, this is Mr. Archie Inch, a regular customer of mine, and a University gentleman like yourself. Mr. Archie Inch—my father ; and this is Cap'n Peters—come in, Cap'n Peters, there's room for a little one —and Cap'n Peters has been everywhere I believe, Mr. Inch, and knows most things, it seems to me, though he doesn't talk about it, and I don't know if he's a University gentleman : and now you all know each other, and whether there's room for the three of you on that old settee, or whether it'll break up, bein' of a weak constitution, if you all sit down on it together, I can't tell till you've tried."

Having got this far, 'Melia stopped for breath, and her father held out an affable hand, while Peters bowed solemnly in the background.

" Of Oxford ? " asked Rivers, taking the hand of the not-very-eager Archie.

" Edinburgh."

" Ah ! her northern sister ! " said Rivers, still affable, but now with a distinct touch of condescension. " I hope to go over your University some day, Mr. Inch. You lose a great deal, my dear sir, by your non-collegiate system. It destroys *esprit de corps.* Have you ever been to Oxford, Mr. Inch ? "

" Yes ! " said Archie, with some asperity, " I went down in the Rugger team that beat 'em last year," after which, for

a moment, there was silence, while Archie condemned
Rivers as an old Bounder, and Rivers, surveying the son of
his intended victim, wondered how he could be made useful.

He knew quite well, without any help from 'Melia, who
Archie was. Like Peters, he had seen him go in and out of
No. 45, and 'Melia had spoken of him casually, when Rivers
was questioning her in idle curiosity concerning her customers.

"Well," said 'Melia, proud at being able to show her
respectable parentage, and hospitably anxious to honor the
occasion, "as Mr. Inch knows very well, this is all of my
establishment that a customer ever sees, but I don't know
that it'll hurt trade, if I throw the whole place open to you
gentlemen for one night only. I shut soon now, anyway,
and p'r'aps if you'll come in a little farther, Mr. Peters,
unless you're shy to-night, and close that there door, and
pull this curtain back, then some can sit inside and some
out here, and you'll all get more room, and be able to talk
just as well."

"I ought to be going," said Archie doubtfully, but when
'Melia said, "Oh, don't, Mr. Inch, please!" and looked at
him in a more friendly way than she generally did, he said
that he supposed he could spare a quarter of an hour, and
sat down.

"You can tell me about my old college, Balliol," said
Rivers sentimentally.

"I didn't see it," Archie told him. "There was too much
on for us, while we were there."

"Well, well!" Rivers shook his head mournfully, and
seemed quite hurt. "Fancy being at Oxford without going
over Balliol! Dear me! I'd like to drink to Balliol if we
were in my little diggings."

"There's a kettle, that I'll boil in a minute!" 'Melia
chimed in, hospitably. "I'll make you all a lovely cup of
tea," and couldn't understand what amused them so much.

"It would certainly be a change," Rivers allowed. "I
don't suppose that Balliol has ever been toasted in tea yet.
But wait!" A sudden idea struck him and he made for the
door, after borrowing five shillings for half an hour from
Mr. Peters. "Put the kettle on, my dear Em'ly!" he told
her, and disappeared, while 'Melia stared from Peters to
Archie and back again.

"What's up?" she asked, and Archie shook his head;
but Peters, settling down on the red settee and puffing great
clouds, said, "Whiskey!" which was the first word he had
spoken since he came in, and which, being very much to the
point, and echoing deeply through the little place, rather
impressed Archie, who now bestowed upon Mr. Peters the
attention hitherto monopolized by Rivers. As for Peters,
he enveloped himself in smoke, through which his eyes
studied Archie unwinkingly, while, to Archie's dismay, he
chatted like an old friend with 'Melia, who seemed to allow
him to do so on a much more friendly footing than Archie
could ever get. His disgust reached a climax when Peters
inquired with solicitude, concerning a fall 'Melia had got
from her bicycle, on the previous Sunday. Archie was
glaring reproachfully at 'Melia, who was not so unconscious
as she seemed, when Rivers returned jubilant.

"I *think*," he told them, "that we might now honor
Balliol, if you will join me. Here is a sufficient quantity of
the National Beverage," and, as Peters had predicted, he
brought out a bottle of whiskey. He also produced three
toddy-glasses. "To be returned," he told them. "Em'ly,
my dear, you will make yourself a cup that cheers but not
inebriates. Here is also a lemon, and I presume that, for
those who like it, you can supply sugar. Balliol ought to
have had champagne, but her sons can but offer libation of
the best they can afford." He sighed at the thought of
such scant honors for Balliol, but brightened as he drew
the cork, and sampled the whiskey before venturing to offer

it for general use. " 'Twill serve," he told them, and fell to
telling Archie the exploits of his youth, while they waited
for the kettle to boil. That young man, however, was not
so attentive as he should have been, considering the importance of the subject. He answered rather at random,
when he answered at all, and Rivers, though inwardly vot-
ing him an unlicked cub, was interested to notice that it
was 'Melia's chatter to her friend " Cap'n " Peters which
distracted Archie's attention.

" In the States," he said, *à propos* of uncomfortable
quarters as compared with life at Balliol, " one must rough
it."

He repeated this valuable information a little more carefully since Archie took no notice of it, and when the latter
at last paid attention, he added, " Have you ever been there,
Mr. Inch ? "

" No," said Archie, wondering what on earth 'Melia
found to interest her in Peters' conversation. " My father
has." he added, as an afterthought.

" You don't say so ! " Rivers was much interested.
" You don't happen to know where he was ? " he asked,
but got no more information. " All over the place," was
Archie's reply. As the kettle was now hissing loudly, and
Peters had ceased talking with 'Melia, Rivers stopped too,
not being quite decided how far to press his questioning,
and suggested refreshment. So the three glasses were filled,
and Rivers having proposed " Balliol ! " it was drunk
though not with any great enthusiasm. Then he insisted
that each should propose a toast, and Archie straightway
suggested " The Ladies." Peters being pressed for his
sentiments, was meditative, and being, as he announced,
" a most damnably stupid foreign man," took some time
to think of anything suitable. He at last proposed, " May
we all get what we deserve ! " which was the most popular
toast of the three, and was drunk with great applause, be-

sides being warmly praised by Rivers as " quite English ! "
This way of putting it, however, evoked a protest from
Archie, who, there being no heeltaps, had now swallowed
three stiff glasses, all prepared for him by Rivers. He
wished, in place of the word " English," to substitute " British," and got angry because he found " British " a difficult
word to negotiate. He produced it, however, at last, with
gravity and extraordinary distinctness, and was proceeding
to argue with Rivers upon the merits of their respective uni-
versities, when 'Melia, who had watched the proceedings
rather anxiously, declared that she must close the shop at
once.

As she proceeded to do so without stopping to argue the
point, Archie and Peters presently found themselves helping her. Then Rivers, who had taken a fourth and a fifth
glass while 'Melia was putting up the shutters, became much
concerned for her safety, and declared that he must see his
only child safe home. It was of no use for 'Melia to point
out that she was accustomed to go alone. He declared it
his duty to go with her, and Peters, in response to an appeal-
ing glance from 'Melia, suggested that he might as well
come too.

This enraged Archie, who straightway declared his intention of joining the party, and 'Melia, provided they cleared
out quietly, was ready to agree to anything.

So she had such an escort as she had never been honored
with before in her life, and the adieux at the foot of the
stair, in Comely Bank, savored of a much earlier and more
ceremonious period in the evolution of manners.

Then Rivers, who by this time was calling Archie his
dear boy, must needs see him home, and Peters, whom
Archie had quite forgiven, went that way also. They parted
on the best possible terms at Lord Inch's door, and Archie
would certainly have made them come in, but for an indistinct idea that, for some particular reason which he couldn't

quite remember, he mustn't disturb his father. So he regretfully watched them go down the street under a cold moonlit sky.

Almost before Archie had lost sight of them, Rivers, hanging heavily on to the arm of his dear friend Captain Peters, was darkly hinting to that attentive gentleman that if he, Rivers, told all he knew, there would be very considerable discomfort in No. 45. After this, assisted by the very little whiskey left in the bottle which he had brought away in his pocket, and by part of another, opened when he reached his room, he became very melancholy, and went to bed weeping for his dead wife.

# CHAPTER XXVII

## PIPES AND PATIENCE

WHEN day dawned, after the symposium already spoken of, Peters was sitting in his room alone. He had pulled one of the two easy-chairs round to the front of the fire, and was stretched out with his slippered feet on the fender, his hands in his trousers pockets, and a long pipe in his mouth, a pipe so long that the little bowl rested on the floor.

The position was comfortable, suitable for meditation or for dreams. The scent of the burning tobacco was peculiar, and had a peculiar effect upon Peters, whose eyes were half closed, while his lips, instead of being kept, as usual, fairly well together, opened often in a lazy, contented smile.

Anyone passing from this room to the next, would have seen that the bed there had not been disturbed, and the room was quite tidy, which was more than could be said of his sitting-room. Peters had come in so wakeful that he had walked up and down for the greater part of the night, and had only taken to this tiny-bowled, long-stemmed pipe when the gray morning was showing over the house-tops. This business of his was dragging desperately, and the man was not so uniformly indifferent to it as he seemed. Sometimes there came to him, without warning, a sudden temptation to settle it in another way than that which he had planned, and to have done with it all. Then, as quickly as possible, Peters betook himself to his room and to the small-bowled pipe, and brought himself down firmly (though this seems a ridiculous contradiction of terms) to a state of mind in which he wandered through strange lands where he ruled alone, and where nothing mattered much except the thousand indescribable delights of the moment.

There were two very great dangers in this last resource of Mr. Peters'. One was that, by repeated use of this key to the gates of strange countries, he might be led to prefer them above this comparatively joyless existence—and to dwell in them continually. The other was, that his most impatient moments came while he fitted the key to the lock, and he was more ready than ever, just then, to settle anything and everything in the quickest possible way. He knew of these two dangers better than anyone else. He did his best to prevent the first, by only using this key when everything else seemed useless. He usually avoided the second, by the very simple expedient of locking his more material door with a more material key, so that no one could come in unexpectedly, and further, by putting away that key in his bedroom, so that a distinct effort was necessary before he could go out. This morning, however, he had forgotten his usual precaution, and the result was that Rivers came in, after an unnoticed single knock, and stood surveying the scene from the doorway.

"I couldn't take any breakfast," he explained to the motionless figure in the easy-chair, "and our friend Mrs. Jimps told me that you had not been down, so I just looked in to see how things were. We were a bit gay last night, weren't we? Some special occasion, I believe. I thought I'd take ' a hair of the dog,' and I find I've none left."

He got no answer, for Peters, though he heard, had too little interest in sublunary matters to reply. Rivers crossed the room, and took the other easy-chair with the familiarity of one who had occupied it pretty often lately. As he did so he sniffed suspiciously, and his eye fell upon the pipe, the peculiar shape of which was not unfamiliar to the Buncombe of other days.

"Hullo!" he observed, "what's your little game?"

The big head rolled a little towards him, the eyes brightened under the half-closed lids, and Peters smiled in sleepy benevolence.

"Patience," was all he answered, and it amused his visitor.

"Patience again ! You play with that pipe, I suppose ? Come now, that won't do, Captain Peters," he went on in a jocular way, " where are your cards ? "

The man lying before him, with the mouth-piece of the long pipe dropping away from his lips, gave a cunning, sleepy smile, and seemed to enter into the joke. " Up my sleeve !" he muttered, and Rivers applauded noisily.

"Excellent, excellent !" he told him. " I hope you've a good hand, I'm sure. May I help myself to whiskey ? "

But the drowsy eyes were beginning to brighten in an odd fashion. If Rivers had been watching more carefully he might have noticed this, and also that they fastened upon his face with a peculiar intentness. Rivers, however, was looking across at the sideboard for something drinkable, and pursued his small joke with the dull pertinacity of the man who does not make one often.

"Show me your hand !" he persisted.

"Soon ! Go away ! "

The man, if he had known how close he sat under the Shadow of Death, would have shown fear, and, doing so, would have roused the hunting instinct in the other, and would have died where he sat. But he had caught sight of a spirit decanter on the sideboard, and that settled the matter.

" Very well," he said, seeing an opportunity, " I'll take the pool this time, and let you have your revenge later " ; and crossing the room, he took the decanter, and, laughing over his shoulder, went off.

As the door closed behind him, the great body in the easy-chair was tense and ready for a spring, and Peters scowled when he realized that his visitor had gone. He half turned in his chair, intending to lock the door now against all comers, but his hand fell upon the pipe, and, raising it to his lips, he allowed a vacant smile gradually to relax his face.

A little later the pipe slid from his open mouth again, but this time Peters did not notice it. He had passed the gates.

14

# CHAPTER XXVIII

### THIEF!

AFTER Rivers had fortified himself from the spirit decanter, he sat and meditated over the doings of the last night, and the more he thought things out, the more pleased he was with his prospects. Archie had done very little to hide his admiration for 'Melia, and Rivers, sitting quietly in his own room and gradually finding all things take a rosy hue, saw great possibilities, and decided that he must at once turn them into certainties. As a first step he twisted the blue-black mustache carefully, and went down to the door with his very glossy hat tipped a little to one side. It was characteristic of Rivers to put on his hat the moment that he decided to go out, not waiting until he reached the door; and it was always his fascinating habit to wear it considerably out of the perpendicular when he was in good spirits. When, in his opinion, a hard world treated him harshly and fortune frowned, he wore the hat pulled forward—a trick which he had copied from the stage—and his mustache drooped despondently, and showed ragged bitten ends.

He met Mrs. Jimps upon the stair, and, his hat being on, he had the opportunity of taking it off with a fine semicircular sweep, as she stopped him to ask whether he had seen Peters—Captain Peters, as Rivers had set the fashion of calling him, following the example of 'Melia.

"Oh yes, I've seen him," Rivers told her. "He does not intend to have any breakfast, Mrs. Jimps."

"Dear me!" said Mrs. Jimps, much concerned, "I've kept a haddock hot for him, and Captain Peters is so fond of a good haddock. Shall I take it up for him, Mr. Rivers?"

" No, I think not," said Rivers, chuckling unpleasantly as he thought of Peters' occupation. " Captain Peters has had all the breakfast he wants, Mrs. Jimps, and I think he has gone to sleep again " ; and with that he went jauntily on his way, before Mrs. Jimps could formulate inquiries concerning Captain Peters' loss of appetite. She thought thereon, however, and decided that he should have lunch in his own room. By that arrangement she could insure his having something extra, without causing discontent among the less-favored Paying Guests, which shows that Mrs. Jimps had a kind heart that did not allow her to regard her visitors from a strictly business point of view, but that she also regulated its promptings by a certain amount of the prudence born of experience. Can we blame her, if her thoughts, during that day, dwelt a great deal upon the possible and probable causes of Mr. Peters' loss of appetite, and if she considered love among the rest ? Love, she knew from experience, could make a difference. For the most profitable visitors she had ever welcomed, were two young people who had become engaged under her roof. But then they didn't make it up in sleep, as Mr. Peters seemed to be doing. On the contrary, they were always the first to meet at the breakfast-table, and the last to leave the drawing-room at night. If Mrs. Jimps could have seen the way in which Peters had paced his room until morning, love would have seemed to her the certain cause. But she knew nothing of that, and could only relieve her mind by poetically expressing her sentiments in a nicely cooked sweet-bread, sent up in a most tempting manner when Peters rang—well on in the afternoon—for hot water.

That morning 'Melia, too, thought over the last night's proceedings, after she had opened the shop and made everything tidy. Rivers was a seasoned toper, and though the one to blame, he had shown very little sign of excess while with 'Melia. He had merely been a little more garrulous

and demonstrative. Peters had not taken so much as either
of the other two, and could have taken more than either
without being affected by it. But Archie had been decidedly excited, and 'Melia was very vexed when she thought
of him. It was she who had asked him to stay, and she knew
that he would not have done so without her invitation. It
was her father who had brought in the spirits and set the example, and 'Melia flushed as she told herself that he and she
were responsible for Archie's condition. The result was,
that when that rather puzzled and very penitent youth, instead of going to his Humanity Class, dropped in at the shop
to find out if he had made a fool of himself, ready, if need
were, to apologize most humbly, he found 'Melia almost in
tears, and could not understand what on earth was the matter, until she tried to explain—and scarcely even then.

"It was me, Mr. Inch, it was all me," she persisted.

"I don't know what you mean," he told her. "You
never asked me to drink. I hope I didn't behave like a cad.
I can't say that I remember anything more than that I was
a talkative ass, but I want to know if there's anything more
I've got to be sorry for."

"No," said 'Melia, and, to her own intense disgust, went
off into an hysterical giggle, as she thought of his solemn
figure bending over her hand in the lamplight, at the door
of her lodgings.

"Well, I mustn't mind your laughing at me," said Archie
humbly. "I know it serves me right, and I'm awfully
ashamed of myself. All I can say is that I was never like
that before."

This was quite true, Archie's weakness not being in that
direction, and 'Melia ought to have been pleased to hear it :
but, to his astonishment, she took the information in a different spirit, and, putting her head down upon the counter,
wept openly.

"What on earth have I said now ?" he asked, "'Melia

dear, for goodness sake, stop crying, and tell me what's the matter."

But 'Melia's feelings had got the better of her for the moment, and she could only cry on. Archie tried to pull away her fingers and make her lift up her face, but he was clumsy, and only succeeded in disarranging her hair, which uncoiled across the counter like a great snake of red gold. That, and her hands, hid 'Melia's face altogether, but they left bare the back of her neck, creamy and tempting. He looked down at that, fascinated, and silently tried once more to make her lift her head and deliver him from temptation. Then, failing in this, he stooped over the counter and kissed that creamy spot once, twice, and raised his head, proud and ashamed—to find his idol's father watching in the doorway.

"Well, sir," said that irate parent, who, as a matter of fact, could have interfered before the climax, had he thought well to do so, "what is the meaning of this?"

'Melia had already straightened herself up at this reckless attack, pale and panting, and was on the point of flaring out in sincere and righteous indignation against the reckless youth, but, at the sound of Rivers' voice, her face crimsoned, and she would have given worlds for the shop floor to gape and swallow her. Almost immediately, however, she realized that she didn't want that to happen unless Archie was saved in the same way, so, at the mercy of very mixed feelings, she neither spoke nor moved, except, with trembling hands, to attempt the capture and restraint of that snaky red coil, and the two young people stood looking very foolish and ashamed before the virtuous Rivers, who made an admirable picture of dignified astonishment.

"What is the meaning of this?" repeated Rivers. "Em'ly, is it possible?"

"It's no fault of Miss Rivers'," Archie stammered, finding his tongue when he saw his beloved questioned. "I'm

sure she never knew what I was going to do. You'd have
seen that for yourself if you'd been a moment earlier. I—
I didn't know myself," he added haltingly, with a look of
entreaty at the still agitated 'Melia.

"Didn't know, sir!" repeated Rivers, with splendid
scorn. "Didn't know! You needn't tell *me* that you took
my daughter by surprise. You needn't tell me that *my*
daughter was not a willing party to this—this infamous attack. But to say that *you* ' didn't know.' Have you no self-
respect, no self-control ? "

"I'm afraid not," muttered the abashed Archie, with
another penitent glance at 'Melia. "I'm more sorry than I
can say."

"Then, am I to understand," asked Rivers, with a gallant
effort at icy politeness, "am I to understand that you regret
the er—embrace that I witnessed, and wish to back out of
this affair ? "

"I regret it only so far as it has hurt Miss Rivers," Archie
told him, never taking his eyes from 'Melia's face, "I—I—
otherwise I mean, I should be only glad to—to—do it over
again," and at this shameless avowal 'Melia was overwhelmed with crimson confusion, and fled past the curtain
to hide herself. There she listened, without in the least
meaning to do so, telling herself all the while that she was a
shameless hussy, and could, nevertheless, never bear to see
Him any more.

# CHAPTER XXIX

IT was very little more that 'Melia heard that morning, for, after another word or two, Rivers suggested an adjournment, and he and Archie left the shop together.

It was characteristic of 'Melia's father, that he should choose a private bar as the spot for a quiet talk, and also that, having suggested the unfortunate necessity for something in the way of refreshment, for the good of the place, he should leave Archie to pay for it.

" And now, Mr. Inch," said Rivers solemnly, after having tasted and approved, " as this young lady's father, I must ask you, speaking as one gentleman and man of the world to another, what do you mean to do ? "

" I'm sure I don't know," said poor Archie dolefully, for the excitement of the moment had gone. " I'm ready to go back and apologize again at once, if you like, and if Miss Rivers will listen to me."

" Apologize sir ! " said Rivers indignantly, twisting his mustache with the most truculent air he could muster. " Apologize ! What on earth are you dreaming of ? Do you think yourself free to kiss my daughter at the price of an apology ? Good heavens ! Why, if it were once known that a handsome girl like that could be kissed for a mere apology, Gad ! sir, there'd be young men dropping in at that place all day and all night, with apologies ready printed and bound in sets."

" What on earth am I to do then ? " asked the unfortunate Archie, shuddering at the brutal way in which the matter was being stated.

"Do!" repeated Rivers, with a fine air of contempt. "'Pon my soul, I thought I was talking to a man! Did you never think of marrying her?" and Archie gasped, partly at the terribly matter-of-fact manner in which Rivers suggested marriage, as if he were trying to sell Paradise by auction and had accused Archie of a bid, and partly because, after all, to hear Paradise spoken of so plainly, seemed to make it less impossible.

"She wouldn't have me!" he answered. "Sometimes she won't even shake hands."

"Quite right too, one begins to think," said Rivers, working himself up into an excited state, in which his voice grew louder, and threatened to be heard beyond the little private box in which they sat. "You acknowledge, then, that my daughter cannot be accused of encouraging you?"

"She's not a bit like that," Archie told him eagerly. "She always made fun of me if I tried to be serious."

"Then what do you mean, sir, by these—these endearments of to-day? Were you serious, or were you merely trying how far a poor unprotected girl would let you go, without being serious?"

It says a great deal for Archie's high opinion of, and respect for 'Melia, that he was able to stand this catechism without rebelling, in disgust, at the idea of such an impossible father-in-law; but, whatever his opinion of Rivers might be, he was quite clear about 'Melia.

"Of course I was serious," he insisted. "I've learned to respect Miss Rivers very much lately. I'd marry her to-morrow if I could."

"Then," said Rivers, suddenly becoming affable, and clutching at Archie's hand across the table, "we understand one another perfectly, and you've shown me that you are the man of honor I took you to be. You ask me for my daughter's hand."

"Yes," said Archie dubiously, "if you like to put it that

way. Of course I can't have it unless she chooses, and, if she chose, I don't know that I'd ask you about it, but I suppose it's all right."

"Of course it is," said Rivers, quite unruffled. "I must see your father, and let him know the proposal which you have done me the honor of laying before me."

"Oh, but you can't," the horror-stricken Archie told him. "He's busy at the Parliament House all day just now."

"Then," said Rivers, "I must inconvenience myself so far as to give up an evening to your affairs."

"He's in the doctor's hands," Archie protested. "I wouldn't have him worried just now for anything. I'd rather even leave Miss Rivers quite free, if it must be so, for the time."

"Will you have me go to your father," asked Rivers impressively, "and tell him of a proposal, and a promise, made and withdrawn ? As a father I am bound, by regard for my daughter's honor, to do one or the other."

"Do as you like then !" groaned Archie, rising. "No, I don't want anything to drink. Have it yourself if you like, I haven't touched it. If I hadn't been an ass last night this would never have happened."

"Am I to understand," demanded Rivers, with Archie's untouched glass half-way to his lips, "that you wish to blame anyone but yourself—my daughter, for example—for anything that happened last night ? "

"No, not at all ! " said Archie, "I was a fool, and I must pay for it."

"Well, my dear boy," said Rivers, raising the glass higher, until the now fiercely twisted mustache just showed over the brim, "it's not my business to know what you mean by saying you were a fool, and I don't ask questions about what does not concern me. If, as you say, you were a fool last night, you've been a very wise and fortunate young man to-day. Gad ! sir, it doesn't become her father to

boast, but I say my Em'ly's husband will be a lucky man.
Be thankful that poverty prevents me from looking higher
than a simple gentleman for her! You don't take the title,
I think? No. Work hard then, Mr. Inch, and let her
old father see his little Em'ly among the nobility, before
he dies."

With that Rivers drained the glass, such a sentiment
being obviously of the nature of a toast, and then he, too,
there being nothing more to drink, rose from the table.

"Let us say half-past eight this evening," he decided. "I
will do myself the honor of calling upon Lord Inch at that
time, my dear boy," and parting from Archie just outside,
he went jauntily away.

It could not be expected that Archie would attend any
lecture that day. He went disconsolately home, and shut
himself up in his own little room, which was supposed to be
a study, but which showed more volumes of the Badminton
Library, and other sporting works, than anything else.
Here he lit his largest pipe, and then, curled up in a fantas-
tic attitude before the fire, he tried to think matters out, and
this is a summary of his meditations and conclusions.

He had been a fool last night, and was glad to have
'Melia's authority for believing, since his recollections were
vague, that he hadn't been much worse. He had apologized this morning, and straightway committed another
crime, for which sometimes he was sorry and sometimes he
was not, according as it happened that 'Melia, or her parent,
her captivating neck, or his aggressive mustache, rose in
his mind. From that point onward, Archie did not see
where he could have stopped. Didn't he love 'Melia? Of
course he did. Why then was he sitting here, trying to think
things straight? They were straight already, if only 'Melia
cared for him—but, nevertheless, when Archie thought of
his father and of hers, he gave another groan, and set to
work, trying to think it all out again. Rivers was "a

Bounder," he told himself, as he had thought directly he set eyes on that individual, and between his father and Rivers there would at once be a row. If only Lord Inch saw 'Melia and knew her for a little while, he would see, Archie fondly protested, that she was a good girl, a clever girl, and a pretty girl, who only needed a chance to be fit for any position, and who was already far too good for his good-for-nothing son. Then Archie thought of Rivers, grasping at the second glass in the bar, and ready to bully as far as he dared, and he, groaning at that unholy vision, turned to the thought of 'Melia as she cried over the counter, with her red hair about her face, and straightway came to a rash, or valorous, determination. He would go back to her now, at once, and they two would decide for themselves what should be done. After all, who was her father, that he should leave her for years and come just when he wasn't wanted—at anyrate by Archie ?

It was a relief to do anything, and to go anywhere. As he went, 'Melia's face grew more and more distinct, and Rivers' face faded, until Archie's foremost thought, as he went into the shop, past the kilted Highlander who had stood still through so much, was merely that he should see 'Melia again.

What he saw of her was not very encouraging.

'Melia, on the departure of Archie and Rivers, had indulged in what she called a good cry. And I daresay, after all, that, physiologically, it *was* good. Then, finding that she could not imagine what was going to happen next, and could not leave the shop to find out, she tried to work off her excitement by a general clean-up, moving everything, and dusting everywhere. The result was that Archie found her on some low steps behind the counter, which was covered with boxes taken down from a shelf that she was dusting.

When she turned and saw who had come in, she and the

low steps nearly toppled over together, but she clutched at the shelf and began dusting again.

" Go away, Mr. Inch," was all her salutation.

" I've come to say how sorry I am," pleaded Archie.

" Very well, Mr. Inch. I don't bear malice. Go away ! "

" But I want to talk, 'Melia."

" My name's Rivers, Mr. Inch—Miss Rivers, and I don't want to talk."

" There's a lot to talk about," Archie assured her.

" I don't want to hear it then." 'Melia retorted obstinately, and still kept her face to the shelf, from which all dust had disappeared long ago.

" I thought," Archie went on, " that you'd like to hear what your father said."

" He'll tell me, p'r'aps."

" I don't believe he'll see you until he has seen the governor."

" Seen who ? " asked 'Melia, now turning about quickly enough, and she almost toppled over again.

" My governor, my father," Archie answered, eying her anxiously, to discover what he could from a somewhat tear-disfigured face.

" What's he going to see him for ? " demanded 'Melia, amazed, and Archie vainly sought for words to explain the situation satisfactorily.

" I don't know how to tell you properly, upon my word I don't," he at last admitted. " I'm an ass, I know, and I've proved that twice, anyway, in the last twenty-four hours. I can't think while you look at me like that, 'Melia."

" You've grown very shy—all of a sudden," said 'Melia sarcastically, forgetting to remind him again that her name was Rivers, and gaining courage as she discovered her own power. " Tell me as much as you can, Mr. Inch, and I'll excuse mistakes. They won't be the first I've had to excuse this morning, anyway."

" Well," Archie told her, " your father, of course, wanted to know what I meant by behaving so badly. I told him I was awfully fond of you, 'Melia, and he asked me what that meant. I said, of course, that I wanted to marry you, only you always laughed at me, and had never given me the chance of telling you so."

Archie stopped here, trying to think what to say next, but 'Melia allowed him no time.

" Well ? " she insisted, stamping her foot.

" Well, your father said he must see my dad about it."

" About what ? " asked 'Melia. Her head was well up now, and she was facing Archie defiantly, one foot tapping impatiently on the floor all the time.

" Go on ! " she insisted, " quicker."

" About my wanting to marry you."

" And where do I come in ? "

" I said," Archie assured her, hurriedly, " that you didn't care for me and never would, and that it wasn't a bit of good unless you were willing, and I told him, too, that the governor's ill, and that I didn't feel that I could bother him just now. But your father seemed to think I was trying to back out, which I never thought of, and said that either way he meant to see the governor. So he's coming to-night, and I don't care much for myself, for I think I deserve it, but I'm afraid it'll make father awfully bad. If he'd only wait a little."

" Seems to me," said 'Melia, keeping her head very high and speaking hurriedly, " there's no need to wait, Mr. Inch, and there's no need for your pa to be bothered just now or any other time. Go you home and see him first. Tell him from me that there was a silly bit of nonsense to-day w'ich meant nothing, and w'ich I don't mean to remember. Tell him I wouldn't have you at any price, and that if he likes, he being a lawyer, I'll put the same on paper to-morrow if he'll tell me how to do it—and now go away."

" 'Melia, I can't go away without explaining," pleaded Archie, not knowing quite what he meant to say, but wanting to gain time.

" *Will* you go ? " asked 'Melia fiercely, " or must I leave you to mind the shop and go myself ? "

So Archie went, dumfounded, and 'Melia collapsed among the boxes.

# CHAPTER XXX

## FATHER AND SON

IT is no doubt an excellent thing to feel and acknowledge the justice of retribution following on wrong-doing. Archie had already declared that he had been a fool and must suffer for it (which awkward way of putting things had not appeared to poor 'Melia as very complimentary). But, whatever Archie might say, he was not much consoled by his abstract sense of justice when he found himself opposite his father at the dinner-table that evening. Lord Inch, too, did, if possible, even less than usual to encourage confidences. As a matter of fact, he was already particularly troubled, and sat thinking gloomily over anxieties of his own, and scarcely touching the different courses of the meal, as they were put before him. For the first time since he had taken his seat upon the bench he was obliged to preside at a trial for murder, which had already lasted through a day. The case had nothing very peculiar about it. A man had, through jealousy, deliberately murdered a woman, and with the details we have nothing to do. Lord Inch expected that next day would see the case ended. On that afternoon he would sum up, and there was no room for doubt, in his mind, but that every word he said would help to convince fifteen men, if they were not convinced already, that only one verdict was possible.

Then would come the sentence, pronounced by himself, and he groaned to think of it. There was no comfort to him in the argument, to which he again and again returned, that he was merely the mouthpiece of the law, putting into effect, against one who had every reasonable help, the con-

clusion arrived at by fifteen reputable citizens. Nor did it
help him to think that his oath of office allowed no alternative. The grim relentless machinery of the law was so
carefully adjusted, the responsibility so divided, each
function so legalized, that when the half-man half-brute
died—as die he certainly would a few weeks hence—each
could say, from the prosecuting counsel through all the rest,
witnesses, judge, and jury, to the common hangman, " It
was not I who killed him." But, to Lord Inch's troubled
mind, it seemed as though a special responsibility attached
to himself. He exaggerated his own importance in the
ceremonial, his own part in the practically inevitable end.

It was not for nothing that the loungers of the Parliament House had, as he knew, called him, though half-laugh-
ingly, the Just Judge. He felt a grim satisfaction in deciding that he would shift no responsibility of his on any other
man's shoulders. He had fought for position, he had
worked for office, and, now that he filled it, no man should
have just cause to say that he shirked any of his duties.
If only he saw an opportunity of so guiding justice, he
thought, as to atone for his sin of twenty-five years ago, how
gladly he would take it ! Then, at once, he laughed a low
harsh laugh, shifting angrily in his chair, and muttering
to himself, entirely forgetful, for the moment, of Archie's
presence as he realized the absurdity of the wish.

What mere justice done to one man, as he was bound to
do it, could go one hair's-breadth to atone for injustice done
to another ? If one word of more than justice escaped
him, tending rather to mercy, then he must of necessity
be unjust, turning a deaf ear to the cry of innocent blood.
As Archie watched his father furtively, and wondered
how to begin his story to so grim a judge, Lord Inch's
thoughts went back to the beginning of his trouble. He
saw it all, he heard the tune of the unknown foreign words
which had rung in his ears so often since, and watched a

something which, but for him, might have been still a man, swinging in the moonlight.

He had tried, when success and money came, quietly to trace the relatives of that murdered man, but there was no more sign of them than of the leaves beneath which the corpse had swung. Still, he thought now, he must try again. Trouble and expense must have no limit in such a matter, and, comforted perhaps a little by this fresh resolution, he put these thoughts away for the time with a sigh, and tried to eat and to be more sociable.

Archie noticed the change, and noticed also, as he gave a side glance at the clock, that in another hour the self-invited visitor would be with them. How should he begin? He had considered and rejected half a dozen circumlocutory ways of approaching the matter, and now there was no time for anything but plain speaking.

"Can I have a talk with you after dinner, father?"

Lord Inch looked across the table, and frowned, inquiringly.

"Yes, of course, if you wish," he said, "but almost any other time would be better. I have to read my notes in the Lawnmarket case, and I must work all the evening."

"I'm afraid it must be to-night," Archie answered in desperation, "but I can tell you here while you're having dessert. Then it will be over quicker."

"What's this?" asked his father stiffly. "You have not been getting into mischief, I hope."

"I'm afraid you'll think so," Archie told him, keen to get on now and have it over without any slow torture. "But," he added, "I know you're not very fit just now, and I've tried to keep the thing quiet until you were better."

"Come away, man, come away!" Lord Inch told him impatiently, "let me hear the worst and have done with it." So Archie floundered on, with one hand clenched under the table and his eyes fixed upon his wine-glass, and, being

15

as anxious as Lord Inch to get it finished, told the bare
facts of the trouble with no comment or excuse.

So unadorned was his story that, when he stopped, his
father knew very little of Archie's own feeling in the
matter.

"What a vulgar intrigue!" he said scornfully, when
Archie was silent. "You fancy a tobacconist's girl, she lets
you kiss her, the father is in readiness, extorts a pretence of
a proposal out of you, and then has the audacity to talk of
coming round here, to see, of course, what he can screw out
of me. I shall not see him!"

"No, no, you're quite wrong, father," Archie insisted, "I
haven't told you all. I've great respect for Miss Rivers,
and I went round to see her again after that."

"Go on, sir!" Lord Inch said, angrily. "Did she get
you to make her an offer of marriage in writing—or did you
declare yourselves Man and Wife?"

"She told me to tell you she wouldn't have me at any
price."

Lord Inch sat back in his chair, and eyed Archie grimly.

"What is the meaning of this?" he demanded.

"It's quite true," Archie insisted. "She doesn't care for
me, and she won't have me. It's no good trying to make
you understand, father, for you've never seen her, but she's
too good for me, and I suppose she knows it. She said that
if you would tell her how to put it, she'd sign a paper saying
there was nothing between us."

"That's easily done," Lord Inch commented, and then
sat silent, looking at Archie curiously, and drumming upon
the table with his fingers. "Then why does the father make
his appearance?" he asked presently, and added at once,
"I will not see him, I tell you. I need not. You have got
yourself into this difficulty. You can see him if you like,
and tell him what his daughter says. Stay, though! Perhaps it would be best for her to sign that paper first!"

"That," thought Archie, "can wait," and he said nothing.

Presently Lord Inch, watching him, burst out into a mirthless, sardonic laugh.

" You're a pretty fellow ! " he told his son impatiently. " I think you must be right in saying the girl is too good for you. Now that you have obtained your kiss, you don't seem to care how the thing goes, so long as you get off scot free ! "

The words stung the young fellow like a whip, but he rose from the table and went across to the fire, before he faced about and answered.

" I'm not such a cur as you think me, sir," he told Lord Inch at last. "Although it doesn't look much like it, I suppose, I'm trying to consider you."

Lord Inch made him a little bow from his seat at the table. " You are quite right to mention that. I had overlooked it. Would it be too much to ask where this consideration has been shown ? "

" I don't know that it's shown at all," Archie told him, " but it's there."

"Really!" said Lord Inch, in a mocking tone. "Where?"

" I'm very fond of Miss Rivers," Archie repeated, facing him steadily, " and if you were all right, father, I should talk differently. As it is, I bring you her message—that she'll have nothing to do with me, and I bring it so that you mayn't have any worry when you meet her father. It wasn't all for my own sake that I wanted you not to hear about this."

" Well, well," said Lord Inch, perhaps a little softened, for Archie spoke manfully enough, " in any case the thing is impossible. You must see that. But if the girl won't have anything to do with you, what is the use of my being worried with the father ? Heavens ! man, I tell you I have matters to think of to-night to which this is the merest child's play ! "

" Her father doesn't know what she said to me," Archie
insisted, " and he mustn't know. I've only seen him twice,
but I believe he'd be awfully hard on her if he knew."

" That is pertinent ! " Lord Inch allowed. " He might
influence her, and it would be difficult to prove her statement to you. I had better see the fellow for a minute."

" You won't tell him what she said ! " Archie entreated.
His father laughed coldly at the idea. " No," he said, " the
man shall hear nothing of that from me."

" I will be in the smoking-room," Archie suggested.
" You'll send for me if you want me."

" I fancy that I shall not need your help," Lord Inch
told him dryly. " You will oblige me by not seeing this
young person, or her father, until I tell you."

" I'll be ready to come to the study directly he's gone, if
you don't send for me before."

" You will do nothing of the kind ! " retorted Lord Inch
sharply, finishing his wine and rising from the table. " I
can see you no more to-night. I do not know that I shall
have any time to talk to-morrow morning, or to-morrow
night either. It seems hard to you, I daresay, but one cannot be a fool without suffering for it. You are fortunate if
the result of your folly lasts only a few hours."

He was thinking of his own burden now, but the effect
was to make his voice and manner more than ever those of
a stern judge, who had no sympathy with human frailty or
folly of any kind, and Archie felt a very weak-kneed young
man as he listened.

" I know you can't understand a fellow making such a
fool of himself," he said dolefully, moving across the room
with his father, and standing aside at the door to let him
pass. " I know it's awfully hard on you to have such a chap
for a son, but one doesn't mean to do mischief."

" No, no ! " Lord Inch said, stopping suddenly in the
doorway, and looking out into the hall. " One does not

mean to do mischief, my boy; one does not mean to do mischief," and then went hurriedly away to his study, while Archie betook himself to the smoking-room, wondering whether he had any good excuse for thinking that his father's anger had lessened a little, just at the last.

# CHAPTER XXXI

### À OUTRANCE

If Lord Inch had, for a moment, been moved by some thought or memory when parting from Archie, he showed no sign of any such weakness to Morris, the footman, who answered his study-bell five minutes later, and received instructions to admit a man Rivers, who would come having business with his lordship.

That estimable parent, being shown in almost immediately after, had no reason to be elated by the way in which he was received. Lord Inch, scarcely looking up from his desk, pointed to a chair and told him to sit down.

" To what do I owe this pleasure ? " he asked ceremoniously, but Rivers made no haste to reply. He was studying the keen face before him, which he tried to recognize, and for the life of him could not. Twenty-five years of a legal atmosphere had made the judge quite unrecognizable. Rivers could only find consolation in thinking that there was still less chance of being himself detected.

The dry inscrutable figure opposite looked so irreproachable, the eyes were so keen, the expression was so masterful, that Rivers found it difficult to assume an air of assurance and equality.

" My young friend Mr. Archibald has told your lordship, no doubt," he said at last, in answer to Lord Inch's question.

" My son has told me that he met you last night—for the first time I believe," Lord Inch told him, dryly. " I must trouble you to state your business quickly, that I may return to mine."

As he spoke he took up the pen, as if his work had still the greater part of his attention, and Rivers cursed him under his breath for a conceited dog of a lawyer, whom he would bring down on his knees presently.

" You can easily understand," he told Lord Inch, " that I must certainly know more of the young fellow before I give my consent. But my daughter has known him longer, and I have great faith in her judgment."

" Your business, sir, your business ! " the other repeated.

" To consider your son's proposal of marriage to my daughter," Rivers told him. " Is that plain enough ? "

" Quite ! "

Lord Inch laughed a little as he acknowledged this.

" We need not talk of your daughter's position or prospects, Mr.——er Rivers," he added, after a glance at that gentleman's card. " Do you know the boy's age ? "

" When I was at Balliol," said Rivers pompously, dragging in Balliol as it was bound to be dragged in, sooner or later " (I am an Oxford man, my lord), I can have been no older, but I knew my mind in these things."

Balliol ! There was something dimly familiar about that word. Somewhere or other Lord Inch had met someone who dragged Balliol into every conversation. But that was immaterial to the present issue.

" My son is not yet twenty-one," he told Rivers.

" He very soon will be," Rivers said, carelessly. " I don't think that would matter, if you and I came to terms."

The growing impertinence of his manner was rousing Lord Inch's temper, which, however, did not yet show itself. The Parliament House had been an admirable school in the practice of an unruffled demeanor, and Lord Inch was now showing just as much, or as little, of impatience as suited him. After all, the affair was very much child's play. It meant a little expense in getting Archie out of such undesirable society, and a little caution in avoiding chatter. It would be easy to bear with this fellow, until one had taken the precaution of getting that absolving note which the girl had volunteered to give. Then the police could take the man in hand if he proved troublesome. These thoughts went on behind an unchanging face, expressionless almost, except for the keen eyes, and then Lord Inch decided that he had spent enough time in enduring this insolence.

" Well," he said, rising from his desk and moving across to the fireplace, within reach of the bell, " in my opinion, you have made a mistake in coming to discuss such a question as you suggest, and perhaps you will think so upon further consideration. I may say privately, and without prejudice, that if you choose, here and now, to drop this matter altogether, I am willing to make you a gift of fifty pounds to have done with it, and I shall think the kiss, which I understand to be the excuse for your visit, very handsomely paid for. I shall not repeat this offer. On the other hand, if you wish uselessly to discuss the matter to a greater extent, I must ask you to let me arrange some other time. I am very busy to-night, and believe that my clerk is waiting to come in. Shall we say fifty pounds ? I have no intention of raising my terms."

He paused with his hand stretched towards the bell, and looked at Rivers for his answer. But that individual did not seem tempted by his offer, and, indeed, was smiling in a way that Lord Inch did not understand.

" Come ! " the latter said, beginning to show impatience. " I will see the girl myself when I have time," he thought, watching Rivers. " If she be as sensible as Archie pretends, she shall have the fifty pounds privately, and this cur shall have none. Come ! " he said again, a little more loudly. " One way or the other, sir; I have other things to do."

" So have I," retorted Rivers, not moving from his chair, " and I mean to do them."

" That is well," Lord Inch told him, coolly. " You will think over this, and see that you have made a mistake."

He turned to the bell once more, promising himself that he would not be troubled with this scamp again, when a word stopped him.

"What about Bonville?" Rivers asked, and saw his question answered without words.

The hand that almost rested upon the bell hung motionless for some seconds, and then, slowly, stealthily, was drawn away. The face which had been turned from him came slowly round, as expressionless as a strong will could make it; as hard, but also as void of blood, as the marble mantel-piece behind it. The lips were set like iron, immovable, unbending. It might have been the still face of a dead man, but for the agonized eyes that glared across the room. Then, before either spoke again, a sharp spasm shot over the Judge's face, making the set lips open and writhe with pain. Lord Inch drew himself up breathless against the wall, standing as one might stand who saw death go by, and who drew away lest he should be touched by the far-sweeping scythe. There was no sound heard in that room except the striking of a clock, until, with a face which was calm again, but damp with sweat, he moved slowly away to a sofa and lay there, waving off Rivers, who moved forward with the notion of doing something, he did not know what. The blow had told far beyond the man's highest expectations. He seemed to be holding a stronger hand than he had imagined.

"That is over," Lord Inch said presently. "Of what were you speaking?"

"Bonville," Rivers told him suddenly, half-frightened by the ghastly effect of the word. "You seemed to hear it all right." And Lord Inch, watching from where he lay, felt that denial was useless.

"What of it?" he asked curtly. "Who are you?"

"You've had my name already," Rivers told him. "As for Bonville——" He stopped, staring hard at the Judge, who, he now felt, was completely in his power. "Well, as for Bonville, you and I were there together, and I thought I would warn you before I told my friend Mr. Archie among the rest."

However much this might hurt Lord Inch to hear, he showed nothing of his pain now.

"We were all there, I suppose," Rivers went on deliberately, "on a certain night that you and I are thinking of. But most of us only looked on. You and I know what *you* did." He was playing his hand now for all it was worth.

Lord Inch, lying back upon the sofa, said nothing, but, stretching out his hand, poured something from a bottle that stood within reach and drank it slowly, while Rivers watched.

"What then?" he asked quietly at last.

"What then!" his visitor echoed mockingly. "Why, nothing, I suppose. Nothing that all Edinburgh, all Scotland, mayn't hear; and, by God, they shall hear it too," he went on, maddened by the quiet way in which this man faced him. "All Scotland shall know that Lord Inch, one of Her Majesty's judges at the Parliament House, the 'Just Judge,' by the Lord! murdered a man twenty-five years ago. It may be nothing to you, but it will be news to a great many."

He finished off with a string of blasphemies and abuse, his voice rising as he went, and Lord Inch, still facing him with a firm air, held up a warning hand.

"You will——," he began hoarsely, and then stopped. His throat and lips were dry, he feared that his voice trembled, and he made another strong effort to pull himself together before he continued.

"You will rouse the house," he said presently, "and everyone will hear you. That, from your point of view, would be disadvantageous at the present stage. What do you want?"

" I'll think about it," Rivers told him. " I might have
let you off easy before, but I won't now. You're too pig-
headed, too high and mighty altogether. I'll take that
fifty pounds in the meanwhile. It will help to make my
Em'ly a little better prepared to sit at your lordship's table."

" Be careful," Lord Inch told him, warningly.

" Give me that fifty," Rivers repeated. " I've only to get
hold of the nearest reporter, and tell him what I know, and
it would ruin you. You could have me up for it if you
chose, and you know you wouldn't. Give me that fifty I
say, and I'll think it over before I come round again."

But whatever Lord Inch's faults might be, want of courage was certainly not one of them, and the same pride that
revolted against the proclamation of a fault a quarter of a
century old, rebelled still more against bending to a vulgar
bully like the one who stood before him.

" Understand me," he told Rivers. " Fifty pounds you
shall not have to-night, for any threat that you can think of,
or utter, or carry out. You fool ! what do you think life or
anything else would be worth to me, if I held them at the
mercy of such scum as you ? Do you think I have never
had such cases to deal with elsewhere ? Do you think I
do not know the tricks of your crew, your constant threats
and your constant extortions, until the man you haunt is
poorer in pocket and in reputation than the most naked
truth could have made him ? Here is a sovereign to keep
you from stealing for a week. Then come back, and you
shall know what I will and what I will not do—and you
can then act as you choose ! "

He tossed a sovereign on to the table, whence it fell to
the floor, and Rivers groped for it upon his hands and knees,
cursing as he crawled.

" It shall cost you thousands," he swore, as he got up
from the floor with the coin, and cursed again when Lord
Inch turned from him contemptuously.

" You have gone too far," the Judge told him as he resumed his seat at the desk. " Of two evils I am likely to choose the lesser. Oblige me by touching the bell, and remember that one word too much from you will at once end all negotiations between us."

Rivers might have power over this man, but he had neither the brain nor the nerve to use it profitably just then. He was prepared for nothing except equivocation and denial. To be defied in that contemptuous and desperate way confounded him utterly. He rang the bell as obediently as any lackey, pouring out threats to which Lord Inch listened outwardly unmoved, and which grew lower and lower, as he realized the danger of their being heard by anyone replying to the signal he had been ordered to make.

When Morris came, as he did presently, the visitor stood like a thunder-cloud at the mercy of the wind—undecided whether to break or be driven farther, while Lord Inch, at his desk, was deep in his papers.

" Ask Mr. McIntosh to be kind enough to come up now," Lord Inch told him. And, turning to Rivers, " I will see you next week at the same time if you wish."

There was no more said. Rivers followed the wondering Morris down the stair, feeling very much as if he had been somehow mastered by a weaker man, and went back to his room cursing all concerned, individually and collectively, 'Melia not excepted, and swearing that next week's meeting should be very much more profitable.

Lord Inch laid himself upon the sofa, and spent a few minutes in fighting down his own wild fears of he knew not what; then turning resolutely to the business in hand, he worked his best and his hardest until he could work no more.

# CHAPTER XXXII

## 'MELIA HAS A NEW CUSTOMER

WHEN Lord Inch came down to breakfast the next morning, he found Archie already in the room, and spoke at once.

" I had a little talk with the gentleman who is anxious to be your father-in-law," he told him, " but you must wait until I have more time to spare before I can talk to you. Meanwhile I rely upon your honor not to hold any communication with these people. That is all," and he said nothing more upon that or any other subject.

Archie having, as he put it dismally to himself, nothing better to do, went off presently to attend lectures, and at ten o'clock Lord Inch was in his place in the Justiciary Court. There, however, things went differently from what he had expected. Not that the case for the accused showed any improvement. Far from it. But his counsel, feeling that no common defence was possible, searched heaven and earth and all time for theories, arguments, and appeals. It was all to no purpose, as Lord Inch knew perfectly well. He would have to clear away every wild proposition a few hours hence, and meant to do so without mercy, but in the meanwhile he told himself that it was a man's life at stake, and sat far on into the evening, allowing the prisoner's counsel great latitude in his evidence, and listening patiently with a faint, almost unrecognized hope, that in the course of his wanderings the advocate might chance upon some point really worth considering. Then, at last, he rose and adjourned the Court. So the prisoner had a night more to hope and to fear in, but, being unimaginative, slept instead, which was quite as good. The jurymen were convoyed away, counsel went home, and Lord Inch, finding that it was a fine evening, sent on his brougham and walked down the Mound alone.

The day's proceedings had added very little to what he had considered fully the night before. There were one or two wild theories, which would collapse at a word. Meanwhile he would be glad if, for a time, he could put the matter entirely out of his mind, and an occupation at once occurred to him. Archie had told him where 'Melia was to be found, and that way he went.

He ran the risk of meeting Rivers, but Rivers, although Lord Inch did not know it, was quite safe for that evening, and indeed had not been near 'Melia for the day. Drink was the only consolation for him after the humiliation he had undergone the night before, and in the privacy of his own room he drank and schemed, and schemed and drank, until he could do neither the one nor the other.

He owed to his dear friend Peters a great part of what he drank, and it was Peters, too, who listened to his muttering, his vague threats, his half-confidences about someone whose name he always held back, but whom he would have down in the mud, or his name was not Rivers. This had lasted far on into the previous night, after his retreat from Drumsheugh Gardens. It began again with little variation the next morning, only he got confused in his maundering before he collapsed, and substituted "Buncombe" for "Rivers," at which the attentive Peters laughed amusedly, but said nothing. Then that morning he had fallen asleep in a drunken stupor, and Peters, after thinking awhile as if not knowing quite what to do, had kicked him very badly, and left him lying where he had rolled. Peters locked the door on the outside, and told Mrs. Jimps, as he went out, that Mr. Rivers wished on no account to be disturbed.

Rivers therefore had not been outside his room ; for, on waking, he had only risen, aching, from the floor, to reach his bed and fall into a less unnatural slumber ; but Peters

on leaving him went up to the Parliament House, which of
late he had visited often, and sat, attentive, until Lord Inch
came away. Then he came too, and followed him closely,
though with no particular end in view just then. It pleased
him, for reasons of his own, to watch this man's comings
and goings, unnoticed and unsuspected. If Lord Inch had
turned and looked, he would have seen nothing more than
the rather bulky figure of a neatly dressed foreign-looking
gentleman, who would have passed him, had he stopped,
with a calm face and no sign of interest.

But Lord Inch neither looked nor suspected. If he had
thought of being followed by anyone, Rivers was the only
man whom he would have suspected, and that would have
been to him a matter of indifference. So he went steadily
and rather slowly on, thinking that it was a good thing,
after all, that he had faithfully promised Maitland to take a
rest with the new year, and that if that scoundrel Rivers
came back to worry him again, Maitland should hear it.
After all, Maitland was a good fellow, and had lived too long
and too wide a life to judge harshly of a fault regretted for a
quarter of a century. Was it not said by some that a man
changed in every atom each seven years? Three times
seven, and over, say four times seven years had gone by,
every year, Lord Inch thought, a year of penitence with attempts at atonement ;—for the man could not help exag-
gerating the interval, and his own remorse, which had really
only reawakened a couple of years ago, just as he exaggerated, let us hope, his own crime, and the danger that he ran
of unending shame if Rivers should tell what he knew. Let
him, at least, have credit for greater courage than you or I
possibly might have shown, had we been in his place, and believed as he did; for Lord Inch was doggedly, desperately
determined that, come what might, Rivers should not be his
master, nor would he let his own trouble come between him
and his legal duties.

He broke off his unpleasant reflections to turn in at 'Melia's open door, another actor in the drama that was going on so slowly and yet so steadily under the indifferent gaze of the wooden Highlander. Peters, following not far behind, came no farther, but, after waiting for a few minutes to make sure that Lord Inch had not gone in by chance but with some intention, put two and two together with the help of what he had heard during the last twenty-four hours from Rivers, and turned homeward to see what the state of that worthy might be, and to tell him, perhaps, who was his daughter's latest customer.

# CHAPTER XXXIII

## AD AVISANDUM

'MELIA had passed a lonely and tearful day. It was one thing to roundly scold an impulsive young man for taking liberties, and quite another thing not to feel entirely deserted in consequence.

'Melia had been honestly angry, and was quite prepared to stand by all that she had said. She was secretly far too fond of Archie to get him into trouble. Still, a two days' absence following upon a declaration was not at all according to Life and Love, as set forth in her novels, nor did it at all agree with 'Melia's own ideas thereon. So she had cried a good deal that day in the little back room, bedewing the red settee with her tears, and drinking more tea than was good for her in vain attempts to keep up her spirits. Now, naturally, she had a bad headache, and was wishing that she could go home to bed, when the sound of a step in the shop brought her out.

It was a tired-looking elderly gentleman, with close-cut gray hair and a clean-shaven face, who asked for a good cigar, and leant upon the counter while 'Melia brought out different boxes from various corners, the dearer-priced cigars not being so commonly in request as mixtures and cigarettes.

Business is business, as 'Melia conscientiously felt, and a new customer must be treated properly, whether one had a headache or no. So 'Melia fetched out a cane-bottomed chair from behind the curtain, and placed it by the counter, so that the gentleman might sit comfortably and turn over the contents of the boxes.

16

" Yes, I'm tired," he told her, and seemed grateful to her for thinking of the chair. Then, after he had chosen a box, which he took a long time to do, asking her advice about them as he turned the cigars over, he began to chat of her work instead of going away.

" You look tired too," he told her, though what made him say that, 'Melia didn't know, seeing that he was always looking at the cigars.

" I'll go home and get to bed soon," she told him. " The place gets on one's nerves at times, sir."

" Yes, yes, I daresay," agreed the gentleman. " Now, I think I will have a box of those also. You said you could recommend them, did you not ? "

" They're milder than those you've got," 'Melia told him, " and fresh in."

" Let me see them again," and he pulled this fresh box over, and sniffed at the contents.

" The box is broken," she pointed out. " It's one short, but if you like them I've got another box not touched."

" I should not have counted," said the quiet gentleman, looking at her.

" You wouldn't need to, if you got 'em from me," said 'Melia.

" Honesty is the best policy, you believe ? " asked her visitor. " May I try one here ? "

" Oh, certainly," 'Melia told him, and snipped off the end of the cigar, and held a light to it, so that the tired gentleman needn't rise from the chair.

" As for honesty," she said, a little dismally, " I don't know if it pays or not. Sometimes it looks like it didn't."

She blinked tearfully, but the stranger was apparently trying his cigar with great care, and didn't seem to notice her.

" I'm sorry to hear that," he told her. " Your business doesn't prosper then ? "

" It's not mine," 'Melia explained, " and I think it's just a fancy of my master's and he can afford it anyway, though I try to make it pay. It wasn't that I was thinking of."

" Honesty has its reward in the long run," said the quiet gentleman, " if only it gain for its exponent an easy conscience."

" P'r'aps," said 'Melia doubtfully, not quite sure whether she understood, " but it's not always easy to say what's honesty. Your cigar's gone out, sir." She gave him another light.

" Oh, come now ! " the strange gentleman insisted, after thanking her, " the path of honesty is always quite plain to everyone."

There was a little hardness or bitterness, something that caught 'Melia's ear as he spoke, but he was looking at his cigar end, and showed no change of expression that 'Melia could see. She just shook her head dubiously, and the other noticed it at once.

" You don't agree with me ? Well, I may be wrong, of course, but I can't think of a case at the moment. I don't think you can either."

" Oh, there must be lots," 'Melia insisted, but, upon being challenged, could remember or imagine none but the particular instance she had in her mind, which she tried to modify for the occasion, since the quiet gentleman was still quite sure that she couldn't give him an example.

" S'posin'," she suggested at last, " that another young lady, only better off you know, say my master's daughter, wanted to be *very* friendly, and s'posin' I felt friendly too, but knew it wasn't for her good, should I show what I feel, or should I pretend I didn't care a fig for her ? "

" But that's an impossible case, my dear young lady," said the quiet gentleman, watching his cigar go out again without any movement to stop it, " your master's daughter could take no harm from you."

"Thank you, sir," said 'Melia, blushing and blinking again. It was so pleasant to have something kind said when everyone was against her. "Let's say my master's son, then. It's all the easier to say because he hasn't got one that I know of, nor any other men-folk."

"Ah! that case is not so easy after all," her visitor admitted, and sat staring at the dead ash of his cigar in silence.

"There, you see, sir, it's easy to think of such a thing," 'Melia pointed out with an air of melancholy triumph, "though, as I say, it doesn't matter, for there's no such gentleman belonging to my master at all."

It might not matter, but 'Melia's voice sounded rather as if it did. She thought as much, and was glad the gentleman didn't seem to notice things.

"Supposing our friend the master's son did exist," he asked presently, "have you got a case then? What would be the good of pretending you had no interest in him, if you were fond of him?"

"When you're fond of people you don't want to hurt 'em, do you?" asked 'Melia rather hotly, and the quiet gentleman looked at her rather curiously again.

"No one ever accused me of being fond of people," he said dryly, and got up to go. "Well," he told her, "the problem of your master's son, who, I will remember, doesn't exist, interests me. I'm often consulted in other people's private affairs, but they're mostly arguing their own interests, and don't say much about those of the other side that sounds as if they cared for them. May I think the thing over and come in again some time?"

"Oh, cert'nly," said 'Melia, "and will you take your cigars with you, or shall I leave them at your house?"

"You might send them," he began, and then stopped, remembering that it involved giving an address.

"No, I'll take them with me," he told her, and then

stopped again, finding that he chanced not to have enough money in his pocket.

"I haven't enough money to pay for them," he added. "I think I must leave them with you till I come again, since I am a stranger."

"Oh, that's all right," said 'Melia reassuringly. "We get to know who's to be trusted. You can take 'em if you don't mind the trouble. Only you might pay for that one extra, though you haven't half smoked it. You won't light up again, will you? They say it's horrid to do that with a half-smoked cigar, but still it's a sixpence half wasted, as you may say."

But her visitor refused to light up again. He laid down a sixpence, and, taking up the two boxes, wished her goodnight.

"The case of this gentleman—who doesn't exist," he suggested from the doorway, "would not be worth thinking out unless one were quite sure that one wished to do the best thing for him. We must look after ourselves, you know."

"Oh, quite sure about that," 'Melia told him, "and you'll come in again if you like the cigars, won't you? I don't always talk such silly stuff with customers either, and I can't tell why you let me."

"Good-night. I'll come again," said the quiet gentleman, and, lifting his hat quite politely, stepped out into the darkness.

"That's a nice sort of gentleman," 'Melia decided. "Nice and chatty, with no nonsense about him. I'd trust him with more than two boxes of cigars. Might as well have had his name though, for all that. What a silly fool I am! As long as anyone 'll talk, or listen, for the matter of that, I'm satisfied. He's made the time pass, anyway, that's one comfort."

Then she made an entry of the two boxes, leaving the

name blank, and was glad to find that her head was not so
bad, and that she could close the place in a couple of hours.
So, determined not to let herself get dismal again, she took
up a book at once to read until she could shut up and go
away " home."

# CHAPTER XXXIV

## MINISTERING TO A MIND DISEASED

LORD INCH went down the street with his two boxes of cigars, feeling rather ashamed. However excellent a man's motive is, he cannot well be proud of having spied upon a girl.

'Melia's friendly way of chatting, and the unsuspicious way in which she let him know just what he wanted, showed the better in contrast with his own methods of procedure.

He had gone there expecting to find a brazen-faced young person who would be ready to deceive him or defy him, whichever she found most easy and most profitable. Instead, here was a pleasant-faced, good-natured girl, whose weak points were probably the result of environment and education, or non-education. It was of no use that he told himself the girl must be a silly fool, to chatter like that with the first stranger who dropped in. Her chatter wouldn't have had the least significance to any other stranger, and Lord Inch felt that her simplicity and honesty had been more apparent than his own during the interview. It was a comfort to know that she would be no consenting party to her father's tricks, and to be sure that, if Rivers could only be cajoled, or thwarted, the whole thing would be settled. It would be quite easy to get a formal note from her, denying that she had the least claim upon the youngster. Lord Inch could remind her, if necessary, not only of her message to him through Archie, but also of this evening's chat.

She was far too simple to think of denying that Archie

was the person whose welfare she was considering so anxiously.

After all, she seemed a well-meaning girl, and she should
be well treated. Lord Inch would call, himself, and talk it
over with her, and see that she was not the loser. On second
thoughts, since there might be a scene (and it was not
pleasant to think of facing her as she discovered who had
been her sympathetic customer), he would write, sending a
cheek for the boxes with such a letter as would bring the
desired acquittal of Archie. Then her father, how could
he be guarded against ? Lord Inch must think that over,
say to-morrow night, if he felt able after his work in Court,
which he doubted. Maitland might be consulted safely.
Maitland never preached, and never set up to be better
than other men ; and by the time these thoughts had
crossed his mind, Lord Inch was at his own door.

It was long past their ordinary dinner-hour, and he was
told that Mr. Archie, after waiting some time, had taken
something to eat and had gone out.

Lord Inch felt that this was a relief. His work justified
a refusal to have any discussion until to-morrow night.
He had no wish for dinner, and went straight to his study,
giving orders that wine and biscuits should be brought
there.

But he could not get the business off his mind to-night
as he had done last night. It kept recurring to him while
he sipped his wine, and at last, dreading lest it should really
affect the careful consideration of to-morrow's work, he decided that he must give his confidence to someone—a sure
way of getting relief. He had promised to let Maitland
know if anything followed the type-written letter. To
share the secret with a cool-headed friend would be to
lessen his troubles, and would clear his mind for his work,
which must have undivided attention.

So he sent round for Maitland, without making any further attempt to put off the evil day, which did not now seem altogether evil, and in a quarter of an hour Maitland came.

" The writer of that letter has followed it up," Lord Inch explained, directly the servant had left the room. " He's at my throat, Alec."

" Well," Maitland told him, quietly, " it's a comfort that he's not at your back. Let's hear the whole story and see what's to be done. That's your notion, is it not ? "

" Yes, it has come to that," Lord Inch told him. " The fact is, I have fought shy of you, Alec, but to-night I have more important matters to think of than how to save my miserable skin, and yet I cannot tackle my work with this thing on my mind. I can try no more ! "

" Come then," Maitland answered, wheeling the sofa round. " Rest you there. I've brought my pipe. I may smoke I suppose ? "

" Of course, do anything you like, so long as you'll bear with me for half an hour, and not be too hard on me after."

" I'm no lawyer ! " Maitland growled under his breath.

" Eh, what's that ? " Lord Inch asked.

" Who am I, to be hard on you or any other body ? " Maitland asked more loudly. " Fire away ! "

So Lord Inch told his story, at first hesitatingly, explaining, excusing, but afterwards speaking more directly, starting from the Bonville days, and bringing the tale up to date. He became half apologetic when telling of that evening's chat with 'Melia, but he missed nothing of importance, and lay back with a sigh of relief when he had finished.

Maitland smoked uninterruptedly through it all, and said nothing until he saw that the story was ended.

" What like is he, this Bonville friend of yours ? " he asked at the end of it all.

"A swaggering bully," Lord Inch told him. "A tallish man with black hair and mustache, and shifty eyes. Calls himself an Oxford man, and dresses like a swell mobsman. He's a broken-down swindler, a low blackguard. Mind you, Maitland, the man shall not rule me. It would be a greater disgrace to be his puppet than to let him say all he could. I've confessed to you, I'll confess to all the world before that!"

"Patience! We'll manage him," Maitland said soothingly, remembering the figure he had looked down upon through the fog from that same room. "What's his own history? A fellow doesn't begin to be a blackguard at his time of life. He's your age or thereabouts, isn't he?"

"He must be, thereabouts," Lord Inch answered, "but what his record is I cannot tell you. I wish I could, though it is not likely that would alter things. If the fellow accuses me publicly, Alec, I'll not deny it, though he be fifty times a liar and a scoundrel."

"D'ye think I'd advise it?" Maitland retorted a little hotly, but quieted down at once. "What I mean is, that a scoundrel like that may have something on his conscience that would clear him out of the country at the double, if he thought it was known."

"I cannot tell," Lord Inch said, gloomily. "I don't remember the man. All Bonville was about, that wretched night. I have not been able to think the thing over yet, since he was here."

Maitland's attention had just been drawn to the decanter and biscuits on the table, and he pointed to them.

"What does that mean?" he asked.

"I was taking some wine just before you came in. Let me ring for another glass."

"Not for me. What I want to know is, when did you dine?"

"Well, I cannot say that I have had a regular dinner.

It is of no use frowning at me, Maitland, for I could not help it. Work is work."

"Ay! and break-down is break-down, as you'll find," Maitland retorted, grimly. "What have you had?"

"Well, I had a basin of soup for lunch," Lord Inch told him with an apologetic air, while Maitland scowled very much as an irate dominie might at a careless pupil, "and a cup of tea later."

"Mere wash!" Maitland told him, scornfully. "I know what you'll have had. As much nourishment in the soup as in the cup of tea maybe!"

"What could I do?" Lord Inch asked, querulously. "I must keep my head clear. You wouldn't have me snore on the bench, would you, while a man's life was fought for? If I fed like a pig, I should judge like a pig."

"If you feed like a woman, you'll judge like one," Maitland snapped at him. "Then, why didn't you have a sensible meal when you came in?"

"I was very late, and I went, as I have told you, to see that girl. I had no appetite after that, and besides I have a great deal to do to-night."

"How are you to do it?" Maitland growled. "Man, you're feeding on your own brains. I'll away down to your kitchen presently, and risk the rolling-pin over my head for being a poking old fool who doesn't know his place. Mind, you'll take what comes up!"

"Yes, I'll take it," Lord Inch promised him. "But what are we going to do about all this, Alec?"

"Nothing—to-night," Maitland declared. "I'm your confessor and your judge. The whole thing's on my shoulders, and I'm away home to smoke a pipe over it, after I've been to the kitchen."

He rose and held out his hand.

"You will shake hands still, then?" Lord Inch asked.

"Havers!" Maitland told him, brusquely. "That comes

of dirty water and tea! D'ye want a penance to satisfy
your soul before I've thought it all out, and had another
chat with you?"

"I will do anything to please you, Alec. It will be little
enough, I know, for the trouble you have with me."

"Be gentle with yon lassie in the tobacconist's then,
Inch. It's not for the likes of you or me to visit the sins
of the fathers on the children. She's a good lassie, I'm
thinking."

"Yes, yes, I believe she is," Lord Inch agreed. "But
what would you have me do, Alec? I mustn't commit
myself."

"Send her a line, man, along with the money for those,"
pointing to the unopened boxes on the desk. "Sign it with
your own name, and tell her you'll be round again at the
week end. Let her know it's private, and if she's the girl
you and Archie have found her, she won't let a soul know,
and she'll respect you all the more."

"Very well, to please you," said Lord Inch. "I must not
commit myself, but I'll do that, Maitland. The girl is a
good girl, and I don't bear her any malice. What she sees
in the boy, I don't know."

"Man," said Maitland, impatiently, "do you think he
shows himself to you as he does to her? The boy's right
enough."

"It is possible the girl is," Lord Inch allowed. "She
might be the making of him, if she had been of decent
people, with a little money of her own. Even as it is, I
wonder at her fancy. It is partly his position, I suppose."

"I never met the man yet," said Maitland, "who wasn't
concerned at the unspeakable blindness of the women-folk
—towards other men. As for his station, d'ye think she'd
be so ready to let him go, if that was all?"

Then, "Havering again, you old fool!" he muttered to
himself, as he made for the door, turning for a last word

when he reached it. " Now this business is off your conscience, Inch, and it has become my affair, I'll think it out, and see you before that blackguard calls for you again. Mind that line to the lassie, and see that you follow cook's orders. She'll get them from me."

He left, and presently some light food came up, with directions from the doctor that he was to take it quietly, and not to begin work for half an hour. Also that there would be something ready for him to take before going to bed. So Lord Inch meekly did as he was told, and then worked away at his papers until far into the night. Then he wrote a little note, inclosing a check, to 'Melia, and, addressing it, put it inside the desk ; and Morris, in the small hours, patient because of a word that Maitland had had with him, brought up something more from the kitchen, and Lord Inch, with a sigh of relief as he thought of the sharer of his secret, went to his bed.

As he passed along the corridor he saw a light in the smoking-room, and hesitated at the door.

Archie must be there, and, if he went in, something would be said of the day's doings. The boy must wait.

He went softly a little way past the door and along the passage, then stopped again. The silly fellow must be sitting up on the chance of seeing him, and, having heard nothing, would wait longer. After all, the youngster had been patient. It was enough to try to court sleep that night burdened with one man's unspoken fate, though that man was a criminal.

The boy, who at any rate was no criminal, should wait no longer, and Lord Inch turned back.

He pushed the smoking-room door open quietly, and went in.

By the ashes of a burnt-out fire, fast asleep, with his yellow head resting on the table, his pipe lying where it had fallen upon the floor, lay Archie. His father stood over him, watching gravely for a moment before speaking. Archie was sleeping so soundly now, his face was so quiet and untroubled, that Lord Inch felt sorry to wake him, and did so gently enough.

The boy started up, rubbing his eyes.

" Hullo ! I didn't hear you, father. What's the time ? "

He looked at the clock, and then at Lord Inch again.

" Two o'clock, and you're not in bed ! What'll Dr. Maitland say to this ? He told me you wanted rest more than anything."

" Never mind me," Lord Inch told him, surprised that Archie should think of him at all. " It is time you were in bed too. We will both go after we have had a talk."

" Not now," Archie declared. " I saw Maitland after he left you, and promised I'd not see you to-night."

" Then, for what are you waiting ? " Lord Inch asked incredulously.

" Oh, well, I thought I might as well stay up a bit," Archie told him in rather a shamefaced way. " I got thinking." and Lord Inch, who, a week ago, would have sneered at the suggestion of thought from Archie, now said nothing. He had no idea that Archie was there because Maitland had told him to keep an eye upon his father that night, and see that he got quietly off to bed when his work was done.

" He shall drop work directly this trial is over." Maitland had told Archie on the doorstep. " Promise me, laddie, that he goes straight to his bed and talks of nothing to-night."

So Archie promised, and had been paying half-hourly visits to the study key-hole until he fell asleep.

" Well." Lord Inch said, curious, perhaps, to see how far Archie's self-control went, " I called on Miss Rivers to-day."

" You did ! "

"I did," said Lord Inch. "She's a good girl, I believe, Archie, and a sensible girl. I've great respect for her. But——"

He was going to seat himself in the easy-chair from which Archie had risen, and to explain matters, who knows how far, but Archie stopped him, having Maitland's warnings still fresh in his memory.

"I'm glad to hear it, father," he said, trying to speak quietly. "You can see she's pretty too, and she's as good as she's pretty. You'll like her more the more you know of her. We can't talk of that now though. You must go to bed. Maitland said so."

Lord Inch stared incredulously, but Archie persisted.

"Doctor's orders," he told his father quietly, and Lord Inch gave way, wondering sleepily where the boy got that new authoritative manner, and where his own will had gone. Perhaps the brew of hot wine, brought up half an hour before from the kitchen, had something to do with it. At anyrate, he did not argue the point, but went to his room, wishing Archie a more affectionate good-night than usual at the door ; and Archie went off, being wide awake now, to smoke another pipe, and wonder, uselessly, about his father's interview with 'Melia.

# CHAPTER XXXV

## LABOR IN VAIN

WHEN Mr. Peters had satisfied himself that Lord Inch was not merely a chance customer for 'Melia, he went back to the House of Residence much more quickly than usual. Still, as he went, he found breath enough to hum the quaint little tune which was, for him, significant of certain trains of thought. The air was a common one, still heard, occasionally, on old barrel-organs. " O bianca e fredda "—(Oh, pale and cold), Mr. Peters hummed, and his thoughts travelled across the sea as his voice rose.

Going up the stairs, he felt in his pocket for the key of Rivers' room, and laughed.

" The good Rivers will be hungry, to despair," he told himself, and seemed pleased at the notion, which, however, was not correct.

He found Rivers crouched over the fire, sober enough now, but not at all hungry, and with a splitting headache that made him quite useless to Peters.

That gentleman saw the state of things, but spoke unconcernedly.

" My poor Rivers," he said, " you are hungry ? "

" I'm not," Rivers told him sullenly, " but I'm as sore as if I had been beaten like a carpet."

" It will be rheumatism," suggested Peters. " You would sleep on the floor, but now you are better, and should take exercise. Will you not come out ? "

" Not I ! " Rivers told him, with an oath. " This climate's killing me. I'll go back to the States. I wish I was dead ! "

This aspiration amused Peters beyond measure. He shouted with laughter, and paid not the slightest attention to the other, who, growing angry, cursed him effusively.

"The good Rivers is ready for Heaven," he announced, "but we cannot let him go yet. What a pity that he cannot take the place of the man who will be told to-morrow that he must die!"

He still laughed, but there was nothing about his face to provoke laughter in others. It had the effect of silencing the curses of Rivers, who looked at him with a maudlin puzzled air.

"What are you laughing about?" he asked. "Who must die?"

"Oh, no one who matters," Peters told him; "they say that at the Court to-morrow a man will be told that he shall die for killing someone. That is all. It is just, is it not? You are a scholar, my good Rivers. Teach a poor foreigner! What is it your Scripture tells you? 'Whosoever slayeth——' How does it go?"

"'Whosoever sheddeth man's blood, by man shall his blood be shed,'" Rivers told him, and bent nearer the fire, shivering.

"Ah! that is just," Peters agreed, and then sat down and bent over the fire too, as if cold, leaning forward until his face was close to Rivers' face.

"That is just," he repeated, "and so it is certain that is what the Just Judge will tell him to-morrow."

He watched, but Rivers had never heard of the Just Judge, and made no movement except to rub his hands, and then stretch them towards the blaze.

"Who was that pretty boy we drank with two nights ago, my good Rivers?" he asked suddenly.

"Mr. Archibald Inch," Rivers told him, his bemuddled brain still occupied with his own thoughts.

17

"Ah, it will be his father, then, who is the Just Judge," Peters observed quietly, and it was now Rivers' turn to laugh, as he twisted round.

"Is that what they call him?" he sneered.

"Yes. Why not?" asked Peters placidly, and Rivers sneered again.

"The Just Judge!" he repeated: "why, I could tell you things—that I may tell you some day, but not now," and with that he lapsed into silence, and brooded over the fire, while Peters watched him.

"They are rich, are they not?" Peters asked presently. "It will be good for your daughter to have the family Inch for customers, is it not so?"

"Perhaps Archie will be a good customer in the end," said Rivers, with a grin.

"And the father," asked Peters, innocently, "does he go to Miss Rivers for his tobacco?"

"He doesn't go there at all," Rivers said. "What do you mean?"

"I saw him there to-night," Peters told him, and with an oath Rivers started from his chair.

For a moment Peters, who had quite given up hope of rousing the man, and was only amusing himself in his own peculiar way, really thought that he was going out, and, laughing to himself, he determined to follow and see what was to be seen. But Rivers sank back into his chair almost at once, too muddled for any prompt action.

"I have not seen Miss Rivers since we had our most merry meeting," Peters suggested, frowning a little. "Shall we pay our respects?"

"You can go if you like," Rivers told him, turning his back and crouching over the fire again. "Give my compliments to Lord Inch if you find him there, and say that I shall do myself the honor of seeing him soon. Goodnight!"

" The good Rivers ! " Peters soliloquized in the softest of
voices, standing over him and smiling down. " He turns
me out ! Ah, well. Good-night, my Rivers ! I will pay
my respects, and yours, to your daughter, and to Lord Inch
if I am not too late," and he went away without remembering, or at anyrate seeming to care, that he, too, had eaten
no dinner.

As he passed down, Mrs. Jimps opened her door, and
beckoned him in.

" I've the tenderest steak, Captain Peters, kept ready to
send up to your room. You aren't going out again surely !
Think ! A rump-steak and fried potatoes."

Mrs. Jimps smiled upon him bewitchingly, and at the
same time with a touch of melancholy, as of one with hope
deferred, but Mr. Peters was obdurate.

" I am away," he told Mrs. Jimps. " I have no heart for
food, my best Mrs. Jimps."

" How is that, Captain Peters ? " Mrs. Jimps asked
tremulously, feeling that the question might seem intru-
sive, the causes for loss of appetite being so various. But
Mr. Peters would not gratify her curiosity. He said merely
that he hoped to be better very soon now, and went on his
way, leaving Mrs. Jimps to wonder, in solitude, whether
anything she could say would be likely to expedite a cure.

# CHAPTER XXXVI

## MR. PETERS MAKES A PROMISE

Do what she would, 'Melia could not settle down to her book that night, after her sympathetic new customer had left. Why hadn't Archie, or her father, or even Cap'n Peters been in? If it had not been for Rivers' strict commands that 'Melia was never to call for him at the House of Residence, she would have made up her mind to go there on her way home. As it was, she was the more restless because she couldn't go. There was a high wind that night, and it made itself heard even in this back street, whistling about the keyholes, and moaning down the chimney of 'Melia's little back-room, now and then puffing out a cloud of smoke, and making her uncomfortable, as well as more nervous and melancholy than ever.

She was beginning to wonder whether, after all, to have a good cry wouldn't be the most profitable way of passing the last half-hour before closing the shop. She was beginning to feel, too, that she had very little choice but to cry, when Peters came in, and had a hearty welcome.

"I thought you'd all forgotten me!" 'Melia told him, and then wondered how much he knew of her last encounter with Archie and her father. "Where's father?" she demanded.

"He has a cold," Peters explained, "and sits by the fire with a hot something-to-drink."

At this 'Melia was no better satisfied. She fidgeted a little, looking at Peters and looking away again, but spoke at last.

"I want to talk to you, straight," she told him. "You and I are friends, aren't we? If I want you to sit still an'

listen, I must make you comfortable, so's you'll be patient.
Come inside an' sit down. I don't think there's any smoke
to speak of in there now."

Peters looked at her, wondering what she was going to
say, but made no answer, and, following her behind the
curtain, sat down upon the old red settee, which creaked
under his weight.

"I can speak plain ?" 'Melia asked. "We *are* friends,
ain't we ?" and waited, somewhat to Peters' surprise, for
an answer.

"How can I tell ?" he said at last, shrugging his shoulders. "A very clever man told me, when I was so high,"
and he held his cigar some four feet from the ground, "that
our friends are those who are useful. Am I useful ?"

"Why, yes !" 'Melia told him, indignantly, "'course you
are. Didn't you teach me to bike, and ain't you a friend of
father's ? I don't like your clever men's sayin's though.
They're like lemonade with the sugar left out. Maybe very
healthy, and maybe not, I can't tell. But there's a nasty
sharp taste. Judgin' by that, I'm no friend o' yours. I'm
never of no use to no one, unless it's those who pay me to
do this job. I've done nothin' for you."

"Pardon ! a great deal," Peters assured her solemnly.
"You introduce me to your excellent father, the good
Rivers, a gentleman of Oxford, and to that clever and
amiable young gentleman, Mr. Archie. They are to me—
the wanderer, the homeless man—as equals. We drink together like brothers."

"That's just it !" 'Melia interrupted. "That's what I
want to talk about. There was a lot too much of it two
nights ago, Cap'n Peters, and I can't have it here again."

"Did I drink too much ?" Peters asked, quietly.

"No, Cap'n Peters, I don't say as you did," 'Melia told
him apologetically. "But Mr. Inch did. *He* came round
an' said so."

"That was foolish of him," Peters suggested. "Why did he come round and say that?"

"Well," 'Melia said, carefully smoothing a crease out of the red table-cloth, "I s'pose he thought I'd like to know he was sorry."

Peters watched, smoking his cigar in silence, until the crease was thoroughly disposed of, and 'Melia looked up at him. She dropped her eyes again, however, on meeting his.

"And the good Rivers," he asked presently, "has he been round to say that he had too much, and is sorry?"

"Now, Cap'n Peters, I won't be talked to in that tone of voice," 'Melia told him, sharply. "No, it's no use," she went on, as Peters seemed inclined to protest, "I won't, and so I tell you. It may be my foolishness, but there's times when I think you're foolin' me. My father's my father, and I won't have him laughed at. So, there!"

"If I laughed to you at your father, I did foolishly," said Peters, and 'Melia was pacified.

"I want to talk to you about 'im," she went on, "now we understand one another, and I can trust you."

"My clever friend," Mr. Peters told her, "said he could trust no one."

"Pore chap!" said 'Melia, pityingly, "he must 'ave 'ad a time, but we can't help that. Now, about father. You know I don't scarcely know him better than you do."

"I know," Peters agreed readily.

"And I'm kept a prisoner in this place too," said 'Melia, looking round with a shrug. "Now, I wish you'd help me with him, Cap'n Peters."

"How?" asked Peters.

"Well, you know, p'raps he's told you, and I can trust you anyway. He's got some business here, Cap'n Peters. I don't know what it is, but he says he's goin' to make a lot of money."

" I know," Peters told her, nodding.

" Well, if he did that," said 'Melia, cheering up at the thought of it, and putting Archie out of the question, at anyrate for the moment, " 'course I'd leave the shop, I s'pose, and look after him ? "

She looked at Peters for approval, and he nodded.

" As things is—are, I mean, I can't," she went on. " Now, you're a big strong man, and when you make up your mind to a thing, you'll do it, won't you ? "

" Yes," said Peters, without any hesitation.

" Well, I want you to keep him out of mischief for me. Will you ? " she continued. " There's been bad times for both of us, you know, and bein' a gentleman, well, he feels more of a difference than me, who've never had things much different, except for mother. Maybe in lively company, like t'other night, he drinks a bit. I don't know, but if he does, it's to drown things, as you may say."

" It is possible," Mr. Peters allowed.

" Well, will you help me ? " 'Melia demanded. " I'd do a good turn for you if I could, Cap'n Peters."

" Help, how ? "

" Keep an eye on him, so that he doesn't get into trouble," 'Melia suggested, " and see if you can help to settle his business."

" That is all you want me to promise ? " asked Peters, rising and stretching to his full height, with his hands above his head as if cramped. " That is all ? "

" That's all ! " said 'Melia, after reflection, " and very kind of you, too, Cap'n Peters, if you'll take the trouble."

" To keep an eye on him," repeated Peters, " and to help to finish his business as quickly as possible ? "

" So as I may take care of him," added 'Melia. " Will you do it ? "

" Yes," Peters promised. " I will always keep an eye on him, and help to finish his business as quickly as possible."

and he added some words that 'Melia didn't understand. " It is an oath," he explained. " I wish all evil may come to me if I break it."

" That's the way, I've read in books, with you foreign gentlemen," said 'Melia, with regret. " It's not English you know, and I don't know as I like it so well."

Mr. Peters shrugged his shoulders, and, seeming to think he heard someone in the shop, pushed aside the curtain and stood looking out.

" There is no one there," 'Melia assured him. " I'm that used to all the noises, that I'd know in a jiffy. Come now, none o' your foreign swears over this little job. I give it you back. Say ' yes,' and shake hands on it, English fashion ? "

Mr. Peters, still looking out into the shop, and not speaking very clearly, assured her that it was " yes " a thousand times, but did not turn round, and seemed to be unaware of her outstretched hand.

He began asking her about her day's work, whether the business was improving fast, and what customers had been in that evening. But he began to move out almost as he spoke, and got beyond the curtain before 'Melia realized that he was going.

" What's the hurry ? " she asked.

" I'm hungry," he told her, over his shoulder. " Talking makes me hungry. Good-night to you, I am going."

Sure enough, he was not only going, but gone, before 'Melia reached the door.

" There's a queer man ! " she soliloquized, watching until he passed under a lamp and disappeared in the shadows beyond. " Talkin' makes 'im 'ungry ! W'y, I b'lieve 'twas me did the talkin.' P'r'aps he meant listening. Or p'r'aps he was sick of it. My, Sandy ! " (addressing the mull-offering gentleman at her side), " it's long after eleven, and a good thing he's gone anyway. If he'd stayed on, I'd have

chattered no end. I expect you're the only safe one to hear
about one's young man, ain't you ? Come awa' ben, then ! "

This invitation was 'Melia's only attempt at the vernac-
ular, and was never addressed to anyone save Sandy. She
wheeled him into the shop, and made a prettier picture than
she knew of, as she went on tiptoe, and bestowed a kiss upon
the unmoved face.

" There ! go to sleep, dearie," she told him. " I'll away
home to my supper and bed, like Cap'n Peters," and five
minutes later she was scurrying down the street, trying not
to worry any more just then about Archie. Thinking grate-
fully, too—while a rude wind whistled about her ankles,
and played pranks with her petticoats—what a good thing
it was that Cap'n Peters had promised to keep an eye on
her father, and wondering whether the pair would have
a chat that night, after Cap'n Peters had got something to
eat.

But, that night, Peters neither took anything to eat, nor
saw her father. He did not even go straight back to the
House of Residence. The promise exacted by 'Melia had
been given by him in a very different spirit from that in
which she had asked it, and Peters, thinking over that and
other affairs, which were creeping to their settlement all too
slowly, felt himself getting beyond control. He would walk
it off, he thought, and hurried away against the wind. But
he only went, scarcely conscious, as far as Drumsheugh
Gardens, where he passed and repassed No. 45, attracted,
time after time, by the steady light in Lord Inch's study,
until at last he remembered that there would be danger in
drawing the attention of the constable on the beat, and
returned, cursing, to his room.

But there, too, torment awaited him. Before he reached
his own door he could hear Rivers, snoring in the room
opposite. Twice he touched the handle of that opposite
door, and twice he drew away. Then with a sudden effort

he tramped noisily into his own room, and, slamming the
door behind him, locked it and threw the key, anywhere,
so long as it was out of his sight.

He took down the long-stemmed, small-bowled pipe from
the mantel-piece, and, filling it hurriedly, began to smoke
even before he drew a chair to the fire, as though he could
no longer live or breathe without the drug. He knew it to
be a dangerous remedy. He knew that in exchange for
present peace he would have greater temptation later, with
a weakened will to withstand it; but the need was urgent,
and he smoked on desperately. Things might have gone
otherwise had he been able to restrain himself that night.
Whether they would have gone better, is another question.
He smoked on and on, until his limbs, big as they were,
could not have carried him across the room. Yet—either
because he miscalculated his dose or because of a long fast
—although the body seemed to sleep, stretched out in the
easy-chair before a dying fire, the brain was more active
than ever. Gorgeous schemes, stupendous ideas, floated
before him, while no difficulty was imagined but what it
was overcome by a single effort of the tremendous will of
which he found himself suddenly possessed. He was the
autocrat of autocrats that night. All the earth was his for
a footstool, and its inhabitants were worms in the dust before him. The cold wintry dawn found Mr. Peters shivering before an empty grate, and promising himself that
never, at least until he had done all that he came to do,
would he be such a weak fool again. But it was too late.

# CHAPTER XXXVII

## VOX, ET PRÆTEREA NIHIL!

It was a gray morning that opened over the gray, cold city. The sky gave warning of snow, and the chill east wind told the same tale.

Lord Inch felt the influence of the weather as he drove up to the Parliament House that morning alone in his brougham, meeting the day's work with a face as gray as the sky, and as cold.

He thought of the prisoner who would presently front him in the dock, and had a grim satisfaction in imagining that surely, on such a day as this, with winter just upon us, it could not be so hard to hear that one must die as it would be when summer was felt through the land.

The Parliament House, too, was cold and shadowy. Gas glimmered in the corridors and in the Courts, with patches of light here and seas of shadow there, but all cold and hard.

When everyone rose at the macer's cry, as Lord Inch came in and took his seat, some faces stood out sharply defined, while others were vague and blurred, and the Judge, peering into the shadows, presently found himself wondering if his private troubles would dog him in his public capacity.

There was no face that he knew, save those already familiar either in connection with the Courts or with this particular case, and having satisfied himself of that, as well as the light allowed, Lord Inch was ashamed at his own weakness, and bent all his attention to the speech of the prosecuting counsel. He already understood that he would

be able to sum up a little after mid-day, and intended to
finish before lunch. He felt that the sooner it was over
the better for all concerned. The verdict could be brought
in at once, and then he would go home and try to make up
for the long hours of the last few days, while the prisoner
there in the dock——!

The Solicitor-General was driving nails into the fellow's
coffin with cold precision. The man himself, dull as he was,
seemed to feel it, and Lord Inch saw him breathe deeply
and look round as though he felt Death's hand upon his
shoulder, and found no one to help him.

The faces of the fifteen jurymen hardened, as they, too,
saw clearly what was to be done, and braced themselves to
do it. When the accuser sat down Lord Inch sighed, partly
from relief. There would be very little left for him to say
after that. Then he changed his position, and faced the
counsel for the defence.

The latter did not take very long. There was no hope in
denying the crime. He dwelt upon the imagined provocation, upon the awful responsibility of condemning a fellow-
man to die, upon the weak barrier, not of their own raising,
which the best of men had sometimes found to be all that
stood between them and like crimes. Let them be merciful,
he begged, as they hoped for mercy ; then he sat down,
thankful that it was over, and feeling sure, from the fifteen
set faces opposite, that his words had been useless.

There was a rustle and a low hum through the Court, as
people shifted in their seats and settled themselves to hear
Lord Inch's summing up. While he glanced at his notes
before addressing the jury, there was a slight scuffle in the
body of the Court, caused by a man forcing himself into
what he thought would be a better position. One, whose
foot was trodden upon as the fellow pushed by, complained
loudly, and Lord Inch, looking up with a frown, saw who it
was that caused all the commotion. It was Rivers.

He had fought into the place he wanted, and sat facing
Lord Inch with a stupid leer of recognition, in which the
latter thought he saw an open threat. Had he the foolish
presumption to imagine that, by sitting there, forcing himself into notice, as Lord Inch saw he did, he could disturb
a judge at his work ? Did the rascal think him so weak a
man as that ? For a few seconds they stared across at one
another, Rivers simply smiling, Lord Inch pale with anger,
while those around wondered why his lordship delayed.
Should he order the fellow to be turned out ? He thought
of doing so, and then put the idea aside as contemptible.
The scoundrel should see how little he could do after all ;
and Lord Inch faced the jury again, and directed them as to
their duty in this matter.

Men said, afterwards, that never had they known the Just
Judge to be so pitiless. None of them knew that, to the
man upon the bench, it seemed as if he saw before him—
though he never turned to look at Rivers again—a sneering
face which dared him to do his duty. His voice sounded
solemnly through the hushed Court, every word falling
separately and distinctly. He pointed out the unfounded
nature of the jealousy which was the prisoner's sole excuse,
the relentless and cold-blooded brutality with which the
crime was accompanied, the absence of all sign of remorse
after it. He put all suggestions of mercy relentlessly
aside.

" We are not here," he told them. " to be merciful, but to
be just, acting in accordance with the laws of our country.
What will follow upon your verdict must in nowise concern
you, provided that verdict is according to your conscience,
as it undoubtedly will be. Think of the consequences to
the prisoner at the bar only in so far as it is needful to make
you weigh the evidence carefully and impartially. It is for
you, as for everyone else concerned in this case, myself included, to do your duty, each man with a solemn sense of his

responsible position, but otherwise careless of all consequences, whether to himself or to another."

He turned for a moment from the jury, and looked across
the Court as though something had disturbed him, but not
a soul there spoke or stirred, and, turning to the jury-box
once more, Lord Inch for an instant spoke in another strain.

It was their duty, he told them, to give a verdict in accordance with the facts which had been so plainly laid before
them. But if, in their opinion, the evidence had not been,
beyond all doubt, satisfactory and conclusive, then it was
equally their duty to say so. There was, he reminded them,
a legitimate manner of expressing their doubts. To do so,
if doubt they had, was no act of mercy ; it was the merest
justice. Let them now retire, and consider their verdict as
it behoved men to do who, all their lives, sat under the
shadow of death, and knew not when they themselves would
be called to judgment.

The jury filed away, and Lord Inch, rising, passed
through one of the doors behind him, and went to his own
room, to wait there until he should be summoned to hear
the verdict. The trial had taken place in the Justiciary
Court, in which Donald Dee had shown the Judge to Lucius
and his party, and Lord Inch, in going away, passed through
the glass door with the bull's-eye through which they had
watched him.

He never looked back across the Court after he had
summed up. He never cast eyes on Rivers again ; he never
glanced up at the gallery, where a more sinister figure now
stood. If he had looked, it would have made no difference,
for it was Mr. Peters who stood frowning down upon him,
and Lord Inch knew nothing of Mr. Peters. So he passed
away to his room, and sat before the fire trying to prepare
himself for what must presently be done, while his clerk,
who thought there never had been and never would be such
another man, hovered a little in the background, fearful of

disturbing his lordship's thoughts, but very anxious to know whether he would not take some of the specially prepared soup, sent up from the house by Dr. Maitland's direction.

But Lord Inch, when he saw what was offered, waved it aside angrily, and then apologized.

" Presently, perhaps, when this business is over," he told his clerk. " It is good of you to think of it, Macintosh : and you must not notice my ways to-day. It is a sad business, but they won't be long over it, and no more will I."

The other drew back, watching secretly from the other end of the little room, and careful not to distract his lord-ship further from the solemn words which, he did not doubt, were being considered.

But his lordship was not thinking of any such thing. His thoughts had turned to Rivers, and his reappearance in Court, with his probable or possible intentions in coming. Would he make any further disturbance there ? If so, he should have no further forbearance shown him, come what might.

The train of thought concerning the fellow, this black-guard who called himself an Oxford man, went on uncon-sciously, stirring long dormant cells maybe, and at least rousing old memories. How it was Lord Inch did not know, but suddenly he remembered the man ! The whole scene came up again. He saw the prisoner with Buncombe—now Rivers—at his side. He saw the judge in the blaze of the smoking pine-knots, sitting with his rifle across his knees as he pointed up to a dangling rope. He heard the trivial yet haunting song of the doomed man as he laughed with his face to the moon, and a moment later he saw the thing— that had been a man—twist and swing in the moonlight.

Then he heard the bell ring, intimating that the jury had decided on their verdict, and, rising, he made his way into the Court again.

Meanwhile Rivers, who had come with no definite intention except to annoy his victim, no longer wished to do so. The proceedings of the last half-hour had sobered him, and Lord Inch had frightened him badly. Not only was he conscious how small his power was over that stern, cold figure on the bench, but he felt, as he had never felt before, that the Law wanted him, and that any move of his which drove Lord Inch to search into his history, might end in his standing before the Judge, charged with the crime that was being considered now. He was so tormented with this idea, that he felt as if branded in the face, and, rather than meet Lord Inch's eye again, would have left the Court, but those whom he had annoyed in passing would not let him move again, and Rivers sat with his head bent, wishing for the end of the scene.

What had passed had quite a different effect upon Peters, looking down from the gallery.

The effects of his night's drugging had not yet worn off, and he had chuckled audibly, to the scandal of the man next him, as Lord Inch summed up. Then, when the jury retired, he stood and brooded contemptuously over the whole thing. Was this justice, that a man with such a past as Lord Inch's should sit and judge and sentence other men ? The more he thought over it, the more absurd it seemed. It was so absurd that he felt Lord Inch must see it, and that everyone else would if he told them. Then they would put his lordship, in his solemn wig and great robes with the big red crosses, into the dock, and perhaps they would put the prisoner on the bench, to judge him.

Just then the jury came back, and then—through one of the two doors with the bull's-eye windows, which Peters recognized—came Lord Inch, and passed, gray-faced and solemn, to his seat.

Then a great anger came upon the man in the gallery. If he stayed there he must shout, and there would be trouble and interference with his business.

He turned, and forced his way out through the dozen or so of people between him and the door, who paid no attention, for the foreman of the jury was giving the verdict.

It was " Guilty," and the strain was nearly at an end now. A moment later Lord Inch, with a face that grew grayer and grayer as he spoke, told the prisoner at the bar what would follow. He would be taken from that place to another, and on such and such a day he would be hanged by the neck until he was dead, and might God have mercy upon his soul.

Every word was distinct, but the voice sank and sank, lower and lower, to the end, so that, at the last, attention was strained to the uttermost, and the slightest sound was heard.

It was then that a curious thing happened.

As one of the newspaper reporters hurried away with the verdict, and swung open a small side door, there came from the corridor the sound of a song. No man afterwards could say that he recognized it, and elsewhere it would have been unnoticed. It jarred here, and there might have been trouble, but that something else happened which made the noise be entirely forgotten. Lord Inch was seen to be ill.

He rose from his seat, gasping, and stared across the Court. Rivers, knowing that song, shivering, caught his glance of agonized wonder. Then Lord Inch staggered back and out at the door, disappearing from sight altogether.

When the general public, pushing and scrambling from their seats, found the way to the back of the Court, they also found it blocked by the police.

His lordship was ill, they were told. But in truth his lordship was already lying dead in his own little room, still in his robes, with the great red crosses lying straightened over his breast.

His clerk and the macers, when they hurried across the dais after him from the Court, had found someone there before them. A foreign gentleman, who afterwards gave his name as Peters, was kneeling at his lordship's side, in the corridor, doing all he could to revive him.

He was trying to find his way out of the Parliament House, he explained later, when a door opened, and his lordship fell at his feet.

When the others came up, Mr. Peters was bending over the Judge, apparently asking what ailed him, and trying to catch his last words ; but they arrived only to see Lord Inch die, obviously in great distress.

"HIS CLERKS FOUND PETERS AT HIS SIDE TRYING TO REVIVE HIM"

# CHAPTER XXXVIII

LORD INCH left the Parliament House for the last time
that night, carried thence to Drumsheugh Gardens in a
hearse that bore a snowy pall before it reached his door.
For the snow that had threatened in the morning had fallen
all through the afternoon, and still drifted down, making
all the streets white and silent for his last home-coming.
Archie and Maitland waited for the body together, and
talked together afterwards in Lord Inch's study, until far
on towards morning.

Besides his wish to pay every respect to his old friend,
and to help Archie in his loneliness, Maitland was anxious
to know whether Archie had been told anything of his
father's troubles. He discovered easily that Lord Inch had
said nothing, and decided to say nothing himself, at anyrate
for the time. It would be so easy to speak at any moment,
and the words would be so irrevocable that it was better to
watch and wait. He had heard nothing of the song that
heralded Lord Inch's death ; he knew nothing of Rivers'
presence in the Court, and it was perfectly natural for him
to certify that Lord Inch's death was consequent upon a
long-standing disease, aggravated by the day's excitement.

So he sat with Archie, talking in a gentle, fatherly way
that surprised the young master of the house, while Lord
Inch, past the reach of blackmailers, slept, let us hope, more
soundly than ever before.

If, going softly through the snow-silenced streets, one
had turned to the House of Residence, and looked for
Rivers, one would have found things less peaceful.

For he, gasping at the sound of that snatch of trivial song,
which he would barely have remembered, but for its effect
upon the man he hunted, had fought his way out of the
Court with the rest, and had waited—had been forced to
wait—until he knew what the end was, although he loitered
with, every now and then, a backward glance, dreading that
presently he should hear that song again, close at his ear,
or that in some other way he should feel that the avenger
was upon him.

All around him they talked of nothing but the sudden
illness, until a whisper came, and spread, and became an
outspoken certainty, that Lord Inch was a dead man. But
no one connected the trouble with that foolish noise. That
had been forgotten in what followed, as Rivers found, when
he plucked up courage to speak with one or two of those
who seemed least likely to have been the unseen singer. By
the time that the death was a certainty, Rivers, finding that
his persistent references to that song drew attention upon
himself, stopped talking, and went hurriedly away home.

What should he do, and where was he safe ? Lord Inch
had known nothing, he was sure, of this voice, until it struck
him down. He, Rivers, might know nothing more until
his turn came for punishment, and—when, where, and in
what form would punishment come ?

The average Briton, being aggrieved or injured, or fearing an injury, appeals to the police, if his grievance be not
such as he can air in the daily papers. But Rivers had to
bear his trouble alone. He could not complain about a song.
Why should the verse of a serenade, sung in a foreign
language—and not unmusically—be as significant of death
as any funeral march ? He would have to answer that, if
he wished for protection. The answer might cause trouble,
and would certainly attract notice. Then too, though he
had not dreaded an exposure as had Lord Inch, being in a
tougher condition, and having no reputation to lose, he felt

more than ever that he was an outcast, who had best not claim any protection from the law. There was still the London affair to account for. If he called in the Law to protect him, it might also detect him. Better to hear a song, mean what it would, than hear a sentence of death, as he had heard it that day.

So the man sat in his own room that night, and shivered and drank, and shivered and drank again, and not even the knowledge that he had locked the door behind him, could prevent him from looking over his shoulder at every sound, and indeed at every silence.

A certain amount of liquor raised his courage, or, more correctly, numbed his fear, for he had no courage to raise, and he crept across the passage to seek the comfort of the society of Mr. Peters. For Peters was big, and strong, and imperturbable, apparently, and sitting opposite to him one would be able to sip away without having first to look behind.

But Peters' door was locked, and no answer came. It was cold there in the passage. So Rivers went back to his own room. Besides turning the key, he dragged a table across against the door, and against the table he tilted a chair, so that a push would make it go over. Then he undressed, and, after turning down the light, looked out quietly to see whether anyone haunted the House of Residence, as he had haunted Drumsheugh Gardens. But the white streets were quiet and empty. To add to Rivers' comfort, he presently saw a policeman, strolling on the opposite side of the street, and he fell into drunken sleep, wondering whether it would attract too much attention if he gave that man a modest tip to keep a special eye upon the House of Residence.

Mr. Peters, too, had come to his rooms after having been examined by the authorities, and locking his door also, though he was afraid of nothing either alive or dead, he

sat motionless in his favorite chair before the fire, and
thought over his own foolishness. One after another, he
recalled his mistakes and self-indulgences, until, at the
thought of twenty-five years of patient waiting, plotting,
working, and suffering, wasted at the mad impulse of a
moment, great tears rolled down his cheeks. Anyone coming in, and knowing what had happened that day, would
have pitied Mr. Peters, thinking he possessed a more tender
heart than most of his fellow-men ; he cried bitterly, however, not at Lord Inch's death, but at the manner of it.

When at last he rose from his chair, it was to get the
long-stemmed, small-bowled pipe, with its fuel. He snapped
the stem with a turn of the wrist, and tossed pipe and all
into the fire. They made a fine blaze of heavy-perfumed,
high-reaching flames, and Mr. Peters, watching until nothing was left, shrugged his shoulders, and turned away with
an altered air, as though he had made a bonfire of regrets,
along with the rest.

Whether this was so or not, at least there were no more
tears then, or at any other time. He, too, went to bed,
pausing in his undressing only for a moment, when Rivers
came to the door. Then he went towards the door, silent,
and bent as a tiger crouching for a spring, but the door
remained shut. Rivers went back, and Mr. Peters, putting
away all thought of yesterday, to-day, or to-morrow, slept
like a child.

# CHAPTER XXXIX

## MR. PETERS MAKES MORE MOVES THAN ONE

THE affairs of the world, even those of the Parliament House, went on after the death of the Just Judge ; nor was anyone absolutely inconsolable. Why should it be otherwise ? Archie, considerably sobered down, and with Dr. Maitland for his guardian, could not sorrow eternally for a man who had never been his familiar friend. But he showed an honest intention of being no disgrace to his name, as far as work was concerned, and went about his studies conscientiously, in spite of a distraction, a tormenting, aggravating, tantalizing distraction, in the shape of 'Melia.

For 'Melia, with very mixed feelings, and from very mixed motives, was not seizing her golden opportunity, and, point-blank, refused to consider Archie's suit seriously.

" Boys shouldn't be so foolish," she told him with a reproving air. " You're old enough to have more sense, Mr. Inch," and would not listen to Archie's meek suggestion that this was rather contradictory. " I b'lieve you're talking like that because you think you must," she added once. " I've told you, over and over, that I've forgotten that foolishness of yours." By which further contradictory statement, 'Melia wished to intimate that she attached no importance to the stolen kiss.

She cried over Lord Inch's note, inclosing a check for those boxes of cigars which still lay untouched in the study, and later on showed it to Archie, but refused to say what they had discussed together. Archie argued with her over his father's probable feeling in the matter of his proposal, but they never came to any agreement. The one thing neither of them ever did was to ask Rivers what had been the outcome of his interview with Lord Inch. Each felt that this matter lay entirely between themselves, and both of them, had they been perfectly frank, would have had to acknowledge that they would not be prepared to pay any attention to Rivers' interference. Neither Rivers nor Peters was so much about the shop now, but one day Mr. Peters went down to Leith again, and called on Moriarty.

Business was still doing " most terrible " well with Lucius. Even the tobacconist's shop began to show signs of coming prosperity, thanks to Nell's careful consideration of its possibilities, and also to 'Melia's pleasant ways with the customers. Nell was considering the question of adding good coffee and the daily papers to its attractions, even a magazine or two, if the thing went well, and threw out occasional hints of the advantage of larger premises.

But latterly Lucius had felt, more than ever, the hollowness of mere worldly prosperity, and the need for cultivating other than business interests. His mind was lingering fondly over that old dream of a little farm, where he could breed honest beef and mutton, to the accompaniment of pastoral poetry. His thoughts were on this and kindred matters when Peters was announced.

" How are ye ? how are ye ? my Christian friend ! " said Lucius, rising from his desk precipitately to shake hands. " Where have ye been this long time, Mr. Peters ? "

" Going about my business," said Mr. Peters, and sat down upon the chair pointed out by Lucius.

" Well, well ! " Lucius told him, " it's business takes the pleasure out of life, isn't it ? You're not in such good fettle as when you came to Edinburgh. You're losing weight, I'll wager," he added, after a critical inspection. " What ails ye, man ? "

Then, as a sudden fear caught him, " Y' aren't in the lawyers' grips ? "

But Peters shook his head at that. " No," he said, quietly. " I keep clear."

" That's well," Lucius told him, emphatically. " Come down here, an' drop your money into the harbor first. ' Cast thy bread '—you know. It might return to you— after many days, at a low tide, or with the dredger maybe, but up there——" and Lucius shook his head emphatically, to show what his experience had been " up there." " I'd have looked ye up before now, if things hadn't been as they are," he went on, nodding his head at the papers before him.

" I should have been happy," said Peters, politely.

" Not at all ! " said Lucius, not as a contradiction, but as a conventional courtesy. " Your landlady's a monstrous fine woman, Mr. Peters ; and I reckon your friends are her friends, from the way she made me welcome last time I looked you up. It's my belief you're a sly dog, Mr. Peters, for all you're so quiet. Are ye thinking of settlin' down here, eh ? "

No, Mr. Peters was not thinking of settling down there, and said so.

" That reminds me," Lucius told him, one thing suggesting another, " there's another good-looking lady, a young 'un too, been inquiring after you twice. It's ' When did you see Mr. Peters, Mr. Moriarty ? ' and ' Has Mr. Peters gone away that I don't ee him here now ? ' Who'll that be, eh ? "

" Miss Murray," Peters suggested, apparently not particularly impressed by the news, and Lucius stared at him.

" You're an icicle ! " he insisted, " or we'll say an iceberg, because of the size of you. Is there never a warm heart outside Old Ireland ? Faith, I begin to think it. Why, the boys of me time would have broken heads, everyone of 'em, for a smile from the likes o' her ! "

"I am not a boy," Peters suggested.

"Maybe that's true," Lucius admitted. "We're boys till we die in Old Ireland. But anyway, you're not looking so well as you were. Maybe it's a change you're wanting?"

"I want more air," said Peters, "and so I want money."

"They sell air compressed nowadays, don't they?" chuckled Lucius. "Will ye order it in like beer?"

"I am going where there is more of it," Peters told him, rising and filling his chest with a deep breath, as if he were stifled.

"Ay! Where?" asked Lucius, interested.

"On your hills," said Mr. Peters, sitting down again. "From here and there, in this city, one sees your hills. From a high window, or a street corner. 'They are the Pentlands,' your people say, when one asks, but not many of them can say much more."

"I've not been there meself for years," Lucius admitted, regretfully.

"Very well, then, I have been," Peters told him, "and I go again. There is air, fresh, and plenty of it, up there."

"Plenty," Lucius agreed, "and nothing to pay."

"I have taken, what you call rented, an empty cottage," Peters explained.

"I see. Rent payable in advance," Lucius supposed. "You'll be wanting a matter of fifteen or twenty pounds then, what with furniture and so on?"

"Two hundred," Peters told him, and Lucius, who had taken out his check-book, dropped his pen in horror.

"What blaggard has been havin' ye?" he demanded. "Two hundred pounds, for a bit of an empty cottage on a hillside! Why didn't ye come to me?"

"I have not told you that it is all for that," Mr. Peters reminded him. "I have my expenses here, and, besides, on account of my business, there have been expenses in London."

" Are ye chucking away money there too, that ye may have the pleasure o' payin' your father's old debts ? "

" It is not thrown away," Peters told him, " I have got the value of my money."

" Well, a man's money is his own, I suppose," Lucius grumbled, filling up a check as he spoke, and then touching his bell. " I'd like to know what you call value for it though. I don't fancy we'd agree on that point."

" That is true," Peters agreed, but offered no explanation, and Lucius, giving the matter up in disgust, relieved his feelings by a short homily to the junior clerk.

" It's from two hundred and fifty to three hundred yards to the bank," he told the boy as he handed him the check. " Maybe, to-day, you'll oblige me by tryin' the nearest way for a change ; and that's not by way of the docks, and you don't go up by Leith Walk either. I give ye twenty minutes. If ye don't——! "

He never finished the sentence, for the clerk, on hearing the time-limit, had taken to his heels, and Lucius was left, staring alternately at Mr. Peters and at the door, which his flying messenger had banged behind him.

" There's manners ! " he observed. " And his mother as decent a woman as ever told me a pitiful story in this room, an' it fair groans with 'em, bein' a shippin' business, and all one's people one's friends."

" You are busy," Peters told him. " Continue ; here is a paper that I will read."

" Not you," Lucius insisted, " you'll talk with me. You're on me conscience."

Mr. Peters looked, first frowning, then raising his eyebrows, but Lucius was undaunted.

" Ay, you're on me conscience," he repeated, " an' you may frown away till I've done. D'ye know how much money there'll be left after this two hundred goes ? "

" About a hundred," Mr. Peters told him, " and the bag."

" And the bag," Lucius agreed, nodding towards the safe.
" It's there, since you said you might want it in a hurry.
Contents unknown, but money in some quantity, from the
feel of it. Still——! "

" Still ? " repeated Mr. Peters, whose face had grown
smooth and unmoved again.

" Well, if you don't look lively," Lucius answered, making a plunge, " I'm thinkin' all the cash may go to the pre-
liminaries, and so forth, and none be left for a settlement.
I could be your father, for age, and your friend Bergen is
my friend. Come, now ! can I help ye to settle up ? After
that, go ducks and drakes with the remainder, an' welcome.
But don't go and spend it all in askin' this, an' askin' that,
and findin' this man, and findin' that, just to tell 'em your
money's all gone in the searching for 'em, when all's said
an' done. It's they ought to spend their money in findin'
you—not t'other way round ! "

" They would not," Peters said. " They do not know,
and my way is best. Things shall go well now."

" That's done with, then," Lucius decided, and they
spoke of it no more, but chatted away about public affairs,
until the clerk rushed in, breathless, and with an aggrieved
air plainly showing that he knew whom he would consider
responsible if any ill happened to him after his hurried
errand.

Then Peters shook hands with Moriarty, and, going
straight back to the House of Residence, wrote a letter and
enclosed four five-pound notes, directing to Mr. Domenico
Selli, No. —— Wardour Street, London. The letter was in
Italian, and ran, roughly, as follows:—

" MY DEAR COUSIN,—

Business here goes slowly, and cannot be pushed. Any
rash speculation would perhaps be fatal, as once before.
I invest in house property, and look for a return, but I am

no more in haste. I have had my lesson. Your information and the paper received are invaluable. Resistance is
crippled thereby, and appeal to arbitration made impossible, which is what I desire. I remit the money, which can
ill be spared, but is most well-spent."

Mr. Peters took this business-like epistle to the post-office,
and registered it. Then he went to his room, and sat thinking. In his hand was a London daily paper of some years
back, which, with a letter, had reached him that morning.
A paragraph in it was marked lightly in pencil. He
rubbed the mark out carefully, and sat thinking again.
Then he put a heavy cross in another part of the news
summary, lower down, where the loss of a ship was announced, and tossed the paper carelessly on the table, beside
that day's *Scotsman*.

After that, he looked across the passage and saw that
Rivers' door was open, therefore that Rivers was out. Then
Mr. Peters sat down by his own fire, it being within, perhaps,
three-quarters of an hour from dinner-time, and, with a
lighted lamp upon the table and drawn curtains, began to
play Patience. As he played, he smoked, but there was no
more to be seen of the small-bowled pipe, and Mr. Peters
smoked nothing but Dream Mixture cigarettes, bought
from 'Melia.

Lucius had been quite right in saying that Mr. Peters was
not in such good " fettle " as when he came to Edinburgh.
There was often a tired look about his eyes. His face was
not quite so smooth and round. Still, he looked easily
good-tempered and imperturbable, as he played, and he was,
to all appearance, comfortable and contented enough when
Rivers came along the passage, went into his own room, and
presently, coming out again, knocked at Peters' door.

" Enter ! " said Mr. Peters, dealing another card, and his
neighbor entered accordingly.

Rivers was recovering his spirits to a great extent, and showed it. His hat was on, glossy, and tipped a little to one side. When Rivers was in good spirits it seemed very difficult to part him from his hat. He would wear it coming up the stair, on returning from a stroll, and forget to take it off for some minutes after, if he happened to look in upon Mr. Peters. He began to doubt his recollection of the scene at the Parliament House. Nothing had happened since to frighten him, and his own affairs prospered exceedingly. He doubted whether his ears had not played him false as to the song. He had been drinking heavily at that time—his imagination was excited by his surroundings— one tune sounds very like another at times—and so on.

At anyrate, he was in luck just now, and luck, backed up by manual dexterity, and a fat, good-natured pigeon eager to be plucked, must be pursued.

" Well ! " he asked, sitting down in the opposite easy-chair, " are we ready for revenge ?  Have we the rhino ? "

" I am ready," Mr. Peters told him.  " I have more money."

" 'Tis well ! " said Rivers, twisting his glossy mustache, glossier and blacker than ever, with a melodramatic air. " R-r-revenge is sweet.  To-night ? "

" If you will," Mr. Peters told him.

" Oh, you shall have your opportunity." Rivers declared. " Luck must turn soon, you know."

" I think it will," said Mr. Peters, and his visitor, still twisting the mustache to a most military point, smiled behind his hand.

" I must win," continued Mr. Peters, with one eye on his game and the other on Rivers, " before all your money goes."

" What d'ye mean ? "

" You have told me of money invested in the States, is it not so ? "

" A trifle, yes, that is so," Rivers acknowledged. " Not much perhaps, but something to a poor man."

" The papers say there is trouble between the two countries," said Mr. Peters, and leaning across lazily to the larger table, without rising, he picked up the nearest paper, and handed it to Rivers.

" Somewhere in the small notices," he suggested, and Rivers, although he had not the remotest pecuniary interest in the relations of Great Britain and the States, looked down the column.

" It would be a bad job for me and my little Em'ly," he announced, " though I hope she'll be provided for soon," and then he became very still and said nothing, for quite another bit of news had caught his eye.

—" The man who is wanted in connection with the murder in the tap-room of the ' Flowing Bowl ' will, it is believed, be speedily in the hands of the authorities, reliable information having been received as to his identity and whereabouts."—

Mr. Peters continued to deal his cards, putting them down rather noisily upon the little table before him, but he was not looking at his game. He was quietly watching Rivers.

" Do you not find it ? " he asked presently, but had to repeat the question before he got any answer.

" Not yet," Rivers said at last, and, sitting back in the chair, with the paper close to his eyes, seemed to search on unsuccessfully.

Mr. Peters played away for a few minutes longer, and then said, " Let me find it." He took the paper, Rivers muttering that his eyes were not so good as they used to be, and that he must really get glasses.

But Peters seemed to look, and then burst out laughing. " I do not wonder," he said, " that you cannot find it. It is not your eyes, my best Rivers. The news is not there.

You are looking in a paper many years old. Did you not
see ? "

" I didn't notice," Rivers admitted. He was leaning back
in his chair, and the mustache was trembling as he answered.

" It will be in this," Peters went on, reaching out for the
*Scotsman* upon the table. " Here it is ! "

He found the paragraph, pointed it out, and handed the
paper to Rivers, who sat and studied it intently, but said
nothing.

" What think you of it ? " demanded Peters, who had
gone back to his game.

" Bad, very bad ! " Rivers told him. " My poor little
Em'ly. It gives me quite a turn. Have you just the least
drop of something, handy ? I'm getting an old man, Captain Peters, and I can't afford to lose money."

Peters got something for him, and Rivers took it with a
hand that still trembled.

" I like to see the London paper sometimes," he told
Peters presently. " It's not worth while going to the library, if you have it in the place. Do you take it in regularly ? "

" No." Mr. Peters took up the old London paper, and
sought for a paragraph in it. " It is my family business,"
he explained. " It is believed that a relative of mine was
drowned in this ship," and he showed Rivers the paragraph
already marked in pencil.

Rivers studied it carefully, and drank again.

" After all," Mr. Peters suggested. " we know what these
newspapers are. It is probably not true about these
troubles. It will be told otherwise to-morrow."

" That is so," Rivers agreed, draining his glass. " It is
of no use to be frightened at these things. It is a father's
foolishness, my dear Peters. Let me see, it's almost dinner-
time, isn't it ? "

" In ten minutes," said Mr. Peters. " Shall I have my revenge after dinner, and here ? "

" Excellent ! " Rivers agreed, cheering up very much. " A good fire, and a comfortable chair, a friend to profit if you lose, and a glass to console you. That is what I call comfort."

He rose to go, evidently relieved about our foreign relations.

" By the by," he told Mr. Peters, " I saw my little Em'ly this afternoon. She tells me that she has seen very little of you lately."

" It is true," Mr. Peters admitted. " I have had my business to attend to, in the day. Our evenings we have spent together of late, have we not ? "

" Yes, yes. Better luck to-night perhaps. It's as bad always to win as always to lose, Captain Peters."

" Is it ? " Mr. Peters asked, simply. " Ah ! but I shall have my turn."

" Oh, surely," Rivers agreed, " and how does your business go on ? "

" Slowly," Peters told him, " but I expect to finish soon, very soon, now."

" Well, well," said Rivers. looking at him as if this interested him very much, " and then you will go away ? "

" Then I shall say good-by, and go away."

" I must give you plenty of opportunity to win back your money," said Rivers, with a regretful air.

" Or to lose some more ? " Mr. Peters suggested, but Rivers objected to this way of putting it.

" No, no. Luck will turn," he insisted, and just then the dinner-bell rang, and he went off to go through the very necessary ordeal of washing his hands, which he did with not much superfluous soap and water, but with many smiles.

" I shall lose to-night," he told his reflection in the looking-glass. " I'm as sure of it, as that I stand here," but

19

this foreboding did not appear to damp his spirits, and he joined the party in the dining-room without a sigh.

He entertained himself, if not Mrs. Jimps, that evening, by recollections of his *Alma Mater*. Mr. Rivers had moved in the wittiest, richest, wickedest, most brilliant set of his college, so he gave Mrs. Jimps to understand. Of the wickedness, of course, he could not give details to a lady, and wit is so like champagne that he was quite right not to repeat jokes which had been uncorked, so to speak, so many years ago. If Mrs. Jimps did not appreciate Rivers' anecdotes so highly as he did, she at anyrate smiled occasionally, and, sometimes, quite in the right place. Many of her obliging sex do no more, and rank as sympathetic for doing so much. Rivers did not know that, behind the attentive manner and the smile, thoughts came and went in Mrs. Jimps' business-like brain which were concerning himself, and were not so complimentary as he would have expected.

Mrs. Jimps had her suspicions of Rivers, and these had been considerably strengthened, quite lately, by hints from the kitchen. Mrs. Jimps thought it permissible, a thing that must be endured, when a Paying Guest, having met agreeable companions, came home once in a way slightly the worse for liquor, or roused suspicion by want of appetite at the breakfast-table. But, if Annie were to be believed, steady drinking, steady and solitary drinking, had gone on lately in Mr. Rivers' room, until, just a few nights ago, matters became even worse. Rivers had migrated to Peters' room, and if Mrs. Jimps could believe her ears, applied in quite a friendly spirit to Captain Peters' keyhole when going her nightly round. Rivers now spent his evenings in drinking Captain Peters' whiskey, and winning his money.

"It would be the ruin of the place if it was known," she said to herself, smiling at the same time because Rivers had just laughed, and therefore must have said something which he thought funny.

" It will be the ruin of poor Captain Peters, if it goes on," she decided, as Rivers launched forth upon another personal anecdote. " I wonder whether he'd be very angry if I spoke of it ? "

She looked down the table at Mr. Peters, who still had the place of honor at the other end, and acknowledged to herself that she did not like the idea of interfering. Finally she made up her mind to wait one night more.

" I didn't think Captain Peters would be so foolish," she acknowledged later, unburdening herself for once to the faithful Annie, who as usual was her companion on the nightly round.

" They're all the same in the end, I think, Mrs. Jimps. Fools to each other, and villains to we poor women," Annie told her gloomily, with a sigh for the dashing dragoon, who had left Piershill for foreign parts.

" I really will speak to Captain Peters to-morrow, if he goes on losing more money," said Mrs. Jimps. " He sha'n't ruin himself in my house, to please anyone. Hush now, Annie, and mind those squeaky shoes of yours."

They had reached Captain Peters' door, and Mrs. Jimps put an ear to the keyhole. It was now half an hour after midnight. Mrs. Jimps had made her visit much later than usual, Annie having told her that the sittings lasted until half-past twelve or one.

Mrs. Jimps listened, and Annie tried to gather information from her upturned face.

Three minutes Mrs. Jimps listened, then started suddenly, and fled more swiftly than she was accustomed to move on her own premises, followed hot-foot by Annie.

They were only just in time. Peters' door opened as they reached the flat below, and Rivers spoke.

" I told you how it would be," they heard him say, be-

tween one door and the other. "Luck must change. I
shouldn't wonder if you had a run of it, now." Then he
went into his own room, and they heard no more.

Mrs. Jimps looked at Annie and smiled.

"Captain Peters has won some of his money back," she
explained. "That's what that means, Annie. It's a wicked
amusement, and I don't know anything about it, and don't
want to. But if, as that man says, the luck has changed,
why, Mr. Peters will very likely get some more, and I won't
stand between him and what belongs to him. I sha'n't say
anything yet, at anyrate. Good-night, Annie. Be sure
you're up in good time, and, if you come to me after breakfast, I'll give you that silk underskirt that I had turned last
year. I've been meaning you to have it, for a long time."

# CHAPTER XL

## THE TROUBLES OF MADGE MURRAY AND MRS. JIMPS

CHRISTMAS was now drawing near ; the days were short and gray ; more snow had fallen, and could be seen from the city lying upon the Pentland Hills ; but Mr. Peters went up the slopes more than once, to make sure that the little furniture he needed was safely delivered, and arranged in his cottage.

Mrs. Jimps was much troubled when he told her of his new quarters, and recovered her spirits only when she heard that, for the present at anyrate, he intended to keep on his rooms in the House of Residence.

" I shall be delighted, Captain Peters," she told him, " and we will arrange for a little reduction on the rent when you are away. I do hope you will be well taken care of, up there in the cold ? "

" A woman is coming from the nearest house," Peters explained, " to clean the rooms. I will do most for myself. One cannot always have a Mrs. Jimps to take care of one."

Ah ! if he only knew how easily One might have a Mrs. Jimps to take care of him. Mrs. Jimps felt this, but, being trammelled by the conventionalities, did not say so.

" We must take special care of you when you are in town, Captain Peters," was her rejoinder. " Are you sure that you have plenty of warm bedding ? "

" Plenty ! " Peters assured her. " Often, too, I shall sleep here. You will keep my rooms quite as usual."

" I will see to it myself," declared Mrs. Jimps, " and you will keep your key, Captain Peters, so that you can come in at any time. You may be sure, whenever you do, that you will find your bed aired, and the fire ready laid, so that you need only put a match to it. And if you happen to want anything in the way of a meal, when you do come in, please come to me. The rules of the House of Residence can be stretched, for friends, Captain Peters."

Mere creature comforts these, which Mrs. Jimps laid so much stress upon, but her intention was as kindly as if she had offered Mr. Peters higher things. He seemed properly to appreciate the intention. He laughed, not unkindly—Mr. Peters had not laughed much of late ; then he bent, and, kissing Mrs. Jimps' plump hand, set her blushing furiously.

" Captain Peters ! "

" Pardon a foreigner," he entreated. " It is a foreign fashion, Mrs. Jimps. You are kind, and I forget. It shall not happen again."

Nor did it. Mrs. Jimps, now on her guard against such liberties, and determined, of course, to allow no more, had no further cause for complaint, and yet seemed no happier. Nor did she hear Captain Peters laugh again, in the pleasant way with which he had met her hospitable assurances.

Now, though he had entered on the possession of his house on the Pentlands, he still came and went almost every day. Perhaps it was his business that brought him in so often, perhaps it was the recollection of his promise to 'Melia, that he would keep an eye upon her father. Once or twice, when he spent a night in town, Rivers visited his room, and won or lost a few pounds over the cards. But Peters declared that he found the nights pleasantest upon the hills, and Rivers began to wonder how he could continue those delightful evenings which had been so regularly profitable a short while ago.

" 'Ow d'you live up there ? " 'Melia asked Peters one day when he looked in for tobacco to take back with him.

" I smoke."

"You're a funny man, Cap'n Peters," 'Melia declared. "You could smoke anywhere else, just as well."

"There is no room," he told her, gravely. "I smell the smoke of one hundred other men, when I smoke in this place. Then I cannot move. I stretch myself, and see! something is spoilt."

He stretched himself, with a hand extended far on either side of him, and swept a box of cigars from a shelf.

"You're a funny one!" 'Melia repeated, going down on her knees to pick up the cigars. "You needn't have done that. I'd take your word for it. What sort of a place is yours?"

"Two rooms only," Peters told her, "and small. There is little in them, but still I cannot stretch there. It is on the outside that I find room."

"What's that like?" asked 'Melia, laying on the counter a damaged cigar, which she meant Peters to pay for presently, and then resting on her elbows, her pretty chin between her hands.

"Behind is the hill-side," said Peters, "and the fir-trees, that whisper all the night, when there is wind. I walk by them, under the stars, when I cannot sleep, and they tell me all sorts of things, and send me back sleepy to my bed."

"That's pretty," 'Melia allowed. "I didn't know you were that sort. Go on, Cap'n Peters. What's in front?"

Peters, upon the leather-covered seat against the wall, leant his head back, and his hat tilted forward over his eyes.

"In front," he told her, "the hill falls and falls away, until it reaches the water. That is frozen now. There will be skating in a few days."

"What besides?"

"There are the rabbits, and the grouse," Peters went on, "and sometimes, by night, I hear the wild duck going over me, or perhaps a goose sometimes; I do not know."

"Do they chatter like the trees?" 'Melia asked. "I s'pose, if they do, they say 'cook me!'"

Mr. Peters didn't laugh. He seemed not to be thinking so very much of 'Melia, and answered quite softly and solemnly.

"No," he said, "they do not say 'cook me.' In the snow, the rabbits and the grouse tell one another that life is a hard thing, and that everyone must fight for himself. But the geese——"

"Yes?" said 'Melia, "I've heard they're not such fools as they look. What do they say?"

"They cry down to me," Peters told her, "that I am a slow fool, a silly stupid, a dull fellow. They tell me of the places where I met them before. Then they call that I must make haste to finish my work and come away, and be free once more like they are."

"And what do you say?" 'Melia wanted to know.

"I tell them patience, and that a fool, to be sure, must go slowly."

He rose now, and picked up his packet of tobacco.

"I must go," he said. "It will snow again to-night, and then I might lose myself."

"This cigar's your's," 'Melia told him. "See how you've spoilt it. Fourpence please, and you'd best wait till you get to your cottage before you stretch again, or it may come more expensive, Cap'n Peters. Now I'd like to see that place o' yours."

"Well," Peters suggested, "so would your father. Make him bring you. I have already told him to come, if he likes."

"I'll talk to him," 'Melia promised, and then remembered something else to speak of.

"You know that time when you came along here, with a lady," she asked him, "an' left her to come in here?"

Peters couldn't remember for the moment, and said so.

"A tall, dark lady. She was dressed in blue and red. Looks like this!" and 'Melia, drawing herself up, threw her head back a little, and surveyed him superciliously from under drooping lids.

"Yes," Peters told her, "I remember now. What of her?"

"Friend o' yours?" asked 'Melia.

Mr. Peters shrugged his shoulders. "Go on!" he said.

"Oh, she's a customer o' mine, that's all," 'Melia told him. "If she smokes all she buys, she's a Wunner, Cap'n Peters."

"Perhaps she does not," Peters suggested.

"That's what I say," 'Melia agreed, and seemed on the point of saying more, but apparently changed her mind.

"Well, it's going to snow, as you thought," she told him, "and you don't want to be found froze in a ditch. Good-night!" and Peters, wishing her good-night in return, went away.

Half an hour later, Madge Murray came in the dusk, and asked for cigarettes, with a patronizing air that would probably have got scant courtesy in return but for 'Melia's axiom that business came before personal feeling.

"Has Mr. Peters been here lately?" Madge asked carelessly, as she turned to go.

"This very afternoon," 'Melia told her, "for half an hour. He uses up his cigarettes a'most as soon as you, Miss. Could I tell him anything for you, when I see him?"

"No, it's just that I want to give him a book he lent me," her customer explained. "I'm afraid he'll go away without getting it. Half an hour, you say? He's very particular over his cigarettes?"

"Oh, that doesn't take a minute," 'Melia assured her, calmly. "I always know just what he wants. But me an'

Cap'n Peters are old friends. We've always a lot to talk about."

"That's very kind of him. I hope he means all he says to you," the other remarked, and sailed out forthwith.

'Melia, to relieve her mind when the shop was empty, came round the end of the counter, and burlesqued Miss Murray's departure, as far as the door.

"Spitfire!" she announced, to no one in particular, and, after watching the stray flakes of snow for a minute or two, she made herself a cup of tea, and settled down as usual over a book; but, as usual, too, nowadays, she got on slowly. There were so many things to wonder over. There was Archie first always. 'Melia couldn't rid herself of the idea that Archie was pressing his suit, partly—at anyrate—because he was being pressed. She had not spoken to Rivers about it, but that was her feeling, and nothing that Archie could say would rid her of it altogether. Rivers had cunning enough not to discuss the thing with her. His hints about the pleasure it would give him, to see her quietly settled down, with a house in which her poor old father might some time find a corner when he felt near his end, were too vague to quarrel over, but quite enough to worry 'Melia. Rivers was, nevertheless, her father, and 'Melia was ready to defend him against all the world, but she had very few illusions left concerning him, and could not persuade herself, as she could once have done, that Archie would be pleased, or honored, in having such a father-in-law. Leave him she would not. Inflict him upon Archie she could not, and poor 'Melia, torn both ways by these contradictory feelings, had of late, in trying to be just to both, been none too sweet-tempered with either.

"You're the best of 'em," she often assured her silent friend "Sandy." "You're the only one I can have about me for very long without wishing you out o' this, anyway."

If it had not been for her doubts about her father, 'Melia

would probably have consulted Nell. But the hours at which Nell came were not those at which Rivers usually made an appearance. Nell had never met him, and 'Melia had not felt bound to mention him, much less to discuss her troubles concerning him with anyone.

# CHAPTER XLI

## CANDIDUM SORACTE

THE next Sunday, the ground being white with a thin covering of snow, 'Melia and her father went across the hills, by invitation from Mr. Peters, to see him in his new quarters.

There was not much talking by the way. 'Melia had learnt that there were not many things which her father cared for which were of any interest to her ; also, that any chat, however it might begin, was apt to end in hints from Rivers that he was getting impatient over her unnecessary delay in providing a comfortable home for both of them.

She went along the slopes, after they reached the open hill-side, looking on the thin, powdery sheet of snow for foot-prints of birds and beasts, drawing deep breaths as she went, and wondering why she had never ventured before into this quiet, white fairyland.

Once she told her father to look at the rabbits, scuttling to their burrows, and at a hawk, hanging against the blue-gray sky, ready for a swoop : but Rivers was unresponsive. He thought the white country-side cold and dull, and wondered, as he went, why on earth he had been persuaded to bring 'Melia : he wondered, too, whether, with her there, he would get any chance of a game at cards, to keep him comfortably in pocket money until 'Melia should make up her mind to stop playing the fool, and take young Inch and his money while she could get them. All this fuss and bother, he was sure, only arose from some silly girlish affectation, and he began to feel that, if separated much longer from his dear friend Captain Peters, and consequently from his dear friend's purse, he would have to speak plainly, and teach 'Melia her duty.

Meanwhile Mr. Peters, sitting at the top of the brae, his big chin propped on the palm of his hand, looked down like another hawk over the valley, and watched the coming of his guests. He would have preferred, vastly, to entertain Rivers alone, but there was no hurry to do that. Mr. Peters had sworn that never again in this world would he press matters or run any risk of seeming to guide anyone's movements. He sat careless of the three or four degrees of frost, watching these two figures gradually grow more distinct, and was quite the hospitable entertainer when 'Melia caught sight of him, and, waving her handkerchief, pushed up the hill before her father.

" This is grand, Cap'n Peters," she panted, when within speaking distance. " My ! to think—o' the times—I spent in my bed—lazy good-for-nothing—when I might have been here ! "

Peters, watching her father come up behind her, did not pay much attention, but 'Melia was too happy to care.

" You're right ! " she told him, still panting, "you *can* stretch here," and with that she plumped down on some heather, from which she beat the snow, and, leaning back with her shoulders against a bank, stretched out her arms as if to embrace the Pentlands as a whole.

A cock-grouse, seeing that there was no gun among the party, called from a bare knoll some fifty yards away, and 'Melia watched him, enchanted, then turned to look at a big hare, that went with little hops across the frozen loch beneath them.

" Better'n Princes Street," she pronounced. " I never saw that chap before—'cept at the poulterer's." and then, getting up, walked behind the two men, looking about her, and taking very little share in the conversation, as they followed the narrow footpath that wound away between the hills.

At the edge of the whispering Scotch firs, silent now in the still, frosty daylight, they came upon the cottage that Mr. Peters had described to 'Melia.

It stood quite alone, a thin line of smoke, unstirred by any wind, mounting straight from its chimney.

Down from the door the ground sloped away, thickly covered with heather and coarse grasses, until it fell to the shores of another little loch, Glencorse Reservoir, in the hollow of the hills, and here 'Melia stood and looked about her, more interested in the outside than the inside of the cottage, for the time, and not very willing to move.

" Come," Peters told her, " the good Rivers is hungry it seems, and something is ready for you to eat, and you can see this again after."

So 'Melia went in, and at once became amused by the household arrangements.

Over the fire stood a big pot, and from it came an enticing odor, as Mr. Peters lifted the lid and peered in.

" My ! you know what's good," 'Melia told him, sniffing the air. " What's in that thing, Cap'n Peters ? "

" A little of all things. It is a stew, into which I have emptied my larder. Go away, and put your hat in the other room, my bedroom. Then dinner will be ready here, in this, the dining-room and kitchen."

So 'Melia went off, and was interested in the simplicity of his sleeping arrangements.

A narrow mattress upon an iron bedstead, a little mirror near the window, a lamp, and a few books in a foreign language—this was nearly all that the room held.

When she went back to the kitchen, or dining-room, the table was laid, but laid only for two, and 'Melia commented, as usual, frankly.

" Who's odd man out ? " she asked. " If you'd told me,

I'd have brought something to make up, Cap'n Peters. Isn't there enough ?"

" Some grouse, some hare, some rabbit, some vegetables and potatoes." Mr. Peters told her, " yes, there is enough."

" Well, then," 'Melia demanded, " what's wrong ? "

" I do not eat now," he explained, " not until night."

" It'll be dull work watching, won't it ? " she asked, but Mr. Peters assured her that it would not be so, and 'Melia tried not to feel offended, and chatted as they ate, while Rivers paid no attention at all, being occupied with dinner and his own thoughts, which began to suggest more golden possibilities.

It was a kind of faint shadow of old custom, superstition, what you will, that held Peters back that afternoon, and kept him fasting. Rivers was—Rivers, or rather, Buncombe ; and, in his host's opinion, had no claim upon the laws of hospitality. But with 'Melia it was different.

True, she was her father's child, and he looked constantly, indeed eagerly, to see her prove it, in some such way as should let him think of the two as one. But 'Melia was rather her mother's child, and her father had had decent people as ancestors. The two were not one, could not be thought of, or treated, as one ; and Mr. Peters, prepared to go very far in the transaction of his business, yet drew the line, oddly enough, at the trivial point of eating in his own house with a girl who knew so little of him and of his thoughts as 'Melia did, and who yet trusted him so much.

So, father and daughter ate by themselves, and Peters talked away so readily about one thing and another that 'Melia, though she was strangely vexed at his fasting, in time almost forgot that.

" Well, we've left some for your supper, anyway," she told him, when they had ended the meal. " Where you get these nice things from, up here, I can't tell."

" They are at my door," said Mr. Peters calmly, lighting

the cigarette, which he had been twisting in his fingers, when he saw they had finished.

"What!" 'Melia had never thought of that. "You don't mean to say you catch 'em?"

Mr. Peters nodded. "Why not?"

"That's poaching, isn't it?" asked 'Melia, wide-eyed.

"I believe so," Mr. Peters allowed. "What then?"

"You're breaking the laws of the country!"

"Not my laws, nor my country," he told her, with a sort of contempt. "Look at your laws. Poof!" and blowing a little cloud of smoke, he waved it away with his open hand. "That for your laws!" he told her. "It is clearer without them."

Rivers, who had been helping himself generously to Mr. Peters' spirits, applauded with vigor. "An effete country, with effete laws, my dear Captain Peters," he agreed. "That is why I left my *Alma Mater* (did I ever tell you?) a little sooner than was customary. Young blood has nothing in common with picturesque ruins, my dear sir. You haven't one of those excellent cigars about you, have you? My little Em'ly has been so carefully brought up that she won't let her father get his cigars on tick! Well, well! we sha'n't be there much longer, shall we, Em'ly?" and Rivers, chuckling, winked knowingly at Peters, who made no response.

"Don't know, I'm sure," said 'Melia, and, to give the conversation a turn, got up from her chair, and, going to the window, asked Mr. Peters the name of the hill opposite.

Mr. Peters didn't know and didn't care, but the question served its purpose, and 'Melia began wandering about the room, with a notion of putting things straight. She cleared the table and went outside, leaving the men for ten minutes or so, but not going out of sight of the cottage. Then she came back, for it was already getting much colder. The two men were still talking and smoking by the fire. Perhaps most of the talking was done by Rivers, who was speaking as 'Melia came in.

" It must be very dull up here alone ? " he suggested.

Peters only shrugged his shoulders, but Rivers protested that it must be.

" Though two," he suggested, " to keep one another company, might be very snug."

Peters, staring at the fire, with his legs stretched out before him, puffed away slowly, and said nothing.

" How do you pass the time alone ? " asked Rivers, anxious for his friend's comfort.

" There is tobacco," Peters told him, after consideration, " there are books, a few, and there are cards. I play alone, you know. You have seen me."

" Ah, yes. I know your game," and Rivers laughed rather condescendingly, having never taken to it.

" Do you ? " Mr. Peters asked gravely, and then, as if recollecting himself, " ah ! I had forgotten. Yes, you know my game."

" We are so thoughtful," said Rivers, in what he intended to be a light, bantering manner, but which had very little ease or carelessness about it. " We are so thoughtful, and so retiring, that, I suppose, we couldn't put up a friend for a night ? "

" I might," Mr. Peters told him, " if he asked me."

" If he asked ! " Rivers' delicacy was shocked at the notion, and, before he could get over it, 'Melia chimed in.

" Go along, Cap'n Peters," she told him, " where'd you put anybody ? "

" It depends," Mr. Peters said, after consideration, " upon who was the body."

" You've only one bed," 'Melia insisted. " I've been in there, you know," jerking her head towards the other room.

" Oh, I could make another," Mr. Peters told her, and then stopped talking suddenly, struck by 'Melia's occupation, just when, for conversation's sake, she was beginning to discuss the point further.

" What are you doing there ? " he asked, harshly.

" Me ?  I'm just putting a stitch in this for you," 'Melia answered, rather surprised at his manner, and held up for inspection a torn flannel shirt, which she had found lying about, and had begun to darn.

To her astonishment Mr. Peters rose, and, crossing the room, took it from her, and not only took it, but deliberately tore apart the stitches which she had already made.

" Well, I never," said poor 'Melia, " what's that for ? "

" I never asked of you to do it for me," Peters told her. " I never asked of you to do anything for me.  You cannot say that I did."

" W'y, no ! " 'Melia allowed, " I never said you did, did I ?  That's no reason for not doing it, is it ?  I don't know what you're driving at, Cap'n Peters.  What have I done ? "

Rivers sat half turned from the fire, watching them without any interference.  'Melia could take care of herself he thought, so far as he thought of the matter at all, and he was not going to run the risk of offending Peters.  When 'Melia looked at him, saying nothing but hoping for help towards an explanation, he moved round again without a word, and 'Melia turned from him.

" I'll have a walk," she announced, to whomsoever it concerned.  " When you're ready to go back, father, you can shout.  It's near time for starting."

She went to the other room, and, putting on her hat, passed out alone, while Peters stared at the hills from the window, and Rivers shifted uneasily by the fire.

" She's a silly, meddling little fool," Rivers said, apologetically, at last.  " What did she do ?  She shall apologize presently."

He did not look round, and so lost the scowl with which

Mr. Peters, at that moment, was favoring him, and, when the latter spoke, there was no sign of trouble in his voice.

" It is your language that I cannot speak," he explained, " and my foolishness. What have I done ? The woman who waits on me, I pay her to do all these things. Why should anyone else trouble for me ? That was all I meant."

" Em'ly's so hasty," Rivers told him. " She didn't wait to understand. It comes from her mother, Captain Peters. She was a good soul, but, well, a rough diamond, you know."

If Mr. Peters thought anything, complimentary or otherwise, of this man who was so ready to summarize the dead woman, his wife, for a stranger's edification, his face did not show it. His features were smooth once more, and so was his voice as he answered—

" I will explain to her presently," he said, " and she shall come in for a cup of tea, before you go."

He filled the kettle, and put it upon the fire ; then went out into the growing dusk, found 'Melia, and apologized for his awkwardness. 'Melia relented at once, and came in.

" I s'pose I'm a silly," she told him as she came, " but truly, I thought I'd make you mad with me, somehow."

" How could you think so ? " Mr. Peters protested.

" I don't know, I'm sure, for I didn't mean any harm. Anyway it's all right, isn't it ? "

Mr. Peters assured her that it was all right, and that everything was due to his ignorance of the niceties of the English language, but nothing would persuade him to let 'Melia perform the little service which she had begun.

She drank her tea in silence, Mr. Peters refusing to join, and then a thing happened to make her wonder more than ever.

Mr. Peters, cutting bread quickly, perhaps to allow some suppressed feeling an outlet, chopped so viciously that he gashed his hand badly. He said nothing, but had to put down the loaf, and 'Melia saw the blood well out before it could be hidden.

" My gracious ! " she exclaimed, and began searching in a pocket till she produced triumphantly a little case of plaster, with a bandage and safety pins.

" I've carried it for years," she exclaimed joyfully, " ever since ambulance lectures, and no one, not a living soul, would ever go and do anything for me to put right."

By this time she was round at Mr. Peters' side of the table, trying to get hold of the injured hand, which he had covered with a handkerchief.

" That's not the way," she told him. " Let me do it," but Mr. Peters waved her off.

" It is nothing," he insisted. " This will do. Go on with your tea."

" Look ! "'Melia answered indignantly, pointing to where the blood already came through the folded handkerchief. " Call that nothing ? " and when he still, none too civilly, told her to let him alone, 'Melia grew sarcastic. " If you're under contract to give that woman who tends you all your cut fingers, as well as your torn shirts, why—I won't steal her customer, and I hope she'll make a good job of it. But if I'm to understand that I'm no friend o' yours, and it's for that you won't lemme touch you, or any o' your belongings, why, speak plain and let's know it."

" Let Captain Peters alone, Em'ly," Rivers told her. " Where are your manners ? "

But Mr. Peters, after frowning back at 'Melia's angry face, gave way, though most ungraciously, and 'Melia had the pleasure of putting on a pad and bandage, *secundum artem*, with many wise words concerning clean cuts and antiseptics.

That done, it was high time to be going, but, after they had gone some steps from the threshold, Rivers hurried back for a last word.

" I'm an old campaigner," he told Mr. Peters, shaking his hand warmly, " and the town stifles me at times. I shall be ready, and glad, to come up for a night, and rough it any time that you'd like a friend for company. What does a bed matter ? With a pipe and a little whiskey, and perhaps a game if we felt we wanted variety, a night would pass up here before a man knew it had begun ! " and then, diving into the white mist that rose from the hollow, he disappeared.

# CHAPTER XLII

THAT Christmas vacation Tom Dunbar declared to his people, in the south of England, that he could take no holidays, and persisted in his heroic resolve, in spite of a pathetic letter from his mother, entreating him to remember that health is the greatest of blessings. The letter included a few words upon the efficacy of a certain tonic, home-made, in which old sherry took a prominent place. She said that two bottles had been packed for him, with a plum-pudding, a cake, and other products of home industry, and that he must be a good fellow, and be sure not to work on Christmas Day at anyrate. She also sent a bank-note for Christmas expenses, and when Tom had mastered the contents of that letter he felt a condemned fraud.

Of course he was going to work; there wasn't a doubt of it in his mind, but whether it was his work that kept him in Edinburgh just then was quite another matter. If it were not for Nell, Tom would have been at home most certainly, shooting, hunting, or skating, according to weather and opportunity.

Troubled with an uneasy conscience after reading the letter, he tried to soothe it by a morning in the infirmary wards, and by that roundabout route he became aware of the existence of 'Melia. For, coming thence, he asked a fellow-student for a cigarette, and was handed a case full of "Dreams."

"Where do you get these?" Tom asked, and his friend told him, adding "Jolly little girl who sells 'em, too, but as hard as nails," and with that verdict went his own way.

So Tom, who had finished the packet of cigarettes presented to him by Lucius, and had gone through a hot discussion with him on their price and merits, which had left him wondering at that worthy's interest therein, went down and made 'Melia's acquaintance, and, having made it, went again at odd times and more frequently than was necessary, scenting a mystery.

" Seems to me you can't be very busy," 'Melia told him with her usual candor one day, but on being assured that it was holiday time, said no more.

By reason of irregularity, he, at one time and another, met 'Melia's other visitors. One morning it was Archie, deep in argument, and Archie glowered when he came, and stayed till he went. Then it was Rivers, who insisted upon introducing himself—and Balliol—to the obvious distress of poor 'Melia. Another time it was Mr. Peters, calling for tobacco on his way hillward, and with him Tom chatted, his professional eye being caught by the bandaged hand.

Then, near mid-day on Christmas Eve, as he passed by " Sandy," he caught sight of a slim, dainty figure that he knew, and heard a familiar voice say, " Very well, I'll tell them to send round two more plants this afternoon." The figure turned, and there was Nell !

'Melia had the edifying advantage of seeing how very confused a young lady may appear when suddenly surprised by someone to whom, at appointed times and places, she can seem indifferent enough. 'Melia had time to store up her impressions, for Tom—to her disgust—forgot all about buying anything, and straightway insisted upon accompanying Nell home.

When Tom came back 'Melia beamed upon him.

" I thought 'twas a packet to the bad—your going off like that," she informed him, and straightway, to Tom's great joy, began talking of Nell, sure that she had an appreciative audience.

"Isn't she pretty?" 'Melia demanded; "and my! but she's got a head too. The tips she gives me about working this place!" and Tom, not having asked Nell what had brought her there, and not having been told, made no comment, but took his packet of "Dreams" and was interested to find rhymes of his own making upon this new lot.

"What d'you think of 'em?" asked 'Melia, when she saw him reading. "Mr. Moriarty's awful pleased. He told me 'twas a real clever young chap that wrote 'em for him," and Tom chuckled, seeing daylight.

"He'll have to pay for things like that, won't he?" asked 'Melia.

"He'll certainly have to pay," Tom told her; "you may be sure of that."

"Well, I don't know whether the packets 'll stand any more expenses upon 'em or not," 'Melia debated; "there isn't much profit, Mr. Dunbar."

"I know the fellow who did the writing," Tom admitted, still grinning. "He must be careful not to overcharge, Miss Rivers."

"P'raps he'd take payment in tobacco?" 'Melia suggested.

"Yes, or something else," Tom thought. "I suppose the fellow who writes the other things on the packets of mixture gets well paid, Miss Rivers?"

"Not he," said 'Melia, promptly, seeing a chance of lessening charges. "He does it just for love, Mr. Dunbar. I know that, because all the expenses go down in a book here. Just for love he does it. P'raps your friend, if you told him that, would do the same."

"Come!" Tom protested, enjoying himself hugely, and chuckling more than ever; "you can't expect much done for love, can you? I think he'll want something in exchange if he can get it; but he shall know what you say." and off he went to spend a good part of the bank-note in something in the shape of a Christmas present, which reached Nell, anonymously, next morning. By the time he had done that, and had thought over his morning's occupation, the voice of conscience was dumb, and Tom was prepared to hold that his virtuous determination, to work through Christmas, was already justified by results.

"That evening, when Lucius called upon 'Melia to give her a Christmas-box, and to find out what she thought of the new wrappers, he got a shock.

"I've sold some already," 'Melia told him, "and I don't think you'll be overcharged for the poetry, sir."

"What d'ye mean?" Lucius asked, staring at her, and running his fingers through his hair, until it stood in an astonished fringe.

"A friend o' yours, Mr. Dunbar, was in to-day, by chance, sir."

"How d'ye know he's a friend o' mine?" growled Lucius.

"Miss Moriarty was here about some more plants—two for the window," 'Melia explained, "and he came in."

"By golly!" Lucius ejaculated under his breath, "the fat's in the fire. I never thought o' that! What next?" he demanded.

"Well, after Miss Moriarty was gone, Mr. Dunbar took one o' the new packets. He smokes 'em regular, sir."

"By golly! the divil he does?"

"And he ses," 'Melia went on, being accustomed to Moriarty's muttered comments, "that he knows the gentleman who wrote this poetry. I told him you said he was awful clever."

"Oh! go on," Lucius groaned.

"And I told him that the poetry upon the packets of mixture was done for love—for nothing I mean—so that his friend must be moderate in his charges." 'Melia concluded triumphantly, and Lucius, finding his feelings too

much for him, hurriedly presented the Christmas-box, told
her not to open the shop next day, and made his escape.
On his doorstep he considered the matter once more, and
summed up thus—

" Th' young rascal has the whip-hand o' me now.   The
other poetry he'll know was mine, if I didn't pay for it.
Good stuff like that isn't got for nothing, though I say it
as shouldn't.   *By* golly !"

# CHAPTER XLIII

WHILE Nelly, on Christmas morning, was smiling over a silver waist-buckle, and blushing a little at the unsigned sonnet that came with it, 'Melia also was rejoicing.

She had decided to take her breakfast in bed that morning "like a lady," and had persuaded her landlady, who had a grim, undemonstrative liking for her, to bring it up.

As the time came for its appearance, there was a bumping and a banging upon the stair outside, and 'Melia, already very wide-awake and hungry, and not sure that breakfast in bed was desirable after all, became anxious for its safety.

"Do be careful," she called out, sitting up in the bed, "or you'll drop the tray, and where'll my tea be then?"

But the banging and the bumping went on, until the door was pushed open, and the panting Mrs. Meiklejohn appeared, struggling, not with the breakfast tray, but with a new bicycle.

"Thocht ye'd maybe like yer Christmas first," she announced, and 'Melia, being untrained in the repression of emotion, fairly yelled.

"Not for me!" she assured Mrs. Meiklejohn. "Oh, it *can't* be for me! Oh, what a beauty! Take it away out of my sight, do!"

"To Miss Rivers," retorted Mrs. Meiklejohn, "and no chairges." 'Melia, still refusing to believe, had her name pointed out, written upon a ticket on the handle-bar.

"Who's it from? Where's it from?"

"A dinna ken. Yer faither, maybe!" suggested Mrs. Meiklejohn, who had once seen Rivers. Then she left the room with what, for her, was a smile, and fetched 'Melia's breakfast up, reminding her, sarcastically, that she had said she was going to church.

" And so I will ! " 'Melia insisted. " Christmas is Christmas where I come from," and then sighed to think that the bicycle must remain untried for three or four hours. So she went to church, and did her best to keep bicycles out of her mind while there ; then, coming home like the wind, changed her dress, and tried her new treasure over three or four miles of the cleanest road obtainable.

She could not decide who had sent it. There were three persons possible—Rivers, Peters, and Archie. She would not let herself acknowledge that Rivers was the least likely, was indeed almost impossible. She determined to say nothing, until she had seen whether anyone would mention the matter.

Then—in the middle of the Queensferry Road—she was suddenly struck by an idea that had never entered her head before. If it wasn't her father—if it was Cap'n Peters— or still worse, if it was Archie who sent the bicycle, what right had she to take such a present ? Poor 'Melia, dismayed, looked down at the flying wheel before her, and saw on it unmistakable signs of her journey.

" What can I do now ? " she wondered. " Any fool can see I've used it. Second-hand ! That's what it is now, and I don't know where it came from, nor if I can keep it."

This rather depressed her, but she got home very hungry nevertheless, and spent a great part of the time between dinner and tea in cleaning and admiring the bicycle.

In the evening, who should visit her but Rivers and Mr. Peters. Rivers would not have come, if it had not been for Mr. Peters. 'Melia thought Mr. Peters had come in from the hills specially for the purpose of wishing her a merry Christmas, and was unnecessarily grateful to both.

" When'll you get back ? " she asked Peters.

" Not to-night," he told her. " I wish to see you good people when you are gay. This is the happy time when you are all gay, and love one another, is it not ? "

" I don't know," 'Melia answered, considering. " It may be so where *you* come from, Cap'n Peters, but here I think one's feelin's is much the same as usual. Friends 'll be kind " (here she thought of the bicycle), and enemies—well, enemies may wish you a merry Christmas, for the look o' the thing, but I don't s'pose it counts for much. Now I come to think of it, *you* never wished me a merry Christmas."

" It is over, is it not ? " asked Mr. Peters. " I hope you have had one."

" Oh, I count it till the New Year," 'Melia insisted. " Wish me a merry Christmas, Cap'n Peters; come, now, or I shall think you're vexed with me still for that," and she pointed to his left hand, now adorned with sticking plaster.

" Ah ! I owe you for that," he told her, looking at it, however, without any great appearance of satisfaction. " From now till the New Year, you say. A whole week ? But I like to pay my debts in full, and over. I wish you a merry Christmas."

" Well, I can't see that it's paying anything very dear, just to wish a body a merry Christmas," 'Melia insisted. " Still, as you don't owe me nothing, we won't quarrel about that."

" Let us make it merry," Peters suggested. " Can we not go anywhere, to see all the good people happy ? Come, I will give you the evening for a Christmas present, and the good Rivers will guard our ways. Where shall we go ? "

" I don't know that father pretends to be good, any more than other people, do you, father ? " 'Melia said, irritably. " I wish you wouldn't be always usin' that word, Cap'n Peters. It makes me cross somehow."

" I thought you and I were going to have a quiet evening by the fire in my room, to-night," Rivers broke in, frowning at Mr. Peters. "It's a beastly night, and there'll be crowds everywhere."

"We want crowds," Peters pointed out, ignoring the signals, "crowds of happy people. Come! It is my Christmas present."

"Oh! *that's* your Christmas present?" 'Melia said. "Well, that settles something else, anyway. Yes, I'll come if father will."

"Oh, he will come," Mr. Peters decided. "We can have a chat by the fire, your father and I, and drink our healths after we have brought you back. He will give you his company for three hours, the good—or, let us say, the generous Rivers. That is his Christmas present."

'Melia looked anxiously at Rivers, who, somewhat cheered by the prospect of a profitable evening later on, said that he would come, of course, and that Em'ly must choose some little thing, not too expensive, say half-a-crown, to-night or to-morrow, as a present from her poor father.

"That settles it!" 'Melia announced, half to herself, and went from Mrs. Meiklejohn's little sitting-room, where she had received her visitors, to put on her cloak. She now knew where the bicycle came from, at anyrate. What she should do about it, 'Melia couldn't decide. It is certain that she never thought of consulting either her father or Mr. Peters, both of whom presently sallied out with her in search of amusement.

It was to the Waverley Market they went that night for their crowd—and found it.

To the sounds of brass bands, hurdy-gurdys, bagpipes, steam-whistles, showmen's calls, the cries of wild beasts, and those of that superior animal, man, on the rampage, 'Melia went the round.

She saw the Beheaded Lady, looking remarkably composed, the Missing Link, the Fat Boy, and the Living Skeleton. She fired six shots at the dancing glass balls, without shrieking, which was considered unwomanly by Annie, from the House of Residence, who stood near and tried to make out what brought together "Old Rivers," the stony-hearted Mr. Peters, and this forward thing, who, the charitable Annie felt certain, was no better than she should be.

But, in the seething mass that filled the place, Annie lost sight of them, shoved hither and thither in a good-tempered way as everyone was, by everyone else.

'Melia afterwards careered in a dignified manner upon the merry-go-round, and at last, when Rivers had begun to grumble, stood before the gypsy-tent.

"*Reel* gypsies?" asked 'Melia. "Oh, my! I've never had my fortune told, Cap'n Peters!"

'Melia's remark was overheard by a man standing at the tent-door, and he turned to her at once.

"Now's the time then, miss! No time like the present. Walk in while grandmother's got the fit on her. Lord! the beautiful things she's promised to-night, to young ladies not half so good-looking. Walk in, miss, and get a golden fortune told you for a bit of silver. You've a lucky face, and don't you go and throw it away."

The fellow had a dark eye and a roguish air. He looked at 'Melia with bold admiration. "You might wait a twelve-month and not get such a chance," he told her. "Will you miss a fortune for a shilling or so?"

"We've spent enough already," said 'Melia, peering into the tent and its mysterious shadows. "Ain't it shuddery-like, Cap'n Peters? Will you get your fortune told? Do you believe in it?"

"No," Mr. Peters said, disregarding the filial pride of the dark-eyed man at the tent-door; "no, it is humbug, altogether."

"Hark to the gentleman!" said the dark-eyed man. "It's easy to see *he's* never had a fortune told. Go in, sir,

and see what the new year'll give to you. There's changes
in it for you. I can read that, though I've not got the sight
like my grandmother, nothing like. Take him in, lady, and
let grandmother tell him what he can expect."

" I'd like to hear your fortune. Cap'n Peters, a'most as
well as my own," 'Melia declared, politely, " but if you
don't believe in it, of course, you won't go in an' throw
money away, as you may say."

Mr. Peters was in a generous mood, however, and looked
at it in a different light.

" If I believed," he explained, " I would not go in, but
since I know it is humbug, what does it matter ? It is
your night, your merry Christmas. Come ! " so they all
three passed in, 'Melia protesting, half-heartedly, against
the extravagance as she went.

A thing, that might be an old woman, or might be a
bundle of old clothes, sat silent and indistinct among the
shadows, just inside the door.

A youngish woman, standing by a little stove, with her
back to the entrance, muttered over the hand of an open-
mouthed, wide-eyed country lass.

She finished hurriedly as the others came in, and turned
to them, but the bundle of clothes near the entrance rose
and came forward, showing itself to be a very old, black-
eyed, skinny creature, wrinkled like a dry apple.

The younger woman drew back, as the other stood before
them, looking with bright bird-like eyes from one to the
other.

" Come along, Cap'n Peters ! she's waitin' for you."
'Melia said in a hushed voice : but Mr. Peters, quite unim-
pressed, " as if he was at 'ome," as 'Melia told him afterwards, insisted that she must be first.

'Melia, still faintly protesting but very much excited,
held out her hand, the necessary silver being produced by
Mr. Peters, while Rivers stood by, and sneered in a superior

manner, listening, nevertheless, to hear what Fortune would bestow upon his daughter. The gypsy waved both the men back, and then gave 'Melia a prediction, concerning fair and dark gentlemen, that kept her alternately smiling and sober-faced for the rest of the evening.

Then came Peters, and while the woman peered into his large hand, 'Melia stood by unrebuked. She heard little of interest.

"Born under Mars and Venus," the woman told him, "and you're a gentleman with a will of your own," which the average observer could have guessed, without seeing his hand. "A free-handed gentleman," the gypsy continued.

"You're that, Cap'n Peters," 'Melia certified. "You know you are. Now, how can she tell?" and was much impressed, not having taken into account the probable effect upon the gypsy's opinions of the two liberal tips out of Mr. Peters' pocket. The woman went on about business, journeys in foreign lands, much to be settled in the coming year, and ended up with a safe prediction.

"You'll take another voyage before the next year's out, Captain," she told him, and Mr. Peters laughed. He certainly would take another voyage, he thought, directly his business was ended, and turned to go.

But the old woman had already fastened upon Rivers, who, although sulky at being kept from a more profitable amusement, was not so determined to resist her blandishments as he had been.

"Come, lady!" the old crone insisted, "make the gentleman listen to me, there's a pretty deary."

"A shilling 'll do it, father, after what she's got from Cap'n Peters already," 'Melia suggested, and Rivers gave way.

"The hand of a gentleman born," the woman told him. "You've had your ups and your downs, you've got your

21

friends and your enemies, but you'll come to your own in the end."

" Own what ? " asked 'Melia, breathless, but the gypsy shook her head.

" His rights, dearie, I don't know what. Maybe a fortune, maybe the House o' Lords. I can't tell. But there's many things 'll happen. I see gold and I see a journey, and I can't see any more for the money."

Finding Rivers regardless of the hint, she dropped his hand, and, collapsing into her seat, became once more a mere bundle of cast-off clothing, inanimate, and deaf to the entreaties of 'Melia for more prophecy.

" It's no use, lady," said the dark-eyed doorkeeper, poking his head inside the tent, with a grin, " the fit's off her now, and she won't say no more, not though the Queen comes an' kneels down before her, she's that contrary. 'Alf-a-crown might do it, but no less."

That sum was not forthcoming, and the three of them went away, Mr. Peters commenting as they went, perhaps to himself, perhaps to 'Melia, upon the dark-eyed man's opinion of the relative persuasive values of Her Most Gracious Majesty and of half-a-crown.

# CHAPTER XLIV

### UNDER EXAMINATION

'MELIA's Merry Christmas time was nearly over, for it was now the day before New Year's Eve. The shortest day having passed, winter tightened his grip upon the land, as a man when past his prime may grip gold, and the lochs and pools were ice-bound. Then (it being an ill wind that blows nobody good), while the aged, the ill-fed, and the weakly cramped themselves together—shrinking from a touch which for them was the touch of death—the lusty and full-blooded, the fittest, fated to survive, came out to face the ice king, and felt the better for doing so.

That day a party met for lunch at Lucius Moriarty's table, with the purpose of skating afterwards on Duddingston Loch.

Madge Murray had persuaded Nell to invite Mr. Peters, and Nell had also invited Tom Dunbar, telling herself that it was his vacation, and that he had been a good fellow to stay and work all through Christmas.

Lucius came up from his office for lunch, certain ships being ice-bound somewhere, and he being in consequence not so busy as usual.

"It's a poor heart that never rejoices," he told Madge Murray. "If I can't see me ships, I can see me friends." and Madge, always quick to see a compliment, whether expressed or implied, laughed, and said she was glad to be a consolation.

"Faith!" Lucius declared. "Consolation, is it? Why, a few smiles like that 'll keep me heart warm for the rest o' this most inclement season. I don't know that I ought to let Nell go wid ye on the ice at all, at all!"

Why not ? " asked Madge, spying another compliment, and smiling upon the gallant Moriarty.

" The ice 'll melt under the eyes of ye ! " Lucius declared, and then, having rebuked Nell for laughing at him, went off to his office again, and the others started for the ice.

Since Madge was now bestowing her smiles and her conversation entirely upon Mr. Peters, Nell felt bound to walk with Tom Dunbar.

" It's awfully good of you to invite me," he told her.

" I wanted to talk to you," Nell explained, and then, seeing he looked unduly jubilant, " to scold you," she added severely.

" Let's put it off until we come back," Tom suggested meekly.

" Best get it over, I think," Nell decided, with great firmness. " Have you been sending any Christmas presents ? "

" Let me see," Tom reflected carefully, with a vacant stare, as at some far distant period. " Yes, I sent the *Mater* a card."

" Anything else ? " Nell demanded, watching him narrowly.

" No," Tom assured her, serenely. " She doesn't like to get more than a card, she says, till I'm in practice."

" I didn't mean that," Nell told him, speaking pretty sharply because she felt sure the scamp was laughing at her. " I mean, did you send any other presents ? "

" Oh, yes," said Tom cheerfully. " I sent a knife to my young brother, and I know he'll cut his fingers before the New Year; I sent a box of chocolate to 'Frida (that's my youngest sister, you know), and a book to 'Trix, who's the eldest."

" Anything more ? " Tom began to feel as if he were at the Confessional.

" Well," he allowed, with an air of polite surprise, " I

sent a card, a funny one, to Mary Ann, but I forget the
words or I'd repeat 'em. You don't know Mary Ann, do
you? She's our old cook. Her surname is Brown. The
errand boys call her Missis Brown—though she isn't married—just to flatter her. She's one of eleven in a family.
I wish I could remember the rhymes, but if you'll let me
think a minute——" He stopped, still showing an air of
innocent and polite surprise, for Nell, much against her
will, had begun to laugh.

"That will do," she told him. "It's very good of you to
tell me so much. You sent nothing else worth mentioning,
I suppose?"

"No," Tom shook his head soberly, after consideration,
"I sent nothing else worth mentioning."

"Christmas presents are a nuisance in some ways, don't
you think?" Nell asked him.

"I don't find 'em so," Tom declared, sturdily. "Sorry
if you do."

"Well, I do," Nell insisted, "particularly when I have to
send them back."

"What do you send 'em back for?" demanded Tom, so
much interested that he cannoned against another man on
the pavement, and had to apologize. "What on earth do
you send them back for?" he repeated, as soon as he had
recovered his balance.

"Oh, well," said Nell, demurely, "I'll tell you what I
mean. Do look where you're going though, or you'll knock
someone down!"

This was probable, for Tom, in his anxiety to watch her
face, had charged another unoffending wayfarer into the
road.

"Deuce of a lot of room these people want!" he muttered to himself, and then asked Nell to explain.

"I had a present sent from a shop in Princes Street," she
told him, "and, of course, I must take it back and explain

to them that I can't keep it, because I don't know from whom it came."

" Would you keep it if you did know ? " asked Tom.

" That depends. What could I use it for ? "

The device was simple enough, but Tom blundered at once. " I should think it might do well enough for a belt," he suggested, and Nell at once turned upon him.

" What might ? "

" You said—didn't you say——? "

" Well ! go on."

" I thought you said what it was." Tom explained.

" What did you think I said it was ? "

" Something for a belt."

" A silver buckle, for example ? No, I hadn't mentioned it. How funny that you should happen to hit upon that ! "

Tom went along in dogged silence for a few yards, and then collapsed.

" I'm an ass," he told her confidentially, " I suppose it's a good thing that I know it. It's no use my trying to humbug anyone. Of course, I know it's a silver buckle. I suppose I thought you'd be more likely to wear it, if you weren't sure that it came from me. But you might keep a trifle like that, anyway."

" A trifle, indeed ! and do you call that a trifle ? " asked Nell severely, comforted to find Tom in such a state of abject humility, and she was proceeding to a lecture upon the sin of thoughtless extravagance when, perhaps to her relief, perhaps to Tom's, Mr. Peters intervened.

He asked some trivial question, but did not quit Nell's side after being answered. Perhaps he thought that a change of society would be pleasant, perhaps he was of opinion that it would be more sociable if the four kept together. At anyrate, he kept near to Tom and Nellie, and, since Madge perforce did the same, the chat became general, and the lecture was indefinitely postponed.

# CHAPTER XLV

## DUDDINGSTON LOCH

IT was a dusky late afternoon, on Duddingston Loch. The air was still, the smoke hung almost unstirred over the city to the northwest, Arthur's Seat towered white and wintry above the Queen's Drive.

But, on the ice below, there was a perpetual hum and movement.

Word had gone abroad that there was skating at Duddingston, and the whole stretch of ice was thrown open to the crowd, save for some fifty square yards, roped off to the north. That lay quiet and bare, temptingly smooth and unmarked. Ambitious skaters, anxious for a clear space, looked at it longingly, but flitted by, threading a way through the swaying, changing, chattering crowd. There was laughing and shouting from end to end of the loch, with the constant swish, swish, of skate-blades, and the rattle and rush of the curling-stones where the Roaring Game was in full swing.

As the dusk crept on, it brought, to some, a feeling of romance—a feeling as if the town, the world, were far away, and they were moving among shadows. Tom, swinging by Nell's side, swayed a little closer, and gripped her hands more firmly, whilst Nell felt that she could not scold him, just now, about the buckle : it was altogether too petty for such a time, and found herself wishing that the ice would stretch farther ahead, smooth and untouched for them alone.

The dusky unreality of everything that night was felt by

Madge Murray too. She looked more keenly for admiration, and, failing to get any satisfactory sign of it from Mr. Peters, fished for it more openly.

She persuaded him to teach her new figures, and showed, recklessly, how far she was ready to depend upon his hand for safety.

" I saw your friend at the tobacconist's shop the other day," she told him, resting after a lesson.

" So I have heard," said Mr. Peters, undisturbed.

" She told you, did she ? The young person seems very friendly."

" With you ? " asked Mr. Peters.

" Don't be ridiculous ! No, with you."

" I find many ready to be friendly," Mr. Peters admitted, without any appearance of gratitude.

" A girl like that, Mr. Peters, soon gets her head turned. She doesn't understand foreign complimentary ways."

" Ah ! the poor foreigner," said Mr. Peters. " He must always make mistakes outside his own country."

" Yes, that's quite true," Madge told him. " We all do, and it's only kind, I think, to warn one's friends."

" I will be more careful," he promised. " Is it right, according to your custom, that I should ask you to skate with me ? "

He hadn't asked her, and Madge frowned at him before answering, but Mr. Peters was engaged in tying his boot-lace.

" Yes, that's all right," she told him. " It's only when you pay too much attention to anyone of a lower class in society, that silly people talk. Come ! show me that figure again."

Mr. Peters showed her, and Madge tried it, but had a collision with a scudding, broom-carrying young ragamuffin, and would have fallen, had she not clutched at the immovable Peters.

" You *are* strong," she said, " but there's no room to do anything here. Let's go just inside that rope."

" You wish to drown ? " inquired Mr. Peters.

" I'm not a bit afraid of that," Madge insisted. " I'm sure it will bear a few, just as well as the rest does. The crowd's afraid to go where there's a rope, and that's all they put it up for."

Mr. Peters made no answer. He was looking at a familiar figure that stood on the ice near the bank—no other than Rivers. That worthy, having met Archie Inch with his skates in Princes Street, had button-holed the young man, and introduced the subject of 'Melia. If anything in the wide world could have made thoughts of 'Melia unpleasant to Archie, the presence of her father would have done it. He could not mention to Rivers her incomprehensible ways —such ways as, for example, her tearful desire to make some arrangement for returning the bicycle, which she had refused to ride again. But Rivers, allowed to maunder on unchecked, might let fall some useful hint for Archie's guidance, and they had come down to the loch together, Archie fervently hoping that he might meet no friends by the way.

Now Archie had become lost in the crowd, and Rivers, when Mr. Peters saw him, was watching the skaters with a critical air, helping himself liberally from a large flask which he had just purchased at the " Sheep's Head," saying, to an acquaintance who had just slowed up to him, that he saw nothing here to come anywhere near Oxford form.

The fellow winked to a friend standing by, having heard frequently of Oxford from Rivers, and thinking that he saw a chance of some fun.

" Skate yourself ? " he asked innocently, and Rivers gave him to understand that, if he chose, he could, even yet, show the skaters of Edinburgh a thing or two.

" Pity you've no skates," suggested the other man, and
Rivers, having no skates, but a fair amount of the flask's
contents, seemed to think it *was* a pity.

" Dab at figures ? " he asked, cutting a couple of threes
without getting out of earshot. Rivers modestly admitted
that he had never been anything extraordinary for pace,
but when it came to figures, well——! " I was president of
our club," he explained, and the man winked at his friend
again.

" A fellow forgets it all in a year or two," the third man
told them. " This gentleman couldn't do a three now to
save his life."

" Oh, nonsense. He could do a simple thing like that
now, if he ever could ! "

" I tell you," declared the third man, " I wouldn't be
surprised if he couldn't go from one side to the other
without a tumble," and, really, taking into account the
crowd, and the flask, and allowing for Rivers' noted men-
dacity, the probability was that he was right.

The end of it was a bet with Rivers of five shillings to one
that he could not skate from one side of the loch to the
other without a fall, and another bet, of ten to one, that he
would not do a figure of three on his return.

Mr. Peters, still watching with interest, saw Rivers begin
to put on skates borrowed from one of his tempters, and
chuckled grimly.

" So long as his neck is not broken," he thought, " I do
not care," and, still watching, repeated his refusal to take
Madge beyond the rope.

" Then I'll go alone," Madge decided.

" I," said Mr. Peters, " will go, then, to the other end."

" Why ? "

" I wish," he told her, " to be as far off as is possible,
when you fall in."

This frank statement, so like the one made upon Leith

Pier in the autumn, must surely be a clumsy attempt at a joke.

Madge faced him, staring, to see whether any smile contradicted the uncomplimentary speech, but smile there was none.

Mr. Peters was closely watching a somewhat unsteady figure that, bumping occasionally against some of the crowd, was now half-way across the ice. No man can lie always and altogether. Rivers had once been a skater, of a sort, and, braced by the flask, and the wish to show what he could do, was making a big effort to win the five shillings, and if possible the ten.

"If other people," said Mr. Peters, still with an eye upon Rivers, "choose to be foolish about their own lives, why should I do anything? Their lives are, perhaps, worth not a sixpence. My life is very valuable to me. I shall keep it."

The woman at his side had often expressed her liking for frankness, but plain speech of this kind was different. It was simple rudeness, and, being angry, she began to tell him so, without his seeming to pay any attention.

Rivers had won his five shillings, and, unduly elated thereby, started to return with bolder more sweeping strokes. He took the edge of the crowd as he came, and, having no collision, increased his speed, passing close by Mr. Peters and Madge. Then, slackening as he reached the disappointed owner of the skates and his friend, he turned on to the outside edge, began the three, tripped over a straw, staggered a step or two backward, was caught behind the knees by the rope, fell over it, and crashing through the ice upon the other side of it, disappeared.

In the rush and hubbub that followed, Madge clung frantically to Mr. Peters, imploring him not to leave her. The crowd first swayed towards the rope, at the spot where Rivers, who had come to the surface again, was floundering

wildly in what would very soon be a death-struggle.  Then
the ice cracked loudly, under the tremendous weight of the
hustling throng, and the people scattered in every direction, lest they, too, should find themselves in the water with
the choking, struggling, spluttering wretch, who now sank
for a second time before their eyes.

Some tried to loosen the rope over which the man had
stumbled, some skated down the ice to fetch other help, but
Mr. Peters never stirred.

At first he laughed, on seeing what had happened, but
when the gasping thing before him fought so impotently,
he laughed no more.

He made no answer to Madge, but when, having got over
the first sudden fright, she turned to make for the bank,
she found that he was leaning one hand heavily upon her,
and slipping off his skates and boots together with the
other.

" Now go ! " he told her, roughly, as the second boot
came off, and she went, breathless.

But Mr. Peters, his eyes fixed upon the rippling, eddying
water which covered the drowning man, ran forward a few
paces, then throwing himself on his face upon the ice
wriggled to the edge of the hole, which now owing to
Rivers' struggles had got much larger.  He hoped that
something would come within reach for him to grip, and
lay peering intently into the black water, while the crowd
shouted and swayed behind him.

Presently a hand rose, gripping wildly at nothing, and
beyond Mr. Peters' reach.  But the man who waited could
wait no longer.  He drew a deep breath, and, sliding into
the water like a huge seal head foremost, clutched at the
other's neck.  If he got, and kept, a hold, it was not because of any help from Rivers, who clutched at him as
only a drowning man can.  Even when his head was above
water, and Peters was shouting in his ear that he was safe,

Rivers struggled as though he would lift himself out altogether by rising on the other, and once sent Mr. Peters bodily under again.

When Mr. Peters rose that time he did not try to say anything, and his face was not pleasant to look upon. He gripped Rivers firmly by the throat with one hand, and the watching crowd saw him deliberately strike the man in the face with his other clenched fist.

Some women shrieked, but Rivers fought no more, being insensible, and Mr. Peters held on to the edge of the ice, silent and grim, until Tom Dunbar, stretching across a hurdle and held by a rope, shuffled his way along, and hauled both of them out.

# CHAPTER XLVI

SEVERAL hours had now elapsed since Rivers had been dragged ashore. As he lay unconscious in his bed, he moaned and muttered more than once, lifting a hand to the great bruise—Mr. Peters' sign-manual—that had risen on his right temple.

Where the thinking, responsible part of him strayed, in the long intervals of dumb stillness, one would like to know. All one can be sure of is that, when that part came back from its wandering, it came back unaltered, and the first use Rivers made of his recovered faculties was to ask for something to drink.

This happened in the small hours of the morning after his exploit. At the querulous sound of his voice, Mr. Peters rose from the fireside, where, by the light of a shaded lamp, he was playing the inevitable game of Patience, and, coming to the bedside, looked down upon him.

" Ah ! the good Rivers. You cannot drown, then ? "

Rivers stared at him vacantly, and, with one hand wandering up to his aching head again, asked where he was.

" In your bed," Mr. Peters told him, and Rivers, looking slowly around, seemed at last to recognize things.

" My head aches like the devil," he said, fretfully. " Have I been drinking ? "

" Quarts," chuckled Mr. Peters, and Rivers, puzzling over things in a drowsy, muddle-headed way, began slowly to remember.

" That was water," he said presently. " It's lying cold on my stomach. Give me whiskey," and Mr. Peters, making a great parade with the bottle, poured out a very small quantity of spirit, and, diluting it liberally, let him drink.

But Rivers was discontented and said so, and Mr. Peters therefore had to explain further.

" It is the doctor's orders," he told his charge, " because of your head."

" What's wrong ? " Rivers demanded, drowsily, his hand still on his forehead.

" You were so strong and so brave," Mr. Peters told him, laughing softly again, " you wished to drown, I think. But I did not, so I hit you."

" What a d—d awkward thing to do," Rivers muttered. " Give me a little more, anyway."

" Not a drop," Mr. Peters declared, not at all troubled by the rescued man's verdict upon his action. " I have pulled you out of the water, my good, grateful Rivers, and you shall not fall into the whiskey. Then I should have got wet for nothing. Now, sleep !" and Rivers, finding that Mr. Peters had returned to the fire and to Patience, and that he would make no reply to any question, presently dropped off to sleep, and woke no more until day had begun.

All that time Mr. Peters kept watch over him, mostly sitting by the fire, amusing himself with the cards, and smoking an occasional cigarette. Now and then he would look across at the sleeper. Twice he rose, and, crossing the room to the bedside, satisfied himself that his patient was doing well. A more attentive nurse than Mr. Peters could not be desired by any man. He trod the room as softly as any cat could have done, and watched the unconscious Rivers as carefully as though he had been a mouse. But when the latter, waking again, was more grateful, and declared himself quite recovered except for a headache, Mr.

Peters watched no longer, but went off to his own room for a nap, contenting himself with Rivers' promise that he would not move until the doctor had called—but taking the whiskey bottle with him.

# CHAPTER XLVII

## NEW YEAR AT THE TRON

LATE on New Year's Eve, Rivers, somewhat against the doctor's orders, left the House of Residence, and, well wrapped up and accompanied by Mr. Peters, went to see 'Melia. He professed himself to be all right again, except for a tenderness where Mr. Peters had made his mark, and was considerably more profuse in his thanks than he had been in the early morning. Mr. Peters took Rivers' expressions of gratitude without any more enthusiasm than he had shown when that gratitude seemed problematical, and was not anxious to call upon 'Melia that night. But Rivers insisted, and so Mr. Peters, shrugging his shoulders with an air of anything but cheerful resignation, yielded.

That night 'Melia sat alone in the little room behind the curtain, and wondered very much what fortune the New Year was going to bring, also what on earth she was to do with Archie. That young man was getting masterful, and, instead of holding to his former humble declaration, that he knew he wasn't half good enough for 'Melia, and that he was sure she couldn't possibly care for him, had lately as good as told her that he felt certain she was not so indifferent as she pretended to be, and that he was determined to make her own to it sooner or later. " Just like his cheek ! " 'Melia said.

Such is the incomprehensible manner of man. So terribly, too, are coy maidens subdued by a lordly manner, that 'Melia, instead of bidding him begone and see her face no more, trembled a little when he came, sighed a little when he went, and altogether behaved as if she were not quite sure but what she liked it It was, at anyrate, difficult

22

to continue to believe that Archie was pushing matters so
far from a mere sense of duty, and, after all, it was pleasant
to be woo'd for one's own sake, and in spite of disadvan-
tages. Still, 'Melia was very vexed with herself for not
being inwardly so stubborn as she seemed, and was scolding
herself well, at the moment when her two visitors from the
House of Residence came in.

Rivers was truly melodramatic in his greeting that night,
and introduced Mr. Peters in a new character, after em-
bracing 'Melia.

" My preserver," he announced, with a hand on Mr.
Peters' shoulder, and 'Melia, being ignorant of recent
events, and possibly suspecting intoxication, said, " Lor !
father, what *are* you talkin' about ? "

" Do not be a big fool ! " suggested Mr. Peters, frowning
impatiently, but Rivers, even with the risk of an unsympathetic audience, was not to be denied his opportunity for a
display.

He told 'Melia the whole story, with many details which
Mr. Peters did not remember, and described sensations
which he himself had never experienced. He drew a vivid
picture of the moment when all his past life had flashed
before him—which it hadn't—and insisted particularly
upon having felt during his struggles, more bitterly than
anything else, that his little Em'ly would be left unprotected. By the time he had ended, poor 'Melia was in tears,
partly because she was an excitable young person, and partly
because she secretly felt that she must lately have been unjust, in her inmost mind, towards a parent who could think
of her with, so to speak, both feet in a watery grave. She
came round the counter, and did her best to secure the hand
of Mr. Peters, who, however, laughing at the beginning of
this dramatic recital, and frowning at the end, stood well
away, with his hands behind his back, and repulsed 'Melia's
advances altogether.

"This is what you call rot!" he announced brusquely. "It is enough, and we will have no more."

"Well, really," protested 'Melia, wiping her eyes, and trying to feel angry with this hero who wouldn't be worshipped, "I never know 'ow to take you, Cap'n Peters."

'Melia's aspirates had much improved lately, but they still played her false in moments of emotion.

"Do not take me," Mr. Peters entreated her. "Leave me alone, that is all."

Then, seeing perhaps that 'Melia was really beginning to feel hurt, "What is it all about?" he went on, less roughly. "A wetting, and nothing more! There was no danger for me. I could have let him go down to the mud and stay there, could I not, if there had been; and you would still have said 'thank you' to me, for pretending to try to fish him out? Come, we have done with it!"

"I sha'n't forgit, anyway," 'Melia declared, "though I dare say, bein' a man, you don't like no fuss made. You've given me my Happy Christmas right through, Cap'n Peters."

"That is it," Peters declared, as if struck by the idea. "I have wished you a Merry Christmas, and I have done my best for you. Now we are quits, as you call it."

"No, we aren't," 'Melia declared, warmly, "not by no manner of means. There's a big balance on your side, Cap'n Peters."

"That is well," Mr. Peters told her. "We will speak of it no more. Good-night. It is time to go home again."

But this by no means pleased the vivacious Rivers.

"Now that I'm out," he insisted, "I mean to stay out, and see the fun, and wish Em'ly here a Happy New Year before she goes to bed."

"This is more humbug!" Mr. Peters declared, and turned away to go off alone, when 'Melia stopped him, anx-

ious that Rivers should have no excuse for roaming alone
that night.

"It's after 'leven now," she told him. "Take me round
to see some o' the streets, Cap'n Peters, an' then you an'
father can get back together. Come, now! my Christmas
isn't done, for more'n half an hour. We don't know where
we'll all be, by this time next year."

"That's true," Rivers agreed. His twenty-four hours in
bed had made him lively, and he was only regretting Mr.
Peters' presence because Mr. Peters would perhaps limit
his drink, according to doctor's orders.

"I'm going a journey next year, remember!" he added.

"Yes, an' Cap'n Peters goes a voyage," 'Melia reminded
them. "Come along, Cap'n Peters, an' see the sights for
once!" and Mr. Peters made no more objections, but went.

The sights were not varied that night, but they saw what
there was to see, with a running commentary for 'Melia's
benefit from Mr. Peters, who was in a very bad temper.

"You've kep' your promise, an' more," she told him,
softly, as they went up the street. "I can't thank you
enough, Cap'n Peters."

"My promise?" he told her, angrily, "I have made you
no promise."

"Oh, but you did," 'Melia insisted. "You promised me
you'd keep an eye on pa. You've done it, too."

"Very well, then," retorted Peters, "if it is done, it is
finished, that is all. I have kept my promise, you say. I
owe you nothing."

"I owe *you* lots," 'Melia declared.

"I promise you no more," Mr. Peters answered loudly,
and then talked to Rivers, though not in a very friendly way.

As for Rivers, his head was aching, and he thought once
more that Peters was a clumsy fellow.

What is the use of pulling a man out of the water, if you
pretty well brain him in doing so? Peters was quite right

to dislike making much of such a rough and tumble affair. No doubt, as he had been frank enough to admit, he would have let Rivers go quickly enough had there been any real danger to himself.

Rivers was quickly getting to think almost as little of the rescue as Mr. Peters seemed to—and his head was really aching terribly.

It would have been a bad job, too, for Mr. Peters, if Rivers had drowned himself, and so had become incapable of playing cards, while still owing Mr. Peters his revenge.

There was now a very tidy little sum of Mr. Peters' money in Rivers' bureau, and no doubt the former recollected that, and gave it due consideration before he came to the rescue.

To know that this was one probable motive made Rivers feel that, after all, it was best, as Mr. Peters had said, to make no more fuss about that clumsy exhibition in life-saving ; also, that if Mr. Peters, unable to take his losses quietly and like a gentleman, should insist upon more play, one need not scruple, from any silly sense of gratitude, to let him have his whim—and take his chance.

These were some of Rivers' reflections as the three went along, and they occupied him as the party proceeded from Princes Street, up the Mound to the Tron Church.

For where else should they go that night, if they wished to go with the crowd ? It moved thitherward from all quarters, and stayed only when it reached the open space about that time-honored landmark, surging and swaying, pushing and reeling, but determined to be—in honor of old custom—within sight of the Tron clock when the hands should mark midnight.

'Melia and her escort drew up at the top of Cockburn Street, and Mr. Peters, surveying the mob, classified its component parts, as he pushed between 'Melia and a hospitable inhabitant of the High Street, who flourished a bottle at her with an invitation to drink.

" Here," said Mr. Peters, " are our good people, here is our happy crowd. Here is fun ! " and he laughed as though he found some amusement, while 'Melia politely declined the offer of the use of another bottle.

" These people," Mr. Peters went on, looking about him, and able to see far, since his head rose well above most of the crowd, " these people are divided into two parts, those who are drunk—and those who are drinking."

" That's not so, Cap'n Peters," said 'Melia, indignantly. " We're not drunk or drinking, an' we don't mean to. I'm sure there's plenty of quiet folks like you an' me, come up just to see things. My ! look ! There's a man working too."

She was quite right. There were plenty of quiet people among the crowd, there, like themselves, out of mere curiosity, but the more objectionable were, as they always are, the more conspicuous. There was also, as she had pointed out, a man working.

He stood at a first floor window of some office facing the Tron, and worked at a desk, with a gas-jet flaring just over his head. The crowd beneath him hummed and reeled. The window at which he worked was now and then opened, and a colored light was pushed out, to blaze for a few seconds and die away without making the man look up. The clock now showed less than five minutes to the new year, but this man worked on methodically, as though, so Mr. Peters thought, his one object in life was to balance accounts.

The hands of the Tron clock moved on towards the hour, nearer and nearer ; the colored " flares " became more plentiful, the crowd grew even noisier, with a continuous roar like that of a heavy sea, but still the man at the first floor window worked steadily on, and still Mr. Peters watched him.

Presently the hour was reached, though one could only

tell it by looking at the clock, for the twelve strokes were unheard in the increased roar.

'Melia, seizing Rivers with one hand, and groping for Mr. Peters with the other, started "Old Lang Syne," as she called it, but Mr. Peters had moved a pace away, and stood nearer under the window, where the book-keeper, with a look of pride, was holding up a sheet of figures for another to see.

" You have balanced your accounts, my friend ! " shouted Mr. Peters to the unconscious clerk, " Bravo ! ! " and then turned away, to go down the street again with the scattering mob, wrapped in his own thoughts, and quite regardless of the good wishes for the new year, shouted at him by 'Melia and Rivers.

That night, 'Melia (who had dreamt almost more in the last three months than in all her previous life) had pleasant visions of a good time coming ; but Mr. Peters dreamt that the man at the window came to him, and asked why his accounts were still unbalanced.

# CHAPTER XLVIII

## QUEM DEUS VULT PERDERE

RIVERS was none the better for his little expedition of New Year's Eve, and kept to his room for a day or two after it. His trouble, however, being nothing worse than a severe cold, he could receive visitors—and entertain them. He entertained Mr. Peters a great deal, at that gentleman's expense. For Mr. Peters, fearing apparently lest life at the House of Residence should be monotonous for Rivers without his society, quitted the Pentlands for a time, and spent social evenings with the invalid, and with the cards.

Fortune, unpropitiated by this self-denial, still went relentlessly against Mr. Peters, with the result that the vigilant Mrs. Jimps determined one night to remonstrate.

" If you could give me just one minute this evening, Captain Peters," she entreated, smiling down the table as she rose from dinner. " I have an application for rooms, and I would like to show it to you," and Mr. Peters accordingly presented himself at her door, half an hour later.

Mrs. Jimps' little room looked very cheerful, and Mrs. Jimps looked cheerful too—more cheerful, indeed, than she felt. She motioned Mr. Peters, who did not seem inclined to seat himself, to the easiest chair, and opened fire at once, lest delay should lead to cowardice.

" We are glad to have you with us again, Captain Peters. We have seen so little of you at the table lately."

She beamed upon him, and Mr. Peters bowed, watching her with a steadfast stare, which Mrs. Jimps found disconcerting.

" Are you likely to be going back to your cottage soon ? "
she asked, and Mr. Peters misunderstood her.

" Do you wish my room ? " he demanded.

" Not for a moment, Captain Peters. I never thought of
it. We are always glad to see you. As I said to Annie
only yesterday " (Fie ! Mrs. Jimps, this is pure inven-
tion), " it seems so natural to have you going in and out.
I—I've once or twice wondered lately whether Mr. Rivers
would be going soon," she suggested.

Mr. Peters remaining silent and sphynx-like, Mrs. Jimps
plunged further, and made further calls (heaven forgive
her !) upon her imagination.

" The fact is, Captain Peters, you must excuse me for
saying that there has been a good deal of gossip, about Mr.
Rivers, just lately. They say that he's very fond of cards,
and—he is most surprisingly fortunate ! "

" Indeed ! " Mr. Peters lifted his thick black eyebrows in
surprise. " With whom does he play ? "

" If you don't know, Captain Peters, then I don't," said
Mrs. Jimps, hurt at this want of confidence ; but she went
on bravely, still determined to save Mr. Peters' money if
she could.

" All I can say is that, while a gentleman who *is* a gentleman, can do what he likes in his own rooms, I can't let
things go on that are talked about, and might get my house
talked about, besides meaning, perhaps, ruin to the other
guests who might be my friends, if you'll excuse my saying
so, Captain Peters."

The wording of this speech was enigmatical, but Mr.
Peters apparently understood, and first frowned, then began to laugh.

" Answer Number One," he told her, checking it off upon
his fingers. " I do not lose, madam. If I lose to-night, I
win to-morrow."

" I never mentioned any names," protested Mrs. Jimps,

"except that of Mr. Rivers," but she was interrupted.

"That is true," Mr. Peters agreed. "I do not accuse you. Answer Number Two. The good Rivers will go in a few days, I think. Do not say so, Mrs. Jimps, or he will be angry, but, lest he should be hurried and forget, you should remind him of that little account."

"He does owe me for six weeks," Mrs. Jimps admitted, "and it's very good of you to think of that, though I didn't suppose he'd tell anyone."

"One may guess," said Mr. Peters. "Is that all?"

"Well," Mrs. Jimps told him, after consideration, "I think that's all, Captain Peters, if you're sure that you're not being deceived."

"And these good people who have talked?" asked Mr. Peters.

"Oh, that will be all right," Mrs. Jimps assured him, careless, apparently, of any possible loss to Rivers. "They never doubted *you*, Captain Peters."

"Did they not? That is good," Mr. Peters decided, and moved to leave the room.

With his hand upon the door, he gave her some further information.

"I owe you nothing?" he demanded.

"Only just for the week, Captain Peters," Mrs. Jimps told him, "and I'm never afraid to leave your little account."

"Still," said Mr. Peters, "I, too, shall perhaps be leaving in a few days. We will settle to-morrow, up to then," and he went away, leaving Mrs. Jimps to take the news as she liked.

He went thence to his own room, and there he found the convalescent Rivers waiting for a game.

That night they played hard and played late, for high stakes, considering their purses, and with heavy bets. Whatever Mr. Peters might tell Mrs. Jimps, his money was going fast, and, between one and two o'clock in the morning, he pushed back his chair and rose from the little table, which had been drawn in front of the fire.

" It is done," he announced ; " I have no more."

" Dear me, now, you don't say so," Rivers lamented. " I've had a most extraordinary run of luck, haven't I ? "

" Most extraordinary ! " Mr. Peters agreed.

" But it couldn't last, you know," Rivers told him. " You really mean to say that you're cleaned out ? "

" Quite, altogether," said Mr. Peters, who stood looking down upon the winner, and on the pile of coins and Scottish bank-notes beside him, without much sign of regret.

He seemed rather excited though. One might almost suppose that play was beginning, instead of having finished, and finished against him. Rivers saw enough of this to be puzzled, and was puzzled enough to show it.

" I will say," he remarked, glancing furtively at Mr. Peters, while he slowly gathered up the spoils, " that I never saw any gentleman take his bad luck better—never."

" All through this life, my good Rivers," said Mr. Peters, sententiously, " one must pay for one's little games."

" That is true," Rivers agreed heartily, helping himself from the spirit decanter as he spoke. " Still, it's deuced hard lines when a man's pluck puts him in such a hole. I'm sorry for you, my good fellow, indeed I am."

Within the last few minutes he had developed an air of patronage most distinctly offensive, or, perhaps one should say, which would have been most distinctly offensive to the average man.

But Mr. Peters was apparently not an average man. He had, to all appearance, not noticed any change in the manner of his guest, and remained quite unruffled. He didn't seem likely to make a fuss over his losses : still, Rivers felt that it would be a nuisance to have the fool about the place, and suddenly decided to be generous.

" Have you squared up with the woman here ? " he asked, suddenly.

" What woman ? " asked Mr. Peters.

" Jimps," explained Rivers, who, with his pocket full of ready money, and with his eye upon Archie as a prospective son-in-law, didn't think so highly of Mrs. Jimps as he had thought a couple of months earlier.

" I owe Mrs. Jimps, so she tells me, for this week," Mr. Peters acknowledged.   " What of that ? "

" Tell you what I'll do.   You'll be wanting to clear out, of course, now, and go to your little country residence, or some other quiet place where living's cheaper, won't you ? If you're in a hurry, being down on your luck, why, I'll square up with the woman to-morrow for you, 'pon my soul I will.   You've been a bit of a fool, you know, not to pay more attention to her.   It might have been worth board and lodging to you, just now, for a week or so, while you looked about you.   Still, as I say, if you're clearing out to-morrow, I'll square up with her for you, so as to make things easier."

He looked up at Mr. Peters, who still stood by the table, and Mr. Peters looked down at him, taking time to consider before he answered, as though the intricacies of our language were, for the moment, too much for his intelligence.

" I shall go to my cottage to-morrow, in the afternoon," he told Rivers, " and I will pay Mrs. Jimps before I go. Why should you do so ? "

" My dear fellow, I thought you said you were cleaned out ? "

" That is true," Mr. Peters admitted, " and, as I told you, my banker has shown me that the money I gave to him is quite done.   But there is something more."

" The deuce there is !  My dear sir, I'm delighted to hear it, really delighted," and Rivers insisted upon shaking Mr. Peters' unresponsive hand.   " Come now, this is good, and

your luck will turn. I'll play you for I O U's. It isn't as
if we didn't know one another. Can you realize this 'something more' easily ? "

" Yes, it will be easy," Mr. Peters admitted, " and I shall
do so to-morrow morning. But I will not play any more,
having no money to show you."

" Oh, nonsense," protested Rivers. " If you're going up
to the hills again to-morrow, who knows when you will be
in again to try your luck ? "

" That is true," said Mr. Peters, " but I cannot play, except with my money upon the table. This house has been
unlucky for me," he added, looking around him ; " I do not
think I will ever play here any more."

" Try my room," suggested Rivers, but Mr. Peters declined.

" It is the house," he declared. " I can feel it. I will
go up to my cottage to-morrow, and play Patience. That is
a game I understand. Shall we say good-night ? "

Rivers was by no means ready to say good-night, Mr.
Peters being apparently not quite plucked, but he was irresolute, because of a new idea which he could not, for the
moment, make up his mind to express. So, with a glance
at the table, perhaps to make sure that he left nothing
behind which it would be possible to carry away, he went
off to his own room.

It was late enough now, surely, to go to bed if one meant
to go at all. The clocks of the city had struck two, and
Mr. Peters' fire had died out. But he did not seem sleepy.
On the contrary, he sat in his easy-chair, looking particularly wide-awake, with his eyes fixed on the door, and his big
black head just a trifle on one side, as though he listened
for something or somebody. He sat thus, quiet, watchful,
untiring, for perhaps another quarter of an hour, listening,
waiting always, though there was nothing apparently moving in the house, and the only sound was that made by the

wind, which rattled a window-sash, and, passing on, whistled down the street. Nevertheless, presently Mr. Peters drew himself up in his chair, turning a little more towards the door, and gripping the chair-arms as though about to rise. He had at last caught the sound of a door handle turning on the opposite side of the corridor, and this was followed by a tap at his door, and the return of Rivers.

" Ah, the good Rivers," ejaculated Mr. Peters.

" What, not in bed yet ? " asked his visitor. " 'Pon my word, I was almost ashamed to knock, but the fact is, I can't find my matches. I've been tumbling about, until I thought I should break my neck."

" I heard you," Mr. Peters told him, and Rivers stared oddly at hearing this simple statement.

" You must not break your neck. Here are matches," said Mr. Peters, reaching up to the mantel-piece, and tossing a box on to the table.

Having done this, however, he waited for further conversation, and presently Rivers, strolling across the room to where Mr. Peters was sitting, unbosomed himself.

" I'm afraid," he announced, " that your luck has taken the pluck out of you. 'Pon my word I am. I wish I knew what to do. I don't see how I can help it though, if you won't have another shot."

" That is true," said Mr. Peters, philosophically. He must have suddenly become tired, else why, instead of looking straight at his visitor, as was his habit, why did he answer with head bent, and with eyes fixed upon the rug before him ?

" Tell you what ! " Rivers suggested suddenly. " I expect you're right in thinking this house is unlucky for you. I've known of similar cases before, and—well, I don't pretend to be more thin-skinned than any other gentleman, but I'm cursed if I care to take advantage of a thing like that. I'll come up and play you at your other place ! "

"It is far," said Mr. Peters, his eyes still fixed upon the carpet. "You might lose, you know. I do not ask of you to come."

"No, no, it's my proposal," Rivers insisted. "After all, it's only fair that I should lose a little. Luck will change up there, I daresay, and I'm quite prepared for it."

"It will change, I think," Mr. Peters told him. "I am glad that you are prepared."

What a fool is a losing gambler! Rivers laughed secretly to hear how this ass, that had been so easily led, now brayed in triumphant assurance of a change.

"There's no accounting for luck," he assured Mr. Peters. "If, as you say, you can raise cash to-morrow morning (not that that would matter, only you tell me you won't play without it), why, what's to prevent me from going up with you in the afternoon?"

"Nothing," said Mr. Peters, and Rivers went away once more. As he went, he laughed, thinking perhaps that, though luck could never be accounted for, a practised hand could be relied upon against a fool.

Mr. Peters, too, was laughing as he rose from the easy-chair, and stretching himself to his full height watched the retreating figure. For a long time he had laughed very little. Perhaps he laughed now, because Rivers, who came for matches, had forgotten to take them away.

# CHAPTER XLIX

## GOOD-BY

THE next morning Lucius Moriarty, busy in his office, and groaning over the briskness of trade and the consequent dwarfing of his higher faculties, was told that Mr. Peters wished to see him.

" Now, this is kind of ye," he declared to Mr. Peters, as they shook hands. " There bein' no money left to draw, I thought, maybe, I'd not be seein' ye so soon. How are ye ? "

" I am well," Mr. Peters assured him, " but, when you say there is no money left to draw, you forget the bag."

" A kill-joy ! " Lucius told him, shaking his head mournfully at his visitor. " That's what ye are, Peters. Do I understand, then, that ye've come for business purposes only ? "

" Not only," Mr. Peters said, " but of that we will talk presently. First, I will consult you about the bag."

" Well, well," grumbled Lucius, going to the safe. " this is a place of business, an' I'm a plain business man, an' if anyone shows his face here, begor ! I suppose it's natural that he comes on business. Here's the bag."

He took it from the safe, rather a large bag, apparently heavy, and dumped it down upon the table. Mr. Peters, for his part, took from his breast-pocket a paper, and handed it to Lucius. " That is your receipt," he explained.

" What next ? " Lucius asked, looking curiously from Mr. Peters to the bag upon the table. The bag was made of strong canvas, in no way remarkable except for the initials J. F.. which stood for Joseph Flinders, and the number

1000, which could probably have been explained only by the former owner. But Mr. Peters, lifting the bag, was looking at the seals of common red sealing-wax, which lay across the string about its neck, and Lucius looked too. What he saw was peculiar. On each seal, roughly and hurriedly written, it would seem, with some sharp point before the wax cooled, was a word, and Lucius spelt it.

"S-t-a-i, Stai! Begor! that's a queer seal. It means 'Wait,' doesn't it?"

"Yes," said Mr. Peters, and began to break the seals, one after another. "When did you learn Italian?"

"I travelled once," said Moriarty, dismally, "before this business got the mastery o' me. But what's the man doin'? That's not waitin', is it?"

"I have waited long enough," Mr. Peters told him, and breaking the last seal, and cutting the string, he quietly emptied the bag out on to the table, before the astonished Moriarty.

"It was a pile of American coins that Lucius saw, gold and silver, with greenbacks showing here and there.

"What's the meanin' of this?" asked Lucius.

"Money," Mr. Peters told him, with a little shrug, as he looked down upon the pile.

"I've got eyes in me head," retorted Lucius, "I can see that much; but what d'ye bundle it up in an old bag, an' carry it round like that for? Ye should have got a draft, man, instead o' bringin' a weight like that across the herrin' pond. What's the meanin' of it?"

"It is a long story," Mr. Peters told him, with grave politeness, "and I must not interrupt you to tell it all. But this was money given to me long ago, to be used for business purposes only, and when I should have no more."

"But what did ye carry a lump like that for?"

"I have carried a heavier weight all the time," said Mr. Peters, evasively. "Will you get it changed for me?"

23

" How much is it ? " asked Lucius, scratching his head, with a discontented air, but Mr. Peters shrugged his shoulders again.

" This is business," he suggested. " Count it ! " and Lucius, grunting, touched his bell.

" Ask Mr. Cairns to step this way," he told the junior clerk, and Mr. Cairns, the cashier, coming in, was asked to take out the pile, count it, and be ready to report its value in coin of the realm, when rung for again.

" I want to talk to ye," Lucius told Mr. Peters, pointing to a chair and seating himself at his desk as the door closed behind Mr. Cairns. " Ye're on me conscience, more an' more. What d'ye mean by this ? Don't frown, now ! "

Mr. Peters was certainly frowning a little. On being admonished, however, he lowered his eyes, and proceeded slowly and laboriously to explain. Sometimes it seemed almost as though Mr. Peters was losing his intimate knowledge of our mother tongue, the words came to him so slowly.

" I will be plain, what you call frank, with you," he said at last.

" Right y'are, me boy." Moriarty told him, settling back in his chair, and assuming an attitude of earnest attention. " Frankness is best, Mr. Peters, I do assure ye."

" This business of mine," Mr. Peters went on, " will be, I think, arranged to-night."

" Without th' help o' the Parliament House lot ? " inquired Lucius, anxiously, and Mr. Peters nodded.

" Glory be ! " ejaculated Lucius. " Man, ye're a smart chap, divil a doubt," and would have liked to praise such a triumph further, but restrained himself to hear more.

" Having settled," Mr. Peters went on, " I must go at once, and so this is good-by."

" Havers ! " Lucius told him. " we can't let ye go, man.

This business has been wearin' ye out these last three months. We're disgraced if ye leave us in sich a demoralized condition."

" I must go," said Mr. Peters.

" Nonsense," protested Moriarty, and then remembered that Mr. Peters, after settling his business, might be very short of cash.

" Leave th' House o' Residence, an' th' Handsome Widdy," he urged, " seein' that's your intention anyway, an' spend a few days with us. We'll have a young lady who's a friend o' yours to come in, an' keep ye from bein' dull," and Lucius winked with tremendous slyness.

" It's my belief she's been fair dyin' o' love," he added, " since that little exhibition o' yours at Duddingston. I told her you'd taken to the cold-water cure in a hurry, to put out the fire she'd raised in ye. Faith, when I told her that, if I'd been fated to be killed by lightnin', Lucius Moriarty would have retired from business that same instant."

Mr. Peters was not very attentive. Lucius even doubted whether he heard.

" Look here, Mr. Peters," he said presently, " Cairns 'll tell us in five minutes what check you should have for that bag, but that's neither here nor there. I don't know what you've got left, of the cash you've had already, or what you've done with it, an' I don't want to know. It's not my business."

It was perfectly true that it was not his business to know how Mr. Peters spent his money, but all the same he wanted to know, being interested in Mr. Peters, and kindly curious about all his affairs. However, he would have bitten his tongue out sooner than ask, unless Mr. Peters should encourage him, and Mr. Peters did nothing of the kind. On the contrary, that self-reliant individual nodded his head slightly, as if agreeing with Moriarty's

statement, and waited in silence to hear what was coming
next.

"What I want to know is," continued Lucius, vainly en-
deavoring to assume an off-hand, dry, business air, but failing utterly, "will you have anything to come an' go upon
when this business of yours is settled?"

"I shall have enough to go upon," Mr. Peters assured
him, and Lucius, to cover a great deal of real regret at Mr.
Peters' departure, and of anxiety as to his prospects,
laughed loudly at this answer.

"Begor, that's good!" he exclaimed. "'Have ye
enough to come and go upon?' says I, an' 'I've enough to
go upon, anyway,' say you, as smart as you please."

The laughter stopped suddenly, being a trifle forced, and
Moriarty returned to his point.

"Here's the question," he went on, "and remember,
Mr. Peters, that of course it's a pure matter of business,
and you're a business man, introduced to me by another
business connection. Will there be enough an' to spare?
Because," and here Lucius produced a check-book, "a hundred pound, one way or the other, is neither here nor there
when you've good security, and it's better to have too much
than too little, when you get among strangers again. It's a
matter o' business, mind you, and we'll charge a small per-
centage if you'd like it so."

Lucius looked across at Mr. Peters as he spoke, showing a
face that was an absolute guarantee against any exorbitant
usury. Mr. Peters eyed him curiously.

"You said, 'good security,'" he reminded Lucius.
"What security could I give, do you think?" and Lucius
set all his fringe of hair on end in considering the matter.

"The fact is, me boy, I don't care what you can give,"
he finally acknowledged. "You've come here after creditors, an' hunted 'em, an' found 'em, where another man
might have let 'em go. Am I right?"

"You are right," Mr. Peters acknowledged, staring at him. "I made an oath, and I will keep it so far as I am able."

"There y'are then," Lucius pointed out. "You've come from the ends o' the earth to pay one debt, not exactly your own, if I understand you, an' I'll go bail you'd do as much to pay me a hundred pound if I lent it."

"By God, I would," said Mr. Peters. It was not often that he showed excitement, but he seemed to catch some of Moriarty's feeling, and said this loudly, rising from his chair as he spoke.

"Whisht, man, whisht!" Moriarty entreated, "or the chaps outside 'll think you're swearin'! Shall it be a hundred? Come now!"

He paused, pen in hand, but Mr. Peters motioned him to put it down.

"I shall, perhaps, get back a part of what I have spent," he said, "but I will not forget."

"No, don't, there's a good fellow," Lucius entreated, taking this as a promise that Mr. Peters would reconsider the offer; then he touched the bell, and the cashier answered the summons. There were a hundred and fifty-one pounds, odd, due to Mr. Peters, and Lucius made out a check for that amount, and was going to call upon the junior clerk to go and cash it, when Mr. Peters stopped him.

"I go that way," he said.

"Oh, let the boy go," suggested Lucius. "He'll be grateful to ye for the job. He jist sits an' boils on his stool there, till I give the young blaggard a run for fear he'll turn Fenian, an' dynamite the whole place."

It was not to his liking, this slipping away of a friend—for so he considered Mr. Peters—without any preliminary warning, or opportunity for the consideration of some last words. But Mr. Peters still refused.

" You'll look us up to-night, maybe," suggested Lucius.
" What'll I say to your lady friends ? "

" My kindest remembrances to Miss Moriarty," Mr.
Peters told him, and held out his hand.

" No one else ? " suggested Lucius, taking him by the
arm and piloting him through the outer office.

" No one else," said Mr. Peters, and held out his hand
again as he reached the street ; but Moriarty stepped out
after, bareheaded, letting the door swing to behind him.
A flake or two of snow fell, and settled upon Moriarty's
head and shoulders, but he didn't notice them.

" Man, I'm sorry to lose ye," he admitted, " and mind,"
lowering his voice and looking behind him as he spoke, lest
the door should swing open, " it's the easiest matter in the
world to remit to ye, if that would be a convenience. I've
correspondents all the world over, I may say. It's not
straight home you're going, is it ? "

Lucius would have been surprised to hear that Mr. Peters
had not yet considered where he was going, and had looked
no farther, as yet, than to the accomplishment of his business, but that was the truth.

" Perhaps not at once," he told Lucius, and this time
gripped the fingers of the latter in a way that made him
wince.

" Man ! ye've *still* the divil's own fist," Lucius told him,
with a memory of the morning of their first meeting when
his composition of poetry was interrupted—and was going
to add some appropriate last words when Mr. Peters turned,
and went steadily away down the street. Lucius watched
him ruefully, with a dim wonderment as to what his own
feelings were in regard to Mr. Peters.

" These partin's are the divil's own trouble," he muttered. " I'm to be thankful, maybe, that, bein' a plain man
o' business, I don't feel 'em. I wonder if he does."

He referred to Mr. Peters, but that individual's broad

shoulders had just disappeared round a corner, and so Lucius, with a grunt that might be a sigh, or might be a mere clearing of the throat, turned back into his office. There he kept everyone very much on the *qui vive* for the remainder of that day, finding no rest himself, and being apparently determined that others should fare no better.

# CHAPTER L

CONCERNING A LITTLE ACCOUNT

MR. PETERS cashed his check, mostly in Bank of England notes and gold, then went along the street, again considering the question put to him by Moriarty.

Where was he going after his business was ended ? It seemed quite natural to him never to have considered this matter. Indeed, from his own point of view, it was not his affair. Mr. Peters was of no religion, and would have laughed, also, at being accused of any superstitious fancies, but superstitious he was, nevertheless. From the time that he had been told he was fatherless, he had also been told that there was a task for him to perform—that the first thing to do, the first piece of work always to consider, to live for, and to finish as soon as might be, shaping his life always to that end, was work which no other man could, or would, do for him. His mother had taught him this thing religiously, mingling it with his prayers and hers, until it became his creed, his one belief, lasting even after his mother, his prayers, and all other beliefs had been long dead. Fate was his god, and he was Fate's servant. He had thought no more of what he should do, after Fate had used him, than he thought of what would happen after the world's end. Everything would go well, provided he only let himself be guided by circumstances, never hasting, never tarrying. If he gave way to childish impatience, or temper, or indulgence, then came trouble, as it had come that dark afternoon in the Parliament House when Lord Inch died. He did not need to have any such lesson repeated. Yet everything else being clear in his mind, this question of his future movements might now reasonably be considered, so he went on to the docks and made inquiries about steamers. He was still too much occupied with thoughts of the immediate business to think, or even to care very greatly, where he should go. Anywhere would do, he felt, out of this place, and free from its associations. Elsewhere he could sit down quietly, a day or two hence, and plot out a new life. Still, it would look too foolish to ask merely what steamer started first to-morrow, so he looked at the lists, and found that a boat would leave for Amsterdam at noon on the following day. That would do, he decided, and was told that he need not engage a berth then. He could pay on board, and as that arrangement suited Mr. Peters very well, since, later, when his mind was more at ease he might find that he would prefer to go elsewhere, he went away without settling anything, taking a time-table of boats with him.

That afternoon, immediately after lunch, Mr. Peters tapped at the door of Mrs. Jimps' private room, and was told to come in. He was expected by Mrs. Jimps, who continued to show a cheerful countenance to the world, but who was inwardly in a melancholy condition, and had startled "our Annie," only that morning, by acknowledging herself to be not so young as she had been. This had made a great impression upon Annie, who secretly considered Mrs. Jimps a marvel both in body and mind, and led her to assure cook, at the earliest possible opportunity, that in her opinion Mrs. Jimps was sick. So she was, poor soul, not in body but in mind, and of a malady that would only provoke laughter if acknowledged. Knowing this, Mrs. Jimps made no fuss, but smiled like the Spartan that she tried to be, and held out the little account for which she knew Mr. Peters had come.

"That is right," he said, after looking at it. "Now do me the favor, Mrs. Jimps, to bring it to my room when I ring."

Hope springs eternal. Can poor Mrs. Jimps be blamed, if her heart fluttered once more?

" Would you prefer to settle it there, Captain Peters? " she asked, hoping that nothing in her voice or manner betrayed her.

" Yes," said Mr. Peters, " I will tell you why." And Mrs. Jimps' left hand stole upward, and, under pretence of searching for a pin, pressed upon a throbbing heart which, she could almost have imagined, he must hear.

" It is of the good Rivers that I would speak," Mr. Peters continued, and Mrs. Jimps' heart sank once more.

" You will come to my room," Mr. Peters told her, " with his account as well as mine, and leave the rest to me."

" Really," Mrs. Jimps protested, " this is too kind of you, Captain Peters," and she seemed to think so, else why did her eyes grow moist, quite unnoticed by Mr. Peters, who was already moving away.

" I brought him here, did I not? " he asked over his shoulder. " Remember, do not speak of my leaving, or of his," and then he went upstairs.

Rivers was in his own room, and, being in extraordinarily high spirits, was humming a popular song, very much out of tune.

To him Mr. Peters listened, with a strange, hard smile, and with his customary patience, standing in the corridor, until a verse ended. Then he rapped, and Rivers poked his head out.

" Come in to me," Mr. Peters told him, " and bring your big flask. We must not go short of whiskey on our way up the hills."

" Heaven forbid! " said Rivers piously, and turned back to fetch the flask, while Mr. Peters, returning to his own room, rang the bell.

The result of this simple expedient was that Rivers, flask in hand, met Mrs. Jimps in the corridor, and, thinking more of his whiskey than of his manners, preceded her at Mr. Peters' door.

"Sit down," Mr. Peters told him, pointing to a chair, "while I pay my little account to Mrs. Jimps," and Rivers sat down, rather wishing that he had not crossed the path of Mrs. Jimps while she was engaged in debt collecting. True, he was in flourishing circumstances just now, but it always went against the grain with Rivers to spend ready money in paying debts, and he decided to get out of the way.

"Excuse me a moment," he said, putting the flask upon the table, and, slipping out, he went quietly down the stair, thinking that he could spend the next quarter of an hour seeing 'Melia, and make that an excuse, if necessary.

At the little tobacconist's shop 'Melia greeted him with an affection which he found rather a nuisance than otherwise, and which had tended to be more demonstrative since the mishap at Duddingston.

"What is the use," he peevishly asked her now, as he had often asked before, "of an affectionate manner in a girl, when her poor father knows her to be selfishly conceited and headstrong? It is the merest hypocrisy, Em'ly," and poor 'Melia, who was being constantly worried by Archie also, until she almost doubted her own good intentions, felt that she must certainly be an undutiful daughter.

"How's your cold, father?" she asked, to change the subject.

"I could throw it off, I think, if there weren't so many things to worry me," said the aggrieved parent.

"I'm very sorry, pa—father I mean," 'Melia told him penitently, and Rivers thought he saw his chance.

"I'm going up to Peters' cottage this afternoon," he announced, "to stay the night, in order to see if the change will do me any good. But nothing would help me so much as to find my Em'ly in a more dutiful frame of mind."

" Why, father, it's awful cold up there," 'Melia objected.
" I can't think what Cap'n Peters is thinkin' of to ask
you."

" He knows I'm too much worried to throw off anything
here," Rivers retorted severely.

" Don't go ! " 'Melia entreated. " You've never been
right since your wetting. Besides, you'll be at those cards
again." 'Melia knew very well that they played, for Rivers
had spoken of it once, before her, when Mr. Peters had
been lucky for a night. " I shall be thinkin' of you all the
time," she added.

" That," said Rivers, with a fine air of cynicism, " is
worth risking something for. I cannot hope for so much
unless I go, I'm quite aware of that. If you really cared for
my health as much as you pretend, Em'ly, you'd be guided
by me, and I might stay at home to please you."

He turned towards the shop door, but lingered for her
reply. She knew very well what he meant, and to make
sure of Archie, he thought, it would be worth while to
drop the profits of an evening's play. But 'Melia couldn't
make up her mind to follow her own inclination.

" I'll think about it," she told Rivers.

" Come ! yes or no," he insisted, seeing her waver.

" No, not to-night," 'Melia begged, and he moved out
with a curse.

" Much you care about my health, or my life either ! "
he snarled, and 'Melia was left to question her own motives,
more than ever.

Once out of the shop, Rivers was not so very despairing
after all. The girl was certainly beginning to listen to
reason, he reflected, and would probably be more dutiful
the next time they met. At anyrate he had not wasted
time, since Mrs. Jimps had been avoided.

He reckoned, however, without Mr. Peters, who called
him in from the corridor, and rang the bell.

" You have come ?  That is right," Mr. Peters told him.
" Here is your flask full, and presently we will go.  Have
you money ? "

" Yes," Rivers answered, slapping a breast pocket, and
then pulling out a bundle of notes.  " Plenty, plenty for the
night, even if the luck turns, as, by Jove, my dear fellow, I
daresay it will."

" That is good," Mr. Peters decided.  " I have rung for
Mrs. Jimps, because she has your little account, and I told
her that you would certainly wish to pay now."

Had there been time, Rivers would have asked Mr. Peters,
in the most forcible terms at his command, what made him
interfere.  But Mrs. Jimps, prompt at the call, came in
while, still showing the notes, he stared at Mr. Peters, and
there was no way of escape this time, except with a fuss.

" You shall pay for this to-night, my fine fool," was
Rivers' inaudible promise to Mr. Peters, as he counted out
the money, and got his receipt and change from the scarcely
grateful Mrs. Jimps.  " What the devil made you do it, I
wonder ? "

Indeed Mr. Peters, by whatever power of good or evil
he might have been adjured, would have found it hard to
say why he had done this thing.  Perhaps there was a
contemptuously kind feeling for the hard-headed and soft-
hearted Mrs. Jimps.  Perhaps, knowing his own plans, he
took a grim pleasure in tormenting Rivers while that was
possible, or in making him be just against his inclination.
At anyrate, it was to Mr. Peters that Mrs. Jimps owed the
recovery of her money, and let us hope that, somewhere, he
was credited for the action, not having many such set down
to his account.

# CHAPTER LI

### A DREAM AND ITS CONSEQUENCES

THAT evening, in the little room behind the shop, 'Melia, after crying all by herself over her troubles and Rivers' reproaches, dozed off upon the red settee. She had slept badly of late, and had fallen into the trick of taking irregular snatches of sleep during her less busy times, to make up for bad nights, and of sipping extra cups of tea, which, in the end, were not satisfactory, for they neither cheered nor inebriated. As she had her father very much upon her mind, there was no supernatural agency necessary, one would suppose, to make her dream of him. Perhaps the extra cups of tea would account for the fact that 'Melia's dreams were not pleasant ones. She dreamt that she was among the whispering Scotch firs of which Mr. Peters had told her, and which she had seen for herself, behind his cottage, when she was there. Now she tried to make her way through them, for Rivers was calling to her, and, as she listened, the call became a long, mournful shriek ; but, whichever way she turned, a whispering tree sprang up, or fell before her. She could hear quite well what they said. They whispered, laughing hoarsely, every one of them, that Mr. Peters and her father were at the cards again. They had both lost, the trees said, which 'Melia, with the brain of a dreamer, didn't think strange. Now—so one whisperer told the other, leaning across above her head—they were playing for their own souls, and would both lose again.

All this time her father was crying for her, and 'Melia, trying to cry back that she was coming, turned this way and that, and all this time the trees laughed and whispered.

and rose and fell before her, until at last one seemed to catch and crush her, and she woke with a scream. She was still alone, of course, in the little back room ; the shop was quiet and empty ; and when 'Melia, trembling a little, went and looked out at the shop-door into the still, frosty night, feeling as though she would like company, a whistling, shouting boy went past, whose noise, as he came, had quite possibly started the dream.

" You baby ! " said 'Melia, angrily, to herself, and looked at the time. It was a quarter to ten, and by Moriarty's latest instructions she now closed the shop at ten o'clock.

She moved here and there, giving fresh water to some violets, and taking out the cash from the till to carry home, as had been her custom since there began to be anything worth carrying. But, all the while, the dream-fancies clung to her, and gave her no peace. The clocks of the city struck the hour, and 'Melia locked up the place and went away down the hill. As she went, alternately shivering over this stupid dream and scolding herself for doing so, she was followed. Archie, who practically believed that all the male portion of Edinburgh's population—the marriageable at anyrate—was capable of entering into conspiracy against his peace of mind, had lately made it his practice to watch her go home, clenching his fists whenever, as sometimes happened, some profane fellow, instead of shielding his eyes on 'Melia's approach, turned as she passed him and looked after her. Archie could not go by her side, for 'Melia had forbidden that, but a fellow, so he told himself, could stroll where he chose and when he chose along the public streets, so he made no complaint, but watched over 'Melia's safety secretly and in silence.

Then, as she went, a harebrained scheme gradually shaped itself in 'Melia's silly head.

" If I'd promised to think *carefully* over what he wants," she told herself, " he'd 'ave stayed by the fire this afternoon, instead o' trampin' over those beastly hills. What on earth made me dream such foolishness, I wonder ? " and she shivered again as she went.

" If I even got out there now," her thoughts ran on, " an' told him I'd come to say I'd really try hard to please him, why, I don't b'lieve he'd be very angry, and 'twould ease my mind. I sha'n't sleep a wink to-night, for fear of another dream like that. I couldn't stand two such. I should die."

This was her conviction, and not a pleasant one with which to face the night. " I won't go to bed," she decided. " I'll ask Mrs. Meiklejohn to let me keep a bit of fire in, and I'll sit up and read. If I'd only a bike I could call my own, I'd go for a ride, an' folks might say what they liked. Ten to one they'd never know," and, with that, a fresh notion flashed into her busy mind, and caused her to bring her teeth together with a snap.

If only she made up her mind, she thought, to do as Rivers demanded, and as Archie implored, with no more fuss, then she could use the bicycle that Archie had refused to take back, and, since sleep was not to be thought of, she could ride it anywhere she chose—even to the Pentlands.

'Melia looked up at the sky. It was cloudless, and the moon shone brightly overhead. She felt the nipping air upon her face, and looked at the ground. It was freezing. A little snow that had fallen was thin and powdery—scarcely thawing now, even in the streets. Once beyond the houses, spinning along on the moonlit lonely road, how quickly one would get past Colinton. Then the bicycle could easily be hidden among the trees at the foot of the hills, and the walk up to the cottage would be nothing. Father wouldn't be very angry, and how Mr. Peters would laugh ! In town they never went to bed before twelve, and she'd be there not much after if she looked sharp. If only she could use that bicycle—but then she couldn't, it wasn't hers to use, and to go riding out at this time of night, on a bicycle that didn't belong to her, to a place where perhaps she wasn't wanted, just because of a silly dream—it was too absurd.

" You silly fool," she said out aloud, " you'll do no such thing," and then and there a trivial thing happened which sent her hurrying along well ahead of the astounded Archie, to do, as quickly as possible, the very thing she had just scoffed at.

It was only a dog that had lost his master. The poor beast stood out in the middle of the street, with his tail tucked in between his legs, his head lifted to the sky, and howled of his loss to an unsympathetic world. But, to the startled 'Melia, her nerves already in a jangling state of discord, it was Rivers' voice again calling her to come, and even as she saw the cause and laughed out hysterically at it, her feet flew faster down the street. Doesn't everybody know—'Melia thought, gasping—that dogs see more than we do, and howl to warn us ? She reached her door breathless, and slipping into the silent house, crept up the stair, and then, changing her dress, wheeled the bicycle out swiftly. Silly or no, welcome or no, wrong or no, she would get up to the cottage that night, to be laughed at or scolded as might be, and afterwards she would confess to Archie, and take the consequences.

Archie, however, came first on the programme, for, following her to her door, he had lounged about as usual for a few minutes, watching the light in her window, as has been done by many young men at many windows before. The result was that, as she brought out the bicycle, coming quickly and quietly lest her landlady should hear her and ask questions, he was the first person she met.

" My ! " said poor 'Melia, and had nothing ready to add to this expression of her astonishment.

" Where on earth ——? " Archie began, equally startled, and then stopped, facing 'Melia's defiant glare in silence.

" Well, I'm glad to see you're using the thing," he added

presently, "but I don't think you ought to be going out now."

"I've not used it before—after the first day," 'Melia declared, hurriedly. "I'd have told if I had."

"Oh, that's all right," Archie assured her, still staring, and 'Melia felt bound to explain further.

"I've got to go somewhere to-night," she told him, "at least, I feel as if I must, and I can't go no other way."

"Where on earth ——?" Archie repeated, returning to, and stopping at, the point at which he began.

"It's the Pentlands," 'Melia told him bravely, but in such a low voice that Archie said "What?" loudly, and she had to say it over again.

"Oh, nonsense!" he declared, when really sure that he understood, "you mustn't do anything of the kind. You can't mean it."

"I do. I must," said poor 'Melia. "I'm not such a fool as I look, Mr. Inch. I *must* go."

"What for?" demanded Archie, wondering whether she could be ill. To do him justice, he was not so foolish as to suspect anything underhand in this harebrained expedition.

"Don't ask me, Mr. Inch," 'Melia implored. "It's too silly, I know," which didn't exactly square with her last statement that she was not such a fool as she looked. "Father's up there with Cap'n Peters," she added.

"Does he know you're coming?" demanded Archie, and 'Melia had to say that Rivers didn't know, and added, to herself, that she wished she knew what he'd say when he did know.

"This is too silly," Archie declared at last, kicking viciously at a curb-stone. "Come, give it up and go to bed," but poor 'Melia grew more excited at the idea of giving it up, and also more obstinate.

"I can't, I can't," she declared. "The bike's yours,

Mr. Inch, and if you choose to take it away, why, of course, I can't stop you. But short of that ——!" and 'Melia looked determination personified.

"I've a jolly good mind to," muttered Archie. "I can't make out what you're driving at, blest if I can. D'you really mean it, honor bright? Must you go?"

"I must, Mr. Inch, and please don't keep me waiting any longer."

"Very well," Archie told her, without any further objection, "I'll come too," and he turned and began walking up the road again as if the whole thing were settled.

It was of no use for the startled 'Melia to raise this and that objection. He was restless too, he said. As for their going together, that was a great deal better than for her to go alone. They would cross up by the house in Drumsheugh Gardens, which he had not yet left, and she should wait at a quiet corner where she wouldn't be noticed, while he fetched his bicycle. 'Melia scolded and implored, all to no purpose. Go he would, "or I'll take away your bike, and you sha'n't go," he added, as the one alternative, and 'Melia, resisting no more, found herself twenty minutes later slipping away through the quieter streets with Archie at her side.

# CHAPTER LII

## A WILD GOOSE CHASE

NEVER, even in the golden days of the good King Arthur, had any knight ridden forth to guard an errant damozel with greater pride in his mission than Archie Inch felt as he went through the streets of Edinburgh that frosty night, with the madcap 'Melia. Between poor Archie and the knights of old, there appeared, however, to be an important difference in at least one respect. According to Sir Thomas Malory and other chroniclers of chivalry, these gentlemen of ancient days were frequently not only daring and courteous, but also eloquent, not to say long-winded, when at a lady's feet or by her side. Archie, alas! grew curt of speech, and gruff in demeanor as the houses became fewer and the road more lonely, scarcely speaking except of the road they should take. He brought 'Melia round by quiet streets, across the Haymarket and past Merchiston Station, and snapped at her when she bent away to the right just afterwards.

" Where are you going now ? " he demanded, crossly.

" Out Colinton way, of course," 'Melia called over her shoulder, wobbling dangerously as she tried to look back at him.

" Oh, rubbish ! " was his gruff criticism. " Come back," and 'Melia came back meekly, explaining, when they were side by side again, that she knew of no other way.

" You'd have more than an hour's climb," Archie deigned to point out, " and the snow will be lying thick between the hills. Come away by Morningside ; we shall get a lot closer with the bikes that way on a frosty night like this."

What he thought was that Morningside, being the Asylum of Edinburgh, ought, properly speaking, to receive them both for the night, but 'Melia was now so humble that he kept this idea to himself, and they whirled down the Morningside hill, and began to skirt the Braids in silence.

'Melia, being fairly started upon the journey, and past all thought of retreat, could now safely give herself up to gloomy reflections upon her own foolishness, and the probable reception awaiting her.

"Jolly night," Archie told her, severely, as they walked up a steep bit of road. "Moonlight's jolly, isn't it?"

The white road stretched out before them in the moonlight, thinly sprinkled with the snow that lay, too, on the silent Braid hills. 'Melia, in the most melancholy voice, agreed that it *was* jolly.

"Not half a bad notion of yours after all," Archie allowed.

"You ought to be in your bed, Mr. Inch," said 'Melia, gloomily. But Archie, whom love was educating, refrained from an obvious retort, and went on in silence.

He would have talked more freely if he had felt less. As it was, there being only one matter worthy of conversation, he could say little, that subject being, in his opinion, at present impossible.

"A fellow can't pretend to look after a girl, and then worry her about his own feelings, when she can't shut him up," Archie decided, and his conversation grew monosyllabic, while his spirits sank as the two neared their journey's end. 'Melia, for her part, didn't understand this dumb service. It seemed hard that, at the very moment she started forth to take her first step towards surrender, Archie should suddenly grow cold. What could she say on

reaching the cottage, with this sulky squire dragged at her
heels ?

"I believe you're sorry you've come," sighed 'Melia.

"Not if you aren't," Archie told her, and 'Melia thought
there was sarcasm in his voice, and meditated thereon.

"P'raps I am," she decided, suddenly stopping and
jumping off, "I don't know that it's any good going on."

Archie, who had dismounted a few yards ahead, having
been unprepared for this sudden change of front, now came
back, staring to see what the moonlight would show him in
explanation.

"If it's no good going on, what was the good of starting ?"

"No good, I suppose," 'Melia allowed, "only I didn't
know."

"You can't know more now than you did then," Archie
told her, stubbornly. "You haven't seen anybody."

"Haven't I ? I've seen you," was 'Melia's enigmatic
rejoinder, and, refusing to face Archie, she stared down the
moonlight road, wishing she could get away and cry by
herself.

"Look here, Mr. Inch," she told him presently. "I
want to go on, but you must go back. You can't come any
farther."

"I'm going if you are."

"I must," 'Melia told him. "I'm silly about father, but
there'll be a fuss, I daresay, and it's no good your being
there now."

"Now ! What d'you mean by now ?" demanded Archie.

"The fact is—well, I was goin' to speak about you, and
now there's nothing to say. I'll make up another story,
that's all."

"What were you going to say about me ?" demanded
Archie, staring more than ever, and coming as close as
the bicycle he held would allow.

"Well," said 'Melia, in a weak voice that she tried to make hard and matter-of-fact, "there was a bit of a fuss about you to-day, and I was goin' up to say I'd think about it, an' try to please you both. But it's no fault o' yours that you've got sick of hangin' about, Mr. Inch, as I see you have by your ways to-night, an' I don't wonder at it. Still, father's on my mind, so please go back, and thank you for coming so far, and I'll go on and tell him something else that'll do, if I may keep this bike till to-morrow, now we're here."

It was a long speech that, and 'Melia panted when she had come to the end. Archie heard it patiently, and said nothing when she had finished, so 'Melia, who was afraid that she would presently make an exhibition of her feelings if she stayed there much longer, said "good-night" and "thank you" once more; then, mounting as well as she could, rode on alone.

"It's all right," she assured herself as she went. "I don't mind a bit. 'Twasn't natural for him to care for me long. If it had been a lady, I s'pose she'd have spoken nicer, an' done it better altogether just now, but I can't do no better than I've been taught. It's done anyhow, that's a blessing."

A blessing it might be, but the blessing was so much in disguise, that, after getting round the first curve in the road, 'Melia found she couldn't see to steer, and jumped off hurriedly to avoid falling, and to wipe her eyes.

"It's best so," 'Melia repeated, using her handkerchief viciously. "I'll be up there alone in no time."

"No, you won't," said Archie, at her elbow. "You don't know the way. I'm coming too, 'Melia"—and he went.

# CHAPTER LIII

At about half-past twelve that night, all was very quiet and still upon the hillside. The whispering firs, of which 'Melia had dreamt, were so perfectly motionless in the bright moonlight that she could have thought they had stopped their whispering to listen. When the moon rose they had ceased talking. They had thrown out upon the snow long feelers of black shadow that, creeping on as the moon went her way, gradually touched the cottage. One could have thought that the still fir-trees, themselves, were crowding silently down the white hillside to hear what was going on in the cottage.

Inside the cottage it was neither cold nor quiet. Mr. Peters and his guest sat in that one, of the two rooms, which served as kitchen and dining-room. They had a big fire, a kettle sang upon the hob, toddy steamed upon the table at each man's elbow, and Rivers chattered persistently.

But Mr. Peters seemed disinclined for conversation, and it was curious that he should be the dull, silent player, while Rivers laughed and talked, loudly and continuously, for Mr. Peters had, with occasional small changes of fortune, been winning all the evening.

"'Pon my soul," expostulated Rivers, cheerful in adversity, as is expected of the virtuous, "you don't seem to like winning. It doesn't agree with you, my dear Peters."

"It is all the same to me," returned Mr. Peters, dealing the cards, and at the same time looking at his watch, which lay upon the table.

"I've known you much better company when all the luck

was coming my way," Rivers grumbled, with a glance at the
pile of notes and coin opposite. " Come now, I wonder if
you'd change if the cards did. I begin to feel as though I
might win yet."

What marvellous intuition some men possess! It is
greatly developed, one is told, by asceticism. Rivers won
the next deal, and Mr. Peters threw down the cards.

" It is time to stop and have a little talk," he announced,
rising from his chair, and moving to the fire.

Now, if those listening fir-trees heard at all, surely, at
that moment, they held their breath, craning in the cold
moonlight over one another's shoulders. Rivers looked up
from his seat at the table, frowning darkly.

" Afraid to lose ? "

" No," Mr. Peters told him. " I cannot lose to-night,"
but the words were scarcely out of his mouth before he felt
that loss was threatening, and ill-luck at his very door.

He listened, motionless, holding his breath and clenching
his hands, while Rivers, desperate at the thought of having,
to no purpose, allowed luck to be so long against himself,
pointed out that, among gentlemen and men of honor, a
night of it meant a night of it—not a throwing down of the
cards directly luck turned.

No doubt his argument was strong. He could not see its
effect by his host's face, for that was now turned away, but
Mr. Peters' next words were sufficient proof of his conviction.

" You are right," he said, " we must play again," and, before Rivers, recovering his good-humor, could invite him
back to the table, there came a rap at the door, and the
sound of voices outside.

It was characteristic of the two men that, while Rivers,
starting in his chair, swore loudly, and made some coins
jingle by bringing his fist down heavily upon the table, Mr.
Peters stood quietly staring at him, and said nothing.

" Who's that ? " Rivers asked, adding a curse for them, whoever they might be.

But Mr. Peters shrugged his shoulders, and moved toward the door. He knew, at anyrate, one of the voices, and if ever his belief in an inexorable fate wavered, it wavered then. Whoever was there was impatient, or else, as might well be, Mr. Peters had hesitated longer, before replying, than he supposed, for the knocking was repeated before he could open the door—to let in 'Melia, followed by Archie.

'Melia stood, flushed with her climb and excitement, the lamplight showing the color in lip and cheek and red-gold hair against the background of the outside shadow. Whatever was thought by Mr. Peters and her father, Archie felt proud as he looked at her.

" What's this, Em'ly ? " Rivers demanded, staring from one to the other, and, probably for the first time since childhood, 'Melia, laughing and blushing, let someone else answer for her, and turned to Archie for words.

He, poor fellow, had been eloquent enough in the last half-hour, but now words seemed difficult.

" The fact is," he stammered presently, " we understand one another now, and 'Melia—that is—we thought you ought to know."

" Two of your geese, Cap'n Peters," 'Melia chimed in, with something nearer shyness, in voice and manner, than she had ever shown to Mr. Peters before. " You told me you heard 'em some nights, you know. Now, here's a pair of 'em."

What thoughts were in Mr. Peters' mind it was impossible to tell. His lips kept together, his eyes roved from 'Melia to Rivers, from Rivers to Archie, and back again, restless and incomprehensible.

All three were affected by those restless eyes, all differently, none knowing why. Archie felt an unreasonable

wrath begin to stir him, and stared back, drawing closer to
'Melia, who shivered a little, almost without knowing that
she did so. Rivers fidgeted on the chair, from which he
had started for a moment as they came in. He was vexed
at the interruption, in spite of the news. Given another
hour or two, with bigger stakes, he had intended his cash
to come back, with that of his host to keep it company.
The news was all very well, but he had known, he thought,
that it must come soon, and it might just as well have been
told a day later. As it was, here was Peters most devilish
vexed, so Rivers told himself, and everything upset by a
couple of silly fools.

"Well," he told 'Melia, fretfully, at last, twisting in his
chair and looking apologetically at Mr. Peters as he spoke,
"this is very nice, of course, and all that, and it's quite
proper that I should know of it. But your way of coming
to tell me is—well, in fact it's dev'lish improper, 'pon my
word it is, Em'ly. Then, what on earth are we to do with
you up here ? That's what Captain Peters is wondering,
and you can't be surprised if he's vexed. 'Pon my soul, I'm
vexed myself, and why the deuce you came at this time of
night I can't think ! "

Poor 'Melia began to partake of the astonishment evidently caused by her unwelcome appearance. She couldn't
think, now, why she had come. It was too ridiculous to say,
or even to think, there, in that cosey, warm, well-lit cottage,
before those three men, that she had defied the winter night,
not to mention the proprieties, for the sake of a silly dream,
now utterly scorned. 'Melia's ready wit had deserted her
that night, and it was Archie who, seeing her confusion,
came to the rescue.

"She wanted to tell you, and I asked her to let me bring
her," he announced, taking his eyes off the silent Mr. Peters,
and turning to the Champion of the Proprieties. He didn't
feel the necessity of explaining at what point in their jour-

ney 'Melia and he had arrived at an understanding, nor did
it seem to him that anyone else need know of 'Melia's first
intention to do that journey alone. Prudence, and a masterful manner, were developing in this pupil of Love. So
much so, that when the plain-spoken 'Melia showed signs of
an uneasy conscience at this sketchy explanation of their
appearance, Archie, to his own astonishment and hers,
frowned so fiercely that 'Melia at once, by her silence,
owned obedience to her newly established lord and master.

It was then that Mr. Peters, recovering apparently from
his surprise, came forward, not only cheerfully, but with
more of his old manner than 'Melia had seen for many
weeks. He congratulated them vociferously, his big voice
booming through the little room, and insisted upon shaking
hands with Archie, who still looked upon him rather as
a dog with a bone might look upon another dog boneless.

He swept up his winnings from the table, shouting down
Rivers' angry objections. He got out fresh tumblers and
mixed for both of his new guests, though not another drop
would he touch himself.

"And how did you come?" he asked 'Melia, while
Archie and her father were apparently trying to find some
topic of common interest.

"On our bikes, of course," 'Melia answered, beaming
upon him, "I couldn't have done it but for you, Cap'n
Peters."

"That is true," Mr. Peters acknowledged, and lapsed into
silence for awhile before he spoke again.

"How did you know where to find him?"

"He told me this afternoon, of course. Didn't you know
that?"

No, Mr. Peters had not known that.

"At what time did you see him?" he asked, carelessly,
being apparently hard up for fresh topics of conversation.

"Three o'clock, maybe," said 'Melia, after meditation.

" I vexed him a bit, Cap'n Peters, an' that partly made me want to see him, I think," so Mr. Peters knew that, while 'Melia could not have come without his help, she probably would not have known where to come had he not also tried to help Mrs. Jimps.

What he thought of all this no one knew. He played the host with patience, and, as 'Melia refused to usurp the other room, they all sat about the fire until she fell asleep in her chair. When the gray dawn came, all of them, except Mr. Peters, looked jaded and rather miserable. 'Melia and Archie yawned over their early breakfast, while Rivers, the gray stubble of a night's growth sprouting on his cheeks, in unpleasant contrast with the limp, blue-black mustache, was openly enraged with everyone. He was angry with 'Melia for coming, with Archie for bringing her, and with Mr. Peters for rattling his, Rivers', money in his pocket, and refusing to let him stay the day.

It was only at the very moment of departure that Rivers cheered up. That was when, Archie and 'Melia having moved off, Mr. Peters explained, still chinking the coins in his trousers' pockets.

" The good Rivers is angry ? " he said, watching the two young people as they went.

" The silly young fools," Rivers told him, following his glance ; " you and I were never like that, my dear Peters."

" Never ! How foolish of you, my friend, to speak to her of coming here ! "

" Gad ! so it was," Rivers admitted. " I won't be such a fool next time, and I suppose I may come again, though you won't let me stay now. I feel it would do me a lot of good."

" You need rest," Mr. Peters told him, " and I could give it to you up here. Only, what is the use if you are always known to be here, and always fetched ? "

" You're a sharp man in some ways, Peters," the other

admitted, looking at him with the air of one who had discovered a new thing. "Are you staying here to-night?"

"Yes," Peters told him simply, without asking the reason for this curiosity.

"I may go through to Glasgow this afternoon, if it's fine
—for a week," said Rivers, with a wink. "I forgot to tell
Em'ly of that sooner, but I'll do so."

"I shall see you, perhaps, when you return," said Mr.
Peters, smiling, and watched the three of them go down
the hill, where Archie and 'Melia hoped to find their bicycles, while Rivers made for the nearest railway station.

# CHAPTER LIV

## A FATHER'S FAREWELL

MR. PETERS stood at his cottage door, and watched until he could see nothing of his visitors. Then he went in again, and, preparing for himself good coffee and other little luxuries, he made a hearty meal. This was in complete accordance with Mr. Peters' rule of life, to take every case and luxury within his reach, to keep his big body in good condition for any demand he might make upon its strength, and to think not at all of the unattainable.

After breakfast he found the list of Leith steamers, and, after looking that through, he smoked, seeing dreams of his own in the smoke of the Dream Mixture. Then he went out of the cottage and plunging among the firs, was at once hidden by them, while they whispered to one another, their swaying heads stirred by the northwest wind, that was now rising.

Mr. Peters was hidden for an hour, unseen except by the rabbits which came out of their burrows for a little food, and which, finding that he took no notice of them, sat up to watch him curiously.

Then, coming back, hot and panting, he took out the cards and tried his old game of Patience, but tried in vain.

He lay back in his chair, jingling what money was still in his pockets, and staring across at the little chest of drawers, in which he had stowed away most of that which Rivers had lost. Then, at last, with a shrug of the shoulders at his own foolishness, he locked the cottage door and started for Edinburgh, although the wind had begun to moan over the white hills, under a dirty gray sky, and a few big flakes of snow drifted against his face as he went.

Early that afternoon, 'Melia sat and shivered in her little room behind the shop. Sometimes the outside shop was not cold enough for her, and at other times that little room, in spite of gas and fire, couldn't keep her warm. Her head ached too, and she felt very tired and stupid after the last night's escapade. She tried to take comfort in thinking of Archie, but could only wonder how she would manage to be a good wife for him without neglecting Rivers.

"Gunpowder and matches 'd go better together," she decided, gloomily, and her head ached more than ever at the thought of what lay before her.

To her came Nell Moriarty, to leave her purse in 'Melia's charge.

"There's a good deal in it," she told 'Melia, "because I had a check from father this morning, and cashed it in Princes Street. Now I'm going to make some calls, and I don't want to carry it about all the afternoon, or to take it home first."

"It'll be safe here, Miss Nelly," 'Melia told her, and put the purse in her pocket, while Nell surveyed her critically.

"I've the awfullest headache." 'Melia explained, dismally, and Nell went off, saying that they must see about that when she came back.

Presently Rivers put in an appearance, in a better temper, and with his cheeks clean-shaven, and, though still frowning, prepared to forgive last night's doings if 'Melia would make reasonable amends.

"I'm going to run through to Glasgow to-night, for a week, on urgent business," he announced, shaking the snow off his coat on to the shop floor.

"Yes, father. I hope you'll wrap up well." said 'Melia,

dutifully. " You'll write, won't you ? and I hope you'll
have a good time."

" I don't know that there'll be any chance of a good
time," Rivers told her, with severity. " The fact is, your
tomfoolery last night lost me a lot of money. It so happened that Captain Peters (you saw we had played a little)
had all the luck, and all my ready money. Things were
just coming right when you turned up."

" I'm so sorry," 'Melia told him, penitently, " though I
wouldn't like you to take Cap'n Peters' money either. Still,
he might have played till you got yours back."

" Well, he didn't, you see," retorted Rivers, viciously.
" To-night, though, it'll be different—in Glasgow ; and I'll
bring you back a wedding present. We won't waste any
more time over that business, will we, hey ? "

'Melia's flushed cheeks could scarcely grow hotter, but
she answered hurriedly that she didn't know about that
business. " Time enough to talk about that later," she
objected.

" Oh, nonsense ! girlish affectation," Rivers decided.
" I'm going to get you a present anyway, my dear Em'ly,
at a sale I know of. But, by the by, that reminds me I
haven't got half enough cash."

" Never mind, father," 'Melia told him, relieved at this
announcement, " you'll get it some other time, when things
are a bit settled."

" Rubbish ! " said Rivers, impatiently. " What money
have you got ? I could return it the next time I come
in."

" Something under a pound," 'Melia thought, and taking
Nelly's purse out, together with the shabby old thing that
held all her worldly wealth, she put the first back into
her pocket, and emptied her own upon the counter, while
Rivers watched.

" Eighteen an' seven," she announced. " You could

25

leave me the three an' seven, couldn't you, father, an'
would you like the purse?"

"Fifteen shillings! What's the use of that to me?"
snarled Rivers. "Fifteen or twenty pounds might do," and
so they might, since Rivers meant to control Fortune early
that evening—at Glasgow.

"My! what a lot," 'Melia exclaimed, "I wish I'd got it
for you, pa, I do indeed, but I never did have so much in
all my life!"

"You soon will, now," Rivers suggested, consolingly.
"Ha! a bright idea," and starting, apparently surprised at
his own fertility of expedient, "I have it!" he announced.

"I'm so glad," said 'Melia, much relieved.

"It's as simple as possible," Rivers went on. "I'll go
round and see Master Archie. He's good for twenty, I
should think," but 'Melia stared aghast.

"You can't do that, not for anything."

"Oh, nonsense!" Rivers insisted, beginning to frown
again. "Women don't understand business. Tell me
where to find him. I've no time to waste in searching all
over the place."

"I don't know," 'Melia told him in a strange low voice.
"I couldn't tell you if I did."

"Wouldn't, you mean." Rivers retorted. His eyes were
bloodshot, his mustache trembled, his hands worked upon
the counter. He was not a good thing to look upon. "The
youngster will have the sense to see that he owes me a
turn, after making a mess of things as he and you did last
night," Rivers went on. "Come!"

But 'Melia, whose face had now gone very white and
stiff, just pressed her lips more firmly together and shook
her head, eying her father steadily. It wasn't worth while,
she felt, to repeat that she didn't know where to find Archie, since, if she had known, she wouldn't have told.

But Rivers, gnawing at his ragged mustache, had another

idea. If 'Melia had not come when she did, he would have
played on pretty safely with what money he still had.
What he felt was that to do the business as thoroughly as
he meant to do it to-night, he must not start to win at once
and win uninterruptedly. Money he must have, to be able
to play a losing game at first.

"What's in that other purse of yours?" he asked, pointing down across the counter in the direction of 'Melia's
pocket.

"I don't know. 'Tisn't mine," she told him, and took
her eyes off his, for a moment, to look towards the door,
wishing that someone, anyone, would come in. As she
spoke, her right hand instinctively stole down to the purse,
careful for its safety, but, before she looked at Rivers again,
he leant across and took her roughly by the wrist.

"Come, let's see that purse," he told her.

'Melia hung back, protesting, but Rivers held on, sure
that there must be something worth having, and made the
more obstinate by her struggles.

"You keep two purses, do you?" he hissed at her,
wrenching at her clenched hand and the pocket, all the
while. "It will be his money, I suppose. You'll take it
from him already, will you? but you're too delicate-
minded to ask for a loan for your father. Let me see it,
I say!"

They wrestled and swung to and fro over the counter,
Rivers, thoroughly maddened now, wrenching at the girl's
wrist, and careless how much he hurt her, while 'Melia,
wild-eyed, and with set teeth, clung by her left hand to a
low shelf, and threw all her weight downward that she
might not be dragged across.

"I must scream!" she panted, at his ear, but Rivers
took no notice, thinking it an idle threat.

"Out with it, you jade," he told her, "or I'll come round
the counter for it."

He had just determined to do that, without any further
waste of time, when 'Melia suddenly ceased to make any
resistance. She caught sight of Mr. Peters standing in the
doorway, and she struggled no more, but when Rivers,
following her gaze, turned, and saw what had happened, his
rage boiled over. He struck 'Melia heavily across the face,
and, cursing her for an undutiful slut, sent her reeling
back among the boxes.

For some seconds after that, none of them moved.
'Melia, half lying, half sitting upon the floor, had struck her
head against a shelf-corner, and, though still clutching the
purse, scarcely knew where she was, or what she did.

Rivers, suddenly looking years older, still muttered and
cursed between his teeth. As for Mr. Peters, he waited,
with a face so immovable that no one could have supposed
he had seen anything.

Presently, when 'Melia began to stir, he stepped past Rivers, and helped her to the old settee in her own little room.

"You are better now," he told 'Melia, and 'Melia said
yes, and thanked him, grateful that he had said no more,
and still fumbling anxiously at the disputed purse.

"I'm a silly, Cap'n Peters," she told him, apologetically.
"I'm always vexin' him with my ways. I don't know how
to put things. He never hit me before, and I'm sure he
won't again."

"I think not," Mr. Peters agreed, and said no more,
excepting that he understood her father to say that he was
going to Glasgow, and, if so, that he would see him to the
station.

"Thank you, Cap'n Peters. I'd be glad if you did,"
'Melia admitted. "I can't put things right now, and he'll
feel different next time we meet."

To this Mr. Peters made no answer, but, after looking
down upon 'Melia for a moment, said good-by, and went
off without offering to shake hands, taking Rivers with him.

" Mark you, Captain Peters," the other began, directly
they got outside the shop, " that girl is a bitter disappoint-
ment to me. You saw me chastise her ? " and Mr. Peters
said that he had seen him.

" I ought to have done so long ago," Rivers declared,
working himself into a passion again ; " I hope I may not
have to do so again."

" I am sure you will not," Mr. Peters assured him. They
were now making for the House of Residence, and Rivers
pointed this out.

" I've nothing to go there for," he said ; " have you ? "

" Just one moment," suggested Mr. Peters, " a little
money and a bag from my room. That is all," and Rivers
agreed to go with him.

They went, and they left, together. It was at the door
that Mr. Peters said good-by to Mrs. Jimps.

" The good Rivers has told you that he goes to Glasgow ? " he asked her.

" Yes, for a week on urgent business," Mrs. Jimps said,
with a little melancholy smile for Mr. Peters, a smile which
meant a very great deal, for it was intended to convey that
Mrs. Jimps remembered the lesson she had got, and neither
expected, nor wished, to see Mr. Rivers return from Glasgow. The smile was also meant to show that Mrs. Jimps
knew Mr. Peters was really saying good-by, and was going
off also, though not to Glasgow. It should, too, have expressed a great deal of honest heart-ache, and a great deal
of warm good feeling, if it were to show half of what poor
Mrs. Jimps felt. But as, for many years, a certain dignity
and coldness of demeanor had been her chief aim, perhaps
a smile that could contain so much was, for her, an impos-
sibility. At anyrate, Mr. Peters did not seem particularly
impressed, and he and Rivers went away together.

As they went, Rivers still grumbled of 'Melia's scandalous
and perverse behavior.

" Gad ! sir, she deserves to be frightened," he told Mr.
Peters. " It would serve the girl right if she never saw her
poor old father again ! "

" It would be what she deserves," said Mr. Peters, and he
said it with a heartiness that pleased Rivers very much.

" She'd think more of me, she'd be a more dutiful daughter, if she thought, for a time, that she had seen the last of
me," Rivers suggested, stopping to stare at Mr. Peters as the
thought came to him, and Mr. Peters stared back, silent,
but very much interested.

" I'll do it ! " Rivers decided, and then and there—in, of
course, a refreshment bar—he called for a pen and paper,
and, dashing off a few lines, handed them to the attentive
Mr. Peters.

" EMILY,—Your disobedience and your distrust have
hurt me more than I can tell you. I feel that there is no
more pleasure in being near you, and that I am better away.
Whether I shall ever return, it is not for me to know. I
shall soon be an old man, and cannot naturally expect to
live many years longer, especially since I have no child to
comfort my old age."

Rivers was very pleased with this composition. So much
was he pleased, that excitement made him forgetful. The
letter which he handed to Mr. Peters was signed " Joshua
Buncombe." But Mr. Peters said nothing, only he put the
letter into an envelope for Rivers directly after reading it,
and it was not until he was alone, later in the afternoon,
that he laughed over this. Then he laughed a great deal,
but he was not mirthful, and if Rivers had heard him, and
had known the cause, he would have felt frightened : but
he never heard it, and no one told him.

When the letter was written and posted, Mr. Peters said
that he could see Rivers no farther on his way to Glasgow.

At this Rivers was disturbed. He had counted upon their going to the hills together, and hoped to work round to the subject of a loan before then, since he knew that Mr. Peters liked money on the table when he played. True, he might go back and talk to 'Melia again, but, after posting the letter, that was to be avoided if possible, and Rivers could not feel at all sure of success with 'Melia in any case.

It was Mr. Peters himself who solved the difficulty.

" The girl was obstinate about money, was she not ? " he asked, casually, as they went along.

" Yes, and she's put me in a devil of a hole," Rivers assured him. " I wanted cash to take to —— Glasgow, in case you had last night's luck again. She refused to lend me one penny, sir, of money, twenty pounds it was, that I had given her two days ago."

Twenty pounds ! Mr. Peters was delighted to oblige the good Rivers, and pressed it upon him at once.

" You will, no doubt, find that enough to begin with to-night," he decided. " You are going to win, are you not ? " and with that they separated, for the time, without Mr. Peters having so much as hinted that he would like an I O U for the twenty pounds.

# CHAPTER LV

WHEN Nell went back for her purse, she found 'Melia shivering worse than ever, upon the old red settee, and decided promptly that she must go home. Not only that, but Nell went out and fetched a cab before she said anything about her decision, and then refused to argue the point, because the cab was waiting.

" But who'll see to the shop ? " poor 'Melia debated. " It can't be left, Miss Nelly, and I've not a soul I can trust to take it on."

" I will," Nell announced. " Off you go, now ! " and laughed to see 'Melia's dismay.

" You can't do it ! " 'Melia declared. " What'd your pa say, Miss Nelly ? I can't think of it."

" Very well, then," Nelly told her, " wait a minute, and we'll manage another way."

She slipped out, and presently returned triumphant.

" Your friend in the smoking-cap isn't such a bad little man, after all," she told 'Melia. " He's coming soon, to put up the shutters. I'm going to close early this afternoon. Now, I won't listen any longer," and, with that, she hustled 'Melia gently into the cab, wondering, as she did so, where on earth the poor girl had got such a swollen face.

But when 'Melia reached the cab, she remembered something important, and insisted upon going back to the little back room, to speak of it.

" You'll remember, the first time you came here, that you found a young gentleman talking to me ? " she asked Nell, and Nell, reflecting, said that she did.

"P'r'aps he'll be here before you close," 'Melia suggested. "I don't know that he will, but he does come in—at times. It's Mr. Inch, from Drumsheugh Gardens, Miss Nelly, and he'd be frightened to see you here, an' me away. Will you please tell him, from me, that I'm all right, only I've got a cold, and I'll be out again to-morrow?"

Nell nodded, with wide-open eyes, and followed 'Melia, as, having relieved her mind, that damsel hurried to the cab. But, being safely ensconced therein, she thought further revelations necessary, and let down the window.

"We're engaged—since last night," she told Nell, and, the cabman being impatient, she was driven off before she could receive congratulations.

As for Nell, she stared after the retreating cab in silence, and then, not having had the advantage of a mother's teaching, and being, moreover, utterly at a loss for words to express the feelings of the moment, she hugely delighted two passing small boys, by a long, low whistle. They imitated her, and Nell retired promptly, not feeling quite sure whether she wanted her ally in the smoking-cap to come at once, or whether she would like him to keep her waiting until Mr. Archie Inch came.

Whatever she might wish, Archie was the first to arrive, and was received with a dignified and strictly business-like air, which Nell found it difficult to preserve as Archie stared about him.

"What can I show you?" Nell inquired politely, thinking at the same time that she knew well enough what he wanted to see.

Archie bowing, and staring more than ever, almost wondering whether he had not lost his wits and wandered into the wrong shop, asked whether Miss Rivers was there.

"Oh, it's Mr. Inch, is it?" Nell suggested, and Archie, blushing, he scarcely knew why, told her that it *was* Mr. Inch, and repeated his question.

" Miss Rivers has gone home, Mr. Inch, and left a message in case you called," Nell told him. " She says that she has a cold, and is sure to be here again to-morrow. But " (and here Nell's manner changed altogether, and she leant over the counter with a confidential air) " I think a doctor had better see her to-night, and I was wondering whether I should send one down, or whether you'd like to do so yourself."

" Oh, I will, of course, at once," Archie told her, and hurried away for Maitland, without paying much attention to Nell's assurance that she only wished to be on the safe side for 'Melia's sake, and that 'Melia wouldn't be allowed to think about her work the next morning, in any case.

" That's a very nice boy." Nell decided, as she went to the door, and watched Archie's long legs flying west. " He's awfully fond of her. I don't believe he looked at me—scarcely. I wonder if anybody would really care like that if I were ill! I suppose the opposition shop may as well come and close this now. Here he comes ! "

But it wasn't the " opposition shop " that came. It was Tom Dunbar, dropping in, on his way to " diggings," for an ounce of Dream Mixture, and Nell, taken very much by surprise, did not face him so coolly as usual.

" Well, I never ! " Tom ejaculated, when he had recovered a little from the shock. " Where's Miss Rivers ? "

" She's ill," Nell told him. " She's only just gone. I'm sorry you've missed her."

At this Tom stared, but, having lately made up his mind to new tactics, he only said that it did not matter.

" I'm sorry she's ill, though," he said, " awfully sorry."

" Oh, I don't think you need trouble," Nell suggested. " She isn't very bad, and besides, she has someone who'll take care of her."

" Yes, I know—her father," Tom decided.

"Oh, no," said Nell, letting the information of 'Melia's having a father go by unheeded. "Perhaps you didn't know Miss Rivers was engaged?"

Tom whistled, just as Nell herself had done.

"Jove!" he remarked, "he's a lucky fellow."

"He's a very nice one," said Nell, "and he'll be very good to her, I'm sure. I never saw a boy so much worried as he was when I told him."

"Yes, she's the sort of girl a fellow could get very fond of," Tom decided. "I don't believe she could humbug a fellow if she tried."

He had lately, with great exertion to himself, avoided Nell as much as possible, and treated her in a merely hail-fellow-well-met style when forced to speak. In accordance with this plan, which he wickedly told himself was mere politeness since she found him such a nuisance, he now wished her good-night, and made for the door.

"I'll look in to-morrow, and congratulate Miss Rivers," he said, as he went.

"She won't be here," Nell called after him. "I sha'n't let her come out. Perhaps I shall have to be here myself," which last remark, one fears, cannot possibly be considered Nell's true belief.

Tom, knowing Lucius as he did, grinned at the notion.

"Ah, well, I'll wait until the day after," he told her, and Nell felt that this was carrying the ideas of mere friendship too far.

"You might stay and help me to put up the shutters," she suggested, but Tom refused calmly, to all appearance, but in reality with remorse.

"Awfully sorry," he told her, looking unconcernedly into the street, "but I promised the Macgregor girls that I'd call to-night on my way down. It's their mother's afternoon, you know."

Now, the Macgregor girls ranked very much with Mrs.

MacQuestra, Moriarty's Widdy, in poor Nell's esteem, and she felt the situation to be desperate.

"I wish you'd help me," she said plaintively, but Tom, standing with his back still towards her, shook his head decidedly.

"I know it seems rude, but you see," he explained, "you want to be just friends and no more, and I daresay you're right, though I didn't think so at first. It's getting easier now, though, and I feel that soon it'll be all right. But I can't trust myself yet not to worry you, and so it's better that I shouldn't be hanging about."

There was no answer, and Tom, under his breath, called himself an unmannerly brute. "Of course," he went on, "there's no such great hurry for me. If you like to go, I'll run this show with pleasure for half an hour, and put up the shutters myself."

Still no answer, and Tom began to think he was being made a fool of.

"By the by," he went on, "I suppose you're right about that buckle I gave you. If you'll let me have it some time, I'll send it to one of the girls at home."

This was carrying his scheme too far, and might easily have been fatal. Perhaps, even, the scamp deserved that it should be. He made a step farther, and then turned with his hand upon the door.

"Do you want this left open?" he asked, but Nell made no reply. Her hands were up to her face, and on her waist, as the front of her jacket opened, shone the silver buckle where it had shone for days past when Tom was not likely to see it.

"D—— the Macgregor girls," said Tom hastily, and I am sure insincerely. . . . The "opposition shop" found him there half an hour later.

# CHAPTER LVI

### A SONG, A JOURNEY, AND A VOYAGE

ALL through the day the snow had been drifting down, and when Rivers, walking up from Colinton, reached the open hillside at Bonaly, he could see no track of any kind —indeed, he could not see far at all. A dazzling, dancing, whirling cloud of snow-flakes troubled his eyes, and confused his brain. It was no ordinary invitation that would have tempted Rivers up the brae that dusky afternoon. Even now he hesitated, standing just on the border of the open moorland, and debating within himself whether this little expedition, profitable though it would be, might not safely stand over until better weather came.

" It would be a great joke," said Rivers, chuckling, " if, after all, I used friend Peters' twenty pounds in a little trip to Glasgow," and he was still chuckling over this idea, when Mr. Peters himself hailed him, and came striding down.

Whence he had risen, and how long he had waited, Mr. Peters did not say. There had been very little time for him to do any business in the city, and yet reach the hills before Rivers did. However, there he stood, snow-covered, a very polar bear in size and shape, explaining that, in such weather, he had feared Rivers would lose his way if left to come alone.

" Gad ! a fellow might miss the path on a night like this," said Rivers, as they climbed, " and be seen no more, until the snow melted."

" That is quite true," Mr. Peters assured him. " I would not have that happen to you for worlds," and they stumbled on, Rivers growing more loquacious as he thought of the

fire, and the whiskey, and the cards, awaiting them at the
end of the journey.

"Did you ever use the dice?" he asked Mr. Peters,
clutching at his arm on making a false step.

"At backgammon, often," Mr. Peters told him, but Rivers didn't mean that.

"It's an amusing thing to put a little money on a throw,
if one gets tired of the cards," he suggested. "Have you
never done that?"

Yes, Mr. Peters had done that, but very seldom. "The
dice always go against me," he acknowledged.

"We'll have a throw to-night, if you care for a change,"
Rivers told him. "I put dice in my pocket," and Mr.
Peters said something to the effect that it was very thought-
ful of the good Rivers, and that they would see.

"I shall be getting an old man soon now," Rivers told
Mr. Peters, stumbling again. "If I'm to take the journey
that gypsy body spoke of, I'd better set about it pretty soon.
Your voyage could wait, for that matter, but they're both
to come off this year, didn't she say?"

Mr. Peters had forgotten all this, and was much interested, making Rivers repeat all that he remembered of their
two fortunes.

"You a journey, and I a voyage—and both this year,"
he repeated. "It is curious. I had forgotten that."

"Yes, I a journey and you a voyage," Rivers insisted,
"and I couldn't make out why she drew that distinction,
you know. Hang me if I do now? A fellow can't travel
far, in this little corner of the earth, without a voyage, can
he?"

But something about Rivers' speech had amused Mr.
Peters, and he began to laugh, as Rivers had once made
him laugh before. Started, he could not stop. He roared,
stumbling and staggering in his walk, and at last, giving
way to the fit altogether, rolled shrieking in the snow.

The thing was not, however, laughter-provoking to see.
Mr. Peters looked scarcely sane, and Rivers' hand closed
upon the butt of the revolver, which he often carried, and
had slipped into a pocket to-night lest a ruined man should
turn restive. Mr. Peters, however, rose from the snow, and
stopped laughing as suddenly as he had begun.

It was nearly six when they reached the cottage, and that
night Mr. Peters, instead of having a quiet meal, and then
leaving it to Rivers to suggest play, as had been done the
night before, insisted upon bringing out the cards at once.

" You can feed afterwards—if you care to," he said, and,
setting down whiskey and biscuits by Rivers' side, began.

The cards were favorable, and he mostly won for the
first half hour or so ; nevertheless, he tossed the cards
across the room, calling upon Rivers for the dice, and they
threw, one against the other, turn by turn, and the luck
changed.

But, whereas at first, while he won, Mr. Peters was eager,
fretful, and impatient, now he grew cool. Throw after
throw went against him. Once, even, a dice that came
from, Rivers only knew where, fell and rattled upon the
floor, and Rivers, to cover it, had to sweep down the two
that were rolling on the table. But Mr. Peters gave no sign
of noticing anything strange. He looked far more often
at the watch, lying upon the table beside him, than at the
dice, and he played for whatever stakes Rivers named.

At last it drew close upon eight o'clock—a time when, in
the cities, people are stirring by the hundred : but eight
is a late enough hour upon the Pentlands, when the snow
lies deep, and before the lambing season drags one out.

It was then that Mr. Peters, answering Rivers' call, carelessly put his hand upon the table where his pile had been
at the beginning, to push his stake forward, and found
nothing there.

His side of the table showed not a note, not a coin.

They were all on the far side, and already being picked up by Rivers and stuffed into his pockets.

When he saw this, however, Mr. Peters, instead of swearing, began to laugh, looking at his watch; and Rivers, seeing him laugh, sniggered too.

"One more," Mr. Peters told him, still laughing, and then, putting a hand to his own throat, he lifted a gold coin, hung upon a silk cord, from under his shirt.

"What's that?" asked Rivers, pushing the dice-box over, and craning across to look at it.

"It is a gold coin, a souvenir," Mr. Peters told him. "—though I did not need one," he added.

"Ha! Parting gift. Tender recollections, and so on." Rivers suggested, leaning back without seeing more than that it was gold. "Here's a sovereign against it. Tell me the story."

"Anything will do against it," said Mr. Peters, "and I will tell you the story presently."

Then they threw, Mr. Peters casting a three and four, Rivers winning with double fives, and Mr. Peters laughed again.

"I will tell you the story," he said, pushing the coin a little way across the table with the tip of one finger.

But when Rivers stretched out a hand to take it, Mr. Peters clutched that hand, and then the other, before it could touch the revolver in Rivers' pocket. Then, throwing all his weight recklessly across, he crushed down his enemy and the table together—he on the top, in some way so twisting and injuring the man's arms that they hung limp as though dislocated at the shoulders; and presently Rivers lay upon the floor with a running knot about his knees and ankles. "Now I can tell you that story quietly," said Mr. Peters.

The man upon the floor shouted, rolling to and fro, but Mr. Peters smiled.

" At the nearest farm," he said, " they go to bed at eight
on these nights. They have told me so. Come now, listen
to my story, for I have no time to lose. I take a voyage
to-night, but first, my good Rivers—or, let us say, Buncombe—I must tell this story and start you on your way."

He twisted another cord about Rivers' arms, useless
though they seemed, pulling the elbows back until the man
writhed with pain.

Then he dragged him up on to a chair, and he finished
with another rope about the neck.

" Listen to the wind," he said. " If an unlucky man
came this way to-night, and heard you, he would only pass
by and make haste to get home, away from the shrieking
devil of a wind."

He stood and looked down, laughing, upon the poor
wretch, who now spoke, promising silence, and begging
Mr. Peters to take all the money and to go. He had no
more, he protested, and he would sit quiet all the night,
if Mr. Peters left him there : but, while he begged, one
arm began to recover a little sensation and power of movement, and that hand shifted, in spite of the cord, towards
the revolver.

Mr. Peters saw this at once, and, leaning over, found
the revolver and laid it upon the table.

" Some one might come," he said, simply. " You remind
me that I have not told my story, and it is getting late.
Listen ! "

If this was a story that Mr. Peters told, he had his own
peculiar way of telling it, for, instead of speaking, he only
began a song. " O bianca e fredda," he sang—the hack-
neyed Italian air which had sounded in a murderer's ears
long ago, when he rode through the night from Bonville
City.

A shepherd from the nearest farm passed by that evening, not far from the cottage, and later, as he supped his

porridge, told his wife of the queer ways of the foreign
gentleman, whom they knew by sight.

The cottage was lit up, the man said, and the foreign
gentleman was singing as merry as might be. He had
thought of knocking at the door to wish him good-night,
but the snow was deep, the wind was skirling around, and
altogether " it wasna cannie."

What he heard was the song that Lord Inch had heard
in the Parliament House, and that Buncombe had heard
then too, as well as before at Bonville.

When Mr. Peters finished singing, the man in the chair
was silent for a moment, staring at him in horror, and Mr.
Peters spoke once more.

" I meant to talk to you," he said, with a glance at his
watch, " but it is time to start upon your travels. Besides,
I see that you understand my story, though how long you
may remember it I cannot tell "—and taking one end of the
rope that was looped about Buncombe's neck, he looked
up at a beam above him.

. . . . . . . . . .

An hour later Mr. Peters, who had carried something
out among the firs, came in from their whispering, tossing
blackness, leaving them to call to the sky, if they could,
what thing it was that lay in the ground at their feet, which
the snow was already covering again.

A few minutes later he locked the cottage door, and went
down the hillside to the Glencorse Reservoir, and there a
cab waited for him, the driver stamping up and down in
the snow.

" I am punctual," said Mr. Peters, and the man acknowledged that to be so, saying at the same time that it was
an awful night, and that he hoped Mr. Peters would remember it.

" I will, if you drive quickly," said Mr. Peters, and stepping into the cab, he went silently away.

"THE MAN IN THE CHAIR WAS SILENT FOR A MOMENT"

The snow still swirled in dancing clouds, confusing to the eye, and confusing also, apparently, to the mind of Mr. Peters. He scarcely knew whether he thought and saw, or whether he dreamt, as he stared out upon the night, and rolled down towards Edinburgh.

Sometimes he could have sworn that his mother, dark-faced and solemn-eyed, looked in at the window and beckoned to him, disappearing and reappearing in a twisted eddy of snow-flakes. Sometimes it was Buncombe as he had appeared before starting upon his last journey.

Over this journey, as he rolled along, Mr. Peters thought with vague regrets. There were so many things that he could have said, so many things that he could have told the Carrion, to show what infinite pains had been taken, and how, even if private vengeance had failed, the law would have had him. The business had been concluded far too quickly. A later boat from Leith would have suited Mr. Peters equally well, yet he had been interrupted at his business before, and he might have been again. Then, too, he thought, with a grudging reluctance, that vengeance could not be called complete at all, since 'Melia's friendliness had made him decide to leave her and Archie, while Lord Inch had died in all the dignity of his office.

Still, it must do, and he thought that his mother's face was not so frowning now, among the snow-clouds, as it had been while she lived, and taught him to live, with this thing ever in mind.

So, first the fields and hedges, then the huddled houses of the Edinburgh streets, slipped by, and at last Mr. Peters, paying his cabman without any such dispute as had heralded his arrival in Edinburgh, stood upon the edge of the Leith docks.

No, that nearest boat was not his, he was told.

To-night she lay in the opposite berth, and he **must** hurry round, for her bell was already ringing.

Mr. Peters, a small portmanteau in his hand, hurried, as he was told. The snow drifted into his face and the wind whistled about his ears, but the bell still rang, and Mr. Peters still hurried.

Then, suddenly, the bell stopped, just as he reached a corner. Mr. Peters, knowing the need for haste, pressed on and took this corner sharply. Another five minutes, and he would be out of this accursed place. These maddening snow-flakes would dazzle him no more, with their whirling fantasies of shrouds and faces. Was this the way—or that, where his mother stood and beckoned? Now he was very near. Were those the ship's ropes cast off, that he heard splashing? Mr. Peters opened his mouth to shout that he was coming—that they must wait another moment—but no man ever heard him. A ship's hawser, snow-covered, lay in his path, and over this he tripped. The portmanteau fell from his hand as he staggered on, clutching at the air, and finding no firmer support. Another step, and his feet had left solid ground, for Mr. Peters had gone head foremost over the side into the dock. If that had been all, there would have been little harm done. He had plunged into ice-cold water before, as deep as this, of his own free will. But, as he fell, the great black head struck heavily against a projecting stone—that stunned him, and the waters, as silent as himself, closed over Mr. Peters.

.    .    .    .    .    .    .    .    .

That night the anxious Archie stood in the little sitting-room of 'Melia's landlady, and listened to the verdict of Maitland, whom he had fetched post-haste to see 'Melia.

" She'll do, laddie," Maitland told him, " you'll see her up in a day or two. What's this I hear about a moonlight ride, you rascal? You must take more care of her. She's a good lassie, in spite of her father, which should just remind us that we've other ancestors besides father and mother. I hope the rascal may have told the truth for

once, and have taken to his heels. She'll need a bit school-
ing, Archie, but we'll be proud to show Mrs. Archie anywhere yet."

At the House of Residence Mrs. Jimps went her rounds,
attended by the faithful Annie, and paused in the corridor
between two rooms.

" You can put fresh bedding into these rooms to-morrow,
Annie," she announced, " Captain Peters has had to go
upon another voyage, and I don't think there'll be room for
Mr. Rivers if he comes back from Glasgow."

That was all she said, and Annie, though she looked
hard, could discover nothing more by any expression in
Mrs. Jimps' face. But Mrs. Jimps sat late that night
pretending to work at her accounts, and really thinking of
Mr. Peters.

In another part of the city Madge Murray thought of him
too, and made fresh plans to attract the attention of this
provokingly cold-blooded foreigner. It was well for her,
maybe, that Mr. Peters would cross her path no more, just
as it was well for Mrs. Jimps that she turned back resolutely
to her care of the House of Residence and her unflown
Paying Guests.

In the house of Lucius Moriarty there was great excitement that night. Lucius having suddenly become aware
that his child was a woman, with a will of her own, and a
heart that she had given away. " Begor ! " said Lucius,
his fringe of hair in a state of wild disorder. " She's a
child, Tom Dunbar, an' you're nothing more," and for
some time he was highly indignant at this juvenile lunacy.

But the two culprits pleaded together, and, being of one
mind, were too strong for him.

" I'll think about it," said Lucius at last in his little
study, taking the pipe out of his mouth and trying to look
severe. " There's your examination first, Tom, anyway.
After that maybe it'll be all right. It's a fine thing to have

# By S. R. KEIGHTLEY

---

THE LAST RECRUIT OF CLARE'S. Being Passages from the Memoirs of Anthony Dillon, Chevalier of St. Louis, and Late Colonel of Clare's Regiment in the Service of France. Illustrated. Post 8vo, Cloth, Ornamental, $1 50.

This is a romance not of love, but of daring adventure, and so well worked as to be profoundly interesting.—*Chicago Inter-Ocean.*

Cleverly told, and enchain the reader's attention immediately, holding him captive to the last page.—*Brooklyn Standard-Union.*

A series of vivid pictures of the life of a soldier who was also a gentleman.—*N. Y. Press.*

THE CRIMSON SIGN. A Narrative of the Adventures of Mr. Gervase Orme, sometime Lieutenant in Mountjoy's Regiment of Foot. Illustrated. Post 8vo, Cloth, Ornamental, $1 50.

Recounts in an able manner the terrible scenes which culminated in the siege and relief of Londonderry, giving his readers a personal interest in the characters he has created, and many and pathetic are the resulting pictures. Mr. Keightley, with a few deft touches of his pen, brings them home to the reader with a force that enables him to realize what such warfare really means. The French soldier is a strange character, strikingly conceived.—*Literary World,* London.

THE CAVALIERS. A Novel. Illustrated. Post 8vo, Cloth, Ornamental, $1 50.

Full of adventure, incident, and the wild spirit of the age, yet written withal in so true, simple, and vigorous a manner that it is the people of the narrative as much as their doings and escapades that interest the reader.—*Chicago Journal.*

Compels immediate and enduring interest on the part of the reader. From an artistic and literary point of view, indeed, the book is entirely noteworthy. It has swing, verve, and genuine force. The interest is cumulative, and the denouement of the story in no wise disappointing.—*Philadelphia Bulletin.*

---

PUBLISHED BY HARPER & BROTHERS, NEW YORK

☞ *The above works are for sale by all booksellers, or will be sent by the publishers, postage prepaid, on receipt of the price.*

www.ingramcontent.com/pod-product-compliance
Lightning Source LLC
Chambersburg PA
CBHW021336110726
47900CB00005B/1501